Praise for Mark My

From the Belly of the Dragon

"Mark Mynheir has been a Florida cop and you can feel it in *From the Belly of the Dragon*. The book oozes with real-life cop talk, cop drama, and cop action. Christian fiction lovers are going to gobble this one up."

CRESTON MAPES, author of *Dark Star* and *Full Tilt*

"A police procedural and family story full of thoughts to chew on. Mark Mynheir has given us a book of excitement and substance. A great read!"

GAYLE ROPER, coauthor of *Allah's Fire*

Rolling Thunder

"A remarkable first novel, with strong action and a solid moral. Readers will eagerly await the next installment from Mark Mynheir."

T. DAVIS BUNN, bestselling author

"*Rolling Thunder* is a compelling story examining the struggles, importance, and power of forgiveness."

BILL MYERS, bestselling author of *Soul Tracker*

"Drawing upon his real-life experience as a police detective, Mark Mynheir has given us a realistic story and characters to care for. Mark presents us with a fresh new voice and writes from a unique perspective."

ANGELA HUNT, bestselling author of *Unspoken*

"Don't get comfortable while reading this book. Prepare to be surprised! Mark Mynheir brings his real-world expertise into the fictional realm with startling clarity. *Rolling Thunder* is fast-paced, raw-edged fiction that carries a spiritual message sure to get you thinking about your own life."

CHUCK HOLTON, author of *Bulletproof*

THE TRUTH CHASERS—BOOK 2

FROM THE BELLY OF THE DRAGON

A NOVEL

MARK MYNHEIR

Multnomah® Publishers *Sisters, Oregon*

This is a work of fiction. The characters, incidents, and dialogues are products of the author's imagination and are not to be construed as real. Any resemblance to actual events or persons, living or dead, is entirely coincidental. Although actual colleges are referenced in this novel, they are merely referenced as fictional background. Author and publisher are aware of no actual connection between the colleges and cult activity.

FROM THE BELLY OF THE DRAGON
published by Multnomah Publishers, Inc.

International Standard Book Number: 1-59052-399-7

Cover photo by PixelWorks Studios, www.shootpw.com
Interior typeset by Katherine Lloyd, The DESK

Printed in the United States of America

For information:
MULTNOMAH PUBLISHERS, INC.
601 N. LARCH STREET • SISTERS, OREGON 97759

Library of Congress Cataloging-in-Publication Data

Mynheir, Mark.
From the belly of the dragon : a novel / Mark Mynheir.
p. cm. -- (The truth chasers ; bk. 2)
ISBN 1-59052-399-7
I. Title.
PS3613.Y58F76 2006
813'.6--dc22

2006006084

06 07 08 09 10—10 9 8 7 6 5 4 3 2 1 0

To Chris, Shannon, and Justin

Trust in the LORD with all your heart and lean not on
your own understanding; in all your ways acknowledge him,
and he will make your paths straight.

PROVERBS 3:5–6

I would like to thank Multnomah Publishers and all the ministries dedicated to propagating the gospel of Jesus Christ and exposing the lies of the enemy.

And I'm especially grateful to my wonderful wife and children, who give me the time and encouragement to write, and to Ron and Judy Mitchell for all their love and support in writing and in life.

1

MELBOURNE, FLORIDA

"I hope this knucklehead doesn't get himself killed before we move in." Agent Robbie Sanchez focused on the driver of a blue pickup with her binoculars.

The man had just pulled into the parking lot of the Royal Palms apartment complex, one of the most dangerous places to be in central Florida after dark. Even though it was two in the morning, the driver's pasty skin shimmered with beads of sweat, and he scratched his face without ceasing, as if scraping some unseen insects from his gaunt, unshaven cheeks. Definitely an addict.

A yellow hue blanketed the parking lot from the corner lamppost, which was the only light on the block that hadn't been shot out. Bullet holes pitted the two-story complex, and most of the apartment windows were cracked or smashed in some fashion. Empty beer bottles and cans littered the parking lot.

A young black man wearing a white T-shirt and low-rider blue jeans eased out from the shadows of the building. He turned toward two black men on the open second-floor walkway.

One man's black leather jacket was stretched to its limits

from a series of prison workouts, and an Uzi dangled carelessly from underneath his jacket. The other man was a bit smaller, wearing a basketball jersey, number 32. He sucked on a lollipop as both leaned on the metal railing, a perfect view for their operation.

The big man nodded to Droopy-Drawers below, who then approached the blue pickup. The driver slipped a rolled-up twenty-dollar bill out the window into Droopy's hand. Droopy checked right and then left. He handed a white pebble-looking object to the driver, who had the truck in gear and sped out of the parking lot before Droopy could back away. The truck rumbled down the road, vanishing into the balmy night.

The two lieutenants kept watch over their turf as the young upstart moved back into his position in the shadows.

Parked two blocks away, Robbie slipped her binoculars underneath the seat and tightened her ponytail, checking her look once more in the mirror. A gaudy amount of makeup to be sure. Porter was gonna pay for this—big-time.

She glanced at her watch; it was go time.

Her heart raced as she drove the red Toyota Celica around the corner. The beater car chugged and sputtered down the street toward the "hole," as it was known around town.

As Robbie approached the complex, she reached under the dash, flipped the switch that killed the engine, and coasted into the parking lot, clunking to a stop.

Everyone was watching. Perfect.

The headlights brightened then dimmed, and the engine howled but refused to start again. She slammed her hands and then her head on the steering wheel. Kicking the door open with her stiletto heel, Robbie stepped out onto the street and adjusted her taut black leather skirt. Her fire-red halter top adhered to her athletic figure like an extra layer of skin.

Enjoy the show, fellas, while you still can. It's about to get real ugly.

With a tug on her skirt and a wiggle, Robbie sashayed to the front of her car, lifted the hood, and leaned inside. She tucked her crucifix back inside her shirt and laid a small cylinder on top of the engine, then pulled the pin.

A loud "pop" followed by a column of smoke chased her back on her heels. She fanned her face and coughed. The two lieutenants roared at the spectacle, the big man slapping the railing.

Droopy-Drawers slithered from the shadows and stalked toward her, fiddling with a toothpick in his mouth with one hand while constantly pulling up his pants from halfway down his hips with the other. He glanced back at his bosses and chuckled as he approached.

"Hey, baby," he said, working his best cool walk. "Looks like you need some help."

"Yeah," she choked out, catching her breath. "This thing's dead." The smoke billowed from her car, creeping through the parking lot like a nefarious fog.

The young man shuffled uncomfortably close to her. "What's such a fine J.Lo-lookin' mama like you doin' out here?" His hand massaged her hip, as if inspecting a prize ham at the deli.

"Trying to find some action." She grinned at the little pig. *Cochino*. Robbie hated the constant J.Lo comparisons from every punk she dealt with. Couldn't they at least be a little more original?

"Oh, I got plenty of action."

Searching over his shoulder and past the parking lot, she watched a man move from the rear of the complex into the front parking lot to gawk at her smoldering car—the sign she was waiting for.

A dozen men emerged from the shadows of the wood line and skulked toward the unprotected stairs on the east side of the building, automatic weapons at the ready. Six of the men crept up the steps to the second-floor walkway; the others hid in the shadows underneath the stairs, covering the front parking lot.

If this was going to work, she needed to move now.

"You look like a man with *a lot* of action." Robbie draped her left hand around the back of his neck and turned him toward her, keeping his back to the building. Her free hand eased down and unsnapped the mini-Glock 9mm from the holster strapped to her inner thigh. When the barrel rested underneath Droopy's chin, his eyes widened as he pulled against her firm grip in a vain attempt to step back.

Squeezing his neck hard enough to raise him to his tiptoes, she drew him even closer and whispered in his ear, "I'm a police officer. If you move or scream, you will *not* live to see tomorrow. *Comprende*?"

"That's not fair. Lady cops ain't supposed to be so hot."

Florida Department of Law Enforcement Agents Tim Porter and John Russell snuck up the stairs as the haze from the smoke grenade Robbie had placed under the hood now loomed over the whole complex, providing the cover and distraction they needed.

Tim led the line of agents single file toward their goal, his MP5 submachine gun secured with a three-point sling wrapped over his shoulder and under his armpit, keeping his weapon tight at the ready for a quick target acquisition if need be. He stepped with care, not wanting to stumble or make any sounds to give away their position. Surprise was crucial.

As they reached the top of the stairs, Tim's pulse throbbed in his ears with the frantic cadence of a war drum. They'd hidden in the woods just after nightfall and waited to execute their plan. This spot was pivotal. If they were seen too quickly, the likelihood of a firefight was good. Tim peeked into the walkway—both thugs still enjoyed the show below.

John had his back, and Alan Cohen followed close behind with the other agents—all wearing Kevlar helmets and black raid vests bulging with stun grenades and extra ammo.

Tim curled around the corner, training his sights on his target—the big man. With two soft steps, he touched the barrel against the man's neck while John wrapped his hand around the other's mouth, snatching him backward.

"Police," Tim whispered. "You move, you die."

Big-Man groaned as his hands went skyward. Grabbing a handful of jacket, Tim forced him to the ground. Russell dragged Big-Man's buddy back to the rest of the agents, who cuffed him and passed both suspects down the stairwell to more officers waiting below.

Now to the guest of honor—Rico Harden. The agents amassed at the side of Rico's heavily fortified door. Tim wiggled the doorknob. No luck. That would have made things a lot easier. Now to plan B.

Tim extracted a long ropelike piece of det-cord from his minibackpack. John took position on one side, Tim the other, and they wedged the sticky pyrotechnic cord into the crack between the thick metal door and the frame. Seven seconds—just as they'd practiced.

Tim stuck the probes in and reeled the line out as the team backed down the hall, as far from the door as possible. When the judge had given permission to use an explosive entry, Tim felt downright giddy. *I love my job.*

He pressed the detonator button. A brilliant flash and deafening explosion rocked the beleaguered building, and the door disappeared into Rico's apartment. A plume of smoke and debris spewed forth like a volcano.

Tim and John ran shoulder to shoulder toward the gaping hole. John lobbed a stun grenade into the apartment, and they both stepped back against the wall. Another blast assaulted the night air.

Raising his subgun to the ready, Tim barreled through the haze into the apartment with the other agents in tow. A lone black male sat on the couch next to the wall, his dreadlocks blown back with pieces of drywall stuck in his hair. He spasmodically clutched the video game remote still in his hands, tremors racking his body.

"Police! Search warrant! Get on the ground now!" Tim sprinted toward Rico, who stared blankly at a television that had been destroyed by the door blown on top of it.

A trail of agents passed Tim and scattered toward the back bedrooms. "Police! Everyone on the ground!"

"I said *get down!*" Tim snatched Rico by the scruff of his neck. Adrenaline pumped as he launched Rico off the couch, through the air, and flat on his face on the floor. Kneeling on Rico's back, Tim brushed the subgun to his side, grabbed both of Rico's hands, and cuffed the stymied felon.

Multiple stun grenades exploded on the first floor as the second team hit the apartments where Rico kept his stash of drugs and money.

"All clear." John Russell's tall, sinewy frame cut through the blast-induced cloud, and he joined Tim in the living room. Russell holstered his pistol, unsnapped his helmet, raking his hand through his thick black hair, and sighed. "The rooms are all clear. Rico's the only one here."

"Wha...what's happening?" Rico's eyes glazed over in the stupefied manner Tim often referred to as post-pyrotechnic stress disorder, a rare condition marked by being a felon in the same room when det-cord and stun grenades explode.

"Rico Harden, it gives me enormous pleasure to place you under arrest for conspiracy to traffic in cocaine, the importation of cocaine, aggravated assault...and the murder of Jamal Collins." Tim rolled Rico to a sitting position, and he hung his head between his legs.

"Your days of mayhem on these streets are over." Tim's stomach churned at the sight of Rico. A young black man tormenting and terrorizing his own people—Tim's people? Made him sick. What might have happened in this lawless young man's life if he'd had direction, some positive influence?

When Tim was young, thugs and gangsters didn't control the streets. They had to answer to Tim's father. Having marched with Dr. King and fought for civil rights long before it was popular, Pastor Porter had been respected and revered in the Parramore district of Orlando. He kept a tight rein on the young men in the neighborhood, often patrolling on Sunday mornings to see who might be skipping Sunday school. No foolin' around on Pastor Porter's watch.

Tim couldn't get away with anything either. If he got the least bit rambunctious, word would always get back to his father. The man had spies everywhere. Then it was off to a "session" with Pop, which usually meant a belt, a hug, and a Bible verse. Tim could still painfully recount Scriptures on self-control and the fear of the Lord.

His pop's faith never wavered, not that Tim could see anyway. But as much as he loved his dad, it had been the things of God that had caused their rift.

"You got a stiff neck, Timmy," he used to say during one of their spirited debates. "That just means God's gonna have to give you whiplash to get your attention."

But after a stint in the marines, over twenty years of law enforcement, and watching his father, who served God faithfully, wither away in an excruciating death, Tim was convinced that God was quite distant from the affairs of men, maybe even cold and indifferent to the suffering of all people.

Even though he didn't share his father's faith, at times like this he appreciated the man's love and discipline, even if it could be…uncomfortable to say the least. That patient, consistent devotion was what separated Tim from Rico Harden.

Special Agent in Charge Alan Cohen walked from a back bedroom, working a rubber glove onto his hand, preparing to search the apartment.

"I told you, Alan." Tim pointed to the huge metal door, now embedded in the fifty-two-inch television. "There is no problem in law enforcement that can't be solved through the proper use of pyrotechnics."

"I guess not." Alan scratched his gray-black beard and removed his black skullcap, revealing a head mostly devoid of hair. He was a good boss, giving his agents a lot of leeway. He trusted them, until they messed up, of course. Then Alan could be an ogre.

Nine people in custody, Rico's entire organization, and not one shot had been fired. Six months of chasing down leads, wiretaps, garbage searches, and wheeling and dealing with witnesses and suspects had played out better than Tim could have asked for.

The "hole" had been the largest crack cocaine distribution center on the Space Coast. Rico had built a criminal empire on the blood and bodies of his rivals. He thought himself untouchable—until now. Sitting on the dirty floor with his head between his legs, Rico Harden was defeated. Tim did love his job.

John slipped on a pair of rubber gloves, and he and his team prepared to have Rico transported to jail while they searched his apartment. Tim waved some of the smoke away from his face; the acidic stench of the det-cord hung heavy in the room.

Robbie appeared in the doorway and slapped her hands on her hips. "Sure, gentlemen, get all the glory, why don't you. While I gotta be out there dressed like this." She passed her hand over her skimpy outfit. "It's demeaning. I have a doctorate in psychology. I've had my work published and peer-reviewed, and I'm out here dressed like a hooker. This is not what I had in mind when I got into law enforcement."

Tim and John snickered, trying their best not to burst out. Alan acted like he was looking at the case file, a broad grin creasing his beard.

"I'm serious, Alan. This is the last time I play bait while you guys get the fun stuff. It was all I could do not to break that filthy little punk's hand. Next time I want on the entry team, and we'll put Porter in the dress."

Tim's smile evaporated.

"That is a hideous thought," John said. "We'll all need therapy after that."

Rico glanced up, checking out Robbie.

"Don't get any ideas, Romeo." Robbie pointed at Rico, who bowed his head. "You've got a date with death row."

2

Daddy!" Ruby Porter jumped from the black BMW and jogged up the driveway toward Tim, who was waiting with arms open wide. He hugged his daughter, lifting her off the ground and twirling her in a circle.

"Oh, baby, I missed you so much." Tim set her down and stroked her ebony cheek. "My goodness, look at you."

He beheld his daughter. She bore his lighter complexion, and her deep brown hair was tied back and gently curled in the long, pencil-thin Sisterlocks that hung past her shoulders like chocolate swirls. She was a woman now, as much as he didn't want to admit it, and a beautiful one at that, like her mother.

"You've lost weight," Cynthia Porter said stepping out of the driver's seat.

His ex had a figure that mocked her age. She straightened her skirt along her nimble build and stopped at the front of the car, crossing her arms. Her hair was pulled back in a bun, looking every bit the college professor, with a few gray streaks sneaking in along her hairline.

"Thanks, Cynth. You look good, too."

She really did look good, and different. But something was going on with her. Even though she had kept her distance from him, for the first time in a long time, she seemed at peace. Part of him was happy for her, but another part wanted her struggling without him, maybe considering coming back.

"Thank you," Cynthia said with enough curtness to indicate she wanted to change the subject. He didn't have to be a cop to see that.

Since the divorce, their conversations had been very cordial, almost formal. The fighting was over. They agreed to be civil, especially in front of Ruby. But it felt odd keeping to formalities with the woman he'd spent twenty years of his life with. It was probably best this way, but he didn't have to like it.

"I'm sooo glad to be home," Ruby said, "even if it's just for the weekend. I can use the break. College is a lot harder than I thought it would be."

"What are you talking about? You're a smart girl. Those classes should be nothin' for you."

"It's not the classes, Daddy. They're easy. It's all the other things—the people, just getting along. Everyone there seems so...different."

"It just takes time to adjust. You'll be fine." He patted her on the back. "Now where we gettin' dinner? I'm starved."

"Well, I'll leave you two here." Cynthia twirled her keys in her hand. "I'll pick you up tomorrow, Ruby, and we can go out then."

"Why don't you come out with us, Cynth?" Tim wrapped his arm around Ruby. "It would be like old times." He held his breath, not wanting to give too much of an indication that he would scream and dance right here if she would only say yes.

"I'm really not up for it. Besides, you two need some time together. Ruby and I got to talk a lot on the way here."

Tim paused and bit his lip. "Okay...we'll see you tomorrow then." The disappointment had to echo in his voice. Cynth could always tease out the unbridled emotion in him, good and bad.

But he didn't blame her for not going, for not trying one more time. After all he'd put her through, he couldn't blame her one bit.

He easily could have blamed their failed marriage on a bank robber's bullet tearing through his stomach and the deep depression that followed, but that wouldn't be honest. He and Cynth's marriage was in trouble long before the shooting.

They'd been drifting apart for years with the lack of true communication, the power struggles, the different expectations. Tiny cracks swelled into gigantic fissures, tearing them away from each other until they were two disconnected people living under one roof. When the fighting had stopped, Tim knew their marriage was dead—all the passion and spirit drained from its lifeless body.

Cynthia stepped forward and kissed Ruby on the forehead, then glanced back at him as if she had something to say. She feigned a smile and then got into her car and backed out onto the street.

Tim watched her drive away. No matter how much time went by, he still couldn't get used to seeing that.

"It's so great to see you, Daddy." Ruby took his hand as the two sat in the small booth at the Wagon Wheel Pizzeria. "I can't believe how good you look. You've lost weight, and something else seems different. I can't quite put my finger on it, but you look happy."

Where had the time gone? It seemed like such a short time ago that she was nothing more than a little pixie sprinting toward him when he got home from work. She used to cling to him, one hand on his badge, the other around his neck, giggling hysterically as he gave her rides on his broad shoulders through the house, chasing bad guys.

"You're sweet. You always know how to butter up your daddy. You want more money or somethin'?"

"But you're just as silly as ever." She shook her head and ravaged the piece of pizza in her hand, steam rolling up her face. "That hasn't changed," she muttered with her mouth full.

"A lot has changed." Tim met his precious daughter's eyes. Could he break the news now? He didn't know if the time was right or not, but he yearned to tell her. Her smile convinced him it was past time. "And it's not just my weight."

Ruby lifted her eyebrows.

"I haven't drank anything in seven months," Tim said in almost a whisper.

Her pizza fell to her plate, her mouth wide open. "Daddy, that's fantastic." She slid her hand into his. "Why didn't you tell me?"

"I didn't want to disappoint you again." Tim squeezed her hand tight. "There's been enough of that. I wanted to be sure that I wasn't just playin' games with myself. I've done that too many times now. I wanted to be sure I'd never go back to drinking...for both of us."

"Daddy, I couldn't be prouder of you. Let me go get another round of root beer to celebrate. I'll be right back." She hurried toward the bar.

He bathed in her words. The fallout from the divorce had crippled Tim and Ruby's relationship for well over a year. She'd blamed him, rightfully as far as he was concerned.

As a marine, a cop, and having been shot and attacked in every kind of way, he thought he knew what pain was. But when his own daughter would have nothing to do with him, he found out how wrong he was. The estrangement nearly killed him, but it also finally helped him.

At his lowest point, he knew he had to do something—anything—to reclaim his life. The drinking had to go. He would do whatever it took to have Ruby back in his life and repair their relationship. He was wholly committed to being the father she wanted and deserved.

Some things were still rough, though. He was a people person, not designed to live alone, but he was starting to get used to it. After so many years with the Orlando PD, he was finally settling in with FDLE in Melbourne. He liked the people and the work, but the absolute best thing in his life, bar none, was having Ruby back. He would never, ever lose her again.

Ruby returned with a pitcher and poured them both a fresh glass.

"So tell me about school." Tim sipped his soda and wiped his mouth with a napkin.

"It's okay, I guess." Ruby leaned back. "It's just a lot different than high school."

"That's why they call it college, honey."

"I know. But being all the way up in Tallahassee, I mean, it's just so far away. I can't come home nearly as much as I want."

"It's not easy being away from home for the first time. There's an adjustment period, but that'll pass. Soon you'll be well on your way to being a doctor."

"That's part of the problem, too." Ruby looked tentative. "I'm thinking about changing my major."

"Really? To what?"

"I'm not sure."

"Your grades have been good; I don't understand." Tim wanted to be quiet and hear her out, but he wasn't terribly surprised by her change. She'd only recently announced that she wanted to get into the medical field. She'd never seemed to have a clear vision of what she wanted to do, but at least now she was opening up to him.

"It's not that. It just doesn't feel right. I don't know if that's what I'm supposed to be doing with my life. I thought it was, but now I'm not so sure. I'm thinking about English lit or education. Maybe I'll be a teacher like Mom."

"That would be a fine field, honey. I'll support you in anything you want to do…other than law enforcement. I didn't raise my baby girl to be no cop."

"No chance of that, Daddy," she said with a giggle. "That much I'm sure about."

"Do you really want to teach?"

Ruby was silent and shrugged. "I want to do something to help people, but I have no idea what that could be right now, so I'm leaning toward teaching."

"Don't worry about that stuff today. You've got plenty of time to decide. Let's figure out what we're gonna do with the rest of our weekend. That should keep us busy enough."

3

SOUTH FLORIDA

Mitch Garrow's lungs burned as he trudged through the waist-deep water, praying no alligators prowled this part of the canal. But maybe it would be better if he ran into one. It might be more merciful.

No moon was out to guide his way. The pungent odor of swamp muck assaulted his nose with every deep breath. He made it to the other side, pulling himself onto the shoreline. Mitch was on his own, and he didn't know how much farther he could go.

The roar of an engine called from the distance.

They were coming.

Forcing himself to his feet, he barreled into the dense south Florida foliage. A spiderweb clung to his face, and he peeled it off as he ran. Branches, vines, and roots slapped and tore at him as he negotiated through the night. Saw palmettos ripped his jeans, and blood trickled down his legs as he climbed and crawled his way through the jungle. Sweat and swamp water soaked his hair.

He didn't have much time left.

How could he have been so stupid? All the signs were there. That nutty chick had been right…about everything. Why didn't he listen earlier? Too late to worry about that now. Someone had to know. That man must be exposed, no matter the cost. "God, forgive me for ever being a part of this."

As the vehicle closed in, the crushing, crackling of the palmettos underneath the massive tires of the monster truck resonated through the night. A spotlight passed to and fro in front of his path, stopping him cold.

He couldn't escape.

Crawling along the moist ground, he propped his back against a pine tree, hoping it would conceal him from their probing eyes. Maybe he could wait them out. He rubbed his hand along his face, smearing mud across his cheeks.

The lights stopped for a moment, and everything went dark. His heart throbbed, drowning out the sounds of the truck creeping toward him. A lone spotlight illuminated the tree he was hiding behind.

Night vision goggles. He lowered his head. *I should have known they'd bring them. They could see me the whole time.*

The truck rumbled toward him. He only had one chance. Pushing himself up from the tree, he sprinted through the foliage.

"There he goes," a voice called out.

Mitch galloped as fast as his legs would carry him while pressing his hand against the notebook concealed inside his shirt, the journal that the world must see. Breathing heavily, Mitch felt like the muggy Florida air never seemed to fully fill his lungs.

He hit a small clearing. If he could just make it past…

Crack. A rifle report fractured the air. The round slapped his left leg, knocking it out from under him as he slid face-first into the dirt, his thigh searing as if a hot iron had been thrust through it. The pain amplified with every heartbeat.

The truck crashed through the dense foliage into the clearing, gobbling up everything in its path.

Mitch pushed himself up and limped into the woods again. Just a little farther and he'd be on the road. Someone could help him there. The pain was so intense he nearly threw up, but he pressed forward, dragging his wounded leg behind him.

He slipped through a cluster of pine trees and stumbled out onto the embankment to the road. The truck couldn't follow him through that, he was sure. He climbed up the embankment and fast-limped down the side of the road.

Almost home.

A spotlight flashed on him. Shielding his eyes, he looked toward the pickup only a few feet away, which had obviously been waiting to ambush him.

A huge figure wearing a cowboy hat stepped into the light. Mitch searched up and down the barren road. There was no one to see, no one to help.

"You've got something that doesn't belong to you, boy." The man aimed a rifle at his chest, the truck exhaust encompassing them both in a surreal haze.

Mitch held the journal close to his chest, and blood gushed freely from his wounded leg, which threatened to give out at any moment.

The cowboy showed no concern for it as he shuffled closer to Mitch, rifle still at the ready. "Put it on the ground and step away."

Mitch closed his eyes as he lowered the book to the road, barely keeping his balance.

The menace snatched up the journal and threw it on the front seat of the truck, then turned his attention and his rifle back to Mitch.

As Mitch stared down the barrel, a strange peace overtook him. "Lord, help them all know the Truth."

4

John Russell turned his gray Buick into his gravel driveway, which wove through the scrub oak and palm trees, opening to a full view of John's house. The light blue two-story home was tucked away in the foliage of the three-acre property, just out of sight of the road. The front of the home was warm and inviting. The white trim and railing of the porch contrasted well with the light blue exterior.

Tim had always liked the warm and inviting look and feel of the Russell home. John and the boys had spent last fall repainting it after John's father passed away.

"Appreciate you and Marie having me over for dinner," Tim said, still in his shirt and tie from work.

"Marie thought it would be nice to see you again. Besides, the boys need someone to play with for a while. They're getting a little rowdy and need to wear off some energy."

Tim chuckled.

They parked in front of the house. Tim got out and stretched the day off; it felt good to work out the kinks in his muscles. He had spent almost the entire day at the computer finishing up the Harden report. Paperwork was the part of being a cop he hated the most—the countless hours spent typing reports, filing things. The field was where real police work was done, and he didn't like anything that got in the way of that. But Tim had to do what he had to do.

John circled around the car, and they walked toward the front door. A palm bush on the side of the driveway rustled at their approach. Tim stopped, grabbing John's arm. A long black barrel extended out from the leaves.

"Watch out!" Tim yelled as he jerked John back behind the car.

The first shot nailed John's chest. The second shot caught Tim in the shoulder before he could get behind the car. A rapid three-round burst ricocheted off the windshield.

"We give up," Tim said. "You got us. We surrender."

"Then come out with your hands up," the youthful voice called from the bushes.

Tim and John stepped out from behind the car with their hands up, stains on both their shirts.

Joshua rolled out from underneath the bush, covering them with his Airsoft pellet rifle. Decked out in full camo wear, the precocious seven-year-old had set up his ambush well.

"I had you guys so bad." A triumphant grin crossed the boy's face.

"You did pretty good," Tim said. "But you moved before you took the shot. You sounded like a herd of elephants stomping around in there. You've got to have more discipline and stay completely still before you fire."

"You didn't hear anything, Uncle Tim. You just don't want to admit that I had you."

"I'm telling you, squirt, you were rampaging and raging like elephants. I bet people shopping downtown heard you jumping around out here."

"Okay, boys," John said, chuckling. "That's enough. Where's my hug, son?"

Joshua dropped his weapon and launched himself at his

father's chest and squeezed tight. John picked up the rifle and carried Joshua into the house, Tim following right behind him.

The aroma of freshly cooked ham and mashed potatoes teased Tim's nose, luring him inside. He inhaled a long, deep breath. His home away from home.

Marie walked down the narrow hallway from the kitchen toward her husband, wiping her hands on a towel as John lowered Joshua to the floor. Her coal-black hair was clipped back, and her thin frame and pretty face didn't give the slightest hint that she'd just turned forty. The fact that she'd recently taken up jogging helped her retain her youthful appearance.

In a moment of self-pity, John had confided to Tim that Marie beat him on their last run together, and he was now secretly training on his lunch breaks so he could keep up with her. Tim would keep that tidbit to himself.

She stepped back and glowered at John, then Joshua, who lowered his head.

"Joshua William Russell." Marie crossed her arms, eyes narrowing at the camo-clad offender. "How many times have I told you not to snipe your father when he comes home?"

"It's all right." John touched his chest. "Don't worry, it didn't leave a mark."

"You're missing the point, honey. He's seven. He doesn't need to be setting up ambushes on his father and whoever else shows up. It's not healthy. He should be building Legos, racing cars, or watching *Barney*."

"Aw, Mom." Joshua shook his head. "That's baby stuff."

"The kid's sneaky, I'm telling you," Tim said. "A natural. He'll make a great sniper or cop."

"Thanks, Uncle Tim." The boy beamed.

"News flash. Tim's not your uncle."

"What do you mean, Marie?" Tim pulled Joshua close to

him. "Can't you see the family resemblance?"

Joshua put his arm around Tim and grinned, mimicking him.

A smile infringed on Marie's scowl, shattering her attempt to be serious. She covered her grin with one hand and whipped an angry finger at Tim with the other. "This is partially your fault, you know. No more countersniper classes or glorious cop stories from you."

Tim surrendered again. "Okay, okay. We'll find something else to play…for a while."

"I've been a cop's wife long enough. I don't think I could handle being a cop's mother." Marie leaned forward and kissed Tim on the cheek. "But it's good to see you regardless. I'm glad you could make it for dinner, even if you are a mischief maker."

"Hey, Uncle Tim." Brandon stomped down the stairs. Marie rolled her eyes as she kissed John.

The eleven-year-old looked like he'd grown three inches in the past six months. Brandon was the spitting image of John. His voice was a little deeper now and fluctuated with the gravelly, uneven pitch of impending male puberty, and his hair appeared to have darkened some since the last time Tim had seen him.

Brandon gave Tim a half-shoulder hug, and they made their way to the table. "He's been lying in that bush out there for an hour waiting for you guys."

Tim caught Joshua's attention and gave him a thumbs-up. Joshua giggled and sat at his place at the table, his face still covered with camouflage paint and his sandy blond hair jetting in several directions like a sandspur.

Marie sawed into the steaming ham, trimming off a thick slice. Squeezing it with the knife and fork, she swung it over to Tim's plate.

"Oh yeah, that looks good." Tim rubbed his hands together.

The table turned into a flurry of dipped spoons and sliced

meat until all the plates were full.

Tim cut a juicy morsel of ham and almost had it in his mouth before he noticed that everyone else had their hands folded. He eased his fork to his plate and bowed his head.

"Joshua," John said, "would you like to say the prayer?"

He nodded. "Dear Lord, thank You for the food, and thanks for Uncle Tim. He's lots of fun. Amen."

Tim messed up Joshua's hair and then picked up his fork. The tender ham melted in his mouth. Boy, that Marie could cook. She was a remarkable woman. The whole family was somethin' else.

Since day one of Tim working with John, they had taken him in as one of their own. Even though John could be a tad bit hyperreligious, the man was the best friend Tim had ever known. Tim respected him for how he'd raised his boys, for being a good husband, and for working so hard at being a good cop. In quieter moments, Tim envied John for being able to balance what he'd let tumble and crash to the ground.

For a time in his life, Tim had been able to balance all things, too. But somehow, slowly, that balance had shifted, and his family teetered and then finally collapsed. Only now were those pieces starting to come back together, though in a different shape. Not exactly the shape he'd like, but better than it was. He didn't begrudge John his great life; Tim was just glad he was part of it.

"Uncle Tim, could you pass the peas please?"

"Gladly, Brandon."

Good friends didn't grow on trees, and good kids didn't happen by accident. Russell had good kids. Tim did feel like their uncle now—a title he carried with pride.

5

MELBOURNE

"You're doing it all wrong, Porter."

John saw Robbie reach over Tim's muscular shoulder and point to the picture in the book propped up between Tim's computer and the cubicle wall.

"Well, comments from the cheap seats don't help." Tim didn't even glance up as he studied the instructions in front of him. "This requires precision of mind, body, and spirit fused into the task at hand. Now back off, Sanchez, and give me some space while I create."

Robbie looked to John for help.

"Let him do it himself. He'll get it. It'll just take some time."

Robbie stepped back and crossed her arms. "But he's messing it up."

"Almost finished." Excitement tinged Tim's voice. "And voilà."

Tim swiveled his chair around and extended his hand, holding a wadded-up piece of paper that John thought resembled…a wadded-up piece of paper.

"So now what do you think?"

Robbie's shoulders quivered, and she pursed her lips, holding back the chuckle.

"It looks...well, nice." John looked at it carefully. "What's it supposed to be again?"

"A knight on a horse. It's plain as day. Can't you see that?" Tim held up the accompanying picture in his book *Origami: The Beginner's Guide*.

The tortured creation bore no resemblance to anything even remotely crafted on purpose. Pride still emanated from Tim's face. John didn't want to tell him the truth.

"It's hideous," Robbie blurted out, her hand still covering her mouth. "It's so awful it *could* be modern art."

Tim glared at her. "You just don't have an eye for true art."

Alan walked into the office cubicles, a cup of java in hand.

Tim stepped past Robbie and John. "Alan, tell me truthfully. What do you think?" He held up the book with the picture in one hand and his "masterpiece" in the other.

Alan paused, scanning the eyes of everyone in the room. "Do you really want the truth?"

"Truth."

Alan rested his hand on Tim's shoulder and sighed. "I think you have far too much time on your hands. And that's the ugliest thing I've seen in a very long time."

"Well, fine." Tim slammed the book shut. "A man tries to expand his horizons a bit, and the least he could expect is a little support from his friends."

"We are supporting you, Tim, but this just might not be your thing," John said.

Their secretary joined them. "John, there's a woman here to see you."

In her early sixties, Gloria Davis had frosted hair and a warm heart. She fussed over the agents like they were her own children. If John brought his lunch to work, he made sure it was healthy, or he'd get an earful from Gloria on the hazards of high cholesterol or too much fat in his diet. She meant well and was loved by all.

"Who is she? I don't have any appointments this morning."

"Nora Garrow? She said it was important and that she wanted to speak only with you."

The name wasn't familiar, but he had time to meet with her. It wasn't uncommon for people to request to talk with him since he appeared on the news intermittently. He would listen patiently, then send them to the appropriate agency or person for help. Sometimes he came across some good information, but most of the time people just needed help with their problems.

"Gloria, what do you think?" Tim held out the paper clump with pride.

"I can take care of that." She snatched it from his hand and dropped it in the trash bin as she walked back toward her desk.

Tim's shoulders slumped, and he sulked out the door toward the lobby with John.

The bulletproof window in front of Gloria's desk provided them a glimpse into the lobby of the FDLE office. A woman in her early- to midfifties stood by the front door, cradling her purse in her arms. She met John's stare with a long, gloomy one of her own.

He walked past Gloria's desk as she hit the buzzer to open the door. John and Tim stepped into the lobby. "Mrs. Garrow?"

"Nora." She extended her hand to John.

He shook her hand. "How can I help you today?"

"Is there anywhere we can talk?" She glanced around the room. "It's a long story."

John escorted her past Gloria's desk and into a small break room off the hallway. He didn't want to bring her back to the formal interview room, which wasn't the coziest place for non-criminal types. They sat at a small round table. He would listen to her, hopefully answer her questions, and then send her on her way.

"This is my partner, Agent Porter."

Nora shook his hand. Tim smiled, nodded his head, but said nothing.

"So how can we help you today?"

She pulled a picture from her purse and slid it across the table. "Find my son...please."

The picture was from a high school yearbook. A young man with sandy blond hair, sharp cheekbones, and a smile much like his mother's might be...if John had seen her smile.

"I think I'll need a little more than this to start with," John said. "Why don't you start from the beginning."

"My son, Mitch, was a sophomore at the University of South Florida. He's such a bright kid. Anyway, he got involved with this...*group*." Nora regarded John then Tim. "Have either of you heard of Dr. Walter Simmons, the self-help guru? He's got a book on the bestseller list now."

"I've heard the name." John had no idea where this was going.

"Mitch got involved with his group, the Higher Learning Method something or other. At first I thought it was a good thing for him, a way to make some friends and such on campus. Since his father left when he was six, Mitch has always been more into academics than people, and he's never been good at making long-lasting friends. But shortly after he joined this group, he quit school and went to their facility down in Highpoint, Florida, near the Everglades. He told me if I couldn't support him in this, he would have nothing to do with me, so he stopped talking with me. That was a little over six months ago."

"What makes you think something's happened? Maybe he's just taking some time away," John said.

"A few weeks ago I got this e-mail from him." She handed him a piece of paper. "It's the last thing I heard. I know something's wrong."

John read it out loud. *"Mom, I'm so sorry. Things have changed. China opened my eyes. Will explain later. Gotta go. Love, Mitch."*

"I don't quite understand this China thing. It doesn't make a lot of sense."

"To me either, Agent Russell, but it's the last thing I heard."

"I don't mean to offend you, but I have to ask. Did Mitch have any mental health issues? Was he ever under the care of a doctor?"

She recoiled and glared at John. "No. His mind was fine—until he met those people."

"Have you gone to Highpoint and tried to talk with Mitch?"

Nora nodded. "I met with a rude little man who told me that Mitch had left on some sort of 'walkabout' to share his knowledge around the world and no one there knew exactly where he was."

"What do you think about that?"

"It stinks. No matter what else has happened between us, Mitch wouldn't leave the country without telling me."

John alternated his attention from Nora to his legal pad as he jotted down notes. "Have you brought this up with law enforcement in Highpoint?"

"Yeah, but I got a we'll-keep-an-eye-out-for-him-ma'am attitude. The chief of police was less than helpful. I've been to the FBI. They were no help. I've written letters to Governor Maclartey. No one seems concerned about what's happened to my son. That's why I came to see you."

"This does make it tough." John rubbed his chin. "Mitch is an adult and is allowed to go off if he wants to."

"You don't understand. Just before he went to Highpoint, Mitch spouted all this gibberish about having a higher purpose and learning past our imperfections to attain our higher being. Once he got involved with these people, he ceased talking or acting like my son at all. They stole his mind, and I'm not about to let them get away with stealing the rest of him."

John didn't know what to make of the woman. She seemed legitimately concerned about her son, but Mitch wouldn't be the first child to rebel against his parents and go off on a tangent. John glanced at Tim, who shrugged.

John leaned forward. "I don't know what we can do for you, Mrs. Garrow."

"Do you have children, Agent Russell?"

"Yes, two boys."

"Then you might be able to understand. It's hard to explain, but I know something is wrong… I can feel it. Please. You found that little boy Dylan; now I'm asking you to find my son. You're the only one who can help me."

John leaned back in his chair and regarded the hurting woman. As happy as he was that the Dylan Jacobs case had turned out so well, sometimes it was a millstone around his neck. Since the case had made national news, Nora wasn't the first person to approach him about a missing loved one. But something about her story tingled in his spirit. Tim would accuse him of being a softy for another hard-luck story. But what else was new? His caseload was light; he could take this on, even if it led to nowhere.

"I can't promise anything, but we'll take a look at it."

6

TALLAHASSEE

Ruby braved the chaotic lunchtime crowd as she entered the cafeteria, an increasingly nerve-racking daily ritual. She hurried into line with a pack of other students. She picked up a banana, a bowl of soup, and a biscuit. She wasn't very hungry, but she needed to eat something.

After she paid for her meal, Ruby searched for an inviting table among the crowd. Nothing. Then she spotted her roommate, Traci Spearman, sitting at a table with two other girls.

Traci rarely spent a full night in their dorm room, but when she did, she usually had a companion—and not always the same one. When she was there with one of her "friends," Ruby had to sleep out on the couch in the lounge.

Most of the "talking" Ruby and Traci did was limited to one-sentence civilities in passing. Though Traci had gotten really chatty one time and told Ruby about her thirteen body piercings. Ruby could only account for ten, but she was perfectly happy not seeing the other three.

She swallowed hard and walked over to their table. "Is this chair taken?"

Traci glanced at her two friends and raised her eyebrows "My roommate." Then she turned back to Ruby. "Go ahead. We were just leaving." Traci and her friends rose together, gabbing as they headed out of the cafeteria.

Ruby sank onto her seat. At least she had found an open table. She tasted her soup, which was bland and cold. Alone in a room full of people, she pulled her jean jacket tight about her and listened to the cheerful chatter of those around her.

Had she made the right school choice? If she had gone to the University of Central Florida, where her mother taught, at least she'd have someone to talk to and spend time with. But she had decided that coming to Florida State, away from her parents, would give her a chance to focus more on her studies and relieve some of the tension from her parents' divorce.

Although she and her mother had been close before the divorce, after her dad left, it just wasn't the same. Her mom threw herself into work to cope with the breakup, and Ruby had been so angry with her dad that she couldn't even bring herself to speak to him for a year. Her entire senior year was spent being estranged from her father, juggling a hectic school schedule, and having hit-or-miss dinners with her mother.

Once they had been a strong, vibrant family, and she'd give anything to have that back. Now only an aching void filled her soul, and college wasn't helping. She had no idea what to do next.

The initial thrill of choosing a school and moving to Tallahassee had worn off, and now she was left with a forlorn reality. Had she made a terrible mistake?

7

John turned off of Interstate 27, and he and Tim headed east toward the town of Highpoint. Even though John was raised in Florida, he'd never been to this side of the state. Situated on the west shore of Lake Okeechobee, Highpoint was an older community, obtaining its name after the killer hurricane of 1928 that caused many survivors to move there because of the slightly higher ground. Urban legend had it that Highpoint was built squarely upon an Indian burial ground.

Entering Highpoint, they turned onto Main Street, and the sign that greeted them read "Welcome to Highpoint. May you stay high and dry." The thoroughfare, with its collection of small storefronts and restaurants on the one-road strip, seemed like it had been transported straight from Mayberry.

John was surprised by how modern much of the small town looked. Almost all the storefronts had new fasciae and signs. Well-trimmed oaks lined the street, something foreign to this part of south Florida.

Lake Okeechobee paralleled Main Street, the water's white-caps breaking a few hundred yards to their left. At the far end of Main Street, a sprawling complex of brick buildings peered down on the town.

John pointed to the horizon. "That must be Dr. Simmons's place."

"Looks peaceful. The whole town seems nice. Maybe I'll move here when we clean this case up. Retire. Fish a little."

"Sounds quaint...and quiet, too. You sure you're ready for something like that, Tim?"

"In a tranquil place like this, I might be able to adjust."

"We better check in with the locals. We don't want to ruffle any feathers while we're here."

At the edge of town, just ahead of them, the police department sign hung on a green lamppost along Main Street. They parked in a visitor spot directly in front of the building. The police department also appeared newer. Fresh stucco adorned the small building with green shutters, and large windows provided an open view into the office, where a lone officer occupied a desk toward the back.

John scanned the case file one last time before closing it. He clipped his badge to his belt and started to slide on his holster and gun but thought better of it. He set them under his seat. He wasn't sure how the local chief of police would react to a couple of state agents coming onto his turf loaded for bear. John would travel light, this visit anyway, until they knew what and who they were looking for.

He and Tim entered the station and stopped in the small foyer. A comfortable bench sat against the wall, and a countertop and gate separated the lobby from the work spaces. The whole office was open and inviting, a far cry from the Melbourne FDLE office, which had bulletproof glass separating the lobby from their offices. Just past the counter, three desks formed an L-shape, and each desk held an up-to-date computer with flat-screen monitor.

They caught the attention of a man at the desk farthest from the door. Working at his computer, he glanced between John and Tim.

"Be with you in one second." He clicked the mouse a few times, stood, then strolled toward them.

"Chief Bennington." He extended his hand over the counter. Every bit as tall as John if not a little taller, six-two maybe, the man carried a lean, muscular build, probably an athlete at one time. His strawberry blond hair had retreated to the sides and back of his head, almost in a horseshoe shape. "How can I help you?"

"Agent Russell." John matched his strong, confident grip. "This is Agent Porter. We're with FDLE."

Porter took the chief's hand as well. "Call me Tim."

"What's FDLE got goin' in our small town?"

John pulled Mitch's picture from his file and handed it to the chief. "We're looking for this young man."

Chief Bennington instantly shook his head. "The Garrow boy."

"You know him?" John laid the file on the countertop.

"I only know of him. Never met him. I suppose his mother contacted you."

John nodded. "She came by our office."

"It doesn't surprise me. She came here, too, then went to the FBI and wrote letters to state officials. She's convinced something wicked has happened to her son." He returned the picture to John.

"You're not?" John slid it back into his folder.

"No. He was a troubled kid. Stopped talking to his mom and took off. It happens all the time in every city in the nation. It's tragic but not a crime."

"Mrs. Garrow said Mitch was staying here somewhere." John feigned a look at his notes, feeling the chief out.

"With Dr. Simmons," Bennington said without missing a beat. "At the Higher Learning Center."

"What do you think of this Dr. Simmons and his…group?" John asked.

The chief paused, then pushed through the gate and joined them in the lobby. "Come with me. I want to show you something." He grabbed his tan Stetson off the hat rack and adjusted it on his head as he led them out the front door.

Outside they were greeted by a robust, humid draft from the lake. Chief Bennington propped his hands on his hips and surveyed the town like a cowboy sheriff from years past. "I grew up here. It's a great place for a kid. All the fishing and hiking you could hope for."

His hand panned toward the giant lake, which looked like an ocean from where they stood. "The most people had to worry about back then were alligator poachers. Things changed through the years—a business would close; a prominent family would move away. Other than some agriculture and fishing, there's no strong industry around here to keep up with the times. There are only so many bass tournaments you can hold to bring the people in. This town was dying a slow, painful death."

John nodded and appreciated the serene morning. He was envious of the chief. He wouldn't mind retiring to Highpoint someday either.

Tim leaned against their car and scanned the area. "So what happened?"

"Dr. Simmons happened." Chief Bennington pointed to the brick buildings about a half mile in the distance. "He started building his place about two years ago. He chose this town because of its name. Highpoint goes well with his Higher Learning Method. It was like a blood transfusion for the town.

"Most of these stores you see along here were empty and boarded up. Now we have students from all over the world coming here. Just last month, Don Mitchell's ice cream shop over there posted its best month ever. The Highpoint Inn is open and filling its rooms to capacity. This town has a chance to survive now, and we owe Dr. Simmons a debt we'll never be able to repay. Some people might not think so, but I surely do."

"So not everybody in Highpoint feels the same way about Dr. Simmons, huh?"

"We've got some busybodies who don't like having the campus in town. Some folks think Dr. Simmons is setting up his own little kingdom. It's just plain unfair. The man has helped thousands of people, and it all comes back to benefit our town."

"Sounds like you got a lot of respect for the man," Tim said. "How well do you know him?"

"We talk all the time. He's a remarkable guy, and I feel lucky to consider him a friend."

John checked his watch. "We'd like to meet with Dr. Simmons. Maybe he can give us some insights into Mr. Garrow's whereabouts."

"You won't be able to meet with him today. He's outta town. Another speaking engagement or something. But I tell you what, if you give me your card, I'll make sure he gets the message and contacts you."

"That would be great." John retrieved his card from his shirt pocket and handed it to him.

"Anything I can do to help. But I think you're wasting your time in Highpoint. If this kid was anywhere near my town, I would know. He'll probably turn up in Miami or somewhere, smoking dope and living like a fool."

"We hope he turns up," John said. "But we still need to check everything out."

"There's one thing I'd like you to do for me, Agent Russell. If you need something on this case or come back to town, I'd appreciate you going through me first. I'll be your contact person on this. I don't like surprises in my town."

John locked eyes with Bennington, who met his stare head-on.

The chief meant business. John didn't know if the man was a micromanager or if something else was at work. Time would tell.

John smiled. "No problem, Chief. We'll let you know when we're in town."

An officer came from behind the police station and headed for the front door.

"Hey, Moses," Bennington called to him before he could enter.

"Yeah, Chief." He let go of the door and strolled toward them.

Chief Bennington made the introductions. "This is Moses Harris, one of our best officers."

"There's only six of us, counting the chief," Moses said, shaking hands, "so we're all 'one of the best.'"

Moses could have been Tim's son. He had the same high cheekbones and perpetual smile, the same light brown skin tone, and they were the same height, although he was considerably leaner than Tim. Very odd.

"Moses, show these men over to Kay's Diner and make sure she takes good care of them. Tell her they're my guests."

"Sure thing, Chief."

Bennington glanced at his watch. "I'm sorry, gentlemen. I have an appointment for lunch. If you-all need any kinda help, call me anytime." His words were not a request. He handed them a business card that even had his home phone number on it.

The chief hurried into the police station and to his desk, picked up the phone, and glanced back at John.

"You-all ready for lunch?" Moses asked.

"Sure," John said as they turned toward the diner across the street. "Your chief seems like a good guy."

"Yeah, he's a good boss. Treats us well. The man's a legend around these parts."

"How so?"

"As quarterback he led Highpoint High to the state championship back in the late seventies. It was the last great thing to happen around here."

"At least until Dr. Simmons and his group came to town, right?" John tilted his head to get a better look at Moses.

Moses shrugged and stayed quiet.

"You don't seem to share your boss's admiration for Dr. Simmons and his work," Tim said.

They all stopped in front of Kay's Diner. Moses folded his arms and leaned one foot against the wall. "Dr. Simmons is whatever the chief says he is."

"That's a very politically correct answer." Tim raised his foot and rested it on the bumper of a car parked at the curb. "Officer Harris, Moses, what do you *really* think of Dr. Simmons?"

Moses shrugged again and rolled his eyes. "I think…we better get inside before Kay serves up all her best food." He pulled open the door and held it for them. "Gentlemen, after you."

8

The Florida State University campus bustled with activity as students scurried along the sidewalks between classes. Ruby Porter walked alone, admiring her beautiful but distant surroundings. She stopped along the walkway and plopped down on a park bench, seeking solace in the shade of a colossal oak whose outstretched branches hung next to her like the arms of a friend.

A groups of students passed by, chatting and carrying on, totally oblivious to her. She used to play a game as a child where she'd pretend to be invisible and prance about in the open, and no one knew she was there. She could be free and independent, outside of the control of anyone—her parents, her teachers. Now she wasn't playing the game, but she was every bit as invisible, transparent in a world that seemed made for connections and relationships.

It didn't make sense. *What's wrong with me? Why don't I fit in?* Everyone else moved along in life just fine. All she wanted was one friend, one person she could actually have a conversation with that included more than what boy was cute or what party they were going to.

Maybe it was her clothes. She looked down at her light brown dress, blue denim jacket, and favorite tan boots. She was never very good with fashion. Perhaps they were no longer in style.

Or maybe it was her grades. She'd been getting straight A's since grade school, and that could intimidate people. She couldn't believe that no one here wanted to study. Was something wrong with her that she actually wanted to succeed in school? She wasn't willing to dumb down just to make some friends, but it was getting tough.

It couldn't be because she was African-American. Ruby had gone to mostly white schools her whole life, and she'd never experienced any serious problems before. She didn't even fit in with the other African-American students. She had to face the only option left—she was just plain weird. Otherwise, she'd have at least one friend.

Slapping her hands on her knees, she let out an exhausted sigh. Oh, well. She was now just a spectator in life.

Ruby glanced at her watch. *Uh-oh. Better get to Biology on time.* She scooped up her assortment of books. As she stood, the stack slipped from her arms and books tumbled to the ground, scattering along the walkway. She threw her arms up in the air. "Great. Perfect. Why not?"

She knelt and picked up a book then reached for another when a girl nearly stepped on her hand as she walked through the mess without stopping or saying anything.

"Hey!" Ruby sat on the sidewalk among her mess and the tears started, a small trickle at first, then streams that flowed freely. She wanted to go home. She wanted to leave all these crazy, self-absorbed people.

"You look like you need some help." A guy bent over and gathered some of her loose papers that were scattering in the wind.

His friendly voice forced her from her stupor. "Huh?"

"Do–you–need–some–help?" He enunciated each word slowly, as if she were hard of hearing.

"Yeah…um, yes." She brushed back her locks and picked up her notebook, glancing back at him.

Still crouched down, he extended his hand. "Byron Macy."

She continued to pick up her things.

"This is the part of the conversation where you tell me your name."

"Oh. I'm sorry. I'm just a little preoccupied right now. You know, classes and all this…stuff."

His black hair was straight and combed nicely to the side, and his light blue shirt matched the color of his eyes. He was cute, for a white guy—then he smiled. Nice. He was confident, like he had all the answers.

"Ruby." She shook his hand. "Ruby Porter. I'm a freshman."

"I figured that. Rarely do you see a senior out here crying on the sidewalk. They reserve that honor only for freshmen."

"You saw that, huh?" She could die at any time during this conversation.

He grinned. "I couldn't help but see you sprawled out here."

"Great." She had all her books and enough embarrassment for one day. Time to leave. "Thank you. Gotta go."

"Wait." He set his hand on her arm. "Where you heading to so fast? I could walk with you, if you don't mind the company."

"Not at all." Maybe she wouldn't die quite yet. "I'm heading to Biology."

"Dr. Horowitz?"

"Yeah."

Byron rolled his eyes. "Oh, boy. I better give you the low-down on her. She's very particular and difficult."

"A real fun teacher, huh?"

"Oh, yeah. About as fun as a root canal."

Ruby giggled. It felt good. She hadn't laughed in a while, and this guy had a silly sense of humor, a lot like her father's.

"Say, Ruby, do you know where Dodd Hall is?"

She nodded.

"Some friends and I are meeting there tonight. We have a study group of sorts. And after we're done, we usually get pizza and talk. Would you be interested in being clumsy there about six-thirty? You could drop your books in the parking lot. Then after I help you pick them up, we could hang out."

"Are you asking *me* to meet with *you*...tonight?"

"I must be worse at this than I thought. Yes, I'm asking *you* to meet with *me* and my friends...tonight."

Ruby stopped and turned toward him. Her stomach flipped. "I guess I can have another accident there."

"Great. See you then."

Her day was definitely looking up.

9

DENVER, COLORADO

Hushed energy vibrated in the packed auditorium. Dr. Walter Simmons sauntered along the edge of the stage and peered out at the eager crowd. He pointed his index finger toward the heavens. "In a world where everyone is searching for *real* solutions to life's most difficult problems, why, then, do we look up to some mythical being for answers?"

He panned the audience and flashed his impeccable smile, and his voice deepened with just the right inflection. "When we talk about all good things, all perfect things, all powerful things, why do we assume that all these qualities reside outside ourselves?"

Flawless again. No matter how many times Cliff Chaffin watched his boss lecture, he was still awed by the man's charisma and power onstage. In his early forties with dark brown hair combed perfectly in place, Dr. Simmons—or Walter as Cliff was privileged to call him—worked the crowd with absolute precision, every movement, every hand gesture and facial expression, seamless in its timing and effect. When he strolled from one corner of the stage to the other, all heads followed him. When he pointed up, they looked up. When he laughed, they laughed.

Cliff loved watching the crowd's reactions nearly as much as he loved watching his mentor reveal his transforming knowledge and power to them. Dr. Simmons was truly gifted beyond imagination.

"He's on fire tonight." Todd Yancey smacked Cliff on the back, knocking him forward. The goofy oaf was too big to know his own strength, or he did it on purpose.

Standing at nearly six-five, with arms too thick to measure, Todd grinned with his jagged-tooth smile as he, too, was mesmerized by Walter. But unlike Cliff, Todd was too dim-witted to really understand the genius before him. How could a man with the IQ of a tent peg truly appreciate Walter's brilliance, his inspired wisdom?

Although Todd had benefited from it greatly, how could this buffoon appreciate such radiance? Walter's CDs had freed this barbarian from years of crime, prison, and drug abuse. As a result, Todd had pledged a life of service to Dr. Simmons.

Not that this hooligan didn't have his uses. There were people in the world who could not understand the luminosity and wonder of what Walter had to offer, like weeds in a garden that can't absorb the sun's sustaining light and magnificence.

And some of them saw Walter as a threat—someone to be feared, not revered—and they might try to harm him. That's where Todd came in. He would gladly rip an attacker's arms off, like a child tearing the wings off a fly for entertainment. For that purpose alone, Cliff tolerated his presence.

Walter's teachings had also set Cliff free from prison—the "prison" of his own mundane, suffocating existence. Fifteen years as an accountant, he droned through audits, unbearable tax seasons, and demanding, overbearing clients.

After hearing Walter speak once, Cliff walked away from his old life, from his wife, from his job, and from obscurity to join something new and vibrant, something that could and would truly change the world for the better. Cliff, too, pledged his allegiance to Walter.

"Do not put that *thing* on your head until we get outside." Cliff pointed to the giant cowboy hat Todd was so fond of. "We need to maintain at least an air of class for the doctor."

"I know, I know, Cliffy. Keep your pants on. I know the doc's rules."

At least Todd was wearing long-sleeved shirts now to cover the grotesque tattoos that painted his arms.

"Now, shush, and pay attention. You might actually learn something…if that's possible."

Todd snarled at him as Cliff returned his focus to Walter's lecture.

"We've been so conditioned to believe that we are inherently fraught with wickedness and folly," Dr. Simmons said. "Ladies and gentlemen, that is just plain wrong. You've been lied to and used by a world that lacks clarity and understanding. Everything you need to find happiness, fulfillment, and yes, inner peace, lies within your own heart. I'm here to tell you the truth. The truth that shall *truly* set you free."

The crowd erupted in applause. Walter stood back and bowed slightly, a look of humility covering his face. After a moment, he held up his hands and the applause stopped.

"Since the beginning of recorded history, archaic dogmas have bound the human spirit, and what have they produced? War. Famine. Turmoil. And the division of people along every line imaginable. Now is the time to throw off the yoke of these backward mindsets and come into the enlightened world so you can enter the next level, the highest level, of human evolution.

"Let not your spirit be bound and attached to the limits other people and their ideas put on you. You are the maker of your own destiny. You are the author of your own story. Have the courage, now, tonight, to reject your old life and run boldly toward the new life awaiting you. Join with me to find the person you were born to be. Dare to discover the higher you."

Walter was greeted with a standing ovation. Again he bowed slightly, a humble blush returning to his face.

Cliff and Todd joined the applause. Walter waved and slowly backed off stage toward them. "How did it go tonight, gentlemen?"

"Need you ask?" Cliff said, still clapping, feeling breathless.

Walter patted him on the back. "Always the supportive friend."

"You were great, sir."

Walter grinned at Todd. "Let's go see if this little talk took root."

They walked down the back stairs to the edge of the lobby, where several stations were set up to sell Dr. Simmons's books and CDs. One series was specifically designed to enhance the mind's ability to focus on the task at hand, a particular favorite with college study groups. Another series taught on the evolution of the human spirit, how man was on the cusp of a major evolutionary jump.

A prolific writer, Walter had authored over forty books, on topics ranging from self-help to the basics of piano playing and even a cookbook. He could do anything.

Dr. Simmons emerged from the shadow of the stairwell into the bustling room. A young woman spotted him. "There he is."

The crowed swelled toward him, pressing in all around him. Todd slid to Walter's side, but Walter forced him back with a glare. Todd rejoined Cliff against the wall to watch.

"Dr. Simmons, you have changed my life," a tearful woman said. "I was on the verge of suicide until I heard your teaching on finding the higher you. I can't thank you enough for saving my life." She broke down and sobbed.

Walter wiped a tear from her cheek and placed both hands on her shoulders. "You're going to be all right now. You're finally going to be okay."

She leaned forward and hugged him. The crowed applauded.

It was going to be a big night.

10

Dodd Hall was crowded with more students filing in, probably heading to the Werkmeister Reading Room, where Byron's group was meeting.

Ruby rested on a bench outside. What was wrong with her? She wanted friends and to fit in, and now that she'd finally gotten her chance, she was hiding outside.

Get your courage, girl, and just do it. What do you have to lose?

She took a determined breath, stood, and jogged up the steps and into the hall, following a group of girls as they walked toward the reading room. The atmosphere was light and inviting, and the room was filled with tables and small couches, some book racks along the wall. She didn't expect so many people.

"Ruby," Byron called from the back of the room. He beamed as he hurried toward her, weaving serpentinely through the crowd.

"Glad you could make it." He stopped, looking up and around the room. He shuffled to her other side, searching intently behind her.

"What in the world are you doing, Byron?"

"Since you have a habit of bringing calamity with you, I'm just making sure the roof's not going to cave in on us or something crazy like that."

"Stop it." She slapped him on the shoulder. She barely knew him, but he made her feel comfortable, like they'd been friends for years. "There are a lot of people here."

"Yeah, we seem to be growing every day. Come on. I'll show you around."

He extended his elbow and escorted her to a group of young women talking. "Excuse me. I'd like to introduce you-all to a new friend of mine. This is Ruby Porter. She's come to see what we're all about."

"Nice to meet you, Ruby," one of the girls said.

Ruby held out her hand, but the girl grabbed it and pulled her close, embracing her. "We hug here." The others introduced themselves and chatted with Ruby as Byron waited patiently.

"Okay, girls. I need to show Ruby the rest of our stuff here."

The group wandered off toward the bookshelf, talking among themselves.

"Wow! They were so nice." These strangers were treating her like lifelong friends. Where had these people been hiding?

"We all try to be nice here."

"Who exactly are *we*?"

"I'm glad you asked." He offered her his elbow again. "Come with me."

What a charmer Byron was. She paused for a moment then took his arm. He guided her to a table at the front of the room. "Do you know who Dr. Walter Simmons is?"

Ruby shook her head.

"He's an amazing man. He has put together study guides and learning methods that our study group employs. He's revolutionizing how people learn and respond to everything in life. I've been using his system for six months now, and all my grades have shot up dramatically. And that doesn't even scratch the surface. There's so much more to his teaching."

She raised an eyebrow. "Sound's interesting. What else is involved?"

"Ruby, you ask all the right questions. Dr. Simmons teaches about the meaning of life, finding the higher you."

She held up her hands. "I'm not a very religious person."

"That's the beauty of his message. It's not about religion; it's about the power and goodness of the human spirit and what man can achieve on his own. Dr. Simmons challenges everyone to look inside him- or herself for the answers, not to any mythical being. He believes the human race is on the verge of something great, a huge leap in the evolution of man."

Ruby considered what she heard. Byron was as passionate as he was funny and really believed what he was saying. Perfection and peace? No more wars, no violence…no divorce? Just everyone living together in harmony? It sounded fascinating.

The study techniques piqued her interest as well. Although her grades had been pretty good for her first semester, there was always room for improvement. She needed to keep her edge. It was all intriguing stuff, but she still wasn't sure.

"Wow, Bryon. I just came for the pizza. I didn't expect to have my life change and evolve, at least not tonight."

"I'll tell you what." He reached over to the table and grabbed a set of CDs. "Why don't you listen to these and then tell me what you think? What's the harm in that? If you're interested, we can get together and talk about it. If you're not, no problem."

Ruby rubbed her chin. What could it hurt? "Sure." She grabbed the CDs. "I'll let you know what I think."

"Great. Now it's pizza time."

11

MELBOURNE

In the briefing room of the FDLE office, Tim took his seat and gave his attention to Robbie, who wrote her final instructions on the whiteboard. The face of their suspect filled the middle of the board with arrows drawn to a time line of events. Lawrence "Crazy Larry" Wilcox was a celebrity in central Florida; his string of used car lots dotted the east coast.

Standing a firm six-foot-seven and tipping the scales at nearly four hundred pounds, with a haircut reminiscent of Mr. Clean's, Crazy Larry entertained thousands with the stunts he pulled in his commercials. He routinely crushed car roofs as he jumped up and down on them, screaming of a sale. The former professional football player had once been sued by an animal rights group because he threatened to bite off the head of a live chicken on television unless he sold a thousand cars that month.

Unfortunately for Crazy Larry, it wasn't his unusual fascination with poultry that had gotten him in trouble. He had a fancy for the ladies as well—something that did not bode well with the current Mrs. Crazy Larry, who was in the process of divorcing him and taking half of his dealerships with her. Robbie had received a tip through an informant that Crazy Larry was seeking assistance to have his wife "disappear" before their divorce hearing.

John, Alan, Tim, and two uniformed officers from the Palm Bay police department settled in for Robbie's briefing.

"Our informant has arranged for our buddy Larry to meet us at the parking lot of the Texaco station on U.S. 1. Tim will be our hit man today."

Tim stood and took a stately bow, to the applause of his coworkers. He hadn't shaved for two days, and his scraggly jeans gave him the ex-con look he was going for. Before the briefing, he had hit the gym and worked out in the same shirt he was wearing. He couldn't just look the part; he needed to smell the part as well. Everything needed to fit if he was going to play a street thug.

He hadn't worked undercover in several years and was excited at the prospect. In his career he'd played pimps, too many drug dealers to remember, and even a fake doctor once, but this was his first stint as a hit man. Everything had to be just right.

"Tim, at 6 p.m. I want you to pull in here." Robbie pointed to the spot on the whiteboard with her black marker. "If you park anywhere on this side of the building, we'll be able to pick you up well. Your car is wired with video and audio as well as GPS should anything go bad."

Tim smiled. "If this guy goes nuts and starts pounding me, it's nice to know you'll be filming the whole thing." The technology today was so much better than even a few years ago. He used to have to wear a wire that felt like he was concealing luggage under his shirt. Very uncomfortable to say the least.

"We'll all be only a few seconds away." Alan adjusted his holster. "If something doesn't feel right, Porter, I want you to back out. I won't risk an agent for this guy. We'll take him down another way."

"I'll be fine, boss." Tim smirked. His team wouldn't let him get hurt. He only had to worry about his part. "I just want to see the look on Mr. Clean's face when we show him the video."

"Well, first things first," Alan said. "Let's be safe."

"After we get Crazy Larry to solicit her murder on tape," Robbie continued, "we'll let him exit Tim's car. Tim, pull out like you're leaving; then the marked units will come in and take him down before he gets in his car. No way are we having a pursuit through town."

Robbie set down her marker. "Everyone understand the drill?"

They all nodded.

"Well, let's step off."

Tim pulled his car into the Texaco parking lot. Crazy Larry leaned against a 2000 Buick with a dealer tag in the window, probably a loaner from one of his lots. He wore a tent-sized white T-shirt and blue jeans, and a fat gold chain dangled around his neck. He held a lumpy manila envelope in his hand. John didn't like it. Anything could be in the envelope.

John keyed his radio. "Tim's pulling in now." Parked a block away in the surveillance van, John had a bird's-eye view of the operation. He controlled the two monitors in front of him. One had a view of the entire parking lot from a camera mounted earlier in the day on a power pole at the intersection. The other screen picked up the signal from the dash-mounted pen camera, which gave a frontal view of the front seat of Tim's car. "Video and audio are all working. It looks like a go."

A Marvin Gaye tune played on the radio and came through loud and clear on the equipment. Tim looked into the dash camera, smiled, and winked. "Piece of cake," he whispered. "Target's here."

John didn't like being the equipment guy, but they all took turns. It was Robbie's case, Tim was undercover, and Alan was supervising, so that left him to run the equipment and provide backup.

He still wanted to be a little bit closer, though. Who knew what this guy was capable of? What if he sensed that Tim was a cop or this was a setup? John didn't like his partner being alone with this gargantuan and him being a good fifteen seconds away. In the real world, fifteen seconds wasn't a long time. In a police operation, it could be a lifetime.

Tim pulled up next to Larry. "How's it going, man?"

"Are you Tim?"

"Yeah."

"I'm Larry."

"Ya think? Everybody around here knows who you are. Get in. You keep standin' out there yakking and you'll draw attention to us."

Larry ambled around the car to the passenger side. He opened the door and used the roof to help squeeze himself into the car, which rocked as Larry filled the passenger seat. He laid the envelope on his lap. Tim checked out the package. His look was subtle; the envelope bothered John, too.

The dash-mounted video camera had a perfect view of both of them. As thick and muscular as Tim was, he looked like a child sitting next to Crazy Larry. Larry looked around the parking lot. Sweat had formed on his shiny forehead, and he swallowed hard. The man was skittish. Tim would have to move very carefully not to scare him off.

"At least you don't listen to that hip-hop garbage," Larry said, breaking the ice.

"Nope, I'm a Motown man." Tim turned down the music. He knew what he was doing. Tim didn't want anything to interfere with the audio.

"Marcus says you need some help with a problem you got."

Tim's street slang was turned on strong, and he'd practiced his felon-walk all day just trying to get in character. His look was even harder. John didn't think he could ever look mean, like Tim looked now.

"I gotta problem. A big problem. But I'm not sure about this, and I'm not sure about *you*. How do I know you're not some cop trying to set me up or something?"

"Well, Mr. Used-Car Man," Tim said, anger leaking out in his voice. "I'm on parole. Just sitting here talking with you like this can get me twenty years. So if you don't feel right with me—" Tim reached around Larry's enormous stomach and opened his door for him—"you can get your chunky butt outta my car. I don't need no games today."

Larry's eyes narrowed at Tim, who met his stare head-on, not giving an inch. John hoped Tim hadn't pushed the man too far.

Larry smiled and eased back in his seat. "I guess we're just gonna have to trust each other."

"I trust no one. You tell me what you want done and show me some cash, then we can get all chummy. Even then, I still ain't gonna trust ya."

Larry nodded, then rubbed his chin. "I think we're gonna be able to do some business."

"I'm listening."

"My wife and me have a hearing for our divorce next Thursday. If she wins, she's gonna clean me out. I built this business from nothing, and I'm not gonna let her steal it from me like that."

"What do you want to happen to her?"

"She can't make that hearing."

"You gotta tell me what you want. If you want her beat down, I can do that. If you want something else...I can do that, too."

"I want her dead. Stone-cold, in-the-ground dead."

Tim paused then nodded. "You know that's gonna cost."

"Not anywhere near what it will if she makes that court date."

Tim shifted in his seat and faced Larry. "What kinda price you lookin' at?"

"Ten grand altogether. Five now, five when the deed is done."

"You want me to risk goin' to death row for ten grand?"

Tim was perfect. If he took the first offer, he'd seem too anxious and might tip the man off. John chuckled.

Larry looked like he was dealing in one of his commercials. "What did you have in mind? Make me an offer."

"At least fifteen. Ten before, five after. And I want my expenses paid if I gotta leave town for a while."

Larry glared at Tim, then bit his lip and nodded slowly. "When can you get this done?"

"I'm gonna need her picture, her address, her work schedule, what kinda car she drives. Anything you can get me about her. This kinda thing ain't as easy as it sounds. I can't just walk up and pop her. I gotta have an escape route. I gotta know what I'm dealing with."

"I figured that." Larry tossed the bulging manila envelope in Tim's lap. "Everything you need to find her should be right here."

Tim opened the envelope and poured the contents on his lap. Pictures of Larry's soon-to-be ex-wife spilled out. Her schedules and acquaintances were all carefully documented for him.

"Man, you must want this woman dead in a bad kinda way." Tim sifted through the pictures and information.

"More than you'll ever know." The big man pulled a wad of cash from his pocket and thumbed through it. "Here's ten grand." He handed Tim the money. "If you finish this and do it right, not only will you get the other five, but I might throw in a bonus as well. Maybe even a new ride for you."

Tim nodded as he counted the money, not even looking at Larry.

John checked the recording machines. Everything was working perfectly. This would make a great courtroom presentation. He could just imagine what Larry would think when he saw himself on video.

"Also, the hit has to be done this week. I'll be at a convention in Chicago all week, which will give me a good alibi. I won't be back until the morning of our court date. You've got to do her before then, or this is all over with."

"That won't be a problem." Tim still rifled through the paperwork.

Larry scooted his body around and loomed over Tim. "And one more thing. Don't even think about double-crossing me." He aimed a cigar-sized finger in Tim's face. "Or I'll find you and take care of you *myself*."

John picked up the radio and kept it in his hand as he watched Tim and Larry. The tense moment passed.

"This is easy stuff, man. When I'm done, I'll contact you through Marcus. And then I want the rest of my money."

Larry eased back in his seat as the car rocked with the weight of him moving around. "We got a deal." That just happened to be the saying he used in his commercials. This would make a classic video.

"Okay, people," Alan called over the radio. "Let's get into position to block in Larry's car."

"See you in a week." Larry opened the door and used the roof to extricate himself. He strolled toward his car and put his key in the door when one of the patrol cars pulled into the parking lot, catching his attention. The patrol car stopped in front of Larry's car, and Robbie skidded her surveillance van in back, blocking him in.

Tim leapt from the driver's seat and pulled his Glock 9mm, pointing it at Larry, who glared back at him. "Smile, Crazy Larry, you're on candid camera. You're under arrest." Tim held up his badge.

Larry growled and his mountainous body quaked, his fault line rupturing.

One of the uniformed officers approached him. "Put your hands behind your back, Larry. You're under arrest."

Crazy Larry shuffled around and placed his hands into the small of his back. John drove into the lot and drew his pistol to cover the officer.

As the officer grabbed Larry's fleshy wrist, he spun around, tossed the officer to the side like a paper doll, and sprinted down the sidewalk.

"Stop!" Alan dived and seized Larry around the waist. "You're under arrest!"

Larry didn't break stride as he dragged Alan down the sidewalk.

"Heeeelp!" Alan tried to plant his feet on the sidewalk behind Larry with no success. Alan had bulked up a bit recently as he hit the weight room with more consistency, but he was no match for Crazy Larry.

Tim, Robbie, and John gave chase after the behemoth dragging their boss away.

John caught up to Larry first and grabbed him by the shirt, tearing it as he yanked backward. Larry whipped his meaty arms back, knocking John off balance. Alan's legs swung back and forth as he tried to get footing, Larry still churning away.

The second patrol car drove up on the curb, herding Larry into the street. Cars whizzed by the fight as the team surrounded Crazy Larry.

Robbie cut Larry off in the middle of the highway and hit him twice in the forearms with her expandable baton. The blows bounced off with little effect. Larry swatted at her with his paws, but she dodged them, just out of reach.

Alan had just gained his footing once more when the monster sprinted down the center of the street, hauling him along for another ride.

John leapt on Larry's back, wrapped his arms around the man's thick neck, and squeezed. Larry thrashed about, trying to shake him off. With Alan locked around his hip and John around his neck, Crazy Larry couldn't run anymore. He reached up, grabbed John by the hair, and yanked.

John yelped.

Robbie stepped forward and smacked him again with her baton, this time in the knee. He released John's hair and grabbed his knee. "Aaaaaaaah!"

Tim lunged and side kicked Larry in the opposite knee, tipping him forward. Tim launched a haymaker toward Larry's jaw, and the powerful punch reverberated through Larry's body.

Larry righted himself and swayed in the wind. John was atop a redwood whose base had just been cut. Larry wobbled back and forward. John released his grip and rolled off just as Larry plunged to the pavement, falling on top of Alan.

"Get him off me!" Alan grunted. "I can't breathe. Off!"

The uniformed officers strained and struggled as they hauled the now tamed Larry off of Alan, who resembled roadkill in the middle of U.S. 1. One of the uniforms tried to secure Larry with his handcuffs, but they were too small. The second officer retrieved a pair of leg shackles from the trunk of his patrol car. They tipped Larry over and cinched the shackles tight on his wrists.

"You can add resisting arrest to the solicitation for murder charge," Tim said, huffing and out of breath.

His arms splayed over his head, Alan lay in the street, gulping in air and groaning.

"Alan." John slapped his boss's leg. "You okay?"

He didn't answer. He just sat up, let his arms fall over his knees, and put his head between his legs. "Eight months" was all he could manage between gasps.

"Eight months?" John massaged the back of his neck, which had been whipped around from his wild ride.

"Yep. In eight months, I retire and never, ever have to fight these psychos again." Alan lifted each foot and inspected his shoes, which had holes scraped in them from his ride. "This is a young man's job." He probed a hole with his finger.

U.S. 1 was cordoned off with patrol cars now as three more screeched up to the scene. Two officers led a groggy Larry, with gravel clinging to his face, into the back of a patrol car.

The street was packed with cars stopped in both directions. Robbie rotated her right arm around as if she'd thrown it out of socket during the fight. She plopped down next to the guys, taking several deep breaths.

Tim shook his right hand, obviously still stinging from his potent lick. He joined their impromptu powwow in the middle of the street, catching a much deserved break. Horns blared from impatient drivers, but everyone was too worn out to move.

Tim rubbed his hand and laughed. "Is it just me, or do we not get paid enough for this job?"

12

"I'm going to be so late." Ruby quickened her pace into Dodd Hall.

She'd gotten swept up in a CD and lost track of time. In the three weeks since she'd met Byron, her life had rocketed on a course she never could've imagined. She immersed herself into the teachings of Dr. Walter Simmons. The man was nothing short of amazing. He saw everything so clearly, not like the muddled thinking and incongruent theoretical ramblings of so many professors she'd been exposed to. They were intellectual lightweights compared to Dr. Simmons. He offered real ideas on study habits, philosophy, life…and the afterlife.

She'd spent most of her time on the fantastic study CDs. He opened her up to new concepts about true knowledge, its roots, and why we grow in our intellectual base. She'd never once asked herself why she learned. She only assumed it was to get a good job and move on in life, never considering that the proper knowledge could move her spirit forward, past all of her imperfections. Revolutionary stuff. The kind of ideas that would place Dr. Simmons among the great philosophers of our time…maybe of all time.

"Ruby!" Brenda nearly tackled her, crushing the air out of her with one of her monster hugs. "Where've you been? I haven't seen you all day."

"I've been in my room, listening to CD twenty-two."

"Oh, that's a good one."

"It's one of my favorites, too," Ashley said, wrapping her arm around Ruby. "Just wait till you get into the next section on evaluating your spirit. It will blow you away."

Brenda and Ashley had really been there for her in the last few weeks. Until they came along, she didn't think she would ever find any friends. They ate practically every meal together, shared class notes, and talked late into the night about Dr. Simmons, life, men, everything imaginable.

"Hey, Ruby, someone's checking you out *again*." Brenda pointed not so discreetly toward Byron, who was in the corner talking with a freshman seeking information about the Higher Learning Method. Byron handed the young man a pamphlet and glanced toward Ruby, then turned away quickly.

"I'm telling you, that boy has it *bad* for you." Ashley circled her finger in Ruby's face.

"No." Ruby shook her head. "We're friends, that's all."

"Yeah, keep fooling yourself," Brenda said, "and before long, you'll be hooked, too. Can't you see it? The man has the hots for you. Every time I see him, all he does is ask where you are and what you're doing."

"Really?" Ruby tilted her head. "You really think he likes me?"

Ashley sighed and laid her hand on top of Ruby's head. "You know, for someone so smart, sometimes you really skip right by the big things. Of course he likes you. Everyone on the planet can see that…except you."

Ruby smiled. She wasn't opposed to the idea of dating Byron. She just didn't think he liked her, more than he liked anyone else that is. He was nice to everyone. Open. Content. He did spend a lot of time with her, though, and she had been going out of her way to spend time with him. But she didn't think he had noticed. She wasn't exactly smooth.

Boys in high school had seemed so intimidated by her. It wasn't fair. The few dates she went on never seemed to end well. Their promises to call again never materialized. Sometimes she thought her intelligence was a curse…until the last few weeks. Byron wasn't intimidated by her at all. Probably because he was every bit as smart as she was, if not smarter.

But there was something else. He was self-assured. He knew what he wanted and where he was headed. He was going to teach for Dr. Simmons. After graduation, he would do whatever it took to carry his message forward.

"Hey, stranger," Byron said, touching her elbow. "Where you been all day?"

Goose bumps sprinted up her arm. "Just studying with Brenda and Ashley, that's all." She giggled. "Did you miss me?"

"Maybe a little." He lifted his chin and grinned. "Can you believe Dr. Simmons will be here this week? I can't wait. I've met him once before, and he's as astounding in person as he is in his CDs and books."

"I'm excited, too. For the first time in a long time, I have something to look forward to."

Byron held his hands out. "Oh, like coming here is something terrible?"

"That's not what I meant, you goof. Coming here is the best thing that's ever happened to me. I wouldn't have survived on campus much longer if I hadn't met you-all."

Brenda gave her another power squeeze. "We look out for each other. We're all family now."

* * *

"Hey, Daddy." Ruby held her cell phone with her shoulder as she packed her books in her bag.

"Hey, baby. It's good to hear from you. What's happening?"

"I just wanted to catch up with you. Things are going so much better now. I met a group of people who are all so nice. It seems like everything's turned around."

"I knew it would just take some time. See, Ruby? Things always seem to work out. So what is this, a study group?"

She slipped her backpack on and switched her phone to her other hand. "Something like that. I'll explain it all when I get home in a couple weeks. I can't wait to tell you everything that's been going on."

"I can't wait to see you, sweetheart. I miss you more than you know."

"I miss you, too, Daddy. See you soon. Love you."

"Love you, too."

13

Chief Bennington," John said as he and Tim approached the Highpoint city limits. "We're gonna be in town to do a little follow-up on the Garrow case. Just thought we'd give you a heads-up."

"When you gonna get here?"

"In about three minutes." John slowed the car. "We're just coming into town now."

The chief's pause told John what he wanted to know—the man wasn't happy. "You sure don't give much of a 'heads-up,' Agent Russell."

"Sorry, Chief. Things have been kinda crazy."

"Yeah, I'm sure. Where you heading to?"

"Oh, here and there. We're going to talk with some locals."

"You going up to the learning center?"

"We might, if we have time." What was it with the twenty questions? Cops are naturally inquisitive, but this guy was all over him.

"Well, I'd appreciate a little more notice when you're gonna be in my town...so I can have someone ready to assist you."

"I'll see what I can do." John didn't like being dictated to on his cases. Why would the chief need to know their every move anyway? He was either a micromanager or a control freak. The call was simply a courtesy, not a requirement. "We'll be in touch if we need any help. Thanks for the offer, Chief."

"Fine."

John closed his cell phone.

"He didn't seem too happy," Tim said as they cruised onto Main Street.

"Yeah, I can't quite get a read on him. He keeps sticking his fingers in our case."

Tim adjusted the holster on his belt. "The man runs a tight ship and doesn't want FDLE in here messing up his little kingdom. If he looks bad to the city council, his job could be all but gone."

"Maybe. I hope you're right." Traffic was light. As they passed the police station, Chief Bennington waited just outside the front door with his arms crossed, his gargoyle expression greeting them. Tim waved. The chief didn't.

Main Street curved slightly, and the red brick buildings of the sprawling complex came into view. They turned onto a long circular driveway and ascended the steady incline, the likes of which John had never seen in south Florida before.

Full oaks garnished the path. The impressive three-story administration building testified to the money and power of Dr. Walter Simmons. Two equally grand dorm buildings flanked each side of the administration building, running perpendicular to the waters of Lake Okeechobee. A covered pavilion with a circular table was off to their right, with several young men and women sitting together, laughing and carrying on.

"Wow." Tim slipped his jacket on as he stepped from the car. "This place is even larger than it looks from the road."

"Yeah." John slammed the car door and gazed at the buildings. "I guess motivational speaking is a bigger business these days than I thought."

A young Asian man rushed out to meet John before he made it to the double doors leading into the administration building. "Good morning, sir. Welcome to the Higher Learning Center."

"Thank you," John said, caught off guard, not expecting a doorman.

"How can I help you today?"

"We'd like to speak with Dr. Simmons."

The young man laughed. "Wouldn't we all. That's why we're here."

"Well, we're here for business," Tim held up his badge, "not pleasure."

"Oh. Dr. Simmons isn't here right now. He won't be back until Friday."

"Who's in charge?" John placed his hands on his hips. "Who else can we speak with?"

"That would be me." Another man strutted toward them. His appearance reminded John of a mole, with his dark hair slicked back; his soft, round features; and his long nose.

"Cliff Chaffin." He thrust out his hand. "Welcome to the Higher Learning Center."

"Agent Russell." John shook his hand. "This is Agent Porter. We're with the Florida Department of Law Enforcement."

Cliff stepped back and faced the young man. "I'll take care of these gentlemen, David. You can go back inside now." He returned his attention to John and Tim. "Is there some sort of problem?"

"We're looking for someone who used to stay here."

"One of our students, you mean." Cliff adjusted his thick glasses and pushed his chin high. "This is an educational campus. Everyone here is a student of Walter's...Dr. Simmons's. Myself included, of course."

John nodded. "Sure, one of your *students*."

"Which student are you looking for? I hope he or she is not in any serious trouble."

John took the picture from his file and showed it to Cliff. "Mitch Garrow."

Cliff didn't appear surprised at all by the name. "Of course, I know Mitch. He was one of our most respected students."

"Was?" Tim raised an eyebrow. "When was the last time you saw him?"

"Oh, three, four months ago. He was a smart but troubled lad. Dr. Simmons suggested that he take a spiritual sojourn."

"What's that?"

"It's a principle clearly spelled out in Dr. Simmons's latest series, The Spirit in Flux, Agent Porter."

"Pretend I haven't heard of the series, and then explain it to me." John put Mitch's picture back in the file.

A sigh escaped from Cliff. "A person like Mitch, whose childhood baggage is so great, should go out into the world and cleanse his mind and spirit by traveling, doing good works, and meditating on Dr. Simmons's teachings."

"Is that common?" Tim asked.

"Of course. It's part of the Higher Learning Method curriculum."

"For how long?"

"For as long as a person needs, Agent Russell. For some, it could be as little as six months. For others, maybe a couple of years."

"That's not what I meant." John shifted his weight to his left leg, easing a little closer to Cliff. "How long has this 'spiritual sojourn' been a part of the curriculum?"

"I'm quite sure I don't know what you mean." Cliff glared at John.

"Do you know where Mitch is now, Mr. Chaffin?" Tim brushed his coat back, hooking his thumbs in his belt. "We'd really like to get in touch with him. His mother is worried sick."

"No. That's part of his sojourn. He must do it alone, without help from anyone. I've explained that to Mrs. Garrow a number of times, but she just doesn't get it. She's been all around the campus, talking with a number of the students, but she's convinced Mitch has fallen prey to some malicious force at work here. She's really becoming a nuisance."

"Mitch is her son," John said. "She wants to know that he's okay. What else would you expect from a mother?"

"Maybe so, but he's not here, and we don't know where he is. I don't know how much plainer I can say it."

"What do you make of this?" John handed him a copy of Mitch's e-mail.

Cliff studied it for several seconds. "Looks like he went to China. Maybe Beijing would be a good place to start looking for him. Dr. Simmons's materials are selling well there also." Cliff flipped the paper at John.

He caught it before it hit the ground. "I don't know what it means. But I've contacted Customs to see if Mitch had a passport or has left the country. We should know that much soon."

"Sounds like you're doing everything you can." Cliff's smile was clearly forced. "I'm sure he'll turn up soon."

"Would you mind if we look around for a while? We'd like to check things out for ourselves."

Cliff considered John's request. "It would be a waste of your time, gentlemen. But if you insist, we have nothing here to hide." He pointed to the door with his chin. "Follow me."

They walked into the administration building, the air-conditioning refreshing John for a moment. The lobby was large and open, looking much like a corporate headquarters. A reception desk was directly in front of them; a heavyset young woman with red hair manned the phones.

Just behind the receptionist, an extended open hall led to a set of double doors to a courtyard. On the left side of the lobby was a sign that pointed to the auditorium; on the other side were Dr. Simmons's and Cliff Chaffin's offices with the cafeteria just past that.

John looked up at the walkways that crossed from one side to the other, connecting each of the three floors. Students milled about, and the entire lobby echoed with the voices of excited young people. "Very impressive."

"A very impressive facility for a very impressive man." Pride shone from Cliff's face. "Dr. Simmons designed much of what you see. We just finished the last phase four months ago."

Cliff pointed to the doors at the back of the building. "We're getting ready to hit our stride, so to speak. Dr. Simmons wants to expand the number of students we currently board here. Highpoint will be the launching platform for Dr. Simmons's latest, most in-depth teachings yet. It's going to truly revolutionize how people grow and learn."

"Interesting." John turned in a circle to take in the whole view. What a facility. Many community colleges would be fortunate to have such a complex. "How in the world did you get this place to look like it's on a hill? This is south Florida. A fire-ant hill is considered a mountain here."

"A mere twenty thousand loads of fill can accomplish that task very well. This whole complex, this sanctuary, is a fitting tribute to a visionary like Dr. Simmons. Setting it on a high place seemed more than appropriate."

Tim dug his hands in his pockets. "Sounds like you're fond of your boss."

"He's not just my boss; he's the most amazing man I've ever

met. You really should take some of his books or CDs. They will change your life; I guarantee it."

"No thanks." Tim patted his stomach without even looking at Cliff. "I'm trying to cut down."

"I'll take a look at them," John said. "If you have some you can spare. I'd like to learn more about Dr. Simmons and your program here. It's all very…fascinating."

"Anything to help." Cliff scurried into his office, returning with a plastic bag in hand. "These are some of his latest CDs and a signed copy of his new book, *The Imprisoned Mind.* It's on the *New York Times* bestseller list. You might want to hold on to that; it will be priceless someday."

"Thanks." John smiled. "I appreciate your help." John and Cliff exchanged business cards. "Would you mind if we take a look out back, to see the whole facility?"

"Be my guest. This is an open campus. You can come by anytime." Cliff glanced at his watch. "I really must be getting back to work. If you have any questions, I'll be in my office."

They shook hands again; then Cliff walked away. As John and Tim headed toward the double doors in the back, John noticed Cliff talking with a huge man at his office door. The guy was about thirtyish with stringy brown hair and a thick torso. He looked more like a domesticated Sasquatch than a student.

The two continued to talk, and the big man glanced over at them. John paused at the glass doors, staring out at the courtyard then down to the lake. He wouldn't go out quite yet; he had to see what the big man was going to do.

Cliff hurried into his office, and Sasquatch stayed put, obviously monitoring their movements. John pushed open the glass door, and he and Tim stepped out into the courtyard.

The buildings formed a horseshoe shape pointing toward Lake Okeechobee. A large covered pavilion sat in the middle of the courtyard, which descended gradually toward the water. A swimming area was cordoned off with a metal fence, probably to keep the alligators at bay. A red lifeguard tower stood on the small beach. A group of students passed them without any concern for who they were.

"Nice place." Tim ambled onto the courtyard grass. The Florida morning was heating up. It was set to be another scorcher.

"Maybe. Did you see the big guy our buddy Cliff was talking with?"

"You mean our shadow?" Tim grinned. "Sure did. He's standing at the glass doors watching us as we speak."

John shouldn't have even had to ask. Tim was on it. The guy didn't miss anything.

"I wonder if our shadow has a name. He doesn't seem too anxious to introduce himself."

Tim shrugged. "Maybe he's just looking out for their interests. They've got a good thing going here and don't want people poking around in their business."

"It's just odd to have a whole 'campus' dedicated to one man's teachings." John frowned. "I don't like the feel of it."

"What's wrong with a man teaching stuff to help people? That's what life's all about. It's not my bag, but it seems harmless enough."

"I don't know. It sounds a lot like New Age gibberish repackaged."

"Well, John, you're not the most tolerant man I've every met. You're as rigid and narrow as a yardstick. I'm surprised you took any of that reading material."

"I'll take that as a compliment." John held his bag up. "I took this to get up to speed on who these people are. I don't like this atmosphere of seclusion and limited teaching. I think it can lead to bad things, that's all."

"You think too much, Johnny Fundamentalist." Tim patted him on the back. "Now let's walk back through the lobby and see if we can shake up our shadow a bit."

They turned and walked up the grassy embankment toward the administration building. Their shadow retreated from the glass doors out of sight.

"Let's go have a little fun." Tim beamed.

As they entered the building, Tim strutted right toward the big man, standing in a corner and acting like he was looking at a table full of brochures, half keeping his eye on them. Tim planted himself right next to him, almost shoulder to shoulder. He reached out and took one of the brochures Big-Man was pretending to read.

Their shadow rubbed the back of his neck and sauntered across the large hallway, pretending to give his attention to the course schedule posted on the wall.

Tim followed him again without saying a word, standing close enough to hug him. John picked up some pamphlets off of a table and watched Tim move Big-Man to two more locations.

His flustered and frustrated expression told John that Big-Man might be a couple sticks shy of a bundle in the IQ department. He slicked his hair back and seemed to have no idea how to handle Tim's persistent dogging of him, a little psychological trick most detectives used to unnerve suspects, intentionally violating their personal space to disrupt their comfort level. It was crude but effective.

Big-Man twisted to flee Tim's presence one more time, and John snapped a photo of him with his cell phone. It would be good to find out who Big-Man was. He e-mailed it to his account.

Tim snickered as he returned to John.

"You are a bad man, Porter. You enjoy this stuff too much."

"Hey, you gotta shake people up every once in a while. It keeps life interesting."

As they drove out of the circular driveway and exited the Higher Learning Center, they stopped at the intersection leading back into town. A young woman, maybe twenty-two or twenty-three, stood on the other side of the street in a wooded lot. Her brilliant blond hair shimmered in the midday sun, and one braided strand dangled down her face. She carried what appeared to be a Bible in her left hand and wore blue jeans and a white T-shirt. She watched them as they turned onto Main Street.

John waved and she waved back, expressionless.

"That's kinda weird, her just standing out here all by herself." Tim shook his head.

"Let's pull up and see what her deal is."

Tim drove the car onto the grass next to her and rolled down his window. "You okay, miss?"

She nodded. "I'm fine. Are you students here?"

"Nope." Tim smiled. "Just visitors."

She slipped a slim piece of paper through the window. He took it and gazed briefly at it. "Oh no, Russell. This is for you." He tossed it to John. It was a Bible tract, explaining the road to salvation.

"I don't need any of those." Tim lifted his hand up. "God has put His *special agent* in the car next to me. All day, I gotta listen to the God stuff."

The woman leaned down to make eye contact with John. "Praise God. Keep up the good work."

"Doing what I can. Are you sure you're okay out here? You looked kinda lost."

"I'm fine, and I'm exactly where I'm supposed to be. Lots of interesting things are going on around here now." She glanced back at the Higher Learning Center.

John nodded. "That's for sure."

"May the Lord bless you and protect you in all you do." She stepped away from the car and returned her attention to the Higher Learning Center.

"You, too."

Tim pulled back onto Main Street. "Strange girl, standing out there all alone."

"Just because she was handing out Bible tracts, it doesn't make her weird."

"Maybe not to you."

They breezed through Main Street, hoping to be back on the interstate by noon. A black Suburban pulled onto Main from a side street and hovered behind them. The driver wore dark sunglasses and had a neck as thick as most men's thighs. John couldn't make out anyone else in the car.

"Take this next left." John looked in the rearview mirror, not moving his head so they wouldn't know he was watching them.

"I've already seen him. That Suburban's got cop antennas on it."

"Think they're one of Chief Bennington's crew?"

"I don't know." Tim eyed the mirror without moving his head. "Seems like a mighty expensive undercover car for a podunk PD like Highpoint."

Tim turned onto a side street, and the Suburban followed them, hanging back some.

"Well, whoever they are, John, they're mighty interested in who we are *and* what we're doing."

"When you get a chance, take another left."

"Gotcha." Tim turned left again onto another side street. The odds against someone who wasn't following them doing the same thing were astronomical. The driver of the Suburban broke the laws of probability and mirrored their turn.

They were being tailed.

Tim drove back onto Main Street, coming around full circle. The Suburban trailed them as Tim stopped at a red light.

"Is there any way you can get behind this guy?" John asked. "We need to get the tag number."

"How bad do you want that tag number?" Tim's grin made John hesitate before he answered.

This could get nasty quick, but John ached to know who they were. "*Really* bad."

"Make sure your seat belt's on. We're going for a ride." The light turned green, and Tim eased their car into the middle of the intersection, stopped, and checked his mirror.

The Suburban started forward, then halted abruptly.

Tim slammed the car into reverse and yanked the steering wheel, backing around and passing the Suburban and its stunned driver.

"Say cheese," Tim yelled as John snapped a photo of the bewildered driver, and then took another of the license plate as Tim pulled behind the Suburban.

"Let's see how they like being followed." Tim slammed the gear into drive.

John snapped several more pictures of the vehicle. There was at least one other person in the car, maybe two. The windows were so tinted that John could hardly make anything out. But he got a good picture of the driver and the tag. That would be enough.

The tires on the Suburban squealed as they hustled to get off Main Street.

"Do you want me to follow them?" Tim revved the engine.

"No." John put his hand on Tim's arm. "Let them go. We got what we need."

"I'll be real curious to find out who that car is registered to."

A nice place to retire? Quiet? Quaint? John was seriously rethinking his small town assessment from earlier. "If nothing's going on here in Highpoint, Tim, why in the world are we being followed?"

14

I *don't know if I'm ready for this.* Ruby rubbed her sweaty hands on her jeans as she chewed on her bottom lip. Her stomach was flipping somersaults.

Pacing around in a circle, she was getting ready to meet the man who in just barely a month had changed her life in ways she never imagined possible. What could she say to a man like Dr. Simmons? How could she even relate to such staggering intellect?

Dodd Hall was packed, buzzing with anticipation. Byron had made sure every single member of the group would be here, as well as anyone else they could find. This event was too important to miss.

Dr. Simmons broached the doorway, and the crowd erupted in applause. Taking a step back, he appeared shocked by the attention and the number of people in the hall. He wore a red sweater and jeans, and his dark brown hair, without even a shred of gray, was perfectly styled. He flashed an amazing smile. Handsome but approachable. Bowing slightly, he gave a short wave to the enthusiasts. He was truly a humble man.

Finally Ruby could meet the man who had opened her eyes to a new vision of the world around her. She wouldn't be the same again.

Byron stepped to the front of the crowd and raised his hands. The applause died down.

Dr. Simmons also stepped forward. "I would like to thank Byron Macy and everyone who came today. It's so wonderful to see what's happening here on campus. Byron's been keeping me updated on the growth and development of the group. I believe that if we truly want the fullest life possible, together we must continue in our personal quest for perfection to uncover all the goodness humankind is capable of. The beginnings of the dream for peace on earth can begin in a campus hall just like this."

The room vibrated with thunderous applause, and Dr. Simmons raised his hands to the audience.

Ruby was now part of something that was so much larger than herself. Peace. Perfection. Misery abolished, banished from the face of earth forever. She could help impact other people with these teachings. If only everyone studied Dr. Simmons's methods and worked past their imperfections, maybe true peace would be possible.

As he spoke, she let those thoughts soak in. Maybe reconciliation could come to wounded hearts as well? What if her parents had attended one of Dr. Simmons's seminars before they split? Where would her family be today? Healthy and strong? Hope filled her like a dry sponge dropped in a deep well. Maybe it wasn't too late for all of them.

"I wish I could stay longer, but I have a late flight tonight," Dr. Simmons said. "But I would like to take some time to meet each of you and get to know you all a little better." He moved into the crowd, shaking hands, signing books, offering words of wisdom. The audience swarmed around him.

Trapped on the periphery of the crowd, Ruby rose to her tiptoes when someone pulled her shirt from behind. She turned to see Byron standing behind her.

"Why don't you move up front and meet him, Ruby? I've told Dr. Simmons all about you."

"Really?" Her smile didn't last long. "I don't know. I mean, what would I say to him?"

"He's a great guy. You don't have to be intimidated. Besides, he wants to meet you."

Ruby remained silent, knowing full well that no matter what she said, Byron would goad her on. He could do that like no one she'd ever met before.

"You're coming with me." He snatched her hand and snaked her through the bustling crowd right up to Dr. Simmons. "Sorry to interrupt, sir, but this is Ruby Porter, the one I told you about."

"Ah yes." Dr. Simmons nodded. "Byron can't stop talking about you. He did say you were as beautiful as you were brilliant, but he even understated that." He took her hand in both of his.

Ruby blushed, then glanced at Byron, who gazed at her as if she were the most important person in the world. Maybe he really did like her.

"Byron also tells me you're an amazing student, that you've even surpassed him with your studies."

Ruby focused on her feet and smiled. "Well, he tends to exaggerate a little."

"I don't think so." Dr. Simmons squeezed her hand, meeting her gaze head-on. "I have something very important to ask the both of you before I leave. We'll meet when I've finished up here."

"It would be our pleasure." Byron led Ruby away as Dr. Simmons autographed a book a student thrust toward him.

"He sounded serious." Ruby finally noticed that Byron hadn't let go of her hand since leading her through the crowd. She liked it—warm, gentle. So Byron thought she was *beautiful*? Maybe Brenda and Ashley were right.

They stayed hand in hand at the back of the hall and

watched with amazement as Dr. Simmons worked the crowd. Patient. Caring. He made eye contact with everyone he spoke with. He made them all feel special. He was gifted.

Dr. Simmons finally hurried over to Ruby and Byron. "Walk with me."

The three exited Dodd Hall, and Dr. Simmons quickened his pace toward the waiting Lincoln Navigator. A huge driver exited the car and threw a cowboy hat on the front seat. He walked around the vehicle and opened the front passenger side door for Dr. Simmons, who stopped short of getting in and turned toward Ruby and Byron, who were still on the curb.

"I want to offer each of you an invitation that will change your lives forever."

"Absolutely." Byron stepped forward. "I'm game for anything you have, Dr. Simmons."

Ruby nodded.

"I have training groups in every major university in the United States. I have students in thirty-one countries now, with more growth every day. I'm on the cusp of moving my system worldwide in an unimaginable way."

Dr. Simmons rested his hand on top of the door. "But I'm going to need trained leaders to move with me as we grow. I want only the best of the best, the very brightest and most motivated the world has to offer. I've built a training facility in Highpoint, Florida, where I'm taking those students for this purpose. I want you two to come to Highpoint with me."

"I don't know what to say." Byron stepped back and regarded Ruby. "I'm honored that you would even ask."

"Say yes, then. I already have your room reserved."

"Yes. Yes. Yes!" Byron clapped his hands together. "Of course, yes."

Dr. Simmons turned to Ruby. "What about you, Miss Porter?

Will you join us for the greatest adventure you could ever imagine?"

"I...I don't know. It's all so sudden." She couldn't just pick up and leave school, could she? What would her parents think? "I haven't had time to think about it."

"What's your major, Ruby?" Dr. Simmons leaned in toward her.

"Well, I haven't decided yet. I'm not sure."

"Why is it that you haven't made a decision on your major?"

She shrugged. "I just haven't found my niche, I suppose."

"Maybe now you have. I don't believe in coincidence; I believe in destiny. I think you are destined to find your inner self with us at the Higher Learning Center. And from there, I believe you are destined to help change the face of the world. Fear is the murderer of dreams, Ruby. Don't let fear kill your future as well." Dr. Simmons extended his hand. "Come with us to Highpoint. Start the rest of your life today."

"Come on, Ruby." Byron nudged her arm. "When will another chance like this ever come again? This is the greatest opportunity imaginable."

Ruby searched her soul. It felt so right. The Higher Learning Method had changed her life, and now she had the chance to pass that knowledge on to others. Finally, something filled her with a sense of direction and meaning. But was she willing to take the risks to see this possible dream come true? Byron and Dr. Simmons smiled at her, waiting for her reply.

"Yes, I'll do it. I'll go to Highpoint with you." Peace overwhelmed her as she spoke the words.

"Excellent!" Dr. Simmons slid into the SUV. "You both need to understand that this will be some very intensive training, maybe the hardest thing you've ever experienced. But when we're finished, you'll be prepared for anything the world can throw at you."

Ruby and Byron regarded each other, smiling. It was everything she was looking for.

"I'll cover all your expenses to get you to the learning center. Once you're there, you will be in want of nothing. You'll see; we're like one big family. I can't wait to have you with us."

Dr. Simmons shut the door, and the driver sped away.

Ruby and Byron stood on the sidewalk waving.

"Ruby Porter." Byron faced her and took both of her hands. "I can't think of anyone I'd rather share this fantastic experience with other than you." He leaned in and kissed her.

She pulled back and explored Byron's caring eyes. Her feeling of purpose in that moment was matched by her yearning to draw closer to him. She couldn't deny it any longer. For the first time in her life, she *really* knew what she wanted to do and who she wanted to be with. She was going to Highpoint with the man she was falling for.

"So they're gonna come to Highpoint with us?" Todd drove the SUV away from the curb.

"Oh yes, my friend." Walter snapped his seat belt. "I'm very much looking forward to having them with us. Byron has done a remarkable job here. He's followed my instructions flawlessly. And this young woman, Ruby, should fit nicely with our core group, wouldn't you say?"

"She's a little hottie."

"Yes, she's quite the striking young lady. She certainly has some qualities that could enhance my facility. Ruby will be a nice addition to my flock."

Walter adjusted the mirror so he could watch her as they drove away. She was much more than Byron had told him about. Much more.

15

COCOA BEACH

"I hate delivering this kinda news," John said as he knocked on the second-floor apartment door.

The ten-story complex was set against the Indian River, and a stiff breeze passed through the hallway, providing a little relief from the muggy summer day.

"Or nonnews, if you want to call it that." Tim straightened his coat.

Nora Garrow answered the door and appeared surprised to see them. Her hair was matted on one side, as if she'd just woken up.

"Agents Russell and Porter." She pushed the hair from her face. "Please come in. Forgive the mess. I wasn't expecting anyone."

"We probably should have called." John entered with Tim on his heels. It was 11:30 a.m., and she was still wearing her robe. Poor woman might be clinically depressed. "I wanted to update you on what we've done so far."

"Can I get cleaned up a little before we talk? I didn't sleep well last night… That's not unusual anymore."

"I imagine so." John nodded. If one of his boys were missing, he wouldn't be sleeping much either. "Please, take your time."

She disappeared into the back bedroom. The apartment was small, two bedrooms probably. Papers were strewn about on a tiny round table in the kitchen dining area. Pictures of Nora and Mitch were all around the apartment. Mitch in a soccer uniform, Mitch and Nora building a sand castle on the beach. Mitch's graduation picture was on a metal shelf in the living room. Nora certainly loved her son.

It must have been tough raising a boy as a single mother. John imagined trying to raise his boys alone. No one to bounce ideas off or to give you a break. You'd have to be on your game 24-7. It had to be exhausting.

Nora came back in the room. Her hair had been brushed, and the smell of perfume trailed her. "I'm a little more alive now. Would you-all like some coffee?"

"No thanks, ma'am." Tim stretched as he continued to scan the room. "I think we're fine."

"So do you have some word on Mitch?"

"Well, we went to Highpoint yesterday." John lowered the case file to his side. "No one there has heard from Mitch in some time."

"Or they don't want to tell you." She shook her head. "There's something really wrong there, Detective. And they've done something with my son. Of course, they won't tell you where he is or what they've done with him."

"We also spoke with the local authorities." John didn't want to share his personal observations or all the information from the chief just yet. He would stay as impartial as necessary, with her anyway. She didn't need to be burdened with every consideration in the case. He had Tim to bounce those off of.

"Chief Bennington, right?" She crossed her arms in front of her. "I don't trust him. I can't prove it, but I think that man's covering for the whole operation."

"I understand your concerns, but do you have any solid information that something's happened to your son?"

His heart went out to the woman. Gut instinct was good, but it didn't rise to the level of actual evidence. They needed more, much more, if they were going to find Mitch.

"I don't think you understand, Agent Russell. Something *has* happened, and no one is helping me. It's like no one wants to acknowledge that my son even exists, like his life means nothing. Mitch can't just drop off the face of the planet and have no one care."

"We care, Nora, but we need help, too. We just can't pull information out of thin air. There has got to be something that can help us track him down. I've put out a statewide intelligence bulletin with Mitch's information on it. I've contacted Customs and the FBI. If he turns up anywhere, they'll contact us. I don't know what else I can do at this point."

"I don't care what you have to do." Nora's gaze locked onto John's. "No matter what has happened, I want my son back with me...even if it's only to bury him."

16

Oh, the joys of paperwork. Tim plopped down at his desk and fired up his computer.

He was a good three reports down. If he didn't finish all of them soon, Alan would be hawking around his desk, looking for fresh meat to rip into until he turned them in. And if he didn't finish the Crazy Larry supplemental report, Robbie would be pestering him, too.

Even though he didn't enjoy it, he could write a pretty fair report. Tim was thankful that his father had pushed him in school as hard as he did.

"No excuse for not working, Timmy," his father had bellowed on occasion. "Don't matter if you're the last hired, first fired. You gotta work and work hard. Men are gonna judge you harshly just 'cause you're black. Can't change that. So you gotta be twice as good at whatever you do to get only half the respect. But you can change minds and hearts with your hard work. People can't argue with that."

Tim respected and admired his father, who was the bravest man he had ever known. Growing up as a young black man in the South and being active in the civil rights movement, his father had been acutely aware of the sinister head of racism. Tim had seen his share, too, although it didn't dominate his existence like it had in his father's time.

His pop had a way of challenging people and standing his ground while at the same time being winsome and humble. A stinging humor and a potent intellect were his weapons of choice, and he wielded them with deadly precision when necessary. But at his core, Pastor Leonard Porter was a man of unwavering peace. He could restrain himself in the worst situations with the worst people, a trait that must have skipped a generation with Tim. He had little patience for foolish or bigoted people.

In spite of their many differences, Tim quietly thanked his pop for giving him the gravel in his gut, and he was proud that the elder Porter's blood surged through his veins. He wasn't sure why he'd been so nostalgic about his father recently. Maybe it was because Ruby was off to school and his life was in upheaval...again. Or maybe he just missed his pop.

Sitting right next to his mouse pad was a small, tightly folded paper statuette of a knight on a horse, just like the one he'd tried to make before, but this one was near perfect in every detail. Someone was in trouble.

"All right, you comedians, who's messing with me?" Tim scanned the suspects' faces. "Which one of you is trying to push my buttons?"

John stared at him from his workstation. He looked like he had nothing to do with it, but behind that goody-goody exterior, John could be sneaky.

Tim regarded Alan, who was talking with John, or pretending to talk with John until his prank was brought to fruition. Although Alan was the oldest in the team, he was often quite wily and certainly unpredictable enough to pull off something like this.

And then there was Robbie. Smart-alecky, belligerent, and

most of all, devious. She was his best suspect.

"So, you want to tell me about this, Robbie?" Tim held up the paper doll for all to see. "Anything you want to confess while you have the chance?"

"I don't know what you're talking about."

"Don't give me that. I know your games. Just the other day, you were over here making fun of me, telling me how to do my origami. You wanna pretend that conversation never took place?"

"Oh, it took place." Robbie slapped her hands on her hips. "And yes, I could do origami much better than you—any day. But you're barking up the wrong tree with this one."

"Will you take a voice stress test on that?"

"Porter, you want to give me a lie detector test on a practical joke?"

"Maybe. I might have crime scene come down and check for prints too...until I find the culprit." Tim turned toward Alan and John. "Either of you have anything to confess or tell me?"

"Whoever created it did a really nice job." Alan examined the figurine. "Look at that detail. The folds are sharp and crisp. Nothing like that monstrosity you made."

Tim threw his hands up. "Everybody's a critic now. I just wanna know who's playin' games with me." He regarded John. "Russell, I know you won't lie to me. Who's behind this?"

John shook his head. "I don't know, partner. But it does look like mighty good work. Whoever made it is a master."

"Well, all of you are still on my suspect list. I'll be watching each of you very closely from now on."

Gloria Davis entered the room. "Tim, I have your daughter on the line. She says it's important. Do you want me to ring her through?"

"Yes, please." Tim sat at his desk and picked up the phone with one hand while panning his coworkers with his index finger, giving them the evil eye. "Hey, baby, what's up?"

"Hey, Daddy."

Uh-oh. Her tentative tone didn't bode well. "You sound down. Is anything wrong?"

"No. As a matter of fact, everything is great. Better than it's ever been."

"You don't sound like it."

"Because I have to tell you something important, and I'm not sure how you're going to react."

This didn't sound good. He drew a deep breath and worked to stay calm, no matter what she had to tell him. He didn't want to shut down any communication with her. She'd just started opening up to him again. "Before you get yourself all worked up, try me."

"Daddy…I'm leaving school."

For the first time in recent memory, Tim was speechless.

"Thanks for meeting with me, Cynth." Tim stood as she approached his table at the Denny's on U.S. 192 in Melbourne.

She'd just come from teaching a class, and dressed in all black, Cynthia looked as if she were in mourning. Regardless of her solemn appearance, she was still a radiant woman. A once familiar warmth coursed through his heart as she drew nearer, but he tried not to let it show.

Tim sat back down. "So you talked with Ruby also. What do you think?"

"I don't know." Cynth slid into the booth with him and tucked her purse next to her. "She's always been so practical. Now this. We don't know anything about this Higher Learning Center. Is it accredited? What is she going to do when she finishes up there?"

A waitress interrupted with two cups of coffee, placing them on the table in front of Tim and Cynth. "Can I get you anything else?"

Cynth answered with a wave of her hand.

"You still take cream and sugar?" Tim tore open a packet for himself and poured it in his cup. He'd ordered ahead for her. After twenty years with Cynth, he knew what she'd want. He figured that much hadn't changed.

"Yes, thank you."

Tim didn't want to worry her. She didn't need that with everything else going on, but she did deserve to know about the Garrow kid. It was probably nothing. Russell was making a bigger deal about it than it needed to be. But still, as Ruby's mother, she had a right to know everything he knew. Even if it wasn't going to be pleasant telling her.

"I've been to this Highpoint place." Tim rearranged the salt and pepper shakers in from of him.

"Really? How's that? Did Ruby tell you earlier what she was planning to do?"

"No." Tim shook his head. The last thing he wanted was for Cynth to think he'd been plotting this with Ruby behind her back. That would make any of their past fights look like Cub Scout meetings. "Nothing like that. John and I are working a case of a young man who's missing from their campus."

"So it *is* a college?"

"Of sorts, I guess. John and I went down there and met with some of the people. It's a training center for this Dr. Simmons."

Cynth took a sip of the coffee. "That's what Ruby said. But it doesn't sound right. How can she be doing something like this and not tell us? All she would say was that she was going to teach Dr. Simmons's system to help people."

"That's what she told me, too. I don't understand it any more than you do, but I told her I'd support her in whatever she wanted to do. I just never imagined it would involve something like this."

"You said a boy was missing from this school. What are the circumstances behind that? Is this anything we should be worried about?"

"I don't think so. Looks like this kid just took off and didn't tell anyone where he was going. When I was down there, it looked like a nice facility. Very new and modern."

"That's not my concern. What is she thinking? We spent countless hours and how many thousands of dollars to get her into Florida State. We made plans, and she just up and leaves on a whim? It's not like her."

"I agree." Tim folded his hands on the table. *We* being the operative word. More like Cynth had made plans. Maybe that was why she was so upset. Because her plans for Ruby had been disrupted. "This is the last thing I would have expected. But maybe we should support her in this."

"I don't know, Timothy. I don't like it."

Disagreement rumbled just underneath the surface of her calm veneer. Anytime she called him by his full name, trouble was brewing. It was one of the few clues she would give when she was angry. Even after all these years, she was still a hard woman to read.

"Maybe we should just wait and see what happens." Tim held her gaze. "Maybe her getting involved with this group will turn out to be a good thing. What if she can really help people?"

"I can't support her in this." Cynth shook her head and rested back against her chair. "We don't know a thing about these people or Dr. Simmons. It makes me very uncomfortable. You've always been the one to give in to anything Ruby wanted. I've always had to be the bad guy, the disciplinarian. And frankly, I'm a little tired of that."

Here we go again. That was a low blow. "I'd rather give in and try to find out what *she* wants instead of planning her whole life out for her like *you* have. You've always pushed and pushed her to do more, work harder, do better. Get the best grades, get in the top schools. You never gave her a break and let her be a kid."

"You're blaming this on me?" She leaned in. "So it's my fault that she's getting involved in goodness knows what?"

"Well, if the shoe fits..." Tim's raised voice caught the attention of the people at the next table. He stopped and closed his eyes. This wasn't going to get them anywhere. It was a cryin' shame that they couldn't spend two minutes talking together without conflict. "I don't want to fight, Cynth. This isn't about us anymore; it's about Ruby. Can we at least agree on that?"

She recoiled back in her seat and crossed her arms. "Agreed. I'm just worried, Tim, that's all. I'm sorry I snapped at you. I just want to know who these people are and what our daughter is getting into. If you can put me at ease with that, I'll support her in this. But I don't like it, Tim. Not one bit."

17

David Ling drove the Suburban into the circular driveway of the Higher Learning Center. Ruby couldn't remember a time when she had been so happy, yet so nervous. The facility was beautiful, with its brick architecture and grand vaulted roofs.

Hustling around to their side of the car, David opened the door for them. Ruby and Byron stepped out of the SUV, leaving the old world for the new. She felt odd having a personal chauffeur drive them all the way from Tallahassee. The eight-hour trip had given Byron and her time to get to know David, who'd grown up in Seattle and heard Dr. Simmons speak at a retreat there. He was hooked.

David had only been at the center a little over three months. The entire ride was spent building their anticipation of Dr. Simmons's newest teachings and insights. Ruby could see why David had been invited to the learning center: He could quote Dr. Simmons and his philosophy from memory.

"We're looking to double the number of students to 180 this fall," he said. "I'm telling you, in a few years, this place will be as large as or larger than the University of Miami. And after that, who knows? We're going to make a difference here. I can feel it."

"I can, too." Byron nodded. "That's why we're here. We want to be a part of this. I'm glad we've gotten to know you. Maybe you can help us get around here. The place is much larger than I thought it would be."

"You haven't seen anything yet." David grinned as he scanned the complex. "Dr. Simmons has already designed the additional buildings for campus growth. The man can do anything."

"If it isn't my new protégés!" Dr. Simmons hurried toward them, arms open wide—every bit as impressive as he was the first time Ruby met him. "Welcome to the Higher Learning Center and to the first day of your new lives."

He grasped Byron's hand and then pulled him close, hugging him like a long lost son. Turning to Ruby, he wrapped her hand in both of his. "And you, Ruby. You are truly as lovely as a rare jewel. Welcome."

"Thank you for inviting us," Byron said. "I hope we don't disappoint you."

Dr. Simmons waved away Bryon's comment. "That's not possible, my friend. The first part of your training is to disregard those negative thoughts and feelings. They have no place here. You will soon learn how to train yourself past those imperfections and develop a clearer understanding of yourself and your potential."

Byron shook his head. "Wow! Every time you speak you just blow my mind."

"Well," Dr. Simmons eased his hand onto Byron's shoulder, "we'll try not to overload you before dinner anyway." Everyone shared a laugh. "David will help you get settled in. He knows his way around here quite well."

David lifted the bags from the back of the SUV and set them on the sidewalk next to the Suburban. "I'd be happy to give you a tour."

"I have some tweaking to do for tomorrow's lectures. We're going to start fast and furious. You won't be disappointed, I can assure you." Dr. Simmons smiled. "David, take good care of them. I have big plans for the lot of you."

"Yes, sir." David saluted and returned the smile.

"We never got a welcome like that at Florida State," Ruby said. "I had to make an appointment just to see a professor."

"This isn't Florida State." Byron slipped his hand into hers. "I don't think there's a campus like this anywhere else in the world. And I can't think of anyone else I'd rather share this moment with either."

She kept her hand in his. His hand felt so good, so strong and confident. No one had ever made her feel like Byron did. She was so at ease around him. It just felt natural, like it was meant to be from the beginning.

"Me, too." She squeezed his hand.

David grabbed one set of bags, and Byron reached over and took the other. They walked into the lobby area.

"Hi." Ruby held out her hand to the receptionist. "I'm—"

"Ruby Porter." The redhead shook her hand. "From Orlando, Florida. The land of Mickey Mouse. I didn't think anyone was originally from there."

"Wow. How'd you know who I was?"

"You're at the Higher Learning Center now. You're special to have been invited, and we all know each other. We're family here."

"Well, since you know who I am, what's your name?"

"Kara Carson." She held out a key. "And here's your room key, roomie."

"Roomie?"

"Yeah, we're roommates. Room 312, on the third floor. It's small but nice. I think you'll like it. I don't snore or anything obnoxious like that."

Ruby chuckled. "I don't either, I think."

"Come on," Kara said. "I'll show you both around."

Byron and Ruby followed Kara out the double doors that led to the courtyard. The warm breeze blew Ruby's hair back as she gazed down at the choppy waters of Lake Okeechobee, which was as large as an ocean, with cattails and reeds lining the shore.

A long dock extended out into the lake with a small covered gazebo and several benches at the end of it. A metal security fence was in the water, cordoning off a swimming area. Groups of students were in a water fight on peddleboats, chasing each other around the lake. Others milled around, talking and laughing. More students sat in a large pavilion in the middle of the courtyard. It was paradise.

"Wow!" Ruby lifted her face to the sun. "This is just beautiful."

"It really is. You just don't want to be out here at night." Kara laughed. "The mosquitoes are so big they can carry you away. Other than that, everything is nearly perfect."

Byron wrapped his arm around Ruby's shoulder. Everything truly did feel perfect. She'd finally found her place, and it was here at the Higher Learning Center.

Walter gazed down from his office window to the students in the courtyard. He'd truly pulled together a superior collection of pupils. This group would launch from Highpoint like a rocket, exploding into the world with wisdom and knowledge for a corrupted humanity. Everything was really coming together. It was a magnificent day.

"Well, it looks like everyone is finally here." Cliff placed a stack of reports on his desk.

"Yes. Byron and Miss Porter have arrived. Everything is complete. Now we need to step into the second phase." Walter turned to Cliff. "Do you have the update on the sales figures?"

"Of course." Cliff grabbed a folder from the desk. "Your book is number three on the *New York Times* bestseller list. It should be number one within two weeks if our projections are accurate. This will be your third number one."

Dr. Simmons eased into his chair and steepled his hands, nodding his approval.

"Your CD series is the hottest selling item in Japan right now, and it's taking off in Europe, as well. The numbers are staggering." Cliff drew a deep breath and pushed his glasses up. "Finally, the world will see you for the true genius you are."

"Yes, but there's so much more to do, my friend. We must keep these sales as high as possible because I'll need a much larger financial push if we're to see my vision carried forward. This facility didn't come cheap, and neither will the rest."

Dr. Simmons spun in a quick circle in his chair. "Have the police returned?" He searched out the window.

An awkward hush enveloped the room. Cliff finally answered. "Not for a couple days."

"You can rest assured, they will be back."

Cliff swallowed hard and lowered the folder to his side.

"Could you leave me for a while? I need to meditate." With all that was happening, he would need to be at his best.

"Certainly." Cliff bowed slightly then hurried from the room.

Even though everything was moving as expected, Walter wished everyone could develop at his speed. But others were simply incapable of excelling like him. His whole life, no one had been able to match him in anything. He'd have to be patient with the others. If they would simply listen to and follow him, they, too, could be as enlightened as he was, or close anyway. He alone had the answers that a suffocating, deluded world needed.

Walter rose, walked to the bookshelf, and slid a set of books to the side. He grabbed a small lever then pulled it. A section of the bookshelf lurched forward then canted open, revealing his inner sanctum—a room even Cliff was forbidden to enter. A man of Walter's stature, his intellect, desired a place to gather his thoughts and not be disturbed. Cliff knew that if he was in his meditation room, he was not to be bothered for any reason.

He entered his sanctuary, which contained a recliner and a desk with a mirror. He sat and plucked a timeworn Polaroid that was wedged in the border of the mirror. Lesley Ann's face could still be made out, her fair skin and feathered blond hair in a seventies style. Her arms were wrapped around her legs, pulling them tight to her chest. She was wearing a T-shirt over her bathing suit. Stunning, nonetheless, no matter the years.

"Lesley Ann." He ran his finger across the picture, as if provoking her memory by touch. "If only you could have been with me all these years. We could have risen together, as we were destined to do."

Arching back in his chair, Dr. Simmons surveyed the murals he'd painted on the walls and ceilings, an exact replica of a day seared into his memory from so many years before. He closed his eyes and envisioned their favorite lake, with the cypress trees dangling over their treasured spot, the lily pads floating carelessly about…

And the violent ripples from Lesley Ann disturbing the tranquil waters of Lake Tarpon. The detail astounded him still. One of his finest works to be sure.

18

Welcome to *America in the A.M.*," the leggy blond woman on the television said. "I'm your host, Angie Wilson. This morning our guest is Dr. Walter Simmons—prolific writer, musician, painter, and all-around phenom."

The audience cheered as Dr. Simmons walked onto the set. John turned up the volume on the TV on his desk. Dr. Simmons was decked out in his usual dark sweater and blue jeans, his hair primped meticulously. He kissed Angie's hand. She fanned herself and faced the camera, blushing.

"Dr. Simmons," her sanguine expression overflowed, "you've published over forty books and numerous articles, developed a self-help philosophy that's changing people's lives, while pursuing your musical and artistic interests as well. You've seemingly mastered so many areas. Where do you get the energy?"

"You're very kind, Angie." He faced the camera. "As I wrote in my latest book, *The Imprisoned Mind*, we have so much more potential in our lives than we ever give ourselves credit for."

"Tell our viewers what you mean by that." She crossed her legs. "How much potential does each of us have?"

"I believe that potential is only limited by the individual himself."

"That's a pretty bold statement, Dr. Simmons."

"I've seen it to be true in my own life as well as others. I've received testimony after testimony from students who've experienced my system firsthand. They've watched their grades dramatically increase and their lives blossom from the concepts about which I've written."

"Your books and CDs do appear to be most popular with college students." Angie smiled.

"Well, college students are the most in need of and often the most receptive to ideas and philosophies that can enhance every area of their lives. But my teachings are not limited to students alone by any means. I've received countless letters and e-mails from housewives, grandparents, and people from every walk of life who have benefited from my life principles and teachings."

"Sounds like revolutionary stuff, Dr. Simmons."

"I most assuredly believe so. I am convinced that most, if not all, of the problems in the world today are directly linked to learned behaviors that can be changed then enhanced through precise, regimented training. If more people could embrace these teachings, we would have a much more stable, peaceful world."

"That's truly amazing." She nodded.

Walter smiled and appeared very humble. The man was good. John was amazed at his communication skills; the poor little reporter was enthralled by his whole presentation.

"I understand you have an educational center in Highpoint, Florida, now, specifically for training others to teach your system," Angie said.

"We put the finishing touches on the center about six months ago. You should really come down and visit." He reached out and touched her elbow. She giggled and shifted in her seat. "It's the most fabulous facility. My vision is to carry my system around the world, to help people in every aspect of their lives. This training center is just the first of many more to be built around the world."

"This is all really fascinating. Dr. Simmons, thank you for being our guest today. It's been enlightening." She rose from her chair and took his hand.

He cupped hers with both of his. "I hope to see you in Highpoint very soon."

Angie gave a sheepish smile.

Enough of that. John turned off the television and grabbed his legal pad with pages of background notes he'd compiled on Dr. Simmons. While all his mannerisms were correct and his communication style impeccable, something about the man unnerved John. Maybe it was his eyes. Maybe it was John's ingrained bias against distorted humanistic worldviews like his.

A stack of Simmons's CDs lay on John's desk. He checked out his notes on the messages. While the ramblings held no interest for him personally, they did offer a lot of insight into Dr. Simmons and his group. The doctor based his teachings on the Six Keys to Unlocking Your Higher Being:

1. Exfoliate Your Soul—scrub away the negative past.
2. Discipline Thyself—personally discipline every area of your life.
3. Fidelity—faithfulness to the teachings and concepts.
4. Good Deeds—work hard for others to purify yourself.
5. Tell a Friend—share Dr. Simmons's concepts with the world.
6. Spiritual Sojourn—a time of separation to meditate and do good works.

Dr. Simmons spoke of the cure for the human condition, and while he didn't directly slander God, his condescending remarks about people of faith and God were ripe. His teachings, a mish-mash of New Age philosophy and psychobabble, could be easily distilled into one theme—man can find perfection and salvation in himself...by following Dr. Simmons's system, of course.

John rocked back and rested his pummeled brain. He had to give the man credit: Dr. Simmons was a very charismatic individual if nothing else. His smooth, soothing, almost rhythmic voice slithered across John's psyche like a snake through a pond, leaving plenty of ripples. And those ripples troubled his spirit.

Anytime he encountered a lie, it was discomforting. But this one in particular shook him. How could so many people follow this man? What made this teaching so appealing? John already knew the answer. It was the lie of the ages, something the evil one had spoken of from the very beginning in the Garden—that man could be like God. There was truly nothing new under the sun.

Tim hurried into the office, disrupting John's train of thought. Porter walked straight to his cubical without speaking to anyone. Two crisp origami figurines decorated his desk—one of an elephant, the other a tiger.

He swiped them onto the floor. "Children will play," he muttered as he flipped on his computer and logged in, still keeping to himself.

"Well, good morning to you, too."

"Sorry, man." Tim pounded on his keyboard without looking up. "I'm just a little preoccupied right now."

"Everything all right, Porter?"

"I hope so." An image of Dr. Simmons from his website came up on Tim's screen.

"I've already bookmarked his site on my computer," John said. "I've been doing some background on the Garrow case. Some pretty interesting stuff."

Tim swiveled his chair around to face John. "I wasn't so much looking for the Garrow case. Something has kinda come up, and I'm not sure what to make of it."

"Wanna talk about it?" Tim was normally an open person, but with some things he could be very private. John certainly didn't want to push where he wasn't invited.

"Tell me what you've come up with first." Tim's sober gaze met John's.

"Well—" John thumbed through his legal pad—"Dr. Simmons is a bit of a virtuoso…at everything it seems. He was a concert pianist at age fifteen, a published author at eighteen, graduated Oxford University with a doctorate in psychology at twenty-two. He's written over forty books and has over two dozen study CDs in circulation, as well as competing in several triathlons."

"Pretty impressive." Tim rolled his chair away from his desk. "Maybe our guy Cliff was right about his boss."

"Maybe." John tapped his pen on his desk. "And maybe not. I've been listening to his CDs and noted some things I'm concerned about."

"Like?"

"His teachings, while they sound innocuous, are laced with references of seeking human perfection and being able to think past all of a person's flaws. Even physical illness can be fended off by a sheer act of will. Pretty dangerous stuff."

"What's so dangerous about seeking perfection? Isn't that what everyone truly wants? Isn't that what most religions teach? Sounds like the man is just trying to help people."

"Don't you think it's kind of odd that all his remedies for the human soul reside in his teachings alone? That's should be enough to send up warning signals for anyone, Tim."

"Look, this guy's stuff is not my bag. But who are we to judge his ideas? Again, there's nothing wrong with people trying to help one another."

"If he really is trying to help." John crossed his arms. "I'm not convinced of that. How many societies have started out with the promise of Utopia only to end up with hell on earth?"

Tim shook his head. "It's not the same thing."

"It's pretty close. Anytime man tries to accomplish what God has promised to do for us, it spells trouble."

"There you go." Tim wagged a finger at him. "I knew it wouldn't be two minutes before you brought the Bible into this conversation. You are consistent, Russell. That's for sure."

"I call 'em as I see 'em. And why are you working so hard to defend Simmons? You're normally more paranoid than I am."

Although Tim was smart and a great cop, he lacked true spiritual discernment. But it was still John's job, as a friend, to give him his best read on the situation, even if it meant riling his partner up a bit…again.

Tim shifted in his chair and cast his eyes away. "No reason. I just don't think we should judge a whole group of people until we know more about what's going on. That's all."

"I'm not judging anyone. We've got a case, and I'm doing the background. Why do I get the feeling we're talking about two different things?"

Porter scrunched up his face. "Ruby's quit school."

"I'm sorry, Tim. What's she going to do?"

He hesitated for a long moment, then faced John. "She's gone to the Higher Learning Center. She left school this week and went to Highpoint."

"Oh, I didn't know." That explained his defensiveness. This case, this situation, was morphing out of control, and Tim didn't have any idea what Ruby was setting herself up for. "I'll be praying for her...and you."

"It's not like she died or something." Tim stood and forced his hands in his pockets. "She's just gone down there to expand her education in a different direction. I promised to support her in whatever she chose, and I'm gonna keep my word."

"You don't sound that confident, my friend. And as your friend, I have to tell you I'm worried."

"What's got your fundamentalist drawers all bunched up this time?"

"I don't think Ruby's involved in just another educational choice." John had to encourage Tim to see the nature of what was going on around him. But how could he convince a nonbeliever to see the spiritual implications of what was happening? *Lord, help us. Open Tim's eyes and protect Ruby. This is not going well.*

"Well, what do you think's going on, John?"

"The Higher Learning Center could be the beginnings of a cult."

"I think you're stretching things." Tim frowned. "I don't see that at all."

"I hope I'm wrong." John stood and faced Tim. "More than you know."

"Ruby's a smart girl, smarter than you or me. She'd never fall for no cult. That's just ridiculous."

"Cults are *spiritual* deceptions." John held his hand over his heart. "It doesn't have anything to do with intellect. Many very smart people have fallen victim to cults. Look at the Heaven's Gate cult from almost ten years ago. Nearly everyone in the cult had a master's degree or higher, but they believed that a spaceship was behind the Hale-Bopp comet and was coming to earth to pick them up. Only a spiritual deception could do that to normal-thinking individuals."

"You're way off on this one, Russell." Tim waved a dismissing hand at him. "That's apples and oranges. Those people were nuts."

"They didn't start out that way. They were intelligent, decent people until they followed one man and his perverted teachings to their deaths. Dr. Simmons is a very charismatic leader; he's separated his top students, alienating them from any other teachings or influences; and all his teachings revolve around his kooky theories of the evolution of man to the next higher level. *And* we have a young man missing from that complex. There's a lot there to be worried about."

Tim was silent. In spite of his protest, he appeared worried. Tim was hitting overload, but John was glad that he'd shared the truth with him, no matter how painful it was. Maybe more opportunities would open up in the future. He would pray for that. But for now, he needed to be there for his partner, his friend.

"I tell you what." John perked up his voice, hoping to raise Tim's spirits, if only a little. "There's one way we can truly find out what's going on."

"How's that?"

"Visit with Dr. Simmons."

19

Ruby and Byron slid sideways down the row of seats in the front of the auditorium. The stage was raised and designed in a half-moon shape, so viewing was optimal from any seat in the house. Track lights hung from the ceiling, illuminating the set below. The lecture hall rivaled any Ruby had been in before.

Dr. Simmons rested in a large chair on the stage as Cliff approached the microphone. "Welcome, ladies and gentlemen. For those of you who haven't noticed, we have thirty new students with us tonight. Would the new students please rise so we can introduce you?"

Byron and Ruby stood along with others and were greeted with roaring applause. The outpouring of affection and warmth flabbergasted Ruby. She'd only met a few students since arriving, but to have the whole assembly embrace them in such a way was...overwhelming.

Cliff silenced everyone with his hands, and the students took their seats again. "Tonight we are going to have a special guest speaker. It's something we do here every Friday. I think you'll find this week's testimony particularly enlightening. I'd like to introduce Todd Yancey, a staff member at the Higher Learning Center."

The audience responded again with the same energy, and Todd sauntered onto the stage. Cliff handed him the microphone and reached up to pat him on the shoulder. The man towered over Cliff.

His hair slicked back, Todd wore a blue long-sleeve shirt buttoned all the way to the top and tucked into his blue jeans. He stared off into the waiting crowd, playing with the rim of his cowboy hat that he held down to his side. He paused for a moment, as if not sure how to begin. He looked to Dr. Simmons, who bowed his head approvingly.

"I…I didn't have any kinda family growing up. My dad walked out when I was four. I don't hardly remember him. I started doing drugs, smoking pot and stuff, when I was eleven. I was arrested the first time when I was thirteen for stealing a car. After that, I spent almost all those years in juvie hall, and then when I became an adult, I went to prison. I couldn't hardly read or write. I didn't care about nothin' or no one."

Ruby knew the pain of a parent walking out of her life, too. Although her situation was not as dramatic as Todd's, the sting was every bit as potent. Todd's testimony lured many of those feelings back to the surface. Why had her father let his personal demons destroy their family? Why couldn't he have been more determined to face the depression and alcoholism head-on? How different things might have been for them all.

Todd wiped the tears from his eyes with his shirtsleeve. He looked more confident, hitting his stride—he was speaking from the heart. "But it was there in prison that I met my future. Another prisoner gave me a bunch of CDs with Dr. Simmons's message to the world. After listening to three CDs, I knew my life had been touched, changed. I couldn't get enough of 'em. Dr. Simmons changed the way I saw myself and other people. He gave me the power to stay off dope and get my life straight. And when I finally left prison, I dedicated my life to the man I see as my true father; that's you, Dr. Simmons. You're my true father."

All the students rose and lifted their ovation and adoration to Dr. Simmons, who remained seated and appeared almost embarrassed by the attention. He finally put his hand up, and the crowd took their seats again.

"You're far too kind, my friend." Dr. Simmons smiled. "It has been my pleasure to see you blossom into the man you've become. You truly are a testament to the transforming power of my system. I'm proud to have you on staff here."

Todd wept even more. "Thank you. Thank you for everything!"

Ruby's eyes welled up, and she looked over at Byron, who was crying as well. This man could change lives.

20

John flipped open his cell phone and answered on the second ring. "John Russell."

"Agent Russell," Chief Bennington said. "I need you to stop by my office before you head up to the learning center."

"How'd you know we were coming down to Highpoint today?"

"I told you—this is my town. I know everything that's going on. Meet me here when you get into town. I'm sending one of my guys with you."

"No problem." John turned off of the interstate onto Main Street. "We'll be about five minutes." John slapped his phone closed, then glanced at Tim. "The good chief has requested—or better said, ordered—that we take one of his officers with us when we go up to speak with Dr. Simmons."

"That shouldn't be a problem. I still think we're barking up the wrong tree with this. That Garrow boy's run off, and we're all wasting our time looking for him."

"I hope you're right, Tim, but I still don't like the chief sticking his fingers in our business."

"You're awfully uppity about that. What if you were in the chief's position? Wouldn't you want one of your people involved, watching over the investigation to make sure everything's going all right?"

"That's beside the point."

"That's exactly the point." Tim laughed. "Hey, I appreciate you not telling Alan about Ruby being up here. That's a hassle I don't need right now. If this case goes any further, which I don't think it will, I'll tell him myself."

"It's no big deal. As far as I'm concerned, we're still fact-finding right now."

"Fair enough." Tim smirked as they pierced the city limits of Highpoint. "But you're still a good egg."

As they turned into the parking spot in front of the police department, Chief Bennington sat at his desk, talking with Officer Moses. Both looked their way, but neither rushed to greet them. It wasn't the warm and cozy welcome John would've hoped for. He'd have to dial down his expectations for future visits.

"Let's see what the good chief has for us." Tim slipped on his jacket.

John and Tim entered the lobby. Chief Bennington didn't rise to meet them. Moses approached and extended his hand. "Good to see you-all again."

"Moses will go up with you to the center." Bennington glanced at them. "He'll introduce you to Dr. Simmons." He gave his attention back to the computer screen. "I still think FDLE is wasting its time down here."

"Hope so, Chief." John placed his file folder on the counter. "We should find out soon."

"Maybe when this is all wrapped up, you FDLE boys can come back and we can do some frog giggin'."

"Sounds great." John was not about to get into an airboat in the middle of the night with Chief Bennington to spear frogs or anything else. He'd really prefer not to be anywhere near the man if there were sharp instruments around. "We'll see what happens when the case wraps up." John checked his watch. "Well, we need to be going."

Moses, John, and Tim walked out to their car; Moses got in the backseat. They made small talk on the way up to the learning center and found out that Moses had been with the force for almost seven years and was in the army before that.

"The students are always walking into town." Moses stretched out in the seat. "They don't cause us any trouble at all. The chief even stops and talks with many of them. He's ordered us to take good care of any and all students when they're in town and to watch over them."

Cliff walked through the double doors and scurried to meet them. "Welcome back to the learning center, detectives." He shook their hands. "Moses, good to see you again. How have you been?"

"Doing well. Thanks for asking. Cliff, these men want to talk with—"

"I know; they're here to speak with Dr. Simmons. You're very fortunate. He's here today and wants to see you. I suggested he seek legal counsel before speaking with you, but Dr. Simmons wants to assist in any way he can. He's a big supporter of law enforcement and believes he can shed some light on Mitch's disappearance."

"I'm glad to hear that." John forced a smile. Cliff's tone grated on him, but they were getting the time with Dr. Simmons they needed, so there was no reason to push it. "Hopefully, Mitch will turn up soon, and we can clear this whole thing up."

"Follow me, gentlemen." Cliff led them inside to the administrative portion of the building.

"I'll stay here while you-all talk." Tim stopped and rested his elbows on the receptionist's counter. "Ruby Porter, please."

John winked at him as they passed. He'd take care of the official business while Tim took care of his personal business.

There was no reason to reveal that Tim was Ruby's father. No need to cause added aggravation. John was still fact-finding more than anything else. This at least gave Tim a chance to spend time with his daughter and check things out for himself.

If their roles were reversed, Tim would do the same for him. Besides, John wanted some one-on-one time with the great Dr. Walter Simmons without the added distraction of another detective standing there. Now he'd get his chance.

Cliff led John and Moses down the hallway to Dr. Simmons's office, which opened up into a vast room, much larger than it looked from the outside. A long oriental rug ran down the middle of the room, pointing straight to Dr. Simmons's polished mahogany desk. Just behind the desk, a rectangular window granted a picturesque view of the courtyard and Lake Okeechobee.

A bookshelf covered one entire wall from ceiling to floor. Everything from the classics to numerous psychology books packed the shelf. A biography of Sigmund Freud caught John's attention as well as Thomas Paine's *The Age of Reason*, displayed in an apparent place of prominence with the cover out.

Dr. Simmons rose slowly and stared eye to eye at John. He carried a lean, agile build, especially for a man in his midforties. He rounded the corner of his desk but stopped short with his hand extended. He wanted John to come to him. He was trying to take control of the interview early. Shrewd.

John crossed the expansive room. "Agent Russell." He took the man's hand. Firm and confident. "Thanks for meeting me."

"Dr. Walter Simmons. A pleasure to meet you." He wrapped John's hand in both of his, then slid his left hand up to John's shoulder, a very confident, comfortable move.

Simmons didn't seem the least bit nervous about their meeting. Maybe he wasn't. Maybe this case was nothing more than a confused young man who decided to disappear on his own.

John smiled then stared at the portrait on the wall of Dr. Simmons. The detail was exquisite. His eyes seemed wide, alive, just like the man standing before him.

Nearly every degree, plaque, book, and picture glorified Simmons in some way. He was an elitist and would be very difficult to pin down. With all their strengths, though, elitists had one severe weakness—their egos. John would sit back and pretend to be in awe of him, get the man talking about himself, and then see what happened.

"Dr. Simmons painted that himself." Cliff grinned with pride. "Just one of his many talents. He also carved most of the woodwork you see in this office. He's quite the phenomenal man, Detective. But if you're any good at your job, you'll discover that yourself."

"Cliff, please, let the man breathe." Dr. Simmons offered John one of the two plush leather chairs in front of his desk. "Have a seat, Agent Russell. Cliff, Moses, would you give us some time alone please?"

"But Chief Bennington told me to—"

Simmons raised his hand, cutting Moses off midsentence. "Don't worry about the chief. I'll speak with him. You're an outstanding officer, Moses. I'll make sure your chief knows this as well."

Moses nodded, and he and Cliff exited the room.

"Please forgive my assistant. He's fiercely loyal and maybe a little too defensive. He serves me well, though."

"I'm sure he does."

"So, Agent Russell. You're here to discuss the whereabouts of Mitch Garrow."

"Please, call me John."

Dr. Simmons didn't reciprocate. With the number of advanced degrees on his wall, it would be *Doctor* Simmons for the rest of the conversation.

"Thank you for seeing me today. I have to say, this is a mighty impressive facility. I'm quite taken aback by everything I see."

"Thank you." Dr. Simmons raised his chin as he spoke. "I developed the concept for this training center years ago. I had a vision of a place where the *true* nature of man could blossom and thrive, setting out from this learning center like roots of a fruit tree growing out into the world, eventually bearing transforming fruit. You're getting an inside look at something that is going to change the world."

"Sounds like amazing stuff." *Give me a break! The* true *nature of man?* Corrupt, fallen, and in desperate need of a Savior—that was the nature of man John understood. And over seventeen years of law enforcement had only reinforced that belief. He resisted the overwhelming urge to debate this man point by distorted point. But that would have to wait. The case came first. "A little over my head, maybe, but amazing just the same. What can you tell me about Mitch Garrow?"

Dr. Simmons smiled, as if provoked by a joyous memory of the boy. "Mitch…a brilliant but troubled lad." He rocked his chair and glanced toward the ceiling, his fingers steepled. "I was grooming him to be my second in charge here someday, but he just couldn't seem to shake the baggage of his youth. He had no real father figure in his life, that is, until he met me. I think that scar was too much for him to overcome, at least for now. I took him under my wing and tried everything in my power, and the boy showed great promise. But he just wasn't ready for the radical change that he was experiencing here. It was all too much for him, I'm afraid."

"When was the last time you saw Mitch?" John brushed some lint from his knee to give the appearance of not paying much attention to the question.

"I'd like to say he left here about two months ago."

He'd like to say 'two months ago'? Why didn't he just say it? John didn't take notes, at least physically anyway, but he would remember that phrase. Dr. Simmons needed to feel comfortable and, most of all, to underestimate him and Tim, so John just let the information flow. Simmons was much more likely to make mistakes then, if any were to be made.

"Why did he leave? Did you two have a falling out?"

"Not at all." Simmons grimaced. "We were never closer than the day he left. He came to me and said he was still struggling with issues of his father's abandonment. It was impeding his mental and spiritual growth here. I suggested he take a spiritual sojourn—a retreat of sorts—to meditate on my teachings until he was clear of the baggage from his past. Only then could he move forward into his future. He was to travel the countryside helping others and growing as a person. When Mitch was ready, he would return."

"How long does this 'spiritual sojourn' take?"

Dr. Simmons shifted his head. "Months. Sometimes years. Maybe a lifetime, depending on the person, of course."

"Did Mitch say where he was going to do this sojourn?"

"No. That's the beauty of it. He is away from any corrupting influences that can derail him from his journey."

"Would his mother be considered one of those 'corrupting influences'?" John probed a little, gauging his reactions. "She's very concerned about her son."

His eyes narrowed at John, and the soft, open features shifted, tightened. He stole a purposed breath. John had struck a bull's-eye.

Dr. Simmons didn't like to be challenged, even in the slightest way.

"A parent or family member *can* be a corrupting influence, though not always. If she doesn't want to see her son grow like he's supposed to, then yes, she could be a hindrance, and thus become a person to be avoided, shunned, as some might say."

"That kind of pits family against family doesn't it?"

"A person should throw off *any* negative influences, family or not. Personal growth and achievement are the most important things, even if it pits brother against brother and a father against his child. Individual perfection cannot be attained without it."

John squirmed in his chair; Dr. Simmons's loose Scripture reference bored into his psyche like a dental drill on a molar. It wasn't the first time he'd heard Simmons twist Scripture to suit his own context, but it irked him nonetheless. He took a moment to compose himself. He couldn't let Simmons rattle him and get him off his game.

"Did you encourage Mitch to *throw off* his mother?"

"No." Simmons eyes trained on him like howitzers. "He must have chosen to do that himself. And from what he told me about his life growing up, I'm afraid, *Agent Russell*, that I would have to support his decision. Although Ms. Garrow appears to be the worried, frightened mother now, she wasn't much of a mother to him in his adolescence. I saw this kind of thing often when I was in private practice."

"That's not for me to judge. My only job is to find him... whatever the outcome."

"That sounds ominous." Dr. Simmons chuckled. "Really, Detective, you're looking for a troubled youth who doesn't want to be found right now. Give him his space, and he'll turn up eventually."

"I hope and pray you're right." John stood up. "Nothing would make me happier."

* * *

Ruby appeared at the second-floor railing overlooking the lobby. "Daddy? I can't believe you're here!" She took the stairs two at a time, not breaking stride until she was in her father's arms.

"Oh, sweetheart, I'm so glad to see you."

"What are you doing here on a weekday? Don't you have to work?"

"Well, John and I have a little follow-up business here. No big deal. So I thought I'd take advantage of it and see you."

"I'm so glad you did. Let me show you around." She linked her father's arm in hers and walked him back toward the glass doors that led to the courtyard.

She was so excited; he wouldn't spoil it. She prattled on about this and that so fast that Tim had a hard time keeping up.

"Slow down, baby. A little bit at a time now. First, how are you?"

"Great, Daddy. I've never been better in my entire life."

"I'm glad to hear that." Tim pursed his lips. Should he go further? Everything seemed to be fine. Why should he risk ruining her joy? But if he didn't have answers after this visit, Cynth would wound him on the spot. "I've got to be honest, your mother and I were a little worried when you came straight here without even seeing or talking to us about it. That kinda caught us by surprise."

Ruby's enthusiasm waned some, and she stepped back. "Well, everything just happened so fast. I didn't have time to come home or anything. Byron and Dr. Simmons wanted me here right away to start my studies."

"I know who Dr. Simmons is, but who is this Byron?" Tim raised his eyebrows.

"He's a…friend." She grinned.

"Well, am I gonna meet this *friend*?"

"Sure. I would have brought him with me, but I didn't know you were coming. He's in a class right now. But you'll meet him. I promise."

Tim locked his thumbs in his waistband and inspected the area. It was quiet and peaceful looking, not some horrible torture chamber. He had let Russell and all his fundamentalist cult gibberish get to him. Why did he always let Russell get him worked into a lather? This could be a good thing for Ruby.

"Are you sure you're doing the right thing here, honey? You know your momma's gonna quiz me when I get home to make sure I asked you that."

"I know. I know. I'm surprised she's not here trying to talk me into leaving and going back to FSU. Which I'm not going to do, by the way."

Ruby's forceful statement surprised Tim. That was unusual for her. She must be spreading her wings. Tim simply wanted her to be happy, no matter what she did. "Your mom loves you, and she just wants what's best for you. You know that."

"But she's always planned my whole life. Now I have the chance to do something for myself and others, even if it's something she doesn't approve of. I'm an adult now, and I can make these decisions myself."

"No one doubts that." Tim took her hand. "I have faith in you, sweetheart. I do. But as your father, I want to make sure this is what you want for your life."

"You always told me that you'd support me in anything I wanted to do…*anything*. Well, this is what I want to do. I want to find purpose in my life. And I think I've found it here, with Dr. Simmons and everyone in Highpoint. I hope you can understand that."

"I think I do," Tim said, nodding. "I'll try to talk with your mother. You know that's not going to be easy for her."

"Thank you, Daddy." She rose to her tiptoes and kissed him on the cheek and nearly tackled him with a well-placed hug. "I'm so glad you came. You don't know how much that means to me."

They sauntered back into the lobby as John, Cliff, Moses, and Dr. Simmons were coming out of the office area.

"Ruby?" Dr. Simmons stopped and alternated his stares between Ruby and Tim, then down to Tim's gun and badge. "Is this detective your father?"

A full-toothed grin creased her pretty face. "Yes. I was just showing him around and telling him all about the Higher Learning Method."

"She seems very excited to be here." Tim extended his hand.

Dr. Simmons's smile overtook his face as he vigorously shook Tim's hand. "What a pleasure it is to meet you. Ruby is our star pupil. She's one of the brightest young ladies I've encountered in a very long time."

"Thank you. We're extremely proud of her." Tim glanced toward John, who held his file down at his side. "Are we done here?"

John nodded. "For now. We might be back later should we need any follow-up information. Is that okay with you, Dr. Simmons?"

"Of course. You are all welcome here anytime. And I hope you find Mitch soon. He was such a fine young man."

John cocked his head and glanced at Tim, a look he'd seen a hundred times before. Something had Russell's goat.

Tim hugged Ruby good-bye. He still wasn't sure about this whole Highpoint thing, but he was sure that he loved his daughter without limits and just wanted the very best for her.

John, Tim, and Moses walked out of the lobby to their car. John hustled ahead of everyone, barely able to contain his thoughts.

They had real problems to deal with, but he needed to drop Moses off before they could discuss it. John didn't want any of his impressions of the case to get back to Chief Bennington just yet.

"So your daughter's staying here?" Moses opened the back door and eased into the seat.

"Yeah. She just came in from FSU." Tim settled into the passenger side.

Moses pulled a business card out of his shirt pocket, scribbled on the back, and handed it to Tim. "This is my cell phone number. If you need anything here, you call me. No need to go through the police department. Call me direct."

"I appreciate that."

"I'm sure it's hard having a child away from home." Moses adjusted his gun belt and snapped his seat belt. "We cops have to look out for each other. I will be praying for you."

"You're starting to sound like my partner here." Tim pointed to John with his thumb. "He's always praying for my soul, though I don't think it's doing any good."

Moses regarded John. "You're a Christian?"

"Yes." John smiled; Moses remained stoic.

Moses drew another business card and wrote on the back. "You can call me, too, if you need something."

John reached around and took the card, but Moses held tight, making sure John made eye contact before releasing it. A serious look covered his face. John flipped the card over.

Don't say anything to your partner. Call me later. Urgent!

John returned his attention to the road leading into Highpoint and then glanced at Tim, who chatted away with Moses, unaware of the note.

This case was getting stranger by the minute, and John had

no idea what to make of Moses. If he was a friend of the chief's, John was inclined not to trust him. But if he was truly a believer, John might have to adjust his opinion. Either way, he'd find out soon enough what Moses thought was so 'urgent.' John pulled into the Highpoint PD parking lot.

"Well, I best be goin'." Moses got out and regarded them both. "My boss will be all over me if I'm not back on patrol soon."

"We need to be going, too." John locked eyes with Moses. "Talk with you *real* soon."

21

The Porter girl needs to go." Cliff slammed the office door. "She'll only be a distraction now. We can just tell her she's not making the grade, cut her loose, and be done with her. The last thing you need is to have her father and those detectives nosing around in your business just as we're getting this training center up and running."

"Have you no sense of vision, my friend?" Dr. Simmons leaned against the ledge of his window and absorbed the precious view of Ruby standing in the courtyard. "Sometimes your failure to grasp even the most insignificant thing is a source of great frustration to me. We've cooperated with the authorities and will continue to do so until they're satisfied and move on. If we dismiss her now, those detectives will stick their fingers in all of our business. Neither of us wants that, now do we?

"We have much more important work to tend to rather than be consumed with their investigation. Larger, life-changing things are happening here. Besides, I'm convinced Ruby could become quite the asset for us down the road. She might be exactly what I need."

Cliff drew a deep breath and exhaled deliberately. "Perhaps you're right."

"I'm always right. And you need to lighten up." Dr. Simmons patted him on the shoulder. "It could only get rougher from here on out. When you signed on with me, I told you I have enemies. People who will use any means, any tactics, to discredit my work here, to slander me in any number of ways."

"You warned me. I just didn't expect it to go like this. I'll do better, and I'll keep a much closer eye on this group. We can move past this into the glorious future you've envisioned."

"That's much better, my friend." Walter peered down at Ruby, her hands in her jeans pockets as she faced the lake, the wind blowing her hair back in a most delicious way. He stroked the glass where she stood.

"Ruby Porter is not going anywhere."

"So how was your talk with Dr. Simmons?" Tim waved to Moses, who hurried to his patrol car.

John barely heard Tim as he focused on Moses' cryptic note. He was dying to call him, but that would have to wait until later. He didn't like keeping secrets from his partner, but until John knew the whole story, he couldn't let on to Tim. The man had enough to worry about.

"*Hello*...John, how was your talk with Dr. Simmons? What do you think?"

"Oh, sorry. I was just deep in thought. There's a lot to process here."

"So what's your opinion?"

"I don't like it." John shook his head. "Not one bit. For a number of reasons."

"I figured you wouldn't. You got that determined look on your face you get, like when you're fixin' to jump on something...or someone."

"Well, first," John looked both ways as he turned onto Main Street, "when I was talking with Simmons, I asked him when the last time he'd seen Mitch was. He told me, 'I want to tell you he left two months ago.' That statement is just a little odd instead of saying, 'He left two months ago.'"

"Yeah, but he coulda just misspoken. Sometimes I think that statement analysis stuff is a bit out there."

"Maybe. But it was the second statement that really concerns me, Tim."

"Why's that?"

"When we were leaving, Simmons wished us luck and then said, 'Mitch was a fine young man.'"

"So? It seems as if he liked the boy. Nothing wrong there."

"It's the word *was*. Under normal circumstances, he would say that Mitch *is* a fine young man. Why would he use the past tense form of the verb? He'd only use that type of description if—"

"If he already knew what happened to him." Tim finished the sentence. He hissed and dropped his face into his hands. "This isn't good, John. What do we do now?"

"We've got problems, and your daughter is smack-dab in the middle of it. I'll talk with Alan and go forward in this case."

"Yeah, but the statement analysis stuff isn't enough to fly in court."

"No, but it does let us know that we could be on the right trail." John raised his eyebrows. "Something has happened to the Garrow kid, and we need to find out what it is. And we have to get Ruby out of there, at least until we clear up this mess."

"I don't know, Russell." Tim shook his head. "I just don't know. She seems so happy there. I find it hard to believe somethin' wicked's going on. I trust my daughter. I trust her judgment and her instincts."

"Do you trust mine?"

Tim paused and regarded him. "Of course I do; you know that. You're the best partner I've ever had. But this is different. I promised I would support her in whatever she wanted to do, and I can't go against my word. You should have seen her face back there. She was so full of life. I don't know if I could ask her to leave something that makes her so happy. I let her down and lost her once; I couldn't survive losing her again."

"I know you're in a tough spot, but I'm telling you the truth: Dr. Simmons is the Pied Piper, whisking these young people away into goodness knows what. That's my read on this, and I'd say it even if we weren't working the Garrow case. This isn't just another educational choice. Ruby's being led astray. I wouldn't be much of a friend if I didn't tell you that."

Tim at least seemed to be considering it; that was all John could ask. The man was in turmoil, seeking to hold on to his relationship with his daughter while at the same time trying to do what was in her best interest, even if she didn't agree.

Silence filled the car as they rocked toward Melbourne, the tension as fat as Dr. Simmons's bank account. Tim gazed at the passing telephone poles and swampland for nearly an hour before speaking.

"I'm too close to get any kind of read on the situation, so I trust your opinion. I want her outta there, but I'm not sure how I'm gonna do it. I need your help."

"You don't even have to ask, partner. Whatever you need you got."

"This favor might be big. I don't want you to tell Alan about Ruby yet. I want one more shot to get her to leave."

"I can do that. But we will have to tell him soon. If this investigation ramps up like I think it might, he'll find out one way or another. I think it should come from you."

"I know, I know." Tim slapped his hands on the sides of his

head, as if to keep it from exploding. "But Alan's not the one I'm worried about talking to. I'll get to him."

"How's that?"

"I've got to break the news to Ruby's momma." Tim sighed. "And that ain't gonna be pretty."

22

John hurried into the Patio Restaurant, hoping that Moses and the answers to some serious questions awaited him inside. The restaurant was a favorite among the locals but was out of the way enough to be a good place to meet. John and Marie loved Vero Beach; they had often come here for anniversary getaways. About an hour away from Melbourne, the drive was easy but still felt far enough away to leave the troubles and craziness of life behind.

Moses had beat him there and occupied a booth at the rear of the restaurant. In typical cop fashion, he chose a seat facing the door with his back to the wall so he could keep an eye on everyone coming in and out.

Moses' resemblance to Tim, with his lighter complexion and higher cheeks, was eerie. His countenance radiated a zest for life. John had noticed it the first time they met. There was a lot going on in this young man's head.

"John." Moses stood at his approach and extended a hand. "Thanks for meeting me here. I figured Vero Beach would be a happy medium for both of us."

"I could have met you in Highpoint." John slid into the booth. "That wouldn't have been a problem."

"It would have been for me." Moses shook a sugar packet and then tore the top open, pouring it into his tea.

"So what's this all about? I don't like keeping information from my partner. You're a cop; you understand these things. The man's saved my life countless times, and he's the best friend I've ever had. You better have a good reason for wanting to see me alone."

Moses remained stoic and matched John's stare. "You said you're a believer, right?"

"Yes."

"How strong of a believer are you?"

"That's a tough question. I'd like to think I'm a strong, passionate believer, but I'll leave that for the Lord to judge."

Moses nodded. "What do you think about spiritual warfare?"

John sighed. "Look, I love to talk about spiritual things; it's probably one of my favorite things to do. But I fail to see the connection between this conversation and why you didn't want my partner here—and why you wanted to meet this far away from Highpoint."

"Please indulge me for a moment." Moses raised his hand. "I promise I'll explain everything to you, but I need these questions answered first. Do you think spiritual warfare is a tangible thing or just some obscure concept?"

"I think it's every bit as real as the physical world."

"And just as dangerous?"

"Absolutely." John nodded. "Probably more."

Moses appeared to contemplate his next sentence carefully. "Your partner's daughter is in grave danger."

John rested back against the wooden booth. "How so?" He certainly had his own worries but wanted to hear Moses' fresh perspective without his own opinions getting in the way.

"I can tell you this now because you seem sincere in your faith, but a lot of people wouldn't understand; they'd think I was nuts. But evil forces have moved into Highpoint that have my skin crawling, as if the Prince of Darkness himself has set up shop."

"Dr. Simmons?"

"And then some. His little rat Cliff as well." Moses took a long sip of his tea and regarded John over the glass. "Simmons is spreading his lies and deceptions to youth all around the world—from *our* town. And our church is not going to just sit by and let it happen. As believers, we're called to do more than talk about it. So we've committed to pray for all the young people at the Higher Learning Center and that Simmons be exposed for what he is."

"How does Chief Bennington shake out in all this?"

"That's a hard one. He's just giggly that his budget has more than doubled in the last two years. New cars. New computers. A makeover of the police station. I don't know what's going on with him, but he sure likes having Dr. Simmons and his people in town."

"Is he in Dr. Simmons's pocket?" John put it bluntly. They were well past the euphemistic stage. "You must have concerns, or you wouldn't have suggested meeting so far away from Highpoint."

"The chief's lived in Highpoint his whole life," Moses said. "He has eyes everywhere. Anything that goes on in that town, or in Glades County for that matter, he's on top of."

"But is he dirty?" John hoped not. Few things in life disgusted him more than a dirty cop.

"I don't know." Moses shook his head. "I just don't know. So I'm being cautious."

John absorbed everything he was hearing. Moses at least confirmed some of his suspicions, but he'd need more than that. "What do you know about the Garrow kid's disappearance?"

"Now we're getting to the meat." Moses smiled for the first time in their conversation. "There's a woman at our church who's part of The Freedom Project, an anticult ministry. She arrived here shortly after Dr. Simmons and has been witnessing to the students when they come into town. She's a spirit-filled woman, to be sure. She was a child in the Branch Davidians in Waco. God protected her through that whole ordeal, she believes, to help others escape the dangerous lies of cults."

John raised his eyebrows. "Sounds interesting."

"Well, she met Mitch and started sharing the gospel with him. And he listened. One day he called her panicked and upset. He said he'd stumbled across something about Dr. Simmons that he had to tell her. Something that proved Dr. Simmons was insane and that could blow the whole lid off his operation."

John laid his elbows on the table. "Did Mitch say what he found?"

"No. He said he'd call her the next day and they would meet. She never got that call and hasn't heard from Mitch since. That was two months ago."

This new information had just ratcheted up this case—and John's blood pressure—to the top level. "Have you told anyone this?"

"The people in our church know, but no one else."

"Chief Bennington?"

"No way." Moses shook his head.

"So Simmons's explanation of a 'spiritual sojourn' is…?"

"Hooey. Something's happened to that poor young man. I've been rooting around, trying to do my own investigation while flying under the radar until I could get some help. Until I found someone I could trust." Moses enjoyed another large gulp of his tea then dabbed his mouth with a napkin.

"My pastor, our church, and I have been praying for God to send the right person to Highpoint to uncover the truth, to find Mitch, and to expose Dr. Simmons's lies for what they are." Moses' eyes locked on John's, and he leaned forward. "John Russell, it looks like you're that person."

23

Ruby hiked down the sidewalk that led from the learning center into downtown Highpoint, if you could call it that. Being raised in Orlando most of her life, for Ruby downtown meant skyscrapers, traffic congestion, and hordes of people scurrying about. Downtown Highpoint–style meant a single row of shops, with a restaurant, a hardware store, a grocery store, the police department, an ice cream shop, a convenience store, a small hotel, and not a whole lot more.

She made the half-mile walk in good time, and the fresh air helped wake her up some, although the summer heat bore down on her. Waking up at 4:30 a.m. and not getting to bed until late was wearing her out. But the studies and meditation times were important.

She picked up the pace a little because she had to be back for her next class, but Ruby was in dire need of some munchies. If she hurried, she might be able to get an ice cream cone before heading back.

The regimen, while strict, was refreshing and provided a certain comfort. She knew where she had to be and when to be there, not like the chaotic schedule she'd kept for herself in high school and the first semester at FSU. Dr. Simmons always said that a well-disciplined schedule was essential to a well-disciplined life.

She entered the Highpoint Trade & Grocery, and the air-conditioning rolled over her like an arctic wave. Not much larger than a convenience store back home, the small aisles were stocked with breads and canned goods. One aisle was dedicated to frozen foods and meats. Ruby picked up a basket by the handle and dangled it at her side as she browsed the shelves.

She chose a package of crackers for a midnight snack. As she reached for a box of cookies, she accidentally knocked it to the floor.

"Oh, boy." She bent down to pick up the box, but another hand beat hers to it.

A young woman, not much older than Ruby, maybe twenty-three or twenty-four, grabbed the box and handed it to her. She wore a maroon beret, and her hair was so blond it shimmered under the fluorescent lighting. A single braid hung down alongside her face with a red bead tied at the end.

"Thanks." Ruby smiled.

"My pleasure." The woman tilted her head. "Are you a student at the learning center?"

"Yes, are you?"

She shook her head and scrunched her face. "So how do you like it up there?"

"I love it. Everything is so fantastic. I'm learning so much." Maybe she could interest the woman in the doctor's teachings. She seemed open and friendly. What a perfect opportunity. "Do you know about Dr. Simmons?"

"A little bit." The woman grinned, exposing her front teeth.

Ruby glanced at her watch; she was running way behind.

"You need to get back soon?" The woman stepped closer to her. "They don't seem to give you much time alone in town, do they?"

"Not really. Well, you know, we do a lot of studying. A tight schedule and all. Maybe we can talk about it sometime." She placed the box of cookies in her basket. "I'm Ruby Porter. Nice to meet you." She extended her hand.

"Good to meet you, too." The woman took her hand. "What are you studying so hard for? What are you seeking in Highpoint, Ruby Porter?"

The question caught her off guard. The woman's voice was strange, probing, yet soothing at the same time. She had a peace about her, and her hazel eyes pierced Ruby's, as if she were staring more through her than at her.

"I...I don't quite know what you mean."

"You're here studying for something, aren't you? What are you seeking? What are you truly looking for?"

"I've gotta go," Ruby said. "I'm running late."

"I understand." She patted Ruby's hand, then released it. "I hope we can talk longer sometime. I'd like to hear more about Dr. Simmons. And I'd love to hear your answers to my questions. Take some time. Think about them. I'm quite sure we'll run into each other again."

"Okay." This was a puzzling woman. Maybe they would talk again, and Ruby could tell her more about the Higher Learning Method. "I'm sorry; I didn't get your name."

"Forgive me." The woman covered her mouth as she smiled. "It's China. China Washburn. Pleased to meet you."

24

MELBOURNE

"Come on in." Alan turned away from his computer and gave John his full attention. "What's happening with the Garrow case?"

"That's what I'm here to talk with you about." John closed the door and eased into the chair in front of Alan's desk. Alan's office was neat and orderly, much like the man himself. Numerous unit citations and personal commendations covered his wall.

Alan's eyes were weary. Nearly thirty years of police work had whittled away his once vibrant spirit, and he just didn't seem to have the energy he'd had when John first started working for him.

"I never like it when you close the door." Alan crossed his arms. "I've got seven and half months till retirement, and I don't need to hear bad things. Only things that don't cause me any grief. Please tell me you've come to share happy news and good tidings."

"I suppose it's all in how you look at it, boss. As the proverb goes, I have some good news and some bad news."

"Okay, let's hear it. Good news first."

John leaned forward in his chair. "I've got some leads that might help me track down Mitch Garrow's last hours."

"What do you mean 'last hours'? I don't like the sound of that. Sounds...criminal."

"The last hours that he was seen, I should say, which leads into the bad news."

Alan regarded John with sagging eyes. He opened a desk drawer and armed himself with a bottle of Maalox. "Okay, go for it."

"I think Dr. Simmons is running an operation that could be considered the precursor to a cult and has kidnapped or killed Mitch Garrow for some reason. I want to open a full investigation on him and his group."

"Dr. Walter top-of-the-New-York-Times-bestseller-list Simmons? The self-help guru who has more money than Disney World? This is the man you want to investigate for murder and goodness knows what else?"

"Mitch is missing, Alan. Simmons has done something with this kid. Every part of my gut tells me so. And I don't care how much money, power, or connection Simmons has. He shouldn't be allowed to get away with it." John threw the last part in as a zinger. No matter how burned out or tired Alan was, he had an abnormally strong sense of justice.

Alan growled and pulled a roll of Tums from his shirt pocket, tore it open, popped two of them into his mouth, and chased them down with a shot of Maalox. He massaged his gray, short-cropped beard with his fingers. The rough, sandpapery sound was the only thing to break the silence.

"How sure are you on this? You know this could potentially blow up in our faces. If we jump all over this guy and we're wrong, we all stand to take a bath on it."

"He's dirty, Alan. The man's a snake in the grass, and he's setting up his own little kingdom in Highpoint.

Alan rocked back in his chair and swiveled to face the wall behind him. "What are you going to need?"

"You're a good man, Alan. I might need to set up a base of operation in a motel close to Highpoint. That'll cut down on the travel and give us time to conduct interviews and such."

"Anything else? Maybe a Learjet? A six-figure expense account?"

"Not right now." John smiled. "Although I might request those later."

"The only consolation I have is that if you mess this up," Alan said, still not looking at him, "we're all going down together."

"Timothy Porter." Cynth folded her long arms and scowled at him. "Why do you always do this to me? You tell me our daughter's in danger, and then you can't tell me why. I'm not one of your suspects, and this is *our* daughter we're talking about. I have a right to know."

Cynth was a pretty woman, except when she was angry. Her ebony scowl could stop Tim in his tracks. Communication was never their strong point. Although not as passionate or outspoken as Tim, Cynth was every bit as stubborn and sometimes downright unreasonable when it came to Ruby.

Propping his back against his car, Tim crossed his arms. "What do you want to know?"

"Everything. I want it all."

He wasn't sure if the parking lot of her apartment complex was the best place to talk about their daughter, but it was unlikely she'd invite him up. She'd kept her distance and boundaries solid since they split. Even more so since the divorce.

"We're working a missing person's case from the Highpoint Learning Center." Tim sighed. "It's starting to look bad. John thinks the people who run it are involved in something wicked."

"What kind of wicked?"

"You gotta understand. My partner's a real Bible-thumper. A good man and a great detective, but he can get off on tangents sometimes."

"What kind of wicked, Timothy? What are you talking about?"

"He believes that the group's involved in the boy's disappearance. And he also believes this Dr. Simmons might be starting a...cult."

"Like a Jim Jones kind of thing?" She rolled her eyes and hissed. "That's not very likely. Ruby's a whole lot smarter than that. She's never been interested in religious stuff. This all sounds like crazy talk to me."

"I hope it is." He nodded. "I truly hope it is."

"What do you think, Tim? Whatever problems we've had in the past, I do trust your opinion in these matters. You've always been an outstanding police officer and a good judge of character. Please, tell me what *you* think. Our daughter's caught up in this, and I need your honest assessment."

"It's tough." Tim shook his head. "I'm so emotionally wrapped up in this that it's hard for me to get a clear read on the situation. I want to trust Ruby and her judgment, but I also know what John thinks. He has some good points on this kid's disappearance that have me concerned."

"What about your partner? Do you trust his judgment? Do you trust him?"

"With my life."

Cynth let her hands fall to her sides as she moved closer to Tim. "What about Ruby's life?"

25

"Walter Simmons, this is your life." John typed the doctor's name in LexisNexis. Eighteen hundred hits appeared in newspapers or magazine articles. He wanted as much in-depth information about Dr. Simmons's background as he could get.

John had come in on a Saturday just so he'd have the office to himself, away from any distractions. He loved searching for the one bit of information tucked away somewhere that could give him the edge he needed. Tedious work, but it had paid off more than once.

For four and a half hours, he scrolled through each website or newspaper account. Most were fluff pieces about what an amazing man he was. John printed out anything that offered a new insight into this Dr. Simmons character. Several articles spoke of the success of his program with drug treatment patients and prisoners; others documented his rise in the publishing world as a pop phenomenon on college campuses. *What a guy.*

John arched his back and rubbed his eyes; he was going to need reading glasses soon. His head throbbed. One more cup of coffee should get him past these last few pages.

In desperate need of a breather, he hit the break room and

poured himself a fresh cup. The aroma seeped into his nostrils and pumped some much needed life back into him.

He settled in again at his desk and pulled up the Nexis screen again. On the last page of his search, an article archived from a 1978 edition of the *St. Petersburg Times* popped up. "Young Woman Commits Suicide." It could be a different Walter Simmons—it wasn't exactly a unique name—but John clicked into it anyway.

> Lesley Ann Patterson, 17, died Tuesday from an apparent suicide. Ms. Patterson was pulled from Lake Tarpon by her boyfriend, Walt Simmons, a local swimming champion. According to Simmons, Ms. Patterson was distraught over their impending breakup and dived into the lake in an attempt to take her own life. He tried in vain to rescue her. Simmons is said to be distraught but cooperating with authorities.

A photo of a young Simmons accompanied the story. He had a blanket wrapped around him and was being walked from the lakeshore by a deputy. He had looked up just as the picture was snapped. It was definitely their man.

"Oh yeah." John smacked his hands together. "Dr. Walter Simmons, I think I've just found the chink in your armor."

"We need to present a united front." Tim drove his blue Honda Accord into the driveway in front of the administration building. After their talk the day before, Tim didn't want them arguing in front of Ruby. "If we disagree on something, we'll talk about it when we leave."

"Agreed. This isn't about us. It's about Ruby."

Cynth wore a navy blue dress and heels. The woman didn't know how to dress or act casual. She was all business all the time, which just might work well today.

She scanned the set of buildings Tim was becoming all too familiar with. "The campus looks nice."

"Looks can be deceiving." Tim worked a more casual look, blue jeans and a button-down khaki shirt tucked in. He also had a mini–Glock 9mm secured in an ankle holster. Not that he expected trouble, but he had a difficult time leaving his gun in the car. He'd feel naked without it—tainted by too many years as a cop, he guessed. Maybe after he retired, he'd get some therapy so he could walk in public without being armed.

They entered the lobby and strolled up to the receptionist on duty. "Ruby Porter please."

"She's in class right now." The young girl picked up a pen and paper from the desk. "May I take a message?"

"It's Saturday." Tim snorted. "Who has classes on Saturday?"

"We do here. And Dr. Simmons doesn't like to have the students' class schedules disrupted. I could have her call you at a later time."

Cynth bent over the edge of the desk, going face-to-face with the young woman. "We are her parents, we're here to visit, and I don't care what Dr. What's-His-Name says. I suggest you do whatever you have to do to get Ruby down here, because we're not leaving until we speak with her. *Capiche*?"

"Yes, ma'am." The girl rolled her chair back to a more comfortable distance and punched a number quickly on the keyboard, keeping a strained eye behind her. "It should be just a few minutes. Please have a seat."

Cynth could be forceful, that was for sure. A trait that could come in handy. It was one of the many things Tim loved about her before, as long as that weapon wasn't aimed at him.

Cliff Chaffin hustled from his office with the shadow lumbering behind him as they both hurried toward the lobby.

"Agent Porter, this is my assistant, Todd. Can we help you?"

So the shadow now had a name. Todd wore a flannel shirt with the sleeves rolled up over his beefy arms. He swayed behind Cliff like a sycamore in the wind and glared at Tim with a felonious gaze he'd seen a thousand times. Todd had definitely done time. Tim would check that out later.

"We're here to see our daughter."

"Now is not a good time, Mrs. Porter." Cliff folded his hands in front of him. "Ruby is in class and won't be finished for some time."

"I don't care if she's in class. Tim and I have come a long way and wish to speak with our daughter."

"May I ask what this is regarding?"

"No, you may not ask." Cynth crossed her arms and tapped her foot with a purposed, increasing beat that echoed throughout the lobby. "This is family business—and none of yours. Please let our daughter know we're here. Now."

"Stay here." Cliff turned to Todd. "I'll be right back."

The large man folded his arms and continued to bore a hole through Tim with his glare, his body language screaming that they were not to move past this point.

Several minutes of discomforting silence passed, then Ruby and Cliff emerged at the top of the stairs. Ruby didn't seem as happy to see them as she had just a week prior. She caught her mother's glower.

"Mom, Daddy?" She negotiated the steps quickly, concern creeping across her normally jovial expression. "What are you doing here?"

"Do we need a reason to see our little girl?" Cynth asked.

"Hey, baby." Tim pulled her in tight for a hug. Her body was rigid, and she didn't hug him back.

"Let's talk outside." Cynth opened the glass double door, and they walked out underneath the carport.

"You want me to leave, don't you?" Ruby crossed her arms. "You've come to talk me into leaving."

"What makes you think that?" Tim asked.

"After seeing the look in Mom's eyes, I could just tell."

"Your mom and I are just concerned that you might've been a little rash in your decision to come here." Tim put his arm around Ruby's shoulders. "We thought you might want to take a few weeks at home with us to relax and rethink everything, to have a clear perspective on the whole situation."

"We really would like you to come home with us for a while, honey." Cynthia stroked Ruby's arm. "If you want to come back at a later time, that would be fine. But we just want to make sure you're making the right decision."

"Why?" Ruby pulled away from both of them. "Why do you want me to leave? Don't you trust me? I'm not a little girl anymore. I can make my own decisions, especially about *my* future."

"We do trust you, baby. But this whole place here, out in the middle of nowhere, studying psychobabble and goodness knows what, it doesn't make any sense."

"I can't believe you, *Daddy*! I knew Mom would have a hard time with my decision, but you promised to support me in whatever I wanted to do. You promised! Well, I want to do this." She pointed to the ground, as if driving a spike at her feet. "I want to be here with Dr. Simmons. I've made so many friends here. For the first time in my life, I feel like I belong, and now you want me to just pack up and go home with you?"

"Just for a little while until we're all convinced this is the right move," Cynth said.

"Dr. Simmons said this kind of thing could happen. That our parents and family wouldn't understand what we're doing here.

That some people just weren't ready for what he has to offer."

"What kind of nonsense is that?" Cynth fixed her hands on her hips. "What else has this *doctor* been filling your head with?"

"For one thing, he said that I shouldn't let negative influences derail me from finding my higher self, no matter *who* they are. And to throw off any of those influences if I have to!"

"Have you lost your mind?" Shock filled Cynthia's expression. "Or have these people stolen it?"

"All I want is to be happy and fulfilled, Mom. Why can't you understand that? Dr. Simmons and everyone here have filled a void in my life that I've felt as long as I can remember. I'm part of something great here; we're going to help a lot of people. I am *not* leaving."

"Ruby Porter, I want you to pick up your things and get in this car right now." Cynthia pointed to her daughter and then to the car, as if she could transport her there through a sheer act of her furious will. "We've had enough of this nonsense."

Ruby dug in defiantly, folding her arms and shaking her head. "I'm not leaving, and you can't make me."

Cliff and Todd pushed through the double doors and stood with Ruby. Cliff leaned in and whispered something in her ear.

"If you can't support me in my new life," she declared, "then I don't want you to come here anymore. I'm not going to let you hold me back from my future."

"What?" Tim stepped toward her, arms extended. "You can't be serious. What have these people done to you?"

Ruby didn't answer but gave him a look he didn't recognize, not from his daughter, his baby girl. He didn't know the stranger standing before him.

"I think you two need to leave the premises, now." Cliff stepped forward.

Todd approached them and reached for Tim's arm.

"If you're thinking about grabbing this arm, big man, I hope your dental insurance is good." Tim's hands curled into vibrating missiles, ready to launch at any second. He zeroed in on Todd's chin, a very easy target should he put his nasty hand on him. "I'll drop you like a bad habit."

Todd regarded Cliff, who held his hand out for him to stop. Todd reluctantly withdrew his hand, but his hateful stare remained.

"Smart move, Shrek." Tim's fists were still at the ready.

"Mom, Dad, you'd better leave now. I have a new life here...and neither of you are part of it."

Cliff inched closer to Ruby and glared at Tim and Cynth. "You're no longer welcome here. If you return, you will be arrested for trespassing. Leave now before I call the police...*Detective*."

Tim growled, ready to explode. In three quick bounds, he could be on top of Dr. Simmons's portly prophet, pounding him into the netherworld. The thought tasted good until he felt Cynth grab his loaded arm, pulling him toward the car. He walked backward, trying to make eye contact with his little girl, who stared at her feet, refusing to look at him.

This couldn't be happening. Not again! He couldn't be losing her, not to these people.

"Tim, this isn't getting us anywhere. We need to go." Cynth turned to Ruby, Cliff, and Todd. "But we will be back. You can bet on that."

Tim and Cynthia got in the Honda. He checked the rearview mirror for one last glimpse of his daughter, who still didn't look their way. The tires squealed as they fled the Higher Learning Center. "What happened to our little girl? She just disowned us. How can that be?"

Tim's stomach knotted like he'd been kicked by a mule. The old wounds and pain from their separation paled in comparison to what his daughter had just done. He'd lost her again, probably forever. How could he have let this happen?

"I don't know," Cynth slumped in her seat, a beleaguered expression covering her face. "I…I've never seen her like that. They've done something to her; they must have. None of this makes sense."

"Cynth, what are we gonna do? How are we gonna fight this?"

"We need help, Tim." She put her hand on his forearm. "I'll do whatever it takes, and I don't care what we have to do or who we have to see to get her out of there, but we need some serious help."

26

The pounding on her dorm room door pried Ruby from her slumber. She rolled over and searched for the clock. 4:43 a.m. They'd overslept! Ruby tossed off her covers and jogged over to her roommate's bed.

"Kara, wake up. We're late."

Kara quivered and sat straight up, gazing at Ruby as if she didn't recognize her. "What? What's going on?"

The knock at the door came again, only louder.

"We overslept." Ruby hurried across the small room and opened the door.

Byron stood posted next to the doorjamb. "Rise and shine, sleepyhead."

"I know; we're getting up. I'm sorry. I'm just so tired. This pace is really wearing me out." She brushed back her hair and wrapped her arm around her stomach. Sweats and a T-shirt—nice impression.

"Dr. Simmons said we'd all get used to the pace." Byron shrugged. "I swear the man doesn't sleep. I don't know how he does it."

"I don't either. Listen, Byron, I've got to get ready. I'm already running behind."

"Hey." He lifted her chin. "Are you okay? You look like something's up."

"My parents showed up yesterday." Ruby leaned against the doorjamb and peered into his eyes. "It wasn't good. They want me to leave."

Byron clasped his hands together. "Please tell me you're not leaving."

"I'm not. Especially now. I thought, hoped, they would support me. If only they'd spent some time here, they would have seen the wonderful things going on. They just don't get it."

"Parents are like that. Hey, at least yours showed up. I haven't talked with my dad in two years, and my mom and stepdad are so busy raising my brothers and sisters, I barely hear from them either."

"Yeah, but your parents aren't busy directing every aspect of your life. Telling you this and that. Treating you like a child, like you don't know anything at all."

"My parents don't know I have a life…or care. I threw them off years ago, long before I even heard of Dr. Simmons. I realized that I was on my own. I'm sorry you're just finding that out now."

"I guess I shouldn't have been surprised. I knew my mom would be upset, but I just expected more from my dad. I really thought he'd be happy for me. In the past he had the habit of disappointing me, but that won't happen now. I can't let them hold me back—I won't. But I do wish they would've tried to understand."

"Don't hold your breath, Ruby. They rarely do."

Maybe Byron was right. Her mom and dad might never understand or accept her new life. Dr. Simmons warned of this happening, but he never said how painful it would be. The sting in her gut rivaled the pain she felt when her parents first split just a few years ago. Only this was different. It was permanent. Her newfound knowledge would help her overcome the wound…eventually. That gave her some solace.

"I'm running late, Byron, so I'd better get ready. See you at breakfast."

He placed his hand on her cheek. "It's gonna be okay. I promise. And for what it's worth, you're not alone." He kissed the top of her head. "See you downstairs." He backpedaled down the hall.

Shivers rippled down her spine, chasing away the sick feeling in the pit of her soul. Things could certainly be worse. She glanced at the clock. She'd have to hurry to get to the kitchen on time. It was her morning to help prepare and serve breakfast.

Dr. Simmons felt that communal service was a pillar to building the "whole" person. Everyone shared in the work and studies. Cliff had arranged the schedules into precise intervals that had to be vigilantly maintained—several workstations during the day, anything from picking up trash to mopping the lobby floor to working the kitchen during meals, with class work and auditorium time with Dr. Simmons intermixed.

Ruby wasn't getting to bed until after midnight only to wake up at four-thirty to start all over. Dr. Simmons said there would be a period of adjustment; she just hoped she'd get used to the schedule soon.

Blue was the color of the day for her work group, so she grabbed her navy T-shirt and wrestled it on. At first the thought of a color of the day was a little hokey, but now it seemed to make sense. Dr. Simmons said that dressing alike built unity among their group. All the studying and work would be worth it someday…she hoped.

What was she studying so hard for? China Washburn's words pinged through her groggy head. *What was she searching so hard for in Highpoint?* Odd questions.

Of course Ruby knew what she was searching for, although she couldn't articulate it quite as well as she wanted. She had to admit that the questions had taken her by surprise at first. She'd thought of her conversation with China often in the last few days. The woman was strange, but she had a certain peace about her. Ruby was eager to talk with her again. Maybe it would be soon.

Kara stumbled as she slipped on her jeans. She definitely wasn't a morning person, even less so than Ruby, and she seemed to be having a much harder time with the schedule. Ruby wanted to be there for her. Born and raised in Cincinnati, Kara had been introduced to Dr. Simmons at the University of Miami, Ohio. Bright and sweet, she'd already proven to be a good friend and roommate.

"We'd better get moving." Ruby scooped her bag off the floor without breaking her stride.

"I know, I know, I'm coming." Kara meandered toward the door. "But I don't know how much more of this I can take."

Cliff eased into the chair in front of Walter's desk.

"Clifford, after yesterday's little incident, I think it's time for Todd to bring the security staff on board that we discussed. We'll need more eyes around here. My enemies are everywhere and are closing in."

"It will be taken care of today. Todd has assured me that he has over a dozen good men ready and willing to do this kind of...business."

"Good." Walter nodded. "See that it's done. Also, I want to speak with Ruby personally. I fear that little incident with her parents might have shaken her confidence. It's always hard to cut the umbilical cord."

"I'll have her sent up at once." Cliff rose and headed to the door, then turned back before leaving. "Oh, there's one more thing: I received an e-mail from a friend at the *New York Times*. Your book just hit number one."

"Of course it did." Walter grinned while steepling his hands. "Should we expect anything less?"

"Congratulations. Another wonderful tribute for you. This should position you well for the worldwide push you were looking for."

"Didn't I tell you that all these things would happen just as I predicted?"

"Yes, Walter. Your vision and clarity never cease to amaze me."

"We're only going to pick up the pace from this point on. That's why I need Todd to hire his men. I also want you to begin phase two of the building program. I fear we might need it sooner than I anticipated."

"It will be done as you ordered." Cliff bowed slightly. "Great things are going to happen now. Great things."

"Yes, now bring Ruby to me. I need to speak with her."

Cliff scurried from the room. Walter turned his chair to face the sun rising off the lake. The brilliant glow on the horizon rivaled the colors he saw in his dreams. If the common man could see his visions, how the world could be changed. But he'd been gifted beyond those around him, so much so that few could even recognize his distinction.

When the visions had first come and clouded his sleep, he knew his destiny was to lead. The voices had told him so. Like a narration to a movie, the voices had guided him since his adolescence. Small whispers transformed into screaming beasts until he followed their directions. They'd become his only *true* friends. They gave him the instructions to show those trapped in archaic religious systems a way to a better, brighter future—with Dr.

Walter Simmons at the helm, steering the human race to the next and highest level of man's evolution. This special wisdom had been imparted to him and him alone. And no one would stand in the way. No one.

Ruby opened the office door a crack. "You wanted to see me?"

Shaking back to the present, Walter stood and straightened his shirt. "Please come in, Ruby dear." He directed her to the chair in front of his desk. "I understand you had a rather rough day yesterday."

"I've had better." She bowed her head. "I'm really sorry about what happened. My parents won't be coming here again. I promise."

"I think you misunderstand." He stepped forward. "I'm not worried about any problems here; I'm worried about you, how you're faring after such a difficult, painful incident."

"I'm doing...okay." She shrugged. "I just expected more from my parents, especially my father."

"This is sad." He pursed his lips and shook his head. "It grieves me when families just can't grasp what we're all about. Please don't feel down. Your parents, especially your father, might not have the capacity to understand what's happening here. Really, Ruby, your father's a police officer. A fine profession, but not one filled with powerful thinkers or visionaries like you. There are few in the world like you, that's for sure. I can see you taking my teachings to the remotest parts of the planet to train others. I see great things in your future."

"Thank you." Ruby smiled. "I'm trying my best. Getting used to all this has been a little rougher than I'd hoped, but I'll catch up."

"You're doing fine." He slipped closer to her, sitting on the edge of his desk. He leaned forward and stroked her wavy hair. "You truly are a precious jewel, even if your family can't see that. I can see that, and I value you here in our fold."

He raised her chin with his hand. "Throw off those who don't support you, Ruby. It's for the best. Someday they might recognize your genius. But for now, they can only hold you back, stifle your growth. You deserve better."

"I know. I've done that, and I'm ready to move forward. Ready to take on whatever you have for me." She gazed up at him with the same childlike look of awe and respect he'd become accustomed to from those in his fold. Ruby Porter had just proved her loyalty, graduating to the next level. Soon she'd receive her reward.

"That's my girl." He rose again, turned to his window, and gazed out at the lake. "Now hurry back to your classes. I don't want you to miss a single moment of your training. Not one moment."

27

John paced in front of the whiteboard in the briefing room as Robbie, Alan, and Tim took their seats in a half circle around him.

His mind whirled through the complex possibilities of the case before him. Mitch Garrow's high school graduation picture was taped to the top of the whiteboard with a line going down to a picture of Dr. Simmons, then a driver's license picture of Cliff underneath him, then a booking photo of Todd. A picture of the black Suburban was off to the side with a close-up of the burly driver next to it.

"Okay, people." John pressed his pen to his lips. "We're gonna switch gears in this investigation from fact-finding to person-finding." John drew a circle around Mitch's picture. "We all know that Mitch Garrow went missing approximately two months ago from the Higher Learning Center. We weren't sure what we had at first, but I'm becoming more convinced that Mr. Garrow definitely did not go on a spiritual sojourn as we were told. Tim and I have been down to the 'learning center' and are less than impressed with their responses to our questions."

Tim perched on the edge of a desk facing John, his legs dangling like those of a puppet without a master. His shirt was wrinkled and his tie crooked; his drawn face slid down toward his chin, as if he'd aged ten years in two weeks.

"First, I'll fill you in on the learning center." John pointed to a sketch of the premises that covered half the whiteboard—the three main buildings of the complex in a U-shape facing Lake Okeechobee. "Dr. Simmons opened this center to train students in his self-help system. All things considered, from the outside it's a nice, modern facility, and it has been a boon for the town of Highpoint, which was almost barren before Dr. Simmons and his group showed up. The chief of police in Highpoint, Chief Bennington, is less than helpful and should be considered unreliable from this point on. I don't know where the man stands, but I'm inclined not to trust him."

"That's going to make things tough if we set up in Highpoint." Alan folded his arms as he studied the flowchart. "Without the help of the locals, it'll double our work."

"I didn't say we didn't have some of the locals on our side." John held out one finger. "It's only the chief I'm worried about. One of his officers who I trust has come forward with some valuable information."

"Where do we go from here?" Alan asked.

"Well, I've done some background on Dr. Walter Simmons and have come up with a few interesting items that need some attention. Robbie, could you create a psychological profile on him from the information available? Do you think you can crawl into this guy's head and give us some insights on the man?"

Robbie nodded and jotted down notes on her legal pad. "I'm somewhat familiar with him. Mostly pop psychology and such. I don't know how seriously he's been taken in the psychology community, but you can bet I'll find out. I'll go back through some of his writings and position papers and see what I come up with."

"Thanks." John smiled. "That would be a big help."

Alan crossed his arms. "I'll make some calls and get us situated in Highpoint for a base of operation."

"We might not want to be in Highpoint itself. Let's try to make arrangements to be close enough to do our work but far enough to be out of the reach of Chief Bennington."

"Makes sense, John." Alan pointed at Cliff and Todd. "What about his cronies?"

"Cliff Chaffin and Todd Yancey." John picked up his folders on the two men. "Cliff, our mole-looking buddy here, is a CPA and Dr. Simmons's second in command. No criminal history or anything significant in his background. But Mr. Todd Yancey is another story. He's got a rather healthy rap sheet with over two dozen arrests, starting as a preteen. He has several arrests for robbery and battery, as well as at least two arrests for battery on law enforcement officers."

"Sweet guy, and cute, too. In that rogue, dim-witted felon kinda way." Robbie slapped Tim on the shoulder and laughed at her own joke. He didn't move. "Well, you're in a pretty lousy mood, Porter, considering we've just been handed a case that should drain the entire agency overtime budget for a year."

Tim shrugged and focused on his feet.

"Anyway," John continued, hoping to give Tim a break. "We need to be very careful with Yancey. He's got a significant history, and I can only guess that Dr. Simmons doesn't keep him on staff for his mental prowess, if you know what I mean. He was our shadow while we were at the facility. I think he's the resident security thug."

"Is there anything else, John?" Alan asked.

"Simmons has built this facility in the middle of nowhere and keeps his 'students' on a pretty short leash. He allows only his teachings at the learning center. I fear the man is starting his own little cult there in Highpoint."

"These things can be tricky." Alan walked over and scanned the photos of the complex. "And if what you're saying is true, the last thing we need is another Waco. Let's concentrate on finding out what happened to the Garrow kid and solving this case. You're getting a lot of leeway here, John, so don't blow it."

John nodded. "Fair enough."

Alan had called in some major favors to release that much in investigative funds. He'd been around the agency a long time and had friends all over the place, all the way up to the governor's offices. John had asked Alan to trust him, and he did. Now it was time to prove what his gut and a load of circumstantial evidence told him.

"What about the Suburban?" Robbie asked. "Anything back on that?"

"I ran the tag through NCIC/FCIC, but it came back as no record found. That leads me to only two conclusions: Either the tag has been altered so it can't be properly identified, or our friends in the Suburban are cops. I'm leaning toward cops. Maybe another local jurisdiction we don't know about, or maybe someone else altogether. Time will tell."

"Is there anything else I need to know about this case?" Alan turned to his agents. "I need to know everything before I can get this rolling. I don't want any surprises."

John regarded Tim, who didn't even raise his head.

John closed his case file. "Everything you need right now."

"Okay, people," Alan said, "we have a lot to get done in a short amount of time. I need everyone at your best...again."

Robbie closed her legal pad and headed for the door with Alan behind her.

"Wait." Tim tightened his grip on the desk. "There's more. A lot more."

Alan and Robbie ambled their way back to their seats.

Alan canted his head. "What do you have, Tim?"

"My daughter, Ruby, is part of this mess." Tim wasn't able to look any of them in the eyes. "She's been at the facility for some time now."

"Oh, boy." Alan swiped his hand across his face. "When were you two going to tell me about this?"

John shrugged. "About now."

"Not funny." Alan stared John down. He was not happy. "Let's hear it all, Porter. I want everything."

"When my wife and I tried to get Ruby to come home with us, she wouldn't leave. It's like she's turned into a different person overnight." Tim teared up. "I'm sorry I didn't tell you earlier. I just didn't want to believe that this was happening to her, to us. But now, I don't know. I'm scared for my little girl, and I don't know what to do."

Alan and Robbie remained silent. This put a whole new twist on an already complicated case. John rested his hand on Tim's shoulder. "We're gonna get this thing done, partner. I give you my word."

"If you want me to stay away from this case, I will. I'll do whatever you want me to do. We just need to find out what happened to the Garrow kid and help my Ruby. Nothing else matters."

John turned to Alan. "I need Tim's experience with me. If he gets out of control or becomes a hindrance, I'll send him home."

"I don't know." Alan frowned. "I don't like it. He's too close to this. It's gonna be tough enough without having an outta control cop running around."

"Alan, we're gonna need everyone we have to cover a case like this." Robbie sauntered closer to Tim. "We can't afford to go down there without him. We'll keep an eye on him."

Alan crossed his arms, a deep belly growl rumbling from

him. It was a Maalox moment. "Seven months. How hard is it to stay out of trouble for seven months? Porter, if you get out of line once in this case, I will ship you home and have you work every nutcase that comes in here until I retire. Do I make myself clear?"

"Crystal." Tim smiled for the first time today.

Alan shook his head as he walked from the room. "You-all are killing me slowly. Case by case."

Robbie went to leave, but Tim grabbed her hand. "Thank you, Sanchez."

She squeezed his hand. "We're gonna do everything in our power to get your daughter out of there."

28

Tim collected his thoughts as he and John drove into the ruddy dirt parking lot of the Mount Carmel Worship Center, just outside the city limits of Highpoint.

Set among the scrub oak and palmetto bushes, the ancient wooden church was propped up by cinder blocks and suffered from a distinct and noticeable lean. Half of the front was freshly painted the other half sanded down to the wood, awaiting a new coat. A thin white steeple pointed toward the heavens. A newer-looking building built of block construction was attached to the back of the church, probably for an office or classrooms.

According to John, who'd checked it out on the Internet like he did everything, the Mount Carmel Worship Center was built in the early 1930s and ministered to migrant farmworkers and the small, close-knit African-American community that resided just outside Highpoint. Most of the families living there were descendents of the original settlers that moved from Miami and Palm Beach after the 1928 hurricane. The sign out front read "Reverend Demetrius Taylor."

"I'm not so sure about this." Tim rubbed his hands along his slacks. He'd probably let Russell talk him into more than he was ready for, but he'd give John his due and see what happened. He didn't have a lot of other options. "What you're tellin' me about spiritual warfare, Moses approaching you, the new information on the Garrow kid—you're creeping me out. I don't know how much more I can handle. This is all so bizarre."

Tim's spirit felt as if it would burst from the pressure. During the two-hour trip to Highpoint, he'd unloaded his soul to Russell—his concerns for Ruby and her safety, his own worries about the Garrow case, and what was happening with Cynth. Russell was a good listener, an attribute he surely picked up in seminary, where they must teach those skills. After examining the dilapidated wooden church in front of him, Tim doubted any serious answers lay waiting for them there, but he would go in anyway. He had nothing to lose.

"Let's just meet with these people and see if they'll be assets for us." John shifted the gear into park. "We're gonna need all the help we can get."

"I know." Tim gritted his teeth. "But it just ain't right. I refuse to believe that Ruby could be involved with something wicked or wrong. We raised her right, with good morals and all. I don't understand any of this." He paused and closed his eyes. "I'm trusting you with everything I have. You've never let me down before, and I can't get a clear fix on any of this. I need your help, Russell."

"You already have it."

As they exited the car, Moses and another African-American man strolled from the front door of the church and down the rickety wooden steps toward them.

"Good to see you again, Moses." John shook his hand.

"You, too." Moses turned to his companion. "This is Reverend Demetrius Taylor, the pastor here at our church. Agents John Russell and Tim Porter, FDLE."

"Demetrius." His deep, rich voice floated in the air as if he'd sung his name. He took John's hand and then Tim's. He was much taller than Tim, a solid six-four, but with extremely thin, sinewy build and an Adam's apple that was pointed and sharp. He was a little younger than expected, maybe late twenties, early thirties.

"Pleased you could come." Demetrius scanned the parking lot. "Sorry about the cloak and dagger routine, but we felt it best to meet outside of Highpoint. Too many eyes and ears in that place. Let's go inside, and I'll introduce you to everyone."

Demetrius directed them up the steps and through the front double doors of the church. The midday sun illuminated the small sanctuary. A set of pews was on either side of the main aisle that ran up to the pulpit, which rose only a step from the floor. A cross hung behind that.

Four stained glass windows lined the length of the walls on either side of the church, and light radiated off of the dust from the wooden floor, giving the room a reddish hue. The inside of the church was every bit as muggy as the outside but without the benefits of occasional breezes.

Tim stopped at the first row of pews and ran his hand across the top of it. "This reminds me a lot of my father's church in Orlando. I sat in these kinds of wooden benches so often I'm surprised my backside isn't shaped like one."

"Your father was a pastor?" Demetrius asked.

"He was a Methodist minister." Tim drew a purposed breath. It even smelled the same. "He headed a church a lot like this one. It brings back a lot of memories."

"Good ones, I hope." Demetrius smiled.

Tim nodded. "Mostly." He recalled playing hide-and-seek with his father in his church. He'd always hide under the pews somewhere and make his father chase him. He'd slither on his belly like a snake down the middle of the rows. His father would walk back and forth between the pews, trying to grab his legs while chuckling. "Gonna getcha, Timmy," he'd say. He could never catch him, though. Tim would almost always escape his grasp. Truth be known, his pop might not have been trying that hard. Good times, good memories.

Demetrius led Tim, John, and Moses down to the front pews, where four older African-American women took up one side and a lone blond woman sat on the other. Who were these people, more witnesses?

"Gentlemen," Demetrius held his hand out toward the women, "this is the Mount Carmel Prayer Team. Miss Edna, Miss Sylvia, Miss Florence, and Miss Isabel. Revelation has its four horsemen of the Apocalypse; we have our four prayer warriors of Highpoint."

Each woman neared or crested eighty years of age, and each wore a bright, colorful dress. Miss Edna was a tiny woman, maybe five feet tall with thick glasses and frost-white hair. Miss Sylvia was considerably taller and heavier with a very light complexion. Miss Florence was the tallest of the group, just a bit shy of Tim's height, with enormous hands that swallowed his. Miss Isabel had a cane with a four-point stand on the bottom. She remained seated.

"These women have committed to pray ahead of us." Demetrius clasped his hands in front of him. "You'll have no better friends in Highpoint than these ladies. When they pray, the Spirit moves."

"Great. We've got the geriatric squad as backup?" *Prayer team? More religious nonsense.* They needed a SWAT team, not four great-grandmas mumbling in a corner somewhere. These people had no idea what they were facing.

"Agent Porter." Demetrius propped his elbow on the pulpit. "I'm not sure you understand what we're up against, the nature of the battle here. This is a spiritual war, not one that can be won by fists or guns, but by prayer and the moving of

God's Spirit. Without it, we can do nothing."

"I deal in reality, Reverend, not games of make-believe." Tim had had enough; all of this pushed him over the edge. "And the reality is, my daughter is tangled up with strange people at a very strange place, and we have a boy who's missing from that same place. I know exactly what I'm up against. This is about the here and now and how I get my daughter out of that crazy complex. No puffy chants to an indifferent God are gonna help here. So you can tell the well-meaning but misguided prayer team that they can head on home and leave the cop stuff to us."

"Oh, child," Miss Isabel called in a feeble voice as she shook her cane. "Can you please come close so I can whisper something to you? I have a message from the Lord I think you need to hear. I'm an old woman and hardly have the strength to come to ya."

Tim sighed. He'd blown his fuse too quick and hurt the old woman's feelings. He'd be nice, make her feel better, and then calmly send them all on their way. "I didn't mean to upset anyone. But this is cop stuff, and it should be left to the professionals." He walked over and bent down. "Now what do you have to tell me, ma'am?"

Miss Isabel eased forward, her head trembling and body appearing too weak to even rise. She cupped her right hand over her mouth. "Please, come a bit closer, dearie."

Tim eased down on one knee next to her and placed his ear within whispering range. Miss Isabel leaned in. *Smack!* Her right hand caught the side of Tim's face so fast he didn't have time to react. The blow lifted him to his feet. "Ouch!"

"Don't you blaspheme in here, young man." Her body rocked and trembled with anger as she wagged a crooked finger at him. "Don't you dare blaspheme in this house of God. You need to pull yourself together. Don't you know that Satan's after your daughter? He wants her soul, and you're here babblin' and struttin' around like you're all that, when you should be on your knees before the Almighty instead."

"Yes, ma'am." Tim stepped back and massaged his cheek. What a lick. He'd known boxers who didn't hit that hard.

"Miss Isabel! You can't be slappin' our guest. That's not the godly approach we're trying to achieve here."

"If'n I had a jawbone of an ass," she wiggled her cane in front of her as if it were having a seizure, "I'da whupped him with that, too. You can't get more biblical than that. The young man needs his attention got. He's trying to war in the flesh, and if he don't change his ways, he could lose everything. Consider that correction from the Lord."

John covered his mouth and snickered.

"It's not funny." Tim worked his jaw back and forth. "She's got a mighty wicked right cross."

"Are you okay?" Demetrius rested a hand on Tim's shoulder. "Please forgive Miss Isabel. She's a might...excitable when it comes to the things of the Lord."

"I can see that." Tim kept a healthy distance from Miss Isabel, whose scowl told him she was contemplating a combination for his next 'correction.' "Let's just get on with what we came here to do."

Demetrius wiped the sweat from his brow and shook his head. "Moses has expressed concerns that we might not be able to trust our local law enforcement to do the right thing to find Mitch. All of us here want to provide you with the shelter, assistance, and prayers you'll need to find this young man and get Ms. Porter out of that place."

Demetrius stretched out his hand to the blond woman. "Gentlemen, this is the young lady who can help you out with the information you need. She had been witnessing to Mitch when he disappeared."

She stood and held a maroon beret in her hand. She was the

woman who was standing across the street from the learning center when they were last there.

"Tim, John, this is China Washburn."

China extended her hand. A braid dangled down her face.

"Your name's China?" John beamed as he pointed to her.

"Yes. China Doll Washburn. My mother said I looked just like a China doll when I was born." She toyed with her braid.

"Nice." Tim raised an eyebrow and regarded John. *China Doll?* Her name was as kooky as her look. But now at least Mitch's e-mail about China made sense. He and Russell would kick that around later.

"Ms. Washburn is a cult specialist, and our church has brought her in to help us minister to the people at the Higher Learning Center. We knew as soon as they started building that wretched place that we would need help. She's been, quite literally, a godsend."

"How in the world do you become an 'expert' in cult stuff?" Tim asked.

"I was born into the Branch Davidians in Waco. I was nine when the siege there began and was one of the few to survive. God sent an angel to protect me and brought me out of the flames alive. The Lord rescued me for a purpose—to help those trapped in the lies of the enemy to escape with the truth of Jesus Christ. It's my calling."

"John." Tim nodded toward the door. "Can we talk outside…*now*?"

"Let's listen to what everyone has to say first."

"In the last five minutes, I've been slapped by Grandma Ali, been babbled to by Ragdoll Something-or-Other, and I haven't heard one thing that can help my Ruby. John, I'm trusting you, but this is nuts. It ain't working."

China stood and faced Tim. "You're Ruby's father?"

Tim stopped cold. "Yes. Do you know her?"

"I've met her. When I saw her walking down the street, God told me to go and speak to her. So I did. She has a very sweet, loving spirit. I could see that right away."

"What did she say? How's she doing?" Tim's angry, defensive stance melted as he inched toward China. *Finally, something useful.* "Is she okay?"

"She seemed fine. But she's a true believer in Dr. Simmons, and she's in great danger. The dragon is on the prowl for her bad."

"What did you say?" Tim stepped toward her. "Why did you say, 'the dragon is on the prowl for her'? Who told you to say that?" How could she know? She had to be messing with him. What was this crazy woman trying to pull?

China shrugged and looked bewildered. She glanced over at John, who appeared just as confused.

"Someone had to tell you to say that." Anger fired up Tim's spine. He didn't know who or what this woman was, but she had to be playing some sort of sick game with him.

"Tim." John grabbed his arm. "Maybe we should take a break. We'll be right back." John pulled him down the aisle, out the front door, and into the parking lot.

"What's going on, partner? You look like you've seen a ghost. What in the world did she say that has you so upset?"

"It's gotta be some kinda joke." Tim grabbed his chin with one hand and planted the other on his hip and turned in a circle. "There's no way she could know. No way. It must've been a coincidence."

"What *are* you talking about, Porter?"

"When my dad was sick, Ruby was only a little girl, four maybe five years old." Tim waved his hands in the air. "Nah, it can't mean nothin'. This is just crazy talk."

"Tell me anyway. At least get it off your chest and then we can meet back with everyone."

"It's just..." Tim rubbed the back of his neck. "My pop loved Ruby to death. She was his whole life those last few years. When he was at his sickest, when the cancer had torn through his body, he was having hallucinations, and he said something that's stuck with me all these years. I had dismissed it as the delusional rants of a dying man. But to hear it again, like this, about my Ruby? It's rattlin' my cage."

"What did he say?"

"It was the night before he passed." Tim wiped his eyes, the memory still fresh. "I was with him, and he was tossing and turning. It was rough. And right in the middle of a fit, he sat up in bed, grabbed my arm, and stared me in the eye with a look as sober as a judge. He said, 'Watch Ruby, Timmy. The dragon wants her, he wants her real bad. He's coming to devour her, son. Don't let the dragon get her.' He flopped back in the bed, and those were the last words he ever spoke. He died early the next morning."

Tim's stomach flipped as he relived the conversation with his pop from so many years before. He'd attempted to forget it through the years, but every once in a while, the memory would creep to the surface of his psyche, taunting him.

"Now Baby Doll says almost that same thing. I thought she was messing with me, but how could she know that? I never told anyone until just now."

"I don't believe in coincidences." John shook his head in that fundamentalist way of his. "And I think I know who your father and China were talking about. But I'm not sure if you're ready to hear it."

"I'm not ignorant, you know. I was raised in the church, with a Bible-thumping father. I know good and well who the Bible says the dragon is."

"Satan."

Tim could only nod his head, lest he give the idea a voice.

"Do you believe it?" John asked.

"I don't know what I believe anymore." Tim didn't want to believe it, or even think about it. But what if there was a real Satan, the facilitator of all evil, and he'd set his mark on Ruby? Tim's body quivered as he worked to shake the wicked thought from his mind.

He suddenly felt very small and powerless, and he didn't like that feeling one bit. "The only thing I know right now is that I want my daughter back. And if I have to storm the gates of hell to get her, so be it."

"Partner—" John placed his hand on Tim's shoulder—"we just might have to."

29

John and Tim coasted into Palm Harbor, practically on empty. Located on Florida's Gulf coast, just north of St. Petersburg, the quiet town was like so many others in Florida—warm and inviting on the outside, but ripe with secrets and untold stories on the inside. Every town has at least one secret, one thing that's only mentioned in whispers, if spoken of at all.

Palm Harbor had a secret. And John wanted to hear all about it.

They turned onto William Patterson's street and slowed the vehicle, scanning the mailboxes for his address. Traditional two-story houses, built mostly in the early seventies, intermingled along the street with elegant one-story homes. Still a nice neighborhood to raise a family, but certainly well past its prime.

The ride over had been mostly quiet, which was unusual for Tim, the chatty one, as John often called him. The man had slipped more and more into a deep depression, and John felt helpless to stop it. The meeting with Demetrius, Moses, China, and the four horsewomen of Highpoint hadn't gone as John had hoped. Maybe meeting with Mr. Patterson would give Tim some relief.

"What are you hoping to get from Mr. Patterson, John?"

"Don't know. That's why we ask questions and dig a little deeper. You never know what you'll find."

"Lesley Ann died a long time ago. This could just open up a lot of bad feelings and emotions for the man."

Sympathy didn't flow freely from Tim often. But John figured Tim had in a sense already bonded with a man who'd lost his daughter, even if the situations were different. "We need some background on Dr. Simmons. This man knew him growing up. I know what the risks are, but I also know the advantages. When I read that article, I just knew we had to come here. It might be nothing. But it might be something as well. Simmons is still a mystery to us. Anything from his past can help."

"It's right here." Tim pointed to a two-story home with wood siding. A rusted basketball hoop was attached to the garage, the net torn and dangling. John pulled in behind a small red Toyota parked in the driveway.

After gathering their belongings, John and Tim walked to the door and rang the doorbell. An older man answered. He wore thick glasses and a sleeveless sweater with a shirt underneath covering his soft, distended middle. A gray comb-over thinly veiled his bald head, and his mustache was neatly trimmed.

"Bill Patterson." He opened the door wider to let them in. "You must be the detectives."

John introduced them.

"Please, come in." Bill stepped out of the way so they could enter.

The hallway from the door to the kitchen was lined with family, school, and sports photos, a thirty-year memorial to the Patterson family. The fresh scent of brewing coffee enticed John to follow. Lesley Ann's photo jumped out immediately, and more pictures of her occupied several prominent places along the route. Based on the pictures, Bill had at least two other children, a son and another daughter.

Bill led them into the kitchen. "Please, have a seat." He indicated the stools surrounding an extended countertop that served as a small table. "Would either of you like some coffee?"

John nodded. "Sure."

Tim agreed as he surveyed the room.

Bill poured two cups and handed them to John and Tim.

"You said on the phone that you wanted to talk about what happened to Lesley." Bill propped himself against the kitchen counter. "Why after all these years would anyone care about what happened to her?"

"Some things have come up." John didn't want to go into too much detail yet. He needed to gauge what Mr. Patterson's thoughts about the incident were first.

"You have a nice home, Mr. Patterson," Tim said, taking Bill off task.

"Thank you."

"I can imagine it's a difficult subject, one you might not want to talk about." John folded his hands in front of him, hoping for a comfortable, humble appearance to put Mr. Patterson at ease. "But since you agreed to meet with us, I was hoping you could shed some light on your daughter's death."

"You'd think after all these years it would be easier." Bill pushed his glasses up on his nose. "But it never really gets easier. You come to terms with the pain, but losing a child leaves a wound that never heals."

"I can't imagine." John really couldn't. He prayed he'd never know the kind of pain Bill had seen. "If you're not up to this, that's fine."

"No. I'm okay." He raised a hand. "Come. I want to show you something."

Bill escorted John and Tim out of the kitchen and through the living room. Although clean, the well-worn furniture and carpet were long out of style, like the house itself. He opened the first door on the left.

John felt as if he'd stepped back into 1978. Posters from the time hung on the wall. Pictures of Lesley Ann at various ages occupied prominent places along her dressers, some of her in cheerleading outfits, others with her swim team. Numerous swimming trophies with medals dangling from them were stacked on the dressers as well. The bed was made with faded pink linens. Her closet door was open, still full of her clothes. Bill stopped at the edge of the room, not broaching the doorway. John took that as a sign that they could look but certainly not enter.

"You've kept her room up nicely." What else could he say? The room was a shrine to a young girl long since passed.

"My son, Billy, thinks I've held on a bit too long. He wanted me to sell this place and move closer to him when my wife, Cathy, died. Too many memories here to lose or sell to someone else."

"Your daughter was a very beautiful young lady." Tim kept his hands in his pockets and worked his jaw back and forth. "We're very sorry for your loss."

Bill shook off his stupor. "Well, it has been a long time. People adjust." He closed the door. "I've been blessed with two other wonderful children. I don't know what woulda happened if Cathy and I hadn't had them. They were our reason to go on. But after Lesley's death, Cathy just seemed to give up, like all the life had been sucked out of her. She went through the motions, smiled when she needed to, loved on our children, and at least acted like she was moving on. But the truth is, she never really recovered. She died of a heart attack about seven years after Lesley's death. I say she died of a broken heart."

John and Tim were quiet for a while to let the moment pass. Bill walked back toward the kitchen, and they followed.

"Can you tell me about that day, if you're up to it?" John

asked. "I know it's been a long time, but we'd like to hear what you have to say."

"Of course I can." Bill dragged a stool closer to him and plopped down on it. "Lesley Ann was dating a boy—you might have heard of him—Walter Simmons. He's a bigwig writer and speaker and such now. Well, they dated for a little over a year. We all thought they'd end up getting married. At first he came off as the perfect young man for my daughter. He was charming, sophisticated, and so very talented at so many things. I really liked the kid."

"At first?" John asked.

"Yes, *at first.*"

"What happened to change your opinion?" John rested both elbows on the counter.

"After a couple months of dating, Walter became more and more possessive. Anytime Lesley Ann went anywhere or wanted to do anything, he had to be right there. If she wanted to try something, it was like she had to ask his permission to do anything. He was smothering her."

John shared a glance with Tim, who nodded.

"Lesley Ann wanted to make it work. She really loved him. But it kept getting more and more bizarre and erratic."

"Did she try to talk to Walter about it?" Tim asked.

"Plenty of times. But he just dismissed it, telling her she was paranoid and didn't understand how much he really loved her. She kept a lot of this from Cathy and me, until it got so bad that she had to give him an ultimatum. We supported her decision."

"That's when they went to Lake Tarpon?"

Bill paused and regarded John. "You've done your homework." A spark of understanding flashed across Bill's face, as if he finally understood where John was going. A hopeful smile grew across his face.

"We know a little bit, but Tim and I need you to fill in some of the pieces."

"Lesley Ann told us that morning that she and Walter were going to the lake. She wanted to talk about their relationship, where it was headed. She said she couldn't continue the way it was going. She left for the lake that morning, and that was the last time Cathy and I ever saw her alive."

"What do you think happened?"

"That's a loaded question, Detective Russell." Bill shifted on the stool. "I don't know for sure. How I wish I did. But I know my daughter. She would not have taken her own life. There's just no way. And she was a tremendous swimmer, as was Walter. Both county champions. So that narrows the options down a little bit, doesn't it? No matter what the police reports said, no matter what the medical examiner said, Lesley Ann did *not* kill herself. Not for him, not for anyone."

"Do you think Walter killed your daughter?" Tim asked point-blank, with a hint of concern, like he really didn't want to hear the answer. He had more than one reason for asking, John was sure.

"I think he's not telling the truth about what happened out on Lake Tarpon." Bill crossed his arms and eyed them both. "When Lesley's death was ruled a suicide, that destroyed Cathy. The mere thought that our daughter could do that to herself broke the woman, I tell you. Walter gave several statements to the police about what happened. He charmed them with his wily, lying tongue."

Bill pushed himself off of the counter and leaned in toward John, holding his hands over his chest. "Detective Russell, the man had scratches on his chest. The police said it was from Lesley Ann pushing him away in the water while she tried to swim away from him, as he told them of course."

"They believed his statements?" John raised his eyebrows.

"They had nothing else to go on." Bill threw his hands up. "They were the only two there. Walter was the one who called the police. Supposedly he cooperated with everything they wanted him to do. There was no evidence to contradict his testimony."

John took a long sip of coffee and attempted not to show too much emotion or surprise to Bill yet. Their workload had just doubled in one conversation, and he couldn't wait to get hold of that police report.

"Detectives, I've been very patient. I've invited you into my home and shared the absolute worst thing that's ever happened in my life. Now can you please answer one question for me?"

"We'll try." John nodded.

"Why are you really here? Why is anyone digging around a twenty-seven-year-old *alleged* suicide case, especially FDLE?"

John and Tim glanced at each another, the silence ringing like an alarm throughout the house. Should they tip their hands? What if they told Bill their suspicions and he ran to the media or contacted Dr. Simmons? Their case could be compromised before it even got started.

"I think I'm entitled to a straight answer."

Bill was right; he'd paid the price in years of pain and staggering losses. The man's life lay half in this world half in the next.

"I tell you this in confidence. If this information gets out, it could severely hamper our case. And, yes, you are entitled to an answer."

"I won't say anything to anyone. I just want to know what's going on."

"We have some concerns about Dr. Walter Simmons and his group." John opened his case file, pulled out a picture of Mitch, and showed it to Bill. "A young man is missing from his campus in south Florida. We're very concerned with the goings-on there as well. I discovered the account of Lesley Ann's death in a newspaper archive and thought of talking with you. That's why we're here."

Bill removed his glasses and wiped them clean with the bottom of his sweater. "When you called, I have to admit I thought that finally someone was reopening this case and the truth of Lesley Ann's death would be known—and justice would be done."

"I imagine you did." John returned the picture to the file. "I can't guarantee anything, but we are going to reopen your daughter's case. There could be information in it that can shed light on our current case, and I think you and Lesley Ann deserve a second look. But are you sure you can go through the ups and downs of our digging back into this case? It probably won't be pretty, and we might come up with an answer you don't like."

"I've lived a long life. I have two wonderful children and five fantastic grandkids. I've seen everything that I need to…except one thing." He held his index finger in the air. "I want the truth—good, bad, whatever. I want to know exactly what happened that day on Lake Tarpon. If you find that out, I can die a happy man."

30

Ruby and Byron strolled hand in hand in front of the learning center. Among the excitement and busyness of the last few weeks, her walks with Byron were the thing she looked forward to most in her day.

When they were alone, not talking about Dr. Simmons or the Higher Learning Method or classes, Byron could be quite shy. Small leaks of insecurity dripped out of his soul. She liked that he could vulnerable with her. She was getting to know him more and more and enjoyed listening to him talk of his school years or the band he used to play in. They weren't very good, according to him anyway, but he had lots of fun onstage. She couldn't imagine Byron not being good at anything. He was so full of life and passion for everything.

She stared at his face and tried to imagine what he must have looked like as a child—his silly expressions, his precocious laughter and impishness. He must have been a handful for his mother.

The bellowing exhaust of a backhoe digging trenches near the road shattered the solitude of their evening retreat. A work crew fastened cameras on the light poles while another group assembled a huge metal gate at the front entrance.

"What's with the new fence, Byron?" Ruby liked the open feel of the campus, and the fence would block the view. It seemed so unnecessary.

"I don't know. But that's not your run-of-the-mill fence. That thing's a sturdy, Berlin Wall kinda fence. "

"It's really odd, don't you think?" Ruby squeezed his hand more firmly. "Why do we need this stuff? I don't understand."

"Maybe it's just part of a future building project or something. I'm sure Dr. Simmons will let us know what's going on eventually."

"I guess, but it all seems so weird."

Byron nodded. "Yeah, real weird."

As they walked toward the administration building, Todd drove into the circular driveway in his monster pickup truck, revving the brawny engine twice before turning it off. Three more pickups followed behind him, all filled with large, rough-looking men, much like Todd himself. Several were dressed in full camouflage attire and had military haircuts.

Ruby waved. Todd glanced at her, and then turned back to the men unloading their duffel bags from the trucks. He didn't wave back; his face was all business. "Come on, boys. We've got to get moved in and set up shifts. I want everyone ready for action by 2300 hours tonight."

"Who are all these people?" Ruby asked.

"They're certainly not new students." Byron pulled Ruby close and wrapped his arm around her shoulder.

It was the first time since she'd been at the Higher Learning Center that she felt a chill. She pulled Byron's arm tight and reveled in the comfort of his embrace. Changes were happening suddenly in her life now. Hopefully for the best.

After the men unloaded the trucks, Todd marched the detachment toward the administration building, duffel bags in tow.

Despite the warmth of Byron's body, the chill still enveloped Ruby.

* * *

Walter and Cliff stood watch in the administration building, waiting for Todd's team to enter and be briefed. Fifteen trained security "specialists" would fit nicely into the plan. Todd assured him that all of these men possessed the expertise and the wherewithal to extinguish any problems the Higher Learning Center might face.

Most were prior military, some former law enforcement, all ready to provide their services to the highest bidder. No one would be creeping around anymore. His enemies would think twice before making a move.

Walter took notice of Ruby and Bryon in the driveway. His body tightened and trembled. What right did Byron think *he* had to Ruby? Just because they came here together didn't mean they were going to stay together. He would have to fix this little problem.

"Ruby and Byron seem to be spending a lot more time together lately, wouldn't you say?"

Cliff nodded. "They do seem rather fond of each other."

"I want Byron moved. I want him on a different schedule. Those two together can be distraction. I want it done now."

"It will be done today. Now we need to greet our guests. They're waiting."

Walter drew a cleansing breath and focused on what lay ahead. Cliff would indeed do as he was ordered, and that should solve the problem for now. Otherwise, he could keep Byron so busy that he wouldn't have time for any such diversions, leaving Ruby in dire need of an acquaintance. This could work out quite nicely.

"We mustn't keep our new friends waiting." Walter checked his reflection off the doors. "I want you to call an assembly for tomorrow. We need to introduce these men to everyone. And I think the students need a little tweaking; they've been getting a little loose lately. This next lecture should wind them tighter than the strings on a grand piano."

31

Thanks for having us over." Tim and Cynth entered the foyer of the Russell home. Tim introduced her to John and Marie, then John led them both into the dining room while Marie hurried into the kitchen.

Tim escorted Cynth over to the long oak dining room table that had become a place of comfort and peace for him in the last year. John was dressed casual, wearing blue jeans and a T-shirt with Bible verses on it. The man never gave up. Tim was positive Russell wore the shirt just for him.

John thought it would be good for everyone to get together and sort through the craziness of the last few weeks. Tim agreed, but he was a little surprised when Cynth did too. But Ruby was their child, so it shouldn't have caught him off guard. At least they were unified in this.

"Tim says many kind things about you and Marie." Cynth adjusted her chair at one end of the table while Tim sat at the other. "He has a lot of confidence in you, John."

"The feelings are mutual. Without getting all sappy, Tim's the best partner I've ever worked with."

Marie crossed into the living room from the kitchen, as if walking on a tightrope, balancing a tray loaded with iced teas.

She passed them around the table and took her seat next to John. Her black hair was clipped back, and her white shirt was tucked into her jeans.

"Thank you, Marie." Cynth took a long gulp of the tea and placed the cool glass on her forehead.

Small strips of hair jutted out from her unraveling bun, and her tired eyes nearly sagged to the floor. The poor woman was coming undone. She'd been teaching classes all day and now had to deal with this. Tim wished he could comfort her in some way. Maybe the best way would be to leave her be.

And he wasn't doing a lot better. Tim had come straight from the office and left his coat and tie in the car, his long sleeves rolled up tight along his forearms. Meaningful work was nonexistent at this point. He droned through the day, going through the motions but not accomplishing a whole lot.

Thoughts and memories of Ruby danced through his mind at all hours of the night, chasing away any possibility of real sleep. The one recurring vision was the look on Ruby's face when she ordered them to leave and never come back. She could have shot him and done less damage.

"So where do we go from here?" Cynthia rested her glass on a coaster on the table. "Ruby has dug in and is not going to leave that place. Reason and logic seem to be out the window with her, so I'm not sure what's left."

"Well, we have to deal with the criminal case first, so while we're doing that, we can develop a plan to get Ruby out," John said. "We're going to set up an investigative headquarters at a fishing motel just south of Highpoint in Hendry County. We should be close enough to get done what we need. I've been in touch with our Fort Myers office. They're going to supply any extra equipment or man power, if we need it. Once we get set up, we'll start turning up the heat on Dr. Simmons and see what shakes out. He truly has a couple of skeletons in his closet."

"In the meantime, what are *we* going to do?" Cynthia glanced at Marie.

"Pray." Marie folded her hands on the table. "Pray a lot."

"I've been doing plenty of that already."

Tim turned to Cynth. "Since when do you pray?"

"For some time now." She rested back against her chair. "I thought I'd forgotten how, but this last year I've picked it up again. It's like riding the proverbial bike, I suppose."

"I woulda never figured." Tim gawked at Cynth. Was this the same woman who used to be his wife?

"Prayer certainly is a good start. It has guided us through some tough spots." Marie took John's hand. "We'll do anything we can to help. I mean that."

Cynth passed her hand across her head in a vain attempt to discipline the errant strips of hair unraveling from her bun. "I appreciate all your help already, but I just don't understand any of this. Ruby is such a smart girl. How could she have fallen in with a group like this? What did we do wrong?"

"I told Tim what I'm about to tell you, and I know it's not easy to hear." John scooted his chair up to the table and gave Cynth his full attention. "This is a spiritual battle, not an intellectual one. Many very smart people have been deceived and followed depreaved leaders, sometimes to an awful end. If your heart is not protected by God's Spirit, you can be vulnerable to anything. That's the truth."

"You see everything as 'spiritual,' Russell. Not everything comes down to the Bible and God." Tim's voice rose, and he was workin' real hard not to get fired up, but the man was so black and white, no in between. Russell was like his pop in spiritual things. He wouldn't give an inch. It was aggravating. "We were good parents. We loved Ruby and taught her right from wrong and how to be a good person. This whole spiritual warfare thing doesn't cut it with me."

"John's right." Cynth nodded. "Everything he's saying is true."

"What?" Tim gazed at her as if she'd suddenly sprouted a second head. "You're gettin' as goofy as Russell."

"We've sinned, Tim. I never thought I would use that word in serious conversation again. But it fits now. You and I were raised in the church. We were taught the ways of God. Even if we didn't believe, we knew what Truth looked like. We had exposure to it. Ruby didn't have that same experience as a foundation. As gifted as she is, she couldn't even tell you who wrote the Gospels or what they are. The only exposure she's had to God was the few stories from your father, if she even remembers them. I was too proud, and you were too angry to give her the same opportunity to hear about the Lord that we had. We always said she could choose her own path. Well, God help us, she has made that choice."

"When did you start feeling like this?" Tim asked. "I've never heard you say anything about church that wasn't derogatory. The whole time we were married, you never wanted anything to do with religion or prayer. It was all about school and knowledge."

"Do you really believe you and Ruby were the only ones devastated by the divorce?" Cynth's arms dropped to her sides. "I've been thinking about this for a while, and now with Ruby—there's a knocking in my soul to return to my roots, to seek the things of the Lord. I can't explain it, but I just want to get back to the place of peace I knew as a little girl, that place of belief and faith, without all the garbage of the world getting in the way. I don't know if I can get there now, but I'm willing to at least try."

Cynth stopped and shook her head as a single tear raced down her cheek. Marie wrapped her arm around Cynthia's shoulders and pulled her close. "I hate to admit it, but we have no control over Ruby…or anything, for that matter. We have nowhere else to go but back to God."

"That might be fine *for you*," Tim seethed. Where was God when Pop withered to nothing and died? Where was He when Ruby was being enticed down this awful path by that vile man? God was a spectator, watching everything in the world play out like a huge video game. Nothing more. He didn't govern the affairs of men anymore. "Pray and babble all you want, Cynth. But I can't just sit here and let my baby girl go down this road."

"She's my daughter, too! And I don't like it any more than you do. But it's the reality we're dealing with right now."

"I'll give you reality." Tim stood and paced into the living room. "I'll go down there tomorrow and snatch her from that place myself. That's the reality. And should that so-called doctor or any of his goons get in my way...well, may your God have mercy on them, because I will not."

"What? You're gonna be the big man and take care of this yourself, right?" Life filled Cynth's face again. "Can't you see that this is larger and more difficult than anything we've ever faced? We have no power here. No control. This is no time for you to stand up and act as your own judge."

"I'm not going to judge anyone. I'm just going to speed up the trial." Tim snarled. "I have to *do* something."

"I want to do something, too. And I am going to do something. I'm going to pray for our daughter—and for us to know how to help her."

"You can keep your prayers, Cynth." Tim flicked a dismissive hand in the air. "We need action here, and action is what I'm going to take."

"All the action in the world won't change Ruby's heart." Marie shook her head. "We love you, Tim, but kicking in all the doors in the world can't save her. The door to her heart has to be opened, and only God can do that."

"Marie's right," John said. "Ruby has to want to leave before we can truly help her. We'll have to wait for that sign."

Tim growled and chewed on what he'd heard. He still wasn't sure about the spiritual warfare baloney, but Marie did make sense. After seeing the look on Ruby's face that day, it was clear she'd never leave until she was good and ready.

He closed his eyes and hoped Russell didn't notice. He hadn't prayed since the day his father had died, but he and God did have business, to be sure. Now wasn't the time, though, but soon they would settle up the account.

Tim turned back to John. "And when that sign comes, what then? Are we gonna just sit on our hands and do nothin'?"

"If we see *any* sign Ruby wants out, I give you my word that we'll storm the gates of hell and Highpoint to rescue her."

Cynth stood and faced Tim. "And we'll do it together."

The packed auditorium rumbled with murmurings about fences and new faces at the learning center. The energy swirled around the huge hall, accelerating Ruby's pulse to a near frantic level. Ruby and Byron sat with David Ling and Kara. Rumors had been circulating all day. Now they hoped they could get some solid answers.

The spotlight illuminated Dr. Simmons as he power walked onto the stage toward the microphone. The crowd erupted, many standing. He held his hands up and gave a slight bow. The applause continued, then slowly died down.

"It's good to be here with you today, my students. As I'm sure you've noticed, there have been a whole lot of changes happening at this facility, and I wanted to let you know personally what's going on."

He lifted a stack of papers from the podium and held them at his side. "When I invited you here, it was with a specific vision and plan for each and every one of you. And when you came here, I was also given the awesome and humbling responsibility to watch over and protect you. I have pledged to honor that responsibility, with my very life if necessary.

"I have tried not to burden all of you with the day-to-day details here. I wanted you to focus solely on your training, and your training alone, but recent events have made that impossible."

Ruby squeezed Byron's hand, and they stole a glance.

"For some time I've received threats against my life." He held up the papers in the air. "I get many via e-mail, some on the phone, and some by mail. I've never been particularly worried about such small-minded individuals. As the head of this organization, I expect such attacks. But something has drastically changed. I've now received threats against you because of your association with me. Because you have dared to dream of a higher life and have given up so much to come here and be the leading force in the human race, anointed to bless the world. Many people just can't understand that. And what they don't understand, they want to *destroy*." He crumpled the papers in his hand.

The students' voices echoed throughout the auditorium as the revelations stirred the crowd into a frenzy. Dr. Simmons held up his hands, and peace entered the hall again.

"They can attack me all they want." He eased to the side of the stage and peered out toward his students. "But when these vile creatures make threats toward you, I cannot and will not accept that."

His voice cracked, and he wiped his eyes. "If any one of you, my friends, were to be harmed because of your courage to be here, I couldn't live with myself. That is why I have insisted on some new security measures. Because some of the threats involve burning down our facility, we will be fencing in our property. And we've added additional security personnel to assist Todd in his very difficult position. I will not be intimidated by those intent on stopping us."

"I can't believe people would want to hurt us just for being here," Ruby whispered. "How can people be so sick and cruel?" Why would such disturbed souls threaten Dr. Simmons? Whoever these people were, they couldn't have actually listened to his teachings. He was a man of peace and unity and gave so much of himself to everyone. He only wanted everyone to achieve the level of excellence he had. Where was the threat in that?

"He's right, you know. People always want to destroy what they don't understand." Byron shook his head. "That makes our presence here all the more important. We have to get his message out to the world. It's the only hope humanity has." They turned their attention back to Dr. Simmons.

"For your safety, I'll also have to restrict our time in town even more," Dr. Simmons said. "I fear our small hamlet of Highpoint might not even be safe right now."

Byron pulled Ruby close to him. "It's probably a good idea. He has to take these steps. Who knows what these nutcases will do?"

"I promise each of you, as I live and breathe, I will let nothing—and I mean nothing—stand in the way of my, *our*, destiny."

32

Marie slipped the pants off of the hanger and folded them on the bed next to a stack of John's shirts. John grabbed a pair of his jogging shoes from the closet and tossed them on the bed as well. He might need them.

Both he and Marie were quiet. He didn't have to leave town for his job often, but when he did, he was usually back in a day or two. This time would be different. They would be out of town until the case was solved.

"I'll see if your workout shorts are in the laundry basket." Marie had been quiet all morning, unusual for her and unnerving for John. But as difficult as it was for him to leave, he wondered how much more difficult it would be for her to stay. They shared duties with the boys, from school to practices of whatever sport was in season to taking time out for the other just to get some breathing room. How did single parents do it? It could be exhausting for both of them.

Marie walked toward the bedroom door, and John grabbed her arm. "Are you gonna be okay?"

Marie turned her head toward John. "Would you like me to lie to you?"

"Of course not."

"No, I'm not going to be okay. I'm going to be running around here like I'm crazy and worried sick about you every minute until this thing is over. And I'm going to be lying up late at night missing the love of my life. The question isn't if I'm going to be okay, but if I'm going to survive. The answer to that question is yes." She crossed her arms and pouted.

Marie was a complicated but wonderful woman. Her strength and commitment to him, the boys, and God made it a little easier to leave. She would definitely survive. He was a blessed man, in more ways than one.

"I'm sorry, hon." John stroked her cheek. "We're gonna try to wrap this up as soon as possible."

"I know. I'm not blaming you. Well, maybe I am. If you weren't such a competent and attractive detective, you wouldn't be getting all of these assignments."

John drew her close, and they kissed.

"Ah, um." Joshua stood in the doorway wearing his camos. His sandy blond hair was frizzed from a boy-whirl around the yard, and he and his backpack were stuffed with the accoutrements of war: several toy rifles and shotguns, an indeterminate number of plastic pistols protruding from his waistband, and at least three rubber swords that could be counted on his person.

"How do kids do that?" John laughed. "How do they know the precise time that we're trying to have a romantic moment? It's like they sense it, and they *must* interrupt us."

"I'll get the rest of your clothes." Marie gave him a peck on the cheek and hurried out the door. She rubbed Joshua's head as he passed her into the room. He hopped up on the bed and watched his father.

"I'm ready to go, Dad. I think I have everything packed."

"Well, champ, I don't think you'll be able to go with me on this one." John picked him up and squeezed him tight.

"But you're gonna need a partner for the bad guys." Joshua drew a sword and held it high.

"I appreciate it, son, but I'm gonna need you here to look after Mom and Brandon. Besides, Uncle Tim has my back. You know he won't let any bad guys hurt me."

Joshua scrunched up his face. "Ahhh, Dad, c'mon. You never take me."

"Sorry, champ." John slid him to the ground.

Joshua smacked Brandon on the leg with his sword as he walked out of the room.

"Hey, Dad." Brandon entered the room with a stack of freshly folded clothes. "Mom said to bring these up."

"Thanks." John took the stack and dropped it in the open suitcase on the bed.

Brandon was sprouting up more and more every day. Life was all happening so fast. It seemed like just months ago he was a toddler, relying on John and Marie for every little thing. Now he was nearly a teenager. Soon he'd be off on his own in college somewhere. Brandon's face was so innocent, trusting. He hadn't been tainted by years of police work in a fallen world.

As much as John wanted to protect him from that world forever, that was simply unreasonable and unbiblical. Brandon would someday leave his and Marie's safe home and plunge into the world head-on. What would John do if Brandon were in the same situation as Ruby? He shuddered at the thought. He prayed his boys would be ready.

"Do you have a minute, Brandon?"

"Sure, what's up?"

"Um, I just wanted to see how you're doing and all."

"I'm fine, Dad. I know you won't be gone too long. I'll still miss you and all, but we'll be okay. Don't worry about us."

"That's good." John fumbled over his words. How could he

ease into this? He'd try to be smooth. "What do you think about truth? You know, the Bible being the Word of God, the ultimate source of Truth?" Well, so much for smooth.

Brandon chuckled and shook his head. "Did you go to another men's retreat or something?"

John cocked his head back. "No. Why do you ask?"

"Because every time you go to a men's retreat or some church seminar, you come home and start quizzing me about your parenting skills." Brandon put his hand on John's shoulder. "You're doing fine, Dad. Everything a good father is supposed to do. But you've really gotta lighten up."

"I'm not uptight or anything." Brandon just hadn't been exposed to all John had seen. If he had, Brandon might understand his concern. "I just want to make sure we're all on the right track. That's my job as a dad, you know."

"You are a tad bit obsessive-compulsive as a parent sometimes, John." Marie entered the room with another armload of clothes.

John slapped his hands on his hips. "I am not."

"You really are, Dad." Brandon jabbed him on the arm. Joshua poked his head around the corner of the doorway, nodding.

"Is this a conspiracy or something?" Maybe they were right, but John couldn't help it. He loved his boys and wanted the very best for them.

"No. Just an observation by your eldest that you're slightly neurotic about your parenting, that's all." Marie smiled and rose to her tiptoes to kiss his cheek. "We love you anyway."

John hissed and plopped down on the bed. "I give up. I admit it; I'm a mess."

"Maybe they have a twelve-step program for frantic fathers." Brandon jumped on the bed with John, who was splayed out next to the suitcase. Joshua took the opportunity and launched himself onto John's stomach, and he and Brandon wrestled with their father.

"Okay, okay." John surrendered as his boys pinned him to the mattress. "You win. I'm a disturbed man."

Ruby hurried with a small group down the winding sidewalk into Highpoint. The early morning sun was heating up already; it was well on its way to being another sweltering day.

Dr. Simmons felt it was best for them to travel in groups now and to have one of Todd's security people with them. She didn't know his name. As wide as he was tall, with a flattop haircut and a goatee, he swaggered behind the group; his large frame tottered to and fro like an elephant on a lazy stroll. He seemed nice enough, although extremely quiet.

She wished Byron could go with her, but his schedule had been changed. Dr. Simmons wanted him to step up and take on more responsibility at the learning center. Byron was thrilled, but it meant less time for them to be together. She'd hardly seen him in the last few days.

Ruby passed the ice cream shop on the way to the grocery store.

"Ruby Porter," she heard from behind her. China jogged toward her.

Ruby's heart warmed. Although she had only briefly met the woman once, Ruby couldn't seem to get her out of her mind. She thought about their conversation often. Her friendly face was nice to see.

"Hi, China. I'm surprised to see you again."

"Oh, I'm not." She brushed the iridescent blond braid from her face. "I knew we'd run into each other again. Highpoint is a very small town. Would you like some water?" She reached into her cloth bag, retrieved a bottle of water, and handed it to Ruby.

It was still cool. Ruby rubbed it along her cheek. "Thanks, but I don't want to take your last one."

"Don't worry, I have plenty. I keep several with me during the day. This heat down here kills me."

"You're not from this area?"

China shook her head. "I'm just in Highpoint working on a project."

"How long are you in town for?"

"As long as it takes to finish what I came here to do. Have you had a chance to think about our conversation, the questions I asked?"

"Well, kinda." Truth be known, Ruby couldn't make sense of what the woman wanted to know. She'd churned the questions over and over in her head, but she still wasn't sure how to answer.

China set her bag down. "Have you figured out what you're looking for here in Highpoint with Dr. Simmons? What you're truly seeking?"

Ruby leaned back against a car parked along Main Street and took another sip of water. Her escort was now several stores away with two other students. He glanced back at Ruby, who nodded and smiled, letting him know that she was fine with China. He stood posted on the sidewalk and watched the students as they split up and hurried to different shops.

She turned her attention back to China. "I want to be a part of something that helps people. That's why I came to Highpoint."

China nodded. She opened her water bottle, took a long chug, and then screwed the cap back on. "That tells me what you want to do but not what you're looking for."

"Well, I guess I don't understand what you're asking then."

"Everyone is searching for something, Ruby. I'm just curious about what you're looking for at the learning center."

Ruby shrugged. If she had asked something about the

Higher Learning Method, Ruby could whip the answer right out, but China kept probing her with the same questions on what *she* was looking for. Ruby didn't want to seem rude, but she didn't know what this woman wanted to hear.

"I've been thinking about you a lot since we met, and I have a gift for you." China reached into her bag and pulled out a Bible. "I'm guessing you don't have one."

So *that* was what her questions were all about. It finally made sense. Ruby held her hand up. "I'm not a very religious person. Thanks just the same. Dr. Simmons said that Christianity and all of the traditional religions have crippled people's growth and evolution. Religion undermines humankind's true potential."

"I'm not overly religious either. I'm just in love with the Truth." China took another drink, gazing over the water bottle at Ruby.

"I've never heard anyone put it that way." Ruby cocked her head. "You are a Christian, though, right?"

"I am a follower of Jesus Christ." China smiled. "Who do you think Jesus is?"

"Dr. Simmons said—"

China held up her petite hand, cutting Ruby off. "I know what Dr. Simmons says. But who does Ruby Porter say Jesus is?"

"Well, I think He was a good man, a moral teacher, I suppose."

"Is that opinion based on your own research or on what others have told you about Him?"

Ruby scrunched up her face; she didn't want to answer. The woman nailed her on that one. "Like I said, I've never been a religious person. So, to be honest, my opinion is mostly based on what others have said."

"So you've never read the Bible?"

Ruby shook her head with reluctance.

"Great. Then I got you a gift you can really use." China

handed the Bible to Ruby, who took it this time. If the woman went to the trouble of buying her a Bible, she could at least accept it. It would be rude at this point not to.

"Jesus said that He is 'the way and the truth and the life.' He also said that 'no one comes to the Father except through me.' That means no one goes to heaven except through Jesus. You are a Truth seeker, Ruby. Seek for yourself what Jesus said and did. Don't rely on others to make that interpretation for you.

"Who is Jesus? It's the most important question you can ever answer. If He's a lunatic or anything other than God, dismiss Him. But if you find that what He says about Himself and salvation is true, give your life over to Him. You'll never regret it."

"Dr. Simmons said—" Ruby stopped herself and smirked. "*I* believe that if you're a good person and help others, you can go to heaven."

"So when you say that you came to Highpoint to help others, would it be fair to say that you're here seeking heaven and the truth about life?"

Ruby smiled and nodded. The realization smacked her in the forehead. She was seeking truth and heaven, something better than she'd known, and helping people was only a part of that. She'd never broken her own thought processes down that far, but it made sense now.

"See, Ruby? You are a Truth seeker. I could see that the first time we met."

"I want to know the truth about life, and Dr. Simmons can help me find it."

China slid next to Ruby. "Turn to the first page."

Ruby opened the Bible. A list of verses filled the cover page.

"I wrote down some verses that might help you in your investigation. I also put my cell phone number there as well. If you just need to talk or have questions, just let me know. You could probably use a friend here in Highpoint."

"Thanks." Ruby smiled. "That's very kind of you."

"My pleasure. I hope we can talk soon."

"Me, too." Ruby glanced at her watch. "Yikes. I can't believe the time. I'm so late. Sorry, but I have to go."

China nodded. "I noticed all the new construction at the learning center, the fence, the cameras. Is everything okay?"

Ruby really didn't want to go into it. Although China seemed caring and kind, she probably wouldn't understand. "Everything is fine. Just a little extra security, that's all."

"If you want to talk about anything, please call me anytime, day or night. I'm praying for you, Ruby."

"Thanks, but I really have to go."

China leaned forward and hugged her. Ruby was tense at first. She'd been a little thrown off when China started talking about Jesus and the Bible, but the woman just seemed so genuine and truly concerned about her. Ruby squeezed her back.

"See you soon." China waved as Ruby jogged toward the store. She only had ten minutes before she had to be back.

It'd been a while since someone told Ruby she was praying for her—not since her grandpa, when Ruby was young. It was odd but comforting. And she'd never met anyone like China either. Ruby had always assumed that devout Christians and other religious people were weak and needed that crutch in their lives. But China challenged her without attacking.

Ruby was surprised she'd opened up so much to a stranger. Since Byron was so busy now, it was nice to have another friend, something to look forward to in Highpoint.

When China spoke, Ruby's spirit tingled as never before.

33

The digs at the Gator Lodge & Inn were less than desirable. Alan had promised accommodations, but he never said anything about *good* accommodations. The cheesy alligator head at the entrance to the single-story motel looked more like an anemic albino gecko with missing teeth than a full-fledged alligator.

"It's really kinda homey." Moses took a box from the trunk of Tim's car and carried it into the motel room.

"I know you're extending yourself for us, and we're much obliged."

Moses smiled at Tim. "We want to get to the bottom of this as much as you do, so I guess we're all in this for the long haul."

"Guess so."

John and Robbie were piecing together a computer in one room and would have to get everything set up and running soon. Gloria had packed all the things they'd need from the office, and Alan was making runs back and forth from Melbourne, coordinating the logistics.

Tim hoped the hookup to the department intranet would work. He'd become spoiled with the easy access to so many databases and wasn't thrilled with the prospect of reverting back to pure gumshoe law enforcement.

"Robbie, do you have the profile ready on Dr. Simmons?" John asked.

"I'm tweaking it now." Her head was stuck under the desk, feeding cords up to John. "But I think you hit the nail on the head. This guy's a couple fries short of a happy meal."

"Tell us something we don't already know." Tim went to move another box and stopped. Sitting on top of the box was a paper elephant, the folds perfect and sharp, its trunk curled just right, with tiny protruding tusks. Origami at its finest.

"All right, Robbie. Enough is enough. We've got serious business here. You can stop with the jokes." He held the elephant up to her face.

"I keep telling you, it's not me, Supersleuth. You need to sharpen your skills. You're following the wrong leads."

"Russell." Tim approached him. "You can't lie to me. Did you put this on my box?"

"I told you before, it's not me. Someone else has your number."

Tim regarded Moses, whose bewildered stare told him everything he needed to know. "Ah, I know it ain't you. It's got to be Alan. That sneaky old man. You never really know what's going on with him. You wait till he gets down here. I'll sweat it outta him on the spot."

A black BMW pulled into the parking lot and was as out of place at the Gator Lodge & Inn as jewelry on a monkey. Tim recognized it at once. He wasn't surprised. Cynth was a determined woman when she put her mind to something.

Stepping out with her long legs, Cynthia straightened her skirt and grabbed a black travel bag from the front seat. She wore one of her navy suits, as if she were heading to teach one of her classes—certainly not the look for the luxurious Gator Lodge & Inn.

Tim met her in the parking lot. "Cynth, what in the world are you doing here?"

"Helping *our* daughter."

"But this is a law enforcement problem." Tim turned in a circle with his arms out. "Look around. We're setting up our base of operations here."

"Good. Then this is exactly where I need to be."

Tim shook his head. "You'll only be in the way. Go home, and I'll call you if anything happens. I promise."

"You're all talk about action." Cynthia set down her bag. "Of course, that only applies to what *you* want to do. I want to be here, close to my daughter. I won't be in the way."

"You can't stay here. I won't have it."

"I already have reservations." She crossed her arms and glowered at him. "I'm not leaving, Timothy, so you might as well get used to seeing me around here." She strolled to the back of her car and popped the trunk, pulling out two more pieces of luggage. "I'm in the room next to yours," she called out as she hurried toward the office.

Tim quaked and snarled. "Ooooh, that stubborn, belligerent, gotta-have-it-her-way woman drives me nuts." In that epiphanic moment, he suddenly understood the wisdom of primal scream therapy. He contained his rage and drew a deep breath while surveying the dilapidated motel.

"This place takes reservations?"

Ruby shuffled down the hall to her room. Exhausted and her head still reeling from the conversation with China, she grabbed the doorknob, but it was locked. It was never locked; she didn't even have her key. She jiggled the handle again. No good. She stepped back and checked the number on the door. Everything was right.

She heard a commotion in the room and a "thump," like

something fell on the floor. She knocked on the door. "Kara, are you in there?"

After a long pause, Kara finally spoke. "Just a minute. I'm busy. Can…can you come back in a little while?"

"Come on, I'm tired and I still need to do some reading. Just let me in."

Several more moments passed, and then the door unlocked. Ruby walked in. Dr. Simmons was straightening his shirt, and Kara looked disheveled, her hair messed up.

"Ruby, dear, what a pleasure to see you. Kara and I were just talking about her progress here at the learning center. We're all so pleased with how she's coming along. Don't you agree?"

"Well, ah, yeah, of course." Ruby attempted to make eye contact with Kara, who gave her attention to her fidgety bare feet.

"Well, ladies, I have to be going. I'm very proud of how both of you are coming along. You will be fine instructors someday." Dr. Simmons walked toward the door but stopped short of the threshold. "Remember what we talked about, Kara dear." He grinned at them both. "Ciao."

The door closed behind him. Ruby walked past Kara and dropped her bag on her bed. She had to be imagining things; she was just tired and a little paranoid. Dr. Simmons was a man of honor and had always been so respectful of all the women here. Maybe he just wanted to talk with Kara alone, as he said.

But that was certainly not how it looked.

Kara brushed her hair back, grabbed her purse from the bed, and slipped into her shoes.

"Everything okay?"

Kara's face was drawn and expressionless. She perked up with a plastic smile, nothing like her normal bubbly one. "Everything's fine. Dr. Simmons and I just had to…talk about some things. He was very helpful as usual. No problem."

"It just seems like you're upset. If there's—"

"I said everything's *fine*, Ruby. I'm going for a walk by the lake. I'll be back later." She rushed out the door, slamming it.

Ruby's stomach churned as the questions buzzed around her head like a stirred-up hornet's nest. She plopped down on her bed. Kara must just be experiencing some difficult times that Dr. Simmons was helping her with. She had said that she was struggling to keep up with all the studying. That had to be the answer. She was foolish for thinking anything else. It just wasn't possible.

Ruby opened the white plastic bag next to her and pulled the Bible out. She ran her fingers over the smooth leather cover. She could go through four good books on a weekend, but she had never read the Bible. Not that she was ready to believe what China had told her, but she did feel silly for never having read the most popular book in the world. For all her attempts to be scholarly and well learned, that certainly wasn't something to brag about.

At least she could give it a shot, in between her other reading, to find out what Christians really believed. She could dissect the material and be ready for more questions from China. The debate could be fun. She looked closer at the cover and noticed some writing at the bottom. Her name had been etched in gold lettering there.

How sweet. I can't believe China did that. I guess she's gonna guilt me into reading this thing. She opened the front, and along with the Scripture references, China had written:

> *To Ruby Porter, seeker of Truth. May God direct your steps toward Him! I'm praying for you. Much love, China Washburn*

A yearning overtook Ruby that she wasn't familiar with; she felt drawn to the pages. Her only experience with the Bible was stories from her grandpa when she was maybe five or six. She'd sit on his lap and listen as he told of David and Goliath, Noah and the ark, and Jesus' death and resurrection.

She loved the time with her grandpa and was fascinated by his pure white, short-cropped beard. She used to think it was snow and would try to wipe it off his face. He'd laugh a deep belly laugh and hold her tight. "Ruby, God loves you," he'd say. "You gotta remember that, no matter what happens."

"Okay, Grandpa." She'd giggle, then run her fingers through his beard again. She wished her grandpa had lived a bit longer. She would've liked to have known him better.

How far away that time seemed. Once Grandpa passed away, there was no more church or talking about God in their home. She followed her parents' lead and hadn't felt the need to know if God even existed, until now.

She looked down at the Bible lying open in her hands. Now her interest was piqued, and she couldn't wait to probe the subject a little.

Drained of all energy, Ruby wanted little more than sleep, but sleep would have to wait. She scrolled down the Scripture references.

It was going to be a long night.

34

We're off to the dragon's lair." Tim unbuckled his seat belt as John parked in a small back alleyway just off Main Street behind some of the stores. They had a clear view of the roof of the learning center from here, and it was maybe a ten-minute walk.

"Let's just hope this one doesn't really breathe fire." John had decided it would be best to keep Alan and Robbie out of the limelight, so no one could later associate them with John or Tim, in case they were needed in a surveillance capacity.

John got out of the car and double-checked his Glock 9mm—locked and loaded—then tucked it into a holster in the back of his jeans. The muggy Florida morning teased sweat from his brow, which he wiped away.

As Tim secured his pistol in the back of his jeans, John grabbed his digital camera from the backseat. Some recon shots of the area wouldn't hurt. After that, they would show some pictures of Mitch to the locals and root around a little.

"Okay, let's take a walk up to the learning center and see what we've got." John said.

As they turned toward Main Street, Chief Bennington leaned against the brick building, as if he were holding it up, staring at them with his arms crossed and tapping his foot. At their approach he removed his Stetson and held it at his side.

"I'm still waiting for my heads-up. You boys at FDLE aren't the most reliable bunch."

"We've got a lot going on, Chief." John stopped a couple yards from him. The man was everywhere and downright devious.

"So I've heard. Your partner is not welcome up at the learning center anymore. He caused a ruckus there the other day, so I don't want to catch him *hanging* around."

"I'll hang around anywhere I please." Tim's hands fell to his sides as he shifted into a fighting stance. "And in case you haven't noticed, you're not *my* chief, *Chief*. We've got a case to work, and we're gonna do that regardless of what you think."

"You got squat. You're just down here fishing, trying to make something out of nothing. Dr. Simmons and his people aren't bothering a soul, so why push something that ain't there? You need to leave them and my town alone."

"How do you know what's going on here?" John asked. "Have you bothered to investigate? Have you interviewed potential witnesses or checked the facts? Or are you too busy spending your bloated budget on new computers and fresh paint jobs?"

Bennington moved nose to nose with John. "You got a charge, Russell? Don't beat around the bush. Just make it."

"Fine. I think you're asleep on the job here…or maybe worse." John jabbed a finger at the chief's badge. "You've been commissioned to enforce the law in Highpoint, not to close your eyes to what's going on. Mitch Garrow didn't go on a 'spiritual sojourn.' You and I both know that."

"I know of no such thing. There's not one shred of credible evidence that the boy didn't take off on his own. And I resent your insinuation otherwise."

"You can resent it all you want, Chief, but it's true. You need to open your eyes—your cop eyes—and see for yourself."

"My cop eyes *are* open, and all I see are two rabble-rousers trying to soil the good name of a great citizen of my community. And for the record, I resent that, too. So, gentlemen, your professional courtesy in Highpoint has been all used up. You so much as jaywalk in my town and you'll get a real intimate view of a Highpoint jail cell, detectives or no detectives."

"I'll take that as a threat." John lifted his chin.

"Take it any way you like." Bennington's bald head glowed like a freshly stoked ember. "You just better watch your step." The chief turned and stomped toward Main Street.

"Hey, Chief," Tim called out.

Bennington turned around.

"When did you stop being a cop?"

The chief snarled and continued marching toward Main Street.

"Let's get going, Tim. It's no use trying to be stealthy anymore. If he knows we're here, everyone knows we're here."

"I haven't seen you get that hot under the collar in a long time."

"I just can't stand a dirty cop. That really pushes my buttons." Chief Bennington was turning into the resident thug and do-boy for Dr. Simmons. It made him sick that the man wore a badge. If he shook out anywhere in this case, John would have no problem arresting him and bringing him before the state board. The man was a disgrace.

They ambled up the small alleyway out to Main Street and turned left. The breeze from the lake was stiff and humid, like a fan in a sauna. About ten minutes later, Tim and John arrived at the roadway in front of the Higher Learning Center.

"When did all this go up?" Tim asked.

A long metal fence with spikes at the top encircled the property. A brick guardhouse had been erected almost overnight, manned by a nonuniformed thug with blond hair crimped into minidreadlocks. His broad shoulders could barely contain the attitude he flashed them from across the street. He stepped out of the guard shack and stood at parade rest, glaring at them.

"What in the world have they done here? This is not good." Someone was getting paranoid. John didn't know if the fence was to keep people out or in—or both. Not only was he concerned about Ruby's safety, but any plans to visit the facility again, covertly or overtly, would have to be modified.

Tim shook his head. "Baby, what have you gotten yourself into?"

John snapped several quick pictures.

Tim stared dumfounded at the stronghold before them. "Russell, I'm scared. I hate to admit it, but I've never been this afraid in my whole life. I never saw this coming."

"Well, we're here now, so we'll do everything we can to get her out. Give it time."

"Are you still prayin' for Ruby, John?"

"Of course. Every day, several times a day."

Tim sighed, and his arms fell limp at his sides. "Add me to your list...please."

"You're already there, partner. You have been for a long time." John patted Tim on the back. "Now we better get going before we draw too much attention. We'll walk back to the car, then drive around to the other side and get some shots from there."

Tim was hurting like John had never seen before; he had to be to ask for prayer. But at least he asked. That was the only good part of the day so far.

Lord, help him...help us. We desperately need You.

John had never worked a case remotely like this. Ruby was in a fortress; Mitch was nowhere to be found; Tim was paralyzed by dread—and John felt powerless to change any of it. He wouldn't let Tim in on his own fears. Tim needed to look to John for strength. From this point on, he would portray nothing but confidence, even if he had to fake it.

They hustled back down the bike path. Tim would walk a few steps, turn back toward the learning center, then start forward again. John purposely picked up the pace to get him away from there.

They rounded the first set of buildings and turned into the alley where their car was parked. A dark blue minivan was next to their car. A tall woman in a dark pin-striped business suit stood next to the van with the side door open. Her scarlet hair hung to her shoulders, and her fair skin shone in the morning sun. She didn't wear any jewelry, not even earrings. Her driver—a white male in his late twenties with curly black hair, a tree-trunk neck, and dark shades—kept the engine running.

"Agents Russell and Porter." She motioned to the van door with an open hand. "Please get in. We don't have much time, and we don't want to be spotted."

"Get in the dark van with you and Dr. Thickneck here?" Tim reached toward the small of his back. "I don't think so."

She had a gun or a huge pager on her belt that formed a lump underneath her jacket. The gun in her ankle holster made her calf look swollen. She stood toward them in a bladed stance like a professional fighter—she was definitely a cop. Then she flashed a cocky smile. No, worse than that…

John eased back. "You're a Fed?"

She brushed her coat back, exposing her badge and pistol. "Special Agent in Charge Kate Sweeney, FBI. Now please get in. We really don't need anyone to see us."

John and Tim slipped into the middle seats, and Kate rolled the door shut. She got in the front passenger seat; then the driver pulled out of the parking lot and through the back alley.

Kate turned around and faced them. Maybe in her mid-thirties, she had freckles that made her look younger; she exuded a determined confidence.

"This is Special Agent Pete Morrison." She pointed to the driver, who nodded but said nothing.

"You-all were following us the other day in the Suburban, right?" Tim asked.

"We were trying to get a line on who you were." Kate brushed her hair back as she gave her attention to Tim.

"Did you like that little driving move I made?" Tim grinned.

Pete chuckled until Kate stared him down; he put his game face back on as he turned onto Main Street, heading out of Highpoint.

"Gentlemen, we have a problem."

John rested back in his seat. "What's the problem, Agent Sweeney?"

"We're working the same case."

"Mitch Garrow?" John crossed his arms. He didn't like the direction of the conversation already. The Feds were notorious for not sharing info…or cases.

"Among other things." Kate nodded as she spoke. "It seems Dr. Simmons has some tax issues as well as his suspicious little facility here. The Bureau is more than interested in the goings-on in Highpoint. We want to head off any problems before we have another Waco. No one wants to see something like that happen again."

"So what's the problem?" Tim scrunched in the seat like a schoolboy being chastised by the principal.

"I've run both your records, and you are fine cops who have served with distinction. But you two are stirring things up. The chatter has it that you've got our guy worried and more paranoid than usual. That could turn really bad for us."

"Chatter?" That could mean only one thing. "You're wiretapping their phones?"

Kate's head tilted, and then she scowled at John. "I'm not at liberty to confirm what investigative techniques we're using or not using, but I can tell you that you two need to walk away from this case."

"How seriously are you taking the Garrow disappearance?" John regarded Tim, who appeared as irked as he was.

"Very. It's part of our overall investigative plan."

"Have you talked with any witnesses in the case?" John waited for the answer he already knew.

Kate was silent and didn't appear to like answering questions. She was not a woman to be messed with.

"I take it you haven't." John raised his eyebrows. "So your plan is to sit and wait and maybe, just maybe, *hear* something?" He didn't like to be sarcastic, but it seemed fitting under the circumstances. The FBI might be too cautious to avoid another incident like Waco, which made sense to some degree. It truly was a precarious case to handle. But to do nothing was unacceptable.

"We're not going public with this investigation and creating a spectacle. I have my directives, and they don't include tipping our hand or pushing Dr. Simmons over the edge. You should understand that."

"Does your investigative plan include any actual investigating?" Tim asked. "Or are you-all just gonna hang out until something else happens...possibly something terrible?"

"I'm going to make my case as I see fit." She narrowed her eyes at Tim. "You're not privy to all of our information, but there is more going on here than you can imagine. This is a courtesy call, nothing more. You need to pull out of this investigation on your own, or I'll make some calls and have you yanked out. Your choice."

Tim grumbled and flexed his chest as he leaned forward. "I

don't care who you call. We're not leaving just 'cause it's inconvenient for the Feds."

"Look, Agent Porter." She shifted in her seat to face him directly. "I know your daughter's in there. I'm real sorry about that, but that's outta my hands. My case comes first."

Sweeney was at least thorough. An arrogant control freak, but thorough nonetheless. John respected that. Maybe he could work with her a bit.

"My little girl is in that *learning center* with a lunatic." Tim bristled like a flustered porcupine. "You couldn't possibly know what that's like. She's my baby, and I ain't going anywhere."

"You are *not* going to be a hindrance to my investigation, and that's all there is to it."

John grabbed Tim's shoulder and eased him back in his seat. "What if we can help each other out? If our presence here has increased the 'chatter,' wouldn't it be a good thing for us to stay around? If we tweak Dr. Simmons in the right way, maybe this chatter will turn into some bona fide evidence."

A smirk grew across Kate's face. He'd made sense, and she knew it. Now it was time to close the deal.

"If we work together, maybe we can both meet our goals—finding Mitch, helping Tim's daughter, and locking up Dr. Simmons for the rest of his natural life. It's a win-win for both our cases."

Kate glanced at Pete, who shrugged. She held John's gaze for a long moment. Slowly, she raised a finger and pointed at John then Tim. "Let's get some things perfectly clear—we aren't a task force and we aren't partners. You have your case and we have ours. *Ours* takes priority. I'll give you a little more time—very little—to ferret something out. But if you two go too far or get in our way—in any way—you will be jerked out of here so fast your little state badges will spin."

"Good enough." Actually it wasn't, but it would have to do.

He'd bought some time before she'd start making calls and arguing jurisdiction, an argument they could very well lose.

"I guess our little talk is over, fellas." She glanced again at Pete, who appeared to have the good sense to stay quiet. "Pull over here, Morrison."

Pete drove the van to the side of the deserted highway that led back to Highpoint. They were a good three miles away from town.

"Hey, don't we get a ride back to our car?" Tim asked.

"We can't risk being seen with you in town again." She smirked. "Looks like you're gonna have to walk."

"That's just wrong, Fed-lady." Tim grabbed the handle of the side door and rolled it open. "Wrong, I tell ya." Tim leapt from the van.

John stepped out and pulled a business card from his shirt pocket. "Here, it has my cell phone number on it in case you need to contact me."

"Don't need it. Believe me, I have both your numbers. And remember, we didn't even have this conversation, and you two are on a very, very short leash." She peered at them through her nearly closed thumb and forefinger, as if there were a rifle sight on their heads.

John understood now why she didn't wear a wedding ring. She was all about the job. "How can we contact you if we need to?"

"You can't." She grinned. "Have a nice walk." She stepped out of the van and closed the door. After returning to her seat, Pete looked back at them and gave a sympathetic shrug as he hastened onto the highway, kicking up a cloud of Fed dust that threatened to choke them.

The air fled Tim's lungs, and his shoulders rolled forward. "I've never liked the Feds. Nothing good happens when they show up." He turned and ambled toward Highpoint. "What did we do to be punished like this? So far today we've teed off two separate law enforcement agencies and gotta walk in this heat. I don't think I've ever accomplished that much in one day before in my life. It must be some kinda record. And we haven't even gotten to the bad guys yet."

The oven of south Florida had been set to broil as Tim and John trekked toward town.

"Let's call Robbie and have her pick us up." Tim swatted at a swarm of gnats buzzing around his head. "I don't want to walk all the way back."

"Nah, by the time she gets here, we'll be in town." John walked along the shoulder. He and Tim had just been introduced into the Florida food chain. "And we certainly don't want her to be seen with us right now. We'll need her later."

"You get the feeling we are about the most unpopular guys in Glades County right now?"

John stumbled over a fire-ant mound, then regained his balance. "Yeah, I don't feel the love anymore."

35

This thing weighs a ton." Ruby hoisted the large metal pot from the dishwater. She propped it on her hip and swung it over to the countertop, where she scrubbed the inside with a wire brush. Pausing for a moment to catch her breath, she finally slid it off the counter and back into the water, a wave of warm suds splashing her face. She blew the lather from her lips.

The talkative students, the clanking and rattling of the pots and pans, numbed any attempts she'd had at serious thought or reflection. Grease lightly covered the tile floor, making each step treacherous. Ruby felt as if she were skating in here instead of walking. The grimy smell clung to her clothes and would surely take two washings to get out.

Two chefs were on staff to oversee the food preparation, but the rest of the work was done by the students. Dr. Simmons wanted everyone to be responsible for each other to help them feel like the family they were.

It just helped Ruby feel exhausted and overwhelmed. As if the constant studying and classes weren't enough, everyone pulled kitchen duty at least once a week. People certainly had to eat, but couldn't they hire more help in the kitchen?

She wiped her hands on her long white apron, adjusted her

hairnet, and fell back against the sink. What was she doing? She'd stayed up until 3 a.m. the night before reading the Bible and was so tired she couldn't even focus on washing dishes. But it wasn't just exhaustion that plagued her. Her soul was troubled—nothing was clear anymore.

"Ruby." A call came from behind her.

She jumped up and spun around.

Cliff rushed toward her. "I didn't mean to startle you, but I have some wonderful news."

"Really?" She flicked some soap off of her hands and into the sink.

"You know tomorrow is Friday, and Dr. Simmons loves to hear testimonies on Fridays. They tend to motivate everyone for the weekend classes."

Ruby nodded.

"Dr. Simmons has chosen you to give your testimony to the whole assembly. He's so proud of how far you've come, Ruby. You will make a wonderful testimonial for him and for everyone here at the Higher Learning Center."

"Well, I don't—"

"I'll be there to prep you before you go on. You're going to do marvelously. I just know it. I'll see you at the auditorium promptly at five-thirty." He turned and hurried out of the kitchen.

"Great, like I need one more thing on my plate." She brushed the sweat from her cheek with her sleeve.

The endless repetition was wearing her out—classes, study, work, classes again. It seemed as if she was getting nowhere. Just when she thought she was learning and growing, Dr. Simmons would throw in a new principle or a different set of classes. The standard was constantly shifting. There was no timetable for when they'd be finished. She didn't want to seem ungrateful, but Ruby was ready and willing to go out and help others now, as had been promised.

She wasn't sure which way she was going anymore. Dr. Simmons's teachings were so powerful and penetrating and felt so right—at first. Lately she'd struggled to find any real meat among the morsels she was being fed in her classes. The Bible was another matter. It seemed so authoritative, sound, intriguing. But most of all, it was starting to make sense.

What's happening to me? She yearned to be with Byron. She hadn't even seen him in two days, and even then, it was just in passing. She didn't know where that relationship was going either. Just when they seemed to be moving ahead, Byron had been promoted and moved. She was happy for him...sort of. She missed him.

She'd never had a real relationship with a guy before. A couple of schoolgirl crushes and a few dates in high school, but never anything that resembled something real, tangible. Then came Byron. Then there went Byron. Like everything else in her life, just a fleeting vision of what she thought she wanted. No real substance. Maybe Byron was wrong for her. Maybe everything else was, too.

She was losing her mind; that was the only rational answer.

She lifted herself onto the edge of the sink and folded her arms. Her dad's face flickered through her mind. The worried look he'd carried the day he and Mom tried to get her to leave. Her stomach writhed as if she'd eaten some putrid fruit. They had just started their relationship over again before all this happened, and now she didn't even have him to talk with. She'd hurt him, and that thought haunted her.

She'd repelled her mother as well. They had a good, strong relationship at one time, long before any of this. Back then, her mother used to be her best friend. Ruby ached for one of their late-night talks over root beer and pizza. Oh, the stories she'd have to tell her now. No chance of that. She'd blown that, too. Ruby was unraveling like a ball of twine rolling down a mountain—and picking up speed—and she had no idea how to stop it.

How was she supposed to get up in front of everyone and talk about how her life had been changed when she felt like such a loser? What could she tell everyone? That she was scarcely keeping her head above water, wondering what her purpose truly was in Highpoint? This couldn't have come at a worse time.

What in the world am I gonna do?

"I'm not sure about this." Tim squirmed in the front passenger seat of John's car. "But I'll give it a shot."

He, Cynthia, John, and Marie drove into the parking lot of Mount Carmel Worship Center. A cloud of dust from the road overtook them as they found their spot. The midmorning sun gleamed against the white face of the tiny wooden church.

Alan had declined the invitation to a worship service rather forcefully and went home for the weekend. Robbie was polite but said she didn't attend services that didn't have a priest. She was heading home for the weekend as well. Marie had come to visit John; they both bit at the chance to go to church. No surprise there.

Tim was ready to decline as well until Cynthia had asked him to come. He was so floored that she wanted him with her that his response leapt from his mouth before engaging his brain. Now he was off to church. And it wasn't the worst thing that could happen to him—he and God still had business. No better place than His office.

"I don't think the roof will cave in." John turned off the car and grabbed his Bible. "Besides, after the service, we'll meet with Demetrius and China and update everyone."

"Fine." Tim worked on his tie. The fool thing was strangling him. Wearing a suit and tie at work was one thing, but at church, it was a source of irritation.

At his father's church, all the men had worn suits, even the young men. Tim fought with his mother every Sunday to keep that tie from going around his neck. "You're not gonna embarrass your daddy while he's preachin'," she used to say. "So stand still, young man." He always lost those arguments.

"It's been some time since we've been to church together." Cynthia stepped out of the car and straightened her dark blue skirt.

"Since my father's funeral, if memory serves me correct." Tim slammed the door.

The dusty parking lot filled up quickly as a line of cars vied for the closest positions to the door. A yellow haze filled the air, as the pine pollen was in bloom, covering several cars with a golden tint. A line formed at the door with Demetrius greeting everyone as they entered.

Most of the men wore dark-colored suits, like Demetrius, and the women wore bright, colorful dresses. Many of the little girls wore bonnets. A gaggle of children chased each other around the front steps. Tim felt transported back to his father's church in the sixties and early seventies. A comfort he didn't expect surrounded him—it felt like home.

Miss Florence, Miss Sylvia, Miss Edna, and Miss Isabel greeted Demetrius with enthusiastic hugs. Miss Isabel used her cane to negotiate the uneven steps up to the small porch where he stood. Tim hung back some, lest he fall victim again to Miss Isabel's chastening right hand. He would definitely sit a comfortable distance from her.

"Tim, John," Moses called as he jogged toward them. He hugged John and went for Tim, who thrust his hand forward. He wasn't much for all that huggin'. Moses shook it as if he were trying to rip his arm outta socket. "Great to see you here, Tim.

Demetrius is a fine preacher. You're in for a real treat."

"We'll see." Tim worked his thumbs into his waistband. It would be hard to beat his pop on preaching. The man could work himself into a sweaty, passionate mess by the time he had finished in the pulpit. Tim would try not to hold Demetrius to his father's energetic standard.

John introduced Moses to Marie and Cynthia. "Glad you-all could make it. Wait till you hear Reverend Taylor speak. The man's anointed, I tell you. We better get a seat while we can."

They ambled up the steps toward Demetrius, who greeted them with a wide smile and a wingspan that would make an albatross envious. "It's so good to have you-all here. Make yourselves at home here among God's people." He extended his long wing out, guiding them toward the entrance, then turned his attention to a group behind them.

Stopping at the threshold, Tim hesitated, unsure if his next step would plunge him off the face of the planet or return him to a familiar, more comfortable time. The modest sanctuary called him forward as he braved the front door.

The tiny church was filling fast as the regulars took their seats. People were creatures of habit. He'd bet that everyone sat in the same seats each Sunday, and he didn't want to upset that balance. They chose a pew near the back.

China was in the front pew, talking with several people behind her. She waved at them. Her radiant blond hair bobbed like a buoy among the sea of African-Americans. She didn't seem to notice or care.

John introduced himself to a couple sitting in front of them. He didn't appear to feel out of place either, but he was like that. He could drop into the middle of a prison camp and in two hours be friends with everyone there. He and Marie were good folks. They chatted away with the couple like they'd known them forever.

Cynth had both her hands on the pew in front of them; her eyes were closed and her head bowed. Although she was a hyper-serious woman, Tim was surprised nonetheless by her quiet, reflective demeanor. She was dressed and ready for church with an almost enthusiastic attitude. Maybe she was sincerely searching out her spiritual roots.

Demetrius strode down the center aisle with grace and confidence until with one long step, he leapt behind the pulpit. He straightened his notes, adjusted his tie, and gazed into Tim's eyes.

"Evil." He rose to his tiptoes as he drew out the word with his lyrical voice. "Evil is on the march here in our fair community. Evil has brought its snares, its deceptions, its lies to cause those who are blind to the Truth to stumble and fall into its clutches. Our enemy prowls the earth, to and fro, searching for souls to devour. Our enemy has landed here in Highpoint."

An "amen" rose from the crowd. Several women nodded approvingly with each statement and made vain attempts at comfort with handheld fans. Air-conditioning was foreign to the building, and the temperature climbed with every strike of Demetrius's fist on the pulpit. The atmosphere was electric, pulsing. Something was happening.

"But we, as people of God, have nothing to fear from this evil. It has no power over us. But it is our duty to resist it with all our strength, with all our hearts, and with all our minds." He pointed a long finger toward Tim's head. "And we have people in our midst today who are here to face this evil. It's their job to face it head-on. And it's our job to pave their path with the prayers of the saints. War has started, ladies and gentlemen, whether we like it or not. And victory is our only option."

Tim felt as if every eye was on him. He tried not to fidget, but the tie was driving him crazy.

"Lord," Demetrius prayed in his powerful voice, "please bless those among us who are here to do battle. Give them protection and wisdom. But most of all, give them victory against the evil one. That no more souls will be lost to this scourge in our midst."

Demetrius raised his head and his hands. "Rise, and let's worship the Lord."

The choir, a dozen men and women onstage next to the reverend, broke into the hymn "Roll, Jordan, Roll" as the walls of the Mount Carmel Worship Center vibrated with the faithful praise.

The congregation stood and clapped their hands in solid unity as a beautiful hymn vaulted toward the heavens. Tim didn't clap along with the rest, but his body instinctively swayed to the rhythm as memories and feelings from so long ago poured into his soul. The image of his father in the pulpit, smiling down at him, wrestled some of the anxiety and anger from him. His soul tingled with unseen things—thoughts and desires that had fled him years before never to be felt again…or so he thought. He bowed his head and his heart. It was business time.

God, I'm so afraid right now. I don't know what to do. I've never understood how You could let a man like my father suffer and die like he did. I don't understand all the misery and pain in this world. But right now, I'm so terrified for Ruby that I'm willing to listen and do anything I can to help her…and me. It kills me to admit that I'm powerless here. I want to believe like Russell does, like my pop did, but I have so many doubts and questions. If You still work in this wicked world, I want to trust You, but I don't know how. I'm not used to it. I need help. I need Your help.

"Trust in the L*ORD with all thine heart; and lean not unto thine own understanding. In all thy ways acknowledge him, and he shall direct thy paths."* The Scripture appeared from the recesses of his memory, a place he'd thought long dead.

His father had pressed him to memorize it time and time again as a boy. It had no meaning then but was dreadfully appropriate now. He hadn't thought about it in over thirty years. It wasn't a coincidence that he remembered it today.

He raised his head to see China's hands lifted high. John and Marie clapped in unison. A woman in the pew in front of his stepped into the aisle and turned in circles, clapping and praising God.

The warm, familiar touch of Cynth's hand wrapped around his. She squeezed it tight. A wellspring of emotion overflowed into his parched spirit. They stole a glance at each other, and Cynth rested her head on his shoulder. The two moved together as one to the praise and worship.

As the music stopped and everyone took their seats, Cynth's hand remained in his. He didn't dare move. He would do nothing to disturb this moment, lest it be only a mirage on the edge of his reality, tempting him to believe it could be real.

He'd hoped daily for restoration, second chances to amend his mistakes with Cynth and Ruby, all the pigheaded, prideful blunders of the past. When times got tough and his spirit was beaten down from depression and alcoholism, he'd walked away from his wife and daughter, much as he'd walked away from God as a young man. Now here he was angry with God for what Tim thought was abandonment, when he was the prime offender in his own life.

He sat guilty before the Lord and his wife, but both seemed to be giving him a second chance. As much as he yearned for reconciliation with Cynth, maybe God truly wanted reconciliation with him even more. Was it possible?

"For the Son of man is come to seek and to save that which was lost." Now that the barrier was broken, Scripture deluged his mind. *"If one of them be gone astray, doth he not leave the ninety and nine, and goeth into the mountains and seeketh that which is gone astray?"*

As low as he felt coming into church, the flicker of hope in his soul flamed up into a roaring inferno, burning with an unquenchable fire.

Demetrius launched into his sermon about Elijah's battle with the prophets of Baal on Mount Carmel, one Tim had heard before from his father. Armed only with his faith and the power of the Creator of the universe, Elijah watched as God consumed the wood and sacrifices on Mount Carmel, utterly defeating Baal's powerless prophets. Demetrius was gifted. Tim's father would have approved.

Reverend Taylor ended his sermon and closed his Bible. "Now, before we go on our way, is there anyone here who has unfinished business with the Lord? Anyone who needs to give his or her life over to the Lord Jesus Christ, who died so that we can have fellowship with God Almighty? He is callin' you now."

The congregation paused, and silence dominated the church for the first time since the service started.

In a second, Tim knew—everything his father had taught him growing up, everything he knew about salvation and the Lord was true. The Truth of that moment pierced his soul from head to toe. The God he'd been running from since his teen years had pursued and laid siege on his soul with a battery of love, forgiveness, healing, and restoration.

As Reverend Taylor went to speak again, Tim rose to his feet. Demetrius smiled a full-toothed grin. Tim stood tall as the congregation turned to see him.

"Come on, brother." Demetrius waved him forward. "The Lord is calling you. He has been for a long time. Come."

Tim nodded and shuffled past Moses. Cynth tugged him back, and they locked eyes; she wouldn't let go. She smiled for the first time in a long while. He loved her smile. He loved her still. She rose to her feet as well. They walked down the aisle and toward the altar together.

Tim knelt first, then Cynth, still hand in hand. Demetrius stepped from the pulpit, laying hands on both their shoulders. Tim felt another set of hands. John knelt beside him, tears flowing down his cheeks. Marie appeared on the other side of Cynthia, wrapping her arms around her. Moses stood behind them.

Demetrius recited the sinner's prayer for him and Cynthia. Tim had heard the words a thousand times before, but they never had meaning until now, as he was broken and humble before the Lord.

Endless sermons from his father flowed into his mind as though a dam had burst in Tim's spirit. Salvation, redemption, justification. He'd been weaned on the words, but for forty-five years they'd escaped his grasp, slipping endlessly away at each prideful turn. As tears raced down his cheeks and all pride was stripped from him, Tim opened his heart to the One who called him.

Lord, I'd be lyin' if I said I understood everything. I still have so many questions and fears. But I know this much is true—You are God and I am not. I've tried it my way and failed at every turn. I'm ready to try it Your way. I know Jesus is Your Son, and I believe what is written, that He died for my sins. Please forgive me, heal me completely. It might not be much, but I give You all I've got. Save me. Save my Ruby. Protect her. Help us. Please help my baby girl.

Tim and Cynth rose together, fresh and cleansed. Cynthia's shoulders trembled as she tried in vain to hold back the tears. They embraced, and John, Marie, Moses, China, and the entire congregation of the Mount Carmel Worship Center gathered around the new creations.

"Take heart, people." Demetrius raised his hands to the heavens. "The Spirit of the Lord is moving here today!"

36

With her hands in her jeans pockets, Ruby kicked the grass as she walked between the administration building and the newly raised fence. The evening sun set low in the sky, giving a temporary stay to the cruelty of the summer heat. She looked back at the road that had brought her to the Higher Learner Center, once so easy to see, now blocked and obstructed by a fence and guard shack. The veiled street could barely be recognized.

One of the new guards rolled past her on an ATV, a rifle slung across his back. Even with her father as a police officer, she'd never liked guns. It didn't help her comfort level. Security, fine. But now it seemed that an army occupied the Higher Learning Center. Could there really be that big of a threat to them?

What had happened? What happened to her? Why couldn't she see anything clearly anymore? At first Dr. Simmons's teachings shone like a beacon, filling her with wisdom and a sense of purpose. Everything made sense. Now? She'd read the Scripture references China had given her and the Gospels over and over the night before, jotting notes and approaching the teachings in as scholarly a manner as she knew how.

Then something happened. She read Jesus' own words, and

she didn't need to take notes anymore. There was a clarity about them that was self-evident, penetrating. His words spoke to her soul. She didn't expect that. She had felt she could coolly dismiss narratives written over two thousand years before as archaic nonsense. But it wasn't that easy now.

Dr. Simmons taught that man was the maker of his own destiny, the creator of his own reality.

She read in the Bible that: "A man's steps are directed by the LORD."

Dr. Simmons believed that: "Man can work and toil himself into the perfect being, without any flaws."

The Bible said: "There is no one righteous, not even one" and "All have sinned and fall short of the glory of God."

Dr. Simmons wrote that: "Truth is relative and arbitrary. Humankind determines what will be the truth for its generation."

Jesus said, "I am the way and the truth and the life. No one comes to the Father except through me" and "You will know the truth, and the truth will set you free."

The civil war raged as she alternated between two diametrically opposed worldviews. Only one could be right. But which one?

"Ruby," Byron called as he jogged toward her.

She stopped and faced him, her hands still in her pockets, drawn into herself.

"Hey, I've missed you." He went to hug her, but she didn't respond. "What's wrong? You don't look so happy to see me."

"I'm sorry." She leaned in and hugged him, holding extra tight. "I am glad to see you." He was the only thing that felt right anymore.

"Are you sure you're okay?"

"No." She shook her head. "I'm not sure I'm okay, but I'm not sure about a lot of things anymore."

He pulled back and took her by the shoulders. "What's going on, Ruby?"

Should she tell him of her doubts? Her fears and insecurities...her questions?

"You don't want to know." She lowered her head. "And I don't want to bother you with what's going on with me. I've got things I have to sort out."

"Hello, Ruby, this is Byron here." He waved his hand in front of her face. "We've told each other every detail of our lives. I've shared things with you I haven't told anyone—ever. So it's not a bother. Whatever's going on, I want to help." He lifted her chin and locked eyes with her. "I care about you more than you can imagine. I want to be here for you."

She took his hand and caressed it with her thumb. It felt warm and strong in hers. "I know. I care about you, too. I really do. But there are some things I have to work out on my own. I'm not trying to weird you out or anything."

"Maybe we can sit down with Dr. Simmons and work through this." A smile crossed his face. "He'll know what to do. He can talk you through whatever's bothering you, as long as it's not me. I don't think he can talk you out of that."

She chuckled for the first time in several days. How could she tell Byron what was going on? He was so locked into Dr. Simmons. How could she tell him what she was really considering? And how could she tell him that Dr. Simmons might be the problem?

"Tim and Cynthia." Demetrius beamed as he leaned against the side of one of the wooden pews. "You've made my day, maybe my month. Yeah, maybe my whole year. I'm so glad you responded to the calling of the Lord. Legions of angels are rejoicing as we speak. I give you my word that we will be here to help you grow in your new relationship with the Almighty."

The rest of the congregation had departed, leaving Tim, John, Marie, Cynth, and China to speak with Demetrius. Tim wiped his eyes. He didn't think he could cry like that, blubbering like a little girl and all. He hoped Russell wouldn't tease him about it. "Thank you." Tim stood, hand in hand with Cynth. "I'm not sure what all this means or where I'm going, but I'm willing to trust God."

"We'll trust the Lord together." Cynthia squeezed his hand. "I feel good, right, for the first time in a long time."

Tim stared at the pulpit, as if his father were standing behind it, smiling down at him. That thought warmed his heart. He couldn't wait to be near his father again, to hug him and thank him for the dedicated life and prayers that finally took root so many years after his death. Tim knew now that that day was going to come. The ways of the Lord were mysterious to be sure, but from this point on, he would do his best to search them out.

"I'm so happy for you both. This is exactly what Ruby needs right now—her family and friends interceding for her with prayer." China clasped her hands together and rested them on top of the pew. "I met with her again. She's really searching now. I think she might be open to the Truth. I sensed it in her spirit."

Tim and Cynthia slid onto the bench next to China, and John and Marie sat in front of them. Demetrius pushed off the pew to stand in the aisle. The Mount Carmel Prayer Team was holding hands in the corners, petitioning the Almighty. Their rhythmic murmurings eased Tim's spirit, even though he couldn't understand a word they were saying.

"How'd she look?" Tim leaned forward with his elbows on his knees. "Is she okay and all?"

"She seemed very tired but okay. They keep turning up the stress and pace there. It's very typical."

Tim stood and turned his back to everyone, jamming his hands in his pockets. "Why are they doing that? Are they just cruel and enjoy hurting kids?"

"I wish it were that simple." China brushed her hair back. "These types of cults usually keep their victims working hard, studying, whatever they can do to maintain a pretty hectic pace. It makes them exhausted, mentally and physically, and helps break down any resistance to their control. Then they can slowly implement more of the corrupt ideology and theology. It's a process, not an overnight transition."

Tim growled and gritted his teeth so hard he thought they'd crack under the pressure. "I can't stand just sitting here while she's up there getting her brain sucked out or whatever they do."

"If you go running in there now when she's not ready to leave, it will only drive her deeper into their clutches." China remained calm, her voice barely carrying above a whisper. "We must be patient and pray that her spirit will be changed and she's willing to leave. That's the only way for her to make it out. But it must be done by God. Anything else is just folly."

Tim craved to argue, scream, and tip things over and storm the Higher Learning Center armed with only a spoon if need be. But as odd as China seemed to be, she spoke with a wisdom he couldn't deny. Just as Marie had told him, God would have to open the door of Ruby's heart.

Tim couldn't get the image out of his mind of his daughter standing defiant against Cynth and him with that snake whispering goodness knows what in her ear as she told them to leave and never come back. Her mind was poisoned against him and everyone else who truly loved her.

But for the first time since all of this began, Tim felt like he'd discovered the antivenin. If God could open his hardened, stubborn heart, He certainly could touch Ruby's. He hoped and prayed it wasn't too late. Tim nodded to China.

"I gave her a Bible, some Scripture references, and my cell phone number. We'll just have to wait on God and pray that He'll do something to crack Satan's spell over her."

"Waiting around for something to happen has never been my strong suit." Tim drew a heavy breath. "But I'm willing to do whatever I have to do…even if it means waiting."

37

Ruby's shoulders slumped forward as she walked down the dorm corridor to her room, the weight of the day oppressing every thought and emotion. She opened the door, flicked on the light, then flung the door shut. She desperately needed some quiet time. She tossed her purse on her bed.

"Ruby," a voice called from behind her.

"Ah!" She jumped and spun around in midair like a cat. Dr. Simmons was sitting on Kara's bed.

He chuckled. "Oh, Ruby, I didn't mean to startle you. I'm so sorry about that." He rose and walked toward her, placing his hands on her shoulders.

"What are you doing here?" Her heart pounded. She stepped back and composed herself. What in the world was he doing in her room at this time of night?

"Do I need a reason to visit my star pupil?" He spoke in a tone she didn't recognize. He let his arms fall to his side. "I've sensed over the past few days that something's been wrong with you. You don't seem like your old self. I just came to check on your well-being."

Ruby sat on her bed. "Well, I have had a lot on my mind. I'm just trying to figure a few things out, that's all. Nothing to worry about."

"That's good," he whispered. "That's very good." He placed his hand on her head, stroking her. "Because you have a special place in my heart, Ruby Porter. You're not like all the others. You are truly the most splendid flower in my garden, and it saddens me so to see you wilting here." He stepped closer to her, almost on top of her and caressed her hair again. His leer rattled her.

"Thank you." Ruby stood and walked to the other side of the room with her back to him, crossing her arms. His creepy gaze never left her; she could feel it settling on her like a lecherous fog. This couldn't be happening.

Both of his hands rested on her shoulders from behind, and he pressed his body against hers. He couldn't be doing this.

"Dr. Simmons." She wiggled to get free from his grasp. She turned and faced him. "I don't think—"

He jerked her forward, pressing his lips against hers. She pushed back, but he pulled her even closer. She couldn't breathe. She yanked her head back and then shook her body free from his grip. She stood in the middle of the room in shock.

"Dr. Simmons!" Her arms flopped to her sides. "What are you doing?"

"I've been dreaming of that since the first time I laid eyes on you," he growled. "I knew then that we were destined to be together."

"But I—"

"There are no buts, Ruby." He stalked around her, his eyes wild. "Just act on your passions. Sometimes if you think too much, you miss out on the best things in life."

"Dr. Simmons, you are not my passion."

"Of course I am." He lunged at her and grabbed her shoulders, pulling her close again.

"Dr. Simmons," she mumbled as he pressed his putrid lips against hers again. "Stop. Stop!"

He pawed at her chest as he sat on her bed, pulling Ruby down with him.

God, help me! "STOP!" she screamed as he bit her lip.

The doorknob jiggled and the door swung open; Kara walked in. Her eyes met Ruby's, and then Dr. Simmons's, who sprang to his feet, brushed his hair back, and straightened his shirt.

"Well, well." He took a deep breath. "My two favorite ladies both here in one room. Aren't I the lucky fellow?"

No one laughed. No one spoke. Kara stood frozen at the entrance to the door; Ruby staggered to her feet. She wiped her hand across her lip. A small trickle of blood smeared her hand. Dr. Simmons grinned at them both.

"Well, ladies, I have to be going. I have a lot of work to do here." He glanced at Ruby. "I am so looking forward to hearing your testimony tomorrow. I believe it will be very encouraging for everyone." He winked at her and pointed his thumb and index finger at her like a quick draw of a pistol. He turned and walked out the door.

Ruby wobbled backward and plopped back on her bed, her head reeling. *What just happened?* Ruby stared blankly at Kara for a moment, too stunned to blink. Why didn't he stop? Who did he think she was?

Kara shuffled over to her bed and sat down slowly. Placing both hands on her knees, she looked at Ruby with sympathetic eyes. "I'm so sorry, Ruby. I thought I was the only one."

"Well, we can eliminate the dark Suburban." John snatched the photo of the vehicle off of the flowchart set up on the whiteboard in their motel room. He crumpled it up and tossed it in the trash. "We know who they are."

At least one unknown had been taken care of. The chart had

a picture of Dr. Simmons at the top, with two lines branching out below—one to Cliff, the other to Todd. Two more lines were drawn toward pictures of Lesley Ann and Mitch. Next to the chart, John posted an infrared aerial photo of the entire Higher Learning Center, its deep red, yellow, and orange hues indicating heat-sensitive areas. Another photo was on the other side of the flowchart, this one a normal satellite view of the complex. John had called in a favor from a friend at the Space Center. It helped to know people.

"I spoke with the FBI division chief." Alan sat on the motel room bed. "He was less than helpful. They have their own investigation going and won't be much help with ours. He didn't reveal anything we didn't already know. They want a cautious approach. They're very gun-shy, pardon the pun, about getting involved in another standoff like the one in Waco. I can understand that, somewhat."

"If their wiretap is successful, they still might be able to help us." John turned to Robbie, who leaned against the wall. "Have you finished your profile on Dr. Simmons?"

"Yeah." She handed him a folder. "And it's not pretty. I went back through as many of his writings as I could and listened to his CDs ad nauseam. His early writings were clear and consistent with most accepted psychological principles. He did some pretty solid research and work with drug addiction and criminal behavioral issues. But about nine years ago, his teachings broke off from the mainstream and started to get into, how shall I explain it, la-la land."

"What do you think his problem is?" Tim straddled a chair backward with his arms resting on the seat back.

"Well, the man uses the pronoun *I* more than any human I've ever seen. It's all about Walter and what he can do. His logic and reason have been taking a hit over the years as well, devolving into the mishmash of beliefs he has now. I don't know if he's slowly losing grip with reality, or if he's always been insane and is just losing his ability to cover it up. But in my professional opinion, the man's a loon. Extreme megalomania with elitist tendencies. "

"What do you think he'll do if he starts losing control at the HLC?" Tim asked.

Robbie shook her head, seemingly reluctant to answer. "You never can tell for sure, but I don't think he will go gently into that good night. I think he'll take whoever he can down with him in a blaze of glory. With someone like Walter, it's all about him."

"Well, we already knew the guy's not right." Alan folded his arms. "So how are we going to link him to Lesley Ann's death, which is still ruled a suicide, or to Mitch's disappearance? Just because he's crazy, it doesn't mean he's guilty."

John stood before his team, quietly contemplating the question. Truth was, he didn't know where to go from here. He was stumped. He had a statement from China that Mitch had found out something and was going to leave the campus and the e-mail from Mitch to his mother that was cryptic at best. Now he'd opened another investigation into a twenty-seven-year-old suicide case that no one seemed eager to reinvestigate.

He'd hoped and prayed for a plan that would neatly tie all these elements together into a coherent case package that would easily sail by a grand jury into first-degree murder indictments. But he didn't know what to do. They'd traveled to Highpoint to find answers, but now his team was stuck in a stinky, run-down fishing motel and had no more answers than the day they'd arrived. Tim stared at him with a hopeful expression. His daughter's life hung in the balance—and John had nothing to offer.

"I don't know, Alan," John whispered. "I don't know where

we go next. Everything we have is circumstantial at best, conjecture at worst."

Alan panned the group as he chewed on his lower lip. "We're running up a mighty expensive tab here, not to mention the fact that we all dropped our cases and families to be here. I don't want to sound like the bad guy, but if we don't get any leads soon, I'm gonna have to pull the plug on this whole operation."

Tim's head sunk, resting on the top of the chair.

38

Darkness shrouded China's small room at the rear of the Mount Carmel Worship Center as she knelt beside her bed. "Lord, thank You for paving my path here with Your grace and making it straight. Bless and protect Ruby and her family, John, and the rest of the officers. And thank You for such godly support at this amazing church."

Demetrius and the wonderful people here had blessed her in so many ways. She was never without a meal or care of any kind, and that made her mission so much easier. She could focus on witnessing to the victims of Dr. Simmons and not have to worry about her needs. In all her travels, she'd never experienced a church as committed to the things of God as this group of devout, passionate believers. Demetrius was an anointed teacher and leader and certainly the right man in the right place at the right time. He was a fearless man of God who never blinked with his faith. He'd become a good friend as well.

The chirping of her cell phone teased China back from her prayers. She groped around on the nightstand until she felt the phone in her hand. She flicked on the light but didn't recognize the number. She sat on the bed and opened the phone.

"Hello?"

She was greeted with silence but could hear someone on the other end.

"Hello." China brushed her hair back and lifted the phone to her ear again.

"Is it true?"

"Ruby? Is that you?"

"Yes." Her voice cracked.

"Are you all right? Are you safe?"

"No and yes. Is it true? Is it all true?"

"Is what true?"

"Is what the Bible says true?"

China sent praises to heaven. How many countless hours of prayer had she sent for this phone call, just as she had for Mitch? "Yes, every word of the Bible is true and can be trusted. Jesus died so you could be with Him in heaven." China sensed Ruby's angst and confusion. "What's wrong, Ruby?"

Her question was met with dead air. Then Ruby finally spoke. "Something's happened, and I'm not sure what to do."

"Meet me and we can talk about it."

"Everything's locked down for the night. And I can't stay on this phone very long."

"Your parents are here, Ruby. They're staying close by."

"They're both here, in Highpoint…together?"

"Yes. They've been here together for some time. They miss you and they love you and they want to see you."

Even though the connection on her cell phone wasn't the best, China could hear weeping on the other end.

"After all I've done? I've turned my back on them both. Why would they ever come to see me?"

"You're their child. The bonds of a parent's love can never be broken, just like the love your heavenly Father has for you. They're both waiting for you, Ruby."

She didn't respond but continued to cry.

"Ruby, I'm worried about you now. I think you should consider leaving the Higher Learning Center until you can work things out."

"I can't leave yet." She sniffled. "I have something I have to do first."

"I was in a situation very similar to yours once. I know what I'm talking about. You *are* in danger, and you need to leave as soon as possible. I will help you. Please, do not stay there any longer."

"I might be in danger." Ruby's voice quivered. "But I can't leave yet. I promise that when I've finished what I need to do, I'll call you."

"I'll be here anytime. We're all praying for you, and your family will be here when you're ready."

"Someone's coming. I have to go."

"Ruby." China squeezed the phone tight. "Read Luke 15."

"I have to go." Ruby hung up.

Ruby skulked down the corridor and slipped back into her room, locking the door behind her. Dr. Simmons surely had a key, but at least she'd be able to hear him if he tried to come in later. Everything she knew—or thought she knew—about him was in question; he was completely unpredictable now.

His eyes were so demented, and he showed no concern for her whatsoever. She was his property, his toy. Once she had revered that man as a giant, a father figure, a…godlike man. Now the mere thought of him repulsed her. Slobbering on her like his little plaything? Disgusting!

Her heart throbbed and ached with pangs that only regret can bring. Her parents had come and stayed; they were together and waiting for her. How could that be? She yearned to be with them, just as it was years before, a whole family. She'd done so much to hurt them that she didn't know if it could ever be the same again.

She looked over at Kara, who was fast asleep. She wouldn't wake her. Kara needed all the rest she could get. The girl had been put through the wringer, and after their talk earlier, Ruby's heart went out to her and the burden she'd been carrying.

She'd had a hard enough life without anything else. Like Ruby, she came to Highpoint to make a difference, to believe in something great and life-changing. Only now those dreams were crashing into the ground of a twisted, wicked reality. But unlike Ruby, Kara had no place else to go.

Lying in her bed, Ruby alternated her stare from the ceiling to the door. The light was on in the hallway, and she could see underneath the door, if someone was standing there.

She lifted the corner of her mattress and retrieved her Bible. She should have known something was wrong with the fact that she even had to hide her Bible. She opened to Luke 15, the Prodigal Son.

It was going to be a long night.

39

"I'm confused, Cynth. I don't quite know what to make of all this...of us," Tim said as they stood in the parking lot of the Gator Lodge & Inn, admiring the view of the ailing alligator head at the entrance to the motel. Hardly a place for a serious discussion, but their options were limited.

All day Tim had felt the burden of sins lifted from him and felt a kinship again with his father on a level he never could have imagined. It was as if the thousands of prayers his father had lifted to the heavens for him were now falling back on him all day, like gentle love letters from the past.

But with all that was happening with Ruby, the investigation, and now giving his life to the Lord, Tim just didn't know where he and Cynth stood. She seemed to be reaching out to him again, but he didn't want to assume anything. His emotions were still fragile, and he didn't know if he could take the pain of her rejection.

"I'm confused, too, Tim." Cynth leaned against her car. "I don't seem to know which way is up anymore. With all this going on, I've had a lot of time to think. I worked too much when we were married. I put so much stock in being a professor and taking care of my students that I forgot about taking care of us."

He rested back against his car. "Don't even go there. Our breakup had nothing to do with your work or anything you or Ruby did. That was my bad, and mine alone." He covered his heart with his hand. "You have no responsibility in that. I'm the one who chose to drink himself into oblivion, disregarding everything and everyone that ever really mattered."

"We were married, Tim. We should have shared everything, even the blame when it went wrong. It's not your fault you were shot. You were lucky to have survived that, and I should have been there for you more during your recovery. I just didn't understand what was happening to us, why you couldn't talk to me about what was going on. I should have backed off and given you the space and time you needed to heal."

"You were with me all day, every day in ICU." Tim leaned forward. "You helped me get back on my feet, and you tried your hardest to get me to open up when I slipped into depression. I was in a dark, dark place then. I just wanted out. I thought distancing myself from you would somehow ease my pain. I've never been so wrong about anything in my life. So I don't know what you're talking about abandoning me; I'm the one who walked away from you and Ruby. This is all my fault."

Cynth giggled, slowly at first. She covered her mouth with her hand but burst into a full laugh.

"What in the world is so funny?"

"We can't even apologize to each other without fighting. We're hopeless."

Tim smirked. "Well, I'm more hopeless than you."

"No, I think I've got the market cornered on hopelessness." She didn't give an inch. "And I'm pretty pathetic, too."

Tim reveled in a deep belly laugh. He'd forgotten what joy was like. It had been an interesting day, to say the least. He gazed up at the stars in wonder. How had God been so patient with him all these years, waiting for him to throw down his pride and anger? He had much to learn about his God. And he was eager to get started.

"I'm really sorry for hurting you and Ruby." Tim shuffled his feet and then looked at Cynth again. "If I could take back anything in my life, it would be that."

"I know. I'm sorry, too. I wish I could change things as well."

"Back to my original question, Cynth. Where does that leave us?"

"Always the detective." She smiled. "You never forget what question you're on."

He bent over and took her hand. "Nope."

"No matter how angry I ever was at you or how much I wanted to shake the life out of you, I never, ever stopped loving you, Timothy Porter."

"You are the only woman I've ever loved, and that hasn't changed since the day we first met."

"Let's make a deal then." Cynth flashed a wry grin.

Tim nodded. "I'm game."

"Let's take care of Ruby first. Then we can see where we're going."

"Agreed." Tim slapped a mosquito on his neck. "Man, these things are vicious. We better get inside."

Ruby spotted Byron in the bustling hallway leading to the auditorium and jogged toward him, grabbing his arm.

"Hey." Byron turned and smiled. Looking left then right, he pulled her into a nook, away from the students filing into the auditorium. "Are you ready to give your testimony? How're you feeling now? You look a whole lot better, not that you looked bad or anything. You just look at peace."

She covered his mouth with the tips of her fingers. "Try not to speak for a moment. I have something very important to say."

He nodded, her fingers still planted firmly against his mouth.

"Do you trust me, Byron?"

"Of course," he mumbled.

"Do you love me?"

His eyes widened, and shock covered his face, as if her head had suddenly caught fire. She knew she'd blindsided him, but there wasn't time to be coy; she needed to know.

He nodded again without saying anything. She had hoped for a loud, affirming "yes," but this would have to do. Soon she would see how much he loved her, or if their feelings were all just a charade, like everything else around her.

"Do you have questions about what's happening here?" She pulled her hand away from his mouth.

"Ruby, you're starting to scare me. What do you mean by all this? I just don't understand. You gotta help me out here. I'm trying."

"Do you really trust me?"

"With everything that I have." His eyes locked onto hers. "Please tell me what's going on."

"I will tell you everything, but you have to promise to listen. That's all I ask."

"Absolutely."

"There you are," Cliff called from down the hall. "Ruby, it's almost time, dear. I need you down here now."

"I have to go." She glanced at Cliff and then turned back to Byron. "Remember, listen to what I say. You promised you'd listen."

"I will, I promise."

She leaned forward and kissed him. "I love you, Byron." She turned and hurried toward Cliff, who held the back door to the auditorium open.

"Come on, Ruby." Cliff tapped his wristwatch. "It's almost time."

Ruby entered the door, and she and Cliff stood at the back of the auditorium stage. She could see all of the students filing in and taking their seats. It was packed. Everyone would be here. Perfect.

"Now, Ruby, have you prepared your speech?"

"I've worked on it all day today." While she had worked on it all day, churning the thoughts and emotions around and around in her head, she hadn't come up with exactly what she wanted to say—what she *had* to say. Oh, well. Nothing like winging it.

"Excellent. Now you know what Dr. Simmons likes to hear. How your life was nothing until you met him and discovered his system. And how he's not just a teacher but more of a father figure. That one always gets to him. And you need to mention how your family has never supported you in anything. You know, just *your* testimony. Dr. Simmons was very excited knowing that you'd be the one speaking. I know you're going to give us a thrilling talk today."

"God willing," she whispered.

Cliff took her by the shoulders. "Are you ready?"

"As ready as I can be."

He straightened his shirt, pushed up his glasses, then strode onto the stage to the applause of the students. He waved and smiled as he ambled toward the microphone.

The cheers erupted even louder as Dr. Simmons entered the stage from the other direction. He bowed slightly toward the crowd and ascended his throne, set on the stage for that purpose.

"Thank you, students." Cliff held up his arms and stopped the applause. "Tonight we have a wonderful treat for you and Dr. Simmons. One of our top students has decided to give her testimony, and I think each of you will benefit from her knowledge and dedication to the Higher Learning Method and to Dr. Simmons himself. So please, let's give our attention to Ms. Ruby Porter."

Cliff backed away as he applauded for her.

Ruby walked to the microphone and tapped on it to make sure it was on; the thump echoed throughout the hall. She smiled sheepishly and rubbed her hand up and down on her jeans. The sweat was flowing before she even started speaking. She didn't know if she could do this. *God, help me here.*

She stared into the eyes of all the students. Everyone seemed so eager to hear what she had to say. In the time she'd been here, she'd grown to know many of them. They were her friends, people who, like her, gave up their lives to come to this place with hopes and dreams of making a difference in the world and to find the truth to guide them in their chaotic, lost lives. They thought that Dr. Walter Simmons was the one man with all the answers, the one who could fulfill their dreams. They needed to know the Truth. That thought strengthened her.

She glanced at Dr. Simmons, who was a mere thirty feet away from her onstage, perched on his kingly chair, as if he were looking down on all the peasants. He smiled at her and then winked. Her stomach tossed.

"Thank you all for being here today." She'd worked on the speech over and over in her mind, but she wasn't positive until that moment, looking into his depraved eyes, what she would say. It was time.

"I really want to share my testimony with you, and I hope it enlightens and encourages each of you here today." Her voice was strong and rang clear throughout the auditorium.

Dr. Simmons bowed his head, giving his approval, and folded his hands over his lap.

"Coming to the Higher Learning Center has changed my life in ways I never dreamed it would. And Dr. Simmons has been the agent of that change."

The crowd applauded, some standing to their feet and yelling out.

Ruby took the microphone off of the stand and sauntered to the opposite end of the stage from Dr. Simmons. "But that change might not be what you-all are thinking."

She shifted and glared at Dr. Simmons, who tilted his head and raised an eyebrow.

"You see, in my home growing up, my parents supported me in everything I ever did. They loved me, nurtured me, and blessed me in so many ways I can't even count. My mother spent every day helping me learn and grow and encouraging me at every turn. My grandfather bounced me on his knees and told me stories from the Bible. My father treated me with respect and showered me with nothing but joy, kindness, and unconditional love. I was his baby girl and could do no wrong in his eyes."

Ruby stopped and glanced down, trying to stay composed. She had to get through this. She looked up and saw Kara sitting in a row near the back. She was crying and nodding to Ruby. An uneasy rustling reverberated throughout the audience.

"And I turned my back on these people to follow you." Ruby turned quickly to face Dr. Simmons. "My father is not perfect. He's made mistakes and stumbled and fell, but no matter what happened, I always knew that he loved me. I know this is the part of my testimony where I'm supposed to say that you've become like my father. But let me tell you something, *Dr. Simmons.*"

She held her finger up, facing his stare head-on. She'd never waver again.

"You, sir, are *not* my father. You bear no resemblance to him in form or character. My father respected me. My father never lied to me. My father never *used* me."

"I think we've heard quite enough of your *testimony*, Ruby." Cliff scrambled across the stage toward her.

"I'll stop when I'm finished." Ruby swung around and pointed an angry, determined finger at him. The blood of her father and mother surged through her veins. And the Spirit of her true Father filled her soul. "So don't even think about coming any closer."

Cliff stayed put as if his feet had suddenly been nailed to the floor. Dr. Simmons squirmed in his chair and clenched the armrests, his knuckles white and shaking.

"And now I'm supposed to tell everyone how you 'saved' me from whatever dysfunction I'm supposed to have come from." She shook her head. "How could I have ever fallen for that garbage? There is only one Savior. And, again, you are *not* Him. You're a cheap imitation, a counterfeit, a phony, and a liar. I came here thinking I was running toward the truth, but what I've discovered is that the Truth has been running after me. There is only one Savior, one God, and one way to peace and salvation. And it's through Jesus Christ. May God forgive me for ever getting involved with a deceiver like you."

"Enough!" Dr. Simmons jumped to his feet, the veins popping out of the side of his neck. "Silence her now."

Todd stomped across the stage and reached for the microphone. Ruby turned her back on him and continued, "Dr. Simmons tried to seduce me, and he raped Kara. He's a liar and a psycho."

The microphone squealed across the speakers as Todd ripped it from Ruby's grasp. He hoisted her on his shoulders, carrying her toward the exit.

Byron jumped onto the stage and sprinted toward Ruby. "Put her down, you gorilla!" Todd turned and punched him in the chest, knocking the wind out of him and sliding him across the stage.

Ruby flutter kicked in his arms. "Let me go. I want to leave."

The crowd rumbled and roared, some leaving their seats, others sitting, stunned at the spectacle.

"Take her to my office." Dr. Simmons thrust his hand toward the door. "We'll deal with her there."

He turned to the distressed crowd. He straightened his shirt and lifted a hand into the air. "Everyone, please calm down. I fear Ms. Porter is suffering from some sort of religiously induced psychosis. We will be treating her accordingly. Please, don't let her breakdown inhibit your training. She will be fine, and everything will be back on track soon. I promise that to each of you. I think it's time that everyone go to their rooms and reflect on their last course of study."

Todd marched with Ruby on his shoulders toward the office as Byron scrambled to his feet and rushed toward them. Cliff stopped him with a hand on his chest.

"What's happening? Where are you taking her?"

"That's none of your business, Byron." Cliff pushed Byron backward. "Now go back to your room, and wait for your orders."

"I'm making it my business." Byron brushed past him and took Ruby by the hand, pulling her back against Todd's powerful stride.

"Ruby, I love you." He locked eyes with her. "I do love you—with all my heart."

"Let me go, you ox." Ruby hammered on Todd's back twice with her petite fists, but the shots ricocheted off like BBs off a grizzly's hide. "I want to leave. You can't keep me here. Now let me down."

Two more security personnel grabbed Byron by the arms and pulled him back. "Let her go! You're hurting her."

Dr. Simmons turned to Byron. "She'll be okay."

"What are you doing to her?" Byron wiggled his arms away from the guards.

"She's having a psychological breakdown." Dr. Simmons set a

hand on Byron's shoulder. "I've seen these things a thousand times. She needs to be taken to a quiet, calm place where she can pull herself together. I know you're concerned for her—we all are—but I give you my word that I will be personally monitoring and caring for her. I will see that she's brought back into the fold."

Byron said nothing as Ruby was ushered into Dr. Simmons's office.

40

"You're hurting me, you big jerk!"

Todd set Ruby down at the door but held firm to her forearm and tugged her into Dr. Simmons's office. She yanked against his meat hooks, but to no avail.

"Shut up," he grumbled. "Don't you think you've done enough damage for one day?"

Cliff trailed them into the room and pointed to a chair in front of Dr. Simmons's desk. "Sit her down there, now."

Todd hauled her over and wrenched her arm down, forcing her to sit.

"Ruby, you are a huge disappointment to Dr. Simmons and me." Cliff was out of breath as he paced in a circle in front of the desk. "And you know he doesn't like to be disappointed, much less humiliated in front of the entire assembly."

"I'll apologize if you can tell me one thing I said that wasn't true." She crossed her arms.

"It's all a pack of lies," Cliff barked. "Someone's gotten to you and filled your head with this religious rubbish and delusional thinking."

The office door swung open and crashed against the wall, almost knocking it off its hinges. Dr. Simmons paused in the doorway, his fists clenched at his sides, quaking at the sight of Ruby.

"Who in the world do you think you are?" He stomped toward her, the whites of his eyes radiating rage. "Who are you, you parasitic little ingrate, to challenge me?"

Ruby stayed calm as he loomed over her. She should have been afraid, but she wasn't. A peace she'd never known settled on her. She stared Dr. Simmons in the eyes. "You didn't say that last night when you were laying your filthy paws on me."

He lunged forward and seized her face, squeezing her cheeks tight, and lifted her to her feet. She grabbed his wrist with both hands.

He wrung ever tighter as he growled. "You will get up in front of everyone tomorrow and recant your nonsense." He was barely able to contain himself.

"Not in a millions years. I'm leaving you and this wicked place, and I will never come back. I've believed your lies long enough."

"You aren't going anywhere, *Ms. Porter*. You will stay here until your sanity returns."

Ruby chuckled; Dr. Simmons was a fine one to be talking about sanity. "You can't hold me here against my will."

"My will is your will. You have no thoughts that I don't give to you. You have no will that I don't give to you. Understand?"

Ruby shook her head. "I don't understand. And I will not follow you or your perverted plan anymore. I'm leaving."

Cliff stepped forward. "Maybe we should—"

"Silence!" Dr. Simmons hissed without even looking at him. "Leave us."

Todd hurried from the room, but Cliff paused at the door, finally closing it.

Dr. Simmons waited as the door closed. As soon as they were alone, he tightened his grip on her, and his face resembled the one she'd seen just the night before—the true Walter Simmons, the one he concealed from everyone, probably even Cliff. His wild, fanatical eyes murdered her again and again in a matter of seconds. The man was more than demented; he was consumed with evil.

"No one ever leaves me." He pulled her close to his face, his hot, foul breath assailing her. He kissed her. She squirmed and struggled, pushing him away. He released his grip.

"You're insane!" She spit on the floor. "I'll never follow you again."

"We'll see about that, Ms. Porter. Todd, come back in here." Dr. Simmons grinned while adjusting his shirt. Todd was through the door and rushing toward his desk in seconds. "Take Ms. Porter downstairs please. She needs some time for quiet reflection."

Dr. Simmons walked over to a door parallel with his desk and opened it, revealing a stairwell.

"Bring her to the basement with me." He disappeared down the corridor.

"I'm not going anywhere with you," she screamed as Todd clutched her arm and dragged her toward the door. "Noooooo!"

Byron shook his head as he fled Dr. Simmons's office. What was happening? How did everything get so crazy so quick? Was Ruby okay? Ruby was many things—vivacious and full of life, beautiful, brilliant, sweet—but she was *not* insane. She didn't look like she'd had any kind of breakdown. She looked…angry.

Her last words onstage careened through his mind. What if it was true that Dr. Simmons had tried to seduce her? And did he attack Kara, too? It couldn't be. There had to be some sort of misunderstanding. Dr. Simmons was gifted, a man light-years ahead of his time. It couldn't be possible that he'd stoop to such a low. There was no way Byron could have been that wrong about him.

One of Todd's monster trucks crept past the front window on the grass with two armed guards inside.

Byron didn't know what to think anymore, but he was willing—and determined—to find out. He bounded up the stairs two at a time toward Ruby and Kara's room. He pounded on the door.

"Who is it?" Kara called out, her voice quivering.

"It's Byron. Open up, Kara. We gotta talk."

"Who's with you?"

"No one. I'm alone. Now open the door."

The door unlocked and opened a crack, revealing just a sliver of Kara's face. "Are you sure you're alone?"

"Yes, please let me in. It's important."

She opened the door, and Byron hurried in. She locked it behind him. Kara was dressed in a black T-shirt and dark jeans. Her eyes were as red as her hair, and mascara streaks striped her face. A backpack stuffed full of clothes lay on the bed.

"You're leaving?"

Kara wiped her face and sniffled. "Yes."

Byron didn't know what to say. How could he ask? But he had to know the truth…even if it was painful for them both.

"What happened, Kara?" Byron managed in a whisper.

Her face clouded over. "What does it matter now? You wouldn't believe me if I told you. You're one of his 'top dogs.'"

"I want to know, and I want to help you and Ruby."

"I have to go." She grabbed her backpack, the tears flowing unobstructed. "If I don't go now, I might never be able to." She walked toward the door, her bag in tow.

Byron stepped in front of her, his hands out. "Please, Kara. Did Dr. Simmons attack you? That's all I want to know."

She held his gaze as the tears flowed down her cheeks. "Yes. He did…a lot. Whenever he wanted to. And I walked in on him when he was groping Ruby, too. There, does that make you feel better? He's a maniac and a pervert and who knows what else."

Bryon staggered back, his hands dropping to his sides, blind-sided by her revelation. He turned away; he was going to be sick. How he wanted to defend Dr. Simmons, convincing Kara—and himself—that she simply misinterpreted what happened, that he would never do such a wicked, vile thing.

But Byron searched her eyes, her body language, her broken spirit. And then there was Ruby, who wouldn't lie, not like that. Kara spoke only the truth. The nausea morphed into disgust, then rage. "We've got to tell someone. We can go to the police and tell them what happened."

"Yeah, like I haven't thought of that. Who are they going to believe? Someone like me?" Kara held her hands out. "*Hel-lo*. A college dropout and loser who chose to come to this awful place on a nutty dream? Or the great and mighty Dr. Simmons? It will be my word against his. They'll crucify me."

She slung her backpack over one shoulder and headed toward the door. He gently grabbed her arm and looked her in the eyes. "I believe you. And if we go to the police, I'll stand by you."

"I can't do that, Byron. I'm not strong enough. He'll buy a pack of lawyers, and they will eat me alive. I just want to leave this crazy place and never come back. I don't know what I was thinking when I came here."

As full of steam and vigor as he was, Bryon respected her predicament. After what she'd already been through, he certainly didn't want to leave her here to possibly fall victim again. She needed to get to safety, and then there was Ruby… First things first.

"The guards are out in full force tonight. How are you planning to get out? They might hassle you if they see you, especially after Ruby's tirade."

"I don't have a plan. I'm just gonna go and see what happens. I don't care anymore. I don't care what happens to me. I just want out."

Byron thought for a moment. "I have an idea."

Byron strolled out the front door of the administration building with Kara ducked down behind him, shielding her from the view of the guard in the shack at the front gate. He was looking at a magazine. Byron scanned up and down the fence line. No roaming patrols in sight.

"Go now!"

Kara peeled off and ducked into a shrub line along the side of the building. Byron continued toward the guard shack and almost made it to the back door before the guard noticed him.

"Hey!" The guard tucked a magazine underneath the table. "No one is supposed to be out here after lockdown. Doctor's orders. It's not safe."

Byron feigned a smile. "I thought I would go for a walk."

The guard tilted his head. "Didn't you hear what I just said? This gate doesn't open for anyone after hours, except Dr. Simmons. It's for your protection. Now you need to go back to your room."

As the guard's attention focused on Byron, Kara slipped from the shadows and hurried toward the fence.

"What are you reading there?"

The guard looked down at the magazine, which sported a scantily clad woman in a seductive pose. "Just a little man entertainment. It gets awful lonely out here on the midnight shift."

"Oh, I can imagine." Byron grinned so hard his face hurt. He hoped he wasn't overdoing it.

Kara made it to the fence and tossed her bag over, the "thud" echoing back to them. Byron coughed twice, hoping to mask the sound. Kara scaled the fence like a spider monkey and jumped down from the top. Snatching her bag, she walked backward for a few steps, locking eyes with Byron. Her devastated expression seared into his soul.

"You need to get moving. I don't want to get in trouble for not doing my job."

"Sure, I understand." Byron turned to catch a fleeting glimpse of Kara's white sneakers fleeing into the night. Now on to the rest of his plan.

41

I can't sleep," Tim called over to John in the other bed.

The motel room was dark, save a golden streak slicing through the curtains from the streetlight in the parking lot. Tucked in the corner of the room on a rollaway bed, Alan snored as if competing with the ancient air conditioner for The Most Irritating Noise Ever Award. Alan's guttural eruptions were winning by a long shot.

"Neither can I." John slapped his arms along his sides. "Mainly because you keep waking me up telling me that you can't sleep."

"I'm sorry." Tim stared at the popcorn ceiling of the tacky motel room. Ruby haunted his every waking thought, as well as his dreams. He wondered what she was doing at that very moment. Was she sitting with friends somewhere, listening to the recorded lessons of the Twister of Truths? Was she sleeping soundly, with no concern for anything? Or was she fighting for her life against a madman? He played the scenarios over and over in his mind. It was exhausting, but he couldn't stop himself. He rolled to his side. "Do you want to do a little recon? Get a look around?"

"I suppose I'm gonna have to." John tossed the cover off. "Because we certainly aren't going to get any sleep like this."

"I figured we could get a look at the nighttime security. It might help down the road." Tim was still committed to waiting to hear something from Ruby or to see some kind of sign, but it couldn't hurt to lay the groundwork just in case.

John sat up and rubbed his eyes. "Well, let's get it done. Do you have the night-vision goggles?"

"Of course." Tim jumped from the bed. That Russell was truly a good egg. The man was beat but still wanted to indulge him in this. The recon wouldn't hurt either. They could get a look at the nighttime patrols and do a little sentry watching. It was boring but revealing work. They might find a weakness at the HLC, or Hideous Lying Center as Tim liked to call it.

And maybe, just maybe, he could catch a glimpse of Ruby.

He'd changed cars and surveillance vehicles so many times driving by that building, hoping and praying to see her. He didn't know what he'd do if he actually did. He might slam on the brakes and sprint toward her and squeeze her tight, never letting go. He could dream.

John dressed quickly and grabbed the surveillance equipment bags on the way out. Alan's nasal waves didn't miss a beat as the door to the motel room shut.

Tim and John decided to use the green minivan. Everyone on the planet it seemed drove minivans these days, so they fit in anywhere, even in Highpoint. In a few short moments, they rumbled toward town.

Tim positioned himself in the backseat as they passed the "Welcome to Highpoint" sign. As they cruised into the sleepy town, the streetlights illuminated their path toward the mind-twisting monolith known as the Higher Learning Center.

They coasted past the front gate; a lone sentry manned the brick guard shack. He didn't look up to see them. Tim snapped a series of shots with the infrared camera. They parked around the curve, just out of sight of the security.

Tim stared at the sprawling campus, its modern buildings and fake trappings enticing those around to come to its gates. "She's right in there." Tim pointed to the roof of one of the buildings. "My baby girl is caught in a web of treachery and lies, and she's in there somewhere, just outta my sight. I could be looking at the very room she's in, and I can't do a thing about it. She might as well be on the other side of the planet."

"I can't imagine what that must be like, Tim. Do you wanna pray?"

"I don't know if I can pray out loud, but I'm willing to try."

"No worries, partner. Just follow the Spirit."

Tim had never prayed with another man, other than as a child with his father. He wasn't sure what to do, but if this was going to work, God would have to be with them. "Okay, Russell. You lead."

"Dear, Lord." John bowed his head. "Lift the scales from Ruby's eyes and bless her. Let her hear Your voice and know that You love her and that we love her and that she belongs to You. And bless Tim, one of Your flock now. Be with him and guide his steps...guide our steps. Amen."

"Amen." Tim wiped his eyes and looked back at the black hole that had swallowed his daughter. "This is tough, John. This waiting around, waiting for something else to happen. Or for her to come to her senses. It's killing me."

"I know, but we have to wait for God to open up the opportunity. We'll know when the time is right."

"Give me something tangible. I mean, how will we know when God is opening up the right time?"

"We both pray and keep our eyes and ears open and listen for His voice." John scanned the area with the night-vision goggles. No movement. How many times had he hoped for a conversation like this with Tim? He only wished it came at a better time and circumstance. But he'd take what he could get. John had prayed long and hard for Tim's conversion; now he'd take that energy and help him grow in his faith.

Tim sighed. "But how will we know when God's talking? How do you know that something is meant for you as a sign, not just some coincidence?"

"Trust me." John scanned the building again. "When God shows up on this case, we'll know it. There will be no doubt that He is talking with you."

"Byron, my friend." Cliff's tone was unconvincing as Byron strolled into Cliff's office. "Did you sleep well?"

"What sleep?" Byron stopped in front of Cliff's desk. "How's Ruby? I want to see her."

"Physically, she's fine." He touched his pen between his lip and nose as Byron glared at him. "But we fear for her mental state right now. Dr. Simmons and I were hoping that you could talk with her, you know, talk some sense into her. She needs to be encouraged to get back on track with her training. This course she's taken has Dr. Simmons quite concerned. Religious psychosis can be a very dangerous thing."

"I'll do what I can. I just want to see her."

"Dr. Simmons has written down some guidelines for you to discuss with her, to bring her back into clear thinking." Cliff handed him three pages of notes.

Bryon thumbed through them quickly. He was to make numerous references to Dr. Simmons's teachings and to assure her that everything would be okay. She would be more than welcome back in the group. Byron didn't know what to think anymore. But he needed to see Ruby.

"Where is she?"

"Follow me." Cliff led the way into Dr. Simmons's office. He wasn't there. Where could he be? Cliff walked toward a door that paralleled the desk. He'd been in the doctor's office a number of times and wondered where that door led, thinking maybe it was a closet or an extra sitting room. Now he would find out.

Cliff opened the door, which revealed a stairway down. They followed the metal stairs to a small hallway with three doors in a row on the right side. The corridor was sterile white, like a laboratory.

One of Todd's security men stood next to the middle door. A tall Hispanic man had a pistol strapped to his side and a Fu Manchu mustache. Gaudy diamond studs adorned each ear. He stepped to the side without saying a word as Cliff and Byron approached the door.

Cliff pulled a set of keys from his pocket. "How's she been?"

The man stepped aside. "Quiet."

"Good."

"What is this place?" Byron checked the corridor from floor to ceiling. In the months he'd been here, he'd never seen or heard of any rooms underneath the facility. What in the world would they need this stuff for? And why was Ruby down here?

"We have some extra rooms and storage down here." Cliff turned the key and opened the thick metal door. "You never know when something like this can come in handy."

Ruby was lying on a small bed next to the wall with her hands folded over her stomach. She was in the same blue jeans and shirt she wore the night before and didn't move when Cliff entered the room, but she sprang to her feet when she saw Byron.

She ran toward him, but the security guard stepped in front of her.

"It's okay, Herb. You can wait outside." Cliff waved him out. The large man walked back into the corridor.

The room was about the size of a jail cell and had a set of dresser drawers on the opposite wall from the bed. A CD player was on top of the dresser with two stacks of CDs, all of Dr. Simmons's teachings. His books, pamphlets, and study guides littered the floor.

"I'll leave you two alone for a few moments." Cliff closed the door behind him when he left.

Ruby threw herself into his arms. "I'm so glad to see you."

"Are you okay?"

"I think so." She brushed her hair back.

"What happened, Ruby? That got all crazy and out of hand last night."

She stepped back, scanned the room in an overly dramatic way, then pointed to her ear and scratched it. She was trying to tell him something. They were being listened to.

"I've found the Truth, and I'm not going to let go now."

Ruby had a determined confidence he'd never heard from her before. It threw him off a little. He wasn't convinced they were being eavesdropped on, but after what he'd learned in the last twenty-four hours, he couldn't be sure of anything anymore.

If someone was listening, Byron would at least make it sound good. He lifted the pages in his hand and tilted his head. "Maybe you should listen to Dr. Simmons's CD on *The Folly of Modern Religion*?"

"Byron, I asked you yesterday to listen to me. Now listen to me, and listen to your heart. What does your heart tell you about what's going on here? Didn't you hear anything I said?"

"I heard every word. And they've been flashing through my mind all night." He felt like a fool. They were playing a word game, a charade of cat and mouse, with someone who might or might not be listening to their conversation. Maybe Ruby had lost her mind? And maybe he had, too?

Byron stared into her eyes, her beautifully alive eyes. He

loved her. And she was no crazier than he was. Someone in this sham was crazy, and it wasn't either of them. He didn't understand all of her God-talk from the night before, but it didn't matter to him now.

"Have you talked with Kara?" she asked.

Byron paused. If someone was indeed listening, he didn't want to give away too much. But he didn't like the idea of lying to Ruby, no matter the reason.

Cliff opened the door and poked his head in. "Are you two finished?"

"No. Could Ruby and I take a walk around the grounds and get her some fresh air?" Byron hoped that he could get her alone and make their break for the gates, but he doubted he'd get that lucky.

"I don't think that's possible." Cliff frowned. "Dr. Simmons feels it's best for Ruby if she stays here."

"But I don't want to stay here." Ruby moved forward. "I want to leave now and leave forever."

"I'm afraid that's not possible, Ruby dear."

Byron turned to Cliff. "Why can't Ruby leave? She should be able to go wherever she wants."

Cliff stepped closer to Byron. "She is under the care of the greatest psychologist ever. If he says she needs to stay indoors for treatment, then she needs to stay indoors."

"Against her will?"

"Byron, I thought you would be an ally in helping us help Ruby. But it appears that your thinking might have become as tortured as hers."

"It just seems to me that if she wants to leave, she should be able to leave...without interference."

"We are responsible for the well-being of every student here." Cliff adjusted his glasses. "And when one of those students has a psychological episode, we must deal with it. It's our responsibility.

She's not well enough to be back with us yet. But we're hopeful, with your help, that she'll be ready to return soon, very soon."

Byron regarded Ruby, who shook her head at him ever so slightly.

"I think it's time for you to go." Cliff grabbed Byron's arm to lead him out of the room.

"Can I say good-bye?" Ruby asked. "Please?"

"Fine then." Cliff rolled his eyes. "Make it quick."

Ruby kissed Byron on the cheek at the same time he felt a piece of paper slide into his hand. He gripped it, keeping it out of Cliff's sight.

"We're all in danger," she whispered in his ear. "Get my father. I love you."

He squeezed her hand and walked backward out of the room, Ruby's forlorn countenance tempting him to run back in, scoop her up, and whisk her away from this place forever. But temperance won out; he'd never be able to accomplish that alone.

Herb slammed the door shut and locked it.

"Don't you *ever* cross me in front of a student again." Cliff pointed a stubby finger in his face. "You need to pull yourself together. Get back to your room right now and meditate. You're losing your focus."

"No problem; I won't do it again." Byron squeezed the note firmly in his hand. *Not to your face anyway, jerk.*

Walter zoomed the security camera onto the northwest corner of the complex. A form crept from the shrubs there and sprinted toward the fence. Byron could be clearly seen as he bounded over the fence with a security guard on an ATV skidding behind him just as he cleared the fence. Byron sprinted toward Highpoint.

"Why do we pay security personnel if they can't do their

jobs?" Walter massaged his temples. Cliff and Todd gathered with him in the security office with a guard at the helm of the elaborate camera system. "Play the tape from last night."

The guard pressed a series of buttons. The main screen showed Byron walking out of the administration building with Kara behind him, then her ducking off into the shadows. Byron proceeded down the sidewalk to the gate and distracted the guard. Kara scaled the fence and disappeared from sight.

Cliff pushed the stop button. "Tell me why no one stopped this."

Todd fumbled and shuffled his feet. "Well, uh, it looks like the night monitor was on a bathroom break when she jumped the fence."

"How convenient," Walter hissed. "I want the guards doubled. I don't care who you have to hire. I will not have these little ingrates just leaving whenever they want to. No one—and I mean no one—leaves this complex, do you understand?"

42

Where is China?" Tim paced the aisles between the bookshelves, grumbling. He checked his watch. "She should be here by now."

"Try to stay calm." John's words bounced off Tim like rain off a duck's back. He couldn't blame him a bit, but Tim still needed to keep composed until they had more information. John took a seat at one of the tables at the Glades County Public Library, just outside of Highpoint.

"How can I stay calm?" Tim held his hands out. "Little miss Barbie doll calls and says Ruby's in trouble and we gotta meet. This seems like a perfect time to get agitated and upset. I promised you I'd wait and be patient. Well, I have been. Now it's time for action."

"Keep your voice down." John nodded to the librarian at her desk. She pushed her glasses up on her nose and glared at them.

Tim crammed his hands in his pockets, and his rigid body continued to pace, his breathing coming in short pants. As much as it pained John to see Tim this agitated, it was somewhat refreshing to see him boil to life again. The weeks of insecurity and fear had taken a toll, dragging him into a depression. Tim wasn't depressed anymore; he was angry.

China hurried through the front door of the library, a dark-haired young man trailing her who shared her purposed gait.

China brushed her hair out of her face. "Thank you for coming so quickly."

"Who's your friend?" John pointed to the young man.

"Byron." He seized John's hand and shook it vigorously. "Byron Macy." He was excited, too, and his hands were sweaty.

"Byron?" Tim marched toward him. "The same Byron who's friends with my Ruby?"

He extended his hand to Tim. "I'm so glad to finally meet Ruby's father."

Tim lurched closer, his fingers coiling into fists. "The same Byron who got my little girl involved in this mess? Who helped those people suck the life outta my child?" Tim went nose to nose with the boy, who swallowed hard and quivered.

"The same." He cast his eyes toward the floor.

"Easy, partner." Seeing that Byron was on the verge of a serious thumping, John rested a hand on Tim's shoulder.

China slipped next to Tim. "He's come to help."

"Give me one reason why I shouldn't rip your head off right now." Tim abused him with his glare, ignoring everyone else. "And you better make it quick."

"I can't." Byron kept his head low. "Everything you said is true. I drew her into this mess. I believed in that lowlife Dr. Simmons and led I don't know how many people into this craziness. I'm responsible, and I hate myself for it." He finally lifted his head and met Tim's stare head-on. "But something else happened along the way. I fell in love with your daughter, Mr. Porter. So you can tear my head off, but my heart will still belong to Ruby."

"You've got a real strange way of showing it." Tim growled.

"Ruby needs help." Byron stepped back. "I would gladly trade my life to make this right."

"Please, let him speak." China's exasperated tone carried throughout the library. "It's important, and we might be running out of time."

Tim backed two steps away, his arms relaxing some. "What do you have to tell us?"

"Ruby went a little crazy when she was supposed to be giving her testimony to the students and Dr. Simmons."

"Tell them what she said." China clasped her hands in front of her and closed her eyes as if in prayer.

"She said Jesus was Lord, not Dr. Simmons." Byron rested back against a table next to them. "He was none too happy about that."

"Praise God!" China rocked back and forth to her own rhythm. "Praise God Almighty. That's answered prayer."

Tim smiled and nodded. "That is good news. I really needed to hear that."

"But something's happened, Mr. Porter." Byron's voice grew more energized. "I think Ruby's in danger."

"Is she okay?" Tim scrunched his face. "What's happened?"

"After she told Dr. Simmons off, she was taken to a room, like a basement, underneath the campus. I never knew it was there. She wants to leave, but they won't let her. She needs our help."

"They're holding my baby against her will?" Tim raised to his tiptoes, his eyes wild, raging. "What are we doing standing around here? We need to get up there now!"

"Let's go." Byron pushed off the table and headed toward the door. "We can be there in less than twenty minutes."

"Where does this *we* come from?" Tim slapped his thick mitt on Byron's chest, stopping him cold.

"If you're going up to help Ruby, I'm going with you." Byron glanced over at John. "Besides, I have some things I need to say to Dr. Simmons...personally."

"You're the reason Ruby's there." Tim locked his arm out

straight. "I think you've done enough."

"If you don't want me to go, Mr. Porter, you're gonna have to stop me yourself." Byron pressed against Tim's hand, meeting him eye to eye. "Because I'm going after Ruby, no matter what you think about it."

Tim grimaced, growled, then grinned. "You've got guts, man. You're dumb as a stump, but you've got guts."

"Okay, let's slow down and do this right." John stepped between the two. Life was returning to John, too, as they finally had something resembling evidence. "Byron, will you be willing to swear out an affidavit on what you saw?"

"Absolutely! Whatever you need me to do." Byron turned back to Tim. "I do love her, sir."

Tim folded his arms. "Yeah, we'll see."

John held fast to the bench he was sitting on as the brakes of the panel truck squealed to a stop at the front gate of the Higher Leaning Center.

The guard swaggered from the shack and greeted the driver. "Do you have a delivery today?"

"Sure do. Can you sign this?" Alan held out a clipboard with a search warrant for the Higher Learning Center attached to it.

"Ah...uh." The shocked guard looked up at Alan.

Alan hopped from the van. "We're agents with the Florida Department of Law Enforcement. You don't want to impede our progress in any way. If you do, you will spend many miserable nights in the county jail. Got it? Now open this gate."

"I...I." The guard held his hand out, a bewildered expression covering his face.

"Never mind. I'll do it myself." Alan jogged into the guard shack and pressed the button that opened the electronic gate.

"Hey, you—"

Alan raised a finger, cutting him off. "Many days in county jail. Now step away from the gate." The guard obliged him and backpedaled down the driveway.

Alan leapt back behind the steering wheel. He could be convincing when he needed to be. Robbie was in the passenger seat; Tim was stuffed in back with John and Byron. They motored ahead through the gate toward the administration building. The first hurdle had been jumped. Now to pierce the interior and move quickly toward the basement.

Two more panel vans followed them in. Fifteen agents from the Fort Myers FDLE office were packed in them, as well as three detectives from the Glades County Sheriff's Department. Representatives from the Highpoint PD were conspicuously absent. John had called Moses and asked him to stay out of the area for as long as possible so they could at least get on the property without a problem.

John was surprised at how fast he had been able to put together the task force and get a search warrant signed by a circuit court judge. He needed to go above a county court judge to get the warrant signed because he didn't know how many connections a man like Dr. Simmons might have. Now if the day went well, they could find Ruby and possibly Mitch, wrap up their case, and head home. John's pulse quickened as they neared the building.

"Tim," Alan barked without looking back. "Stay low and stay quiet. We'll head straight for the room she's being held in. If we encounter any problems, let us deal with it. Understand?"

"No problem, boss." Tim fiddled with a zipper on his raid vest. "I'll behave. Just get my Ruby outta there."

John was proud of Tim. He'd promised to contain himself, and he even agreed not to carry his standard MP5 submachine gun. He just needed to be with his daughter, and he'd do whatever was necessary to accomplish that.

"Byron." John adjusted the ammo pouch on his raid vest. "It's a huge facility, so I want you to lead us right to the room. We don't want to be messing around and wasting time."

"No problem. I can't wait to see the looks on their faces."

The vans skidded to a stop, and everyone leapt from the vans and marched into the lobby, where a stunned receptionist froze at their sight.

"We need Dr. Simmons right now," John ordered.

"I'm right here, Agent Russell." Simmons sauntered from his office with Todd on one side and Cliff on the other. "How can I help you gentlemen today? Maybe some regressive therapy?"

"We have a search warrant for the entire campus for one Ruby Porter and any and all evidence that would support her kidnapping and false imprisonment."

Dr. Simmons covered his mouth as he chuckled. "False imprisonment? Kidnapping? You *gentlemen* certainly do have vivid imaginations."

"You need to order your security team to stand down while we're here." John faced Todd. "We're here for lawful purposes and certainly don't need an incident."

Dr. Simmons gave Todd a nod.

"All security personnel report to the office and stow your weapons," Todd called over his handheld radio. "We've got a load of cops running around out here. I'll let you know when all is clear."

"Very good. Now we'll be heading to your office." John held a copy of the warrant at his side. Tim hovered just behind him. "And please don't resist."

"Resist?" Dr. Simmons held his stomach as he laughed even harder. "I'll lead the way."

John and half of the detectives followed Dr. Simmons into his office. The other half fanned out across the complex. Robbie led two other agents to secure and search Ruby's dorm room. Several more conducted corridor searches and kept security at bay while interviewing other students.

John's cell phone vibrated. He opened the phone and was greeted with a deafening, "What do you think you're doing?"

"Special Agent Sweeney." John had grown increasingly familiar with the tartness in her voice. "I'd love to chat, but we're busy right now executing a search warrant at the Higher Learning Center."

"That's why I called. If you had enough information to get a search warrant, why didn't you contact me first?"

"I couldn't." John caught Tim's attention. "Remember, you didn't give me your number."

John's answer was greeted by an infuriated hush. He imagined she was searching for a way to strangle him through the wireless connection.

"Are you looking for the Porter girl?"

"Yes, and I have to go. We're a little busy solving this case."

"I hope you find what you're looking for. Because if you don't, you are so off this case."

"Thank you…I think." John entered Dr. Simmons's office. "Gotta go."

"Save this number in your cell. Call me when you're done." She hung up.

"So what's this all about, officers?" Dr. Simmons stood in front of his desk with Cliff at his side.

"You don't have to answer any of their questions without an attorney present." Cliff panned the crowd of officers and Byron.

Tim remained behind John. He figured it was Tim's way of keeping an obstacle between him and Dr. Simmons lest he give in to the temptation to pounce on the man. "I'm quite aware of my rights, my friend." Dr. Simmons waved him down. "First, you come here looking for a missing student; now you accuse me of holding another. Really, gentlemen, can't you get your accusations straight?"

"She's in a room right through that door and down a flight of stairs." Byron pointed to the door.

"We're very disappointed in you." Cliff glared at Byron. "We had such big plans for you, and you turn around and accuse Dr. Simmons of something like this?"

"Well, let's just go downstairs and find out who's telling the truth." Byron walked toward the door.

"Doctor." John held out the warrant. "I think you need to open that door, or we'll tear it off its hinges."

"No need for such drama, Agent Russell." Dr. Simmons retrieved a key from his pocket and unlocked the door. He leaned in the darkened corridor and flipped the light switch that illuminated the stairwell. Tim whisked around John and hurried ahead of everyone to the bottom step.

"Ruby!" Tim's voice echoed in the hallway. "Ruby, where are you?"

The three doors on the right were all open, and John smelled fresh paint.

"She was here." Byron directed them to the middle door. "She was right in here."

The group surveyed the room, which had a small bed and a dresser in it. Numerous books and CDs were lying around. The wooden door was flimsy, not the strong metal one Byron had described, and certainly not one that could hold a prisoner against her will.

No sign of Ruby.

"I'm telling you, she was here, and they wouldn't let her go.

And this door was metal and had a thick lock on it." Byron turned to Dr. Simmons. "What have you done with Ruby?"

"You've got about three seconds, Dr. Jekyll, to cowboy up and tell me where my daughter has gone, or we're gonna have a big problem." Tim brushed past John into the hallway.

"You probably should have called first." Dr. Simmons folded his hands in front of him. "Ruby and I had a wonderful talk last night. She's so insightful. She told me she needed to take some time away to meditate on her studies. She's left on a spiritual sojourn. I don't know where she is right now."

"Another 'spiritual sojourn'?" Tim quaked. "You better give me my daughter."

"*Your* daughter?" Dr. Simmons smirked. "I don't think so. She's *my* daughter now, Detective. I'm her *true* father."

Tim lunged, hands outstretched, at Dr. Simmons's neck. John and Alan grabbed him, holding on for the ride. "If something's happened to her, so help me, I'll kill you with my bare hands."

"Bring it on, cop." With his fists up, Todd leapt in front of Dr. Simmons. "I'll take you out right here."

Chief Bennington jogged down the stairs and barged into the room with Moses right behind him. "You need to settle Agent Porter down. I can't believe you even let him come in here. Your agency is harassing an innocent man."

"That means a lot coming from his lapdog." John's disgust rang throughout the hallway. The man had no shame showing up to defend Simmons.

"You, *Agent Russell*, are about this close to seeing the inside of the Highpoint city jail." Chief Bennington pinched his fingers together.

"You better think long and hard about that decision, Chief." Alan posted in front of Bennington. "If you hamper my agents' investigation one iota, I'll have your law enforcement certification yanked so fast it'll make your head spin like a cue ball. You wouldn't even be able to work as a meter man when I finished with you."

"You need to control your men." Chief Bennington jabbed his finger at Tim, who was still in John's grasp and snarling at Dr. Simmons.

Alan glanced over his shoulder. "Tim, stand down or leave. Those are your only options."

Tim stepped back, eyeing Dr. Simmons and Todd. "Something's happened to her. I know it. And these guys know where she is."

Dr. Simmons shrugged. "It appears your information is not accurate, Agents. Ruby left the campus last night and has started her spiritual sojourn. We wish her well. That's all the information I have for you."

"I think you need to come to our office to make a formal statement." John needed to get Simmons somewhere away from his turf so John could shake him up a bit, maybe get the truth from him, if Simmons had any idea what truth sounded like.

"I'll contact my attorney about that." Dr. Simmons crossed his arms. "But I'm quite sure he'll tell me not to give any more statements in this case or in any other. I've been more than cooperative every time you've talked with me. But this is harassment, and I won't stand for that. Now, I want you off my property—pronto."

"We'll leave when we've finished searching." John squeezed the warrant in his hand. "And not one second before."

"Very well, search to your hearts' content." Dr. Simmons tossed his hands in the air. "But Ruby Porter is nowhere near Highpoint anymore. And that's all I have to say on this issue."

John couldn't make him talk, but he could certainly make

him uncomfortable. They'd take their time and conduct a methodical, room by room search. As irritated as he was with Dr. Simmons, John's concerns bubbled to the surface. The man was too cool about the agents searching around, and the door on Ruby's "cell" had been replaced along with the addition of a fresh coat of paint.

The two other rooms off the hallway ended up clear as well. John had hoped for any bit of information tucked away in there, but nothing surfaced, not for Ruby or Mitch. Was John losing his mind? Were all of his suspicions pointless? Or was Dr. Simmons much craftier than he even suspected?

John cleared the other rooms and stomped his way back upstairs with the others behind him. Maybe he'd waited too long. It had taken twelve hours to put the task force together and get the search warrant signed. He should have just come straight here like Tim wanted to, but they were way outmanned and outgunned. John wanted everything legal and in place to fry Dr. Simmons.

Where in the world could Ruby be? Could this Byron have come along just to throw off the investigation? John had more questions than answers. The group reassembled in Dr. Simmons's office.

"You need to stay here while we search the rest of the complex." John told Dr. Simmons, whose maddening smirk remained painted on his face like some deranged circus clown. Alan stayed in the room to watch over Dr. Simmons, Cliff, and Todd.

John, Tim, and Byron left the room. "Take us to Ruby's room." Byron nodded at John, and they all hustled toward the dorms.

"This cannot be happening, John." Tim jogged next to him. "That maniac has done something. I can feel it."

"Stay calm, partner." They were running out of time, but he needed to keep Tim sane. "She's gonna turn up."

Two agents from the Fort Myers office stood sentry duty at the door to Ruby's room. One guy opened the door at their approach. Robbie was inside, searching the dresser drawers with her rubber gloves on.

"I found this under the bed." Robbie handed John Ruby's Bible. He opened it, revealing the inscription from China.

"Well, Ruby was definitely here." John tucked the Bible under his arm. "Anything else turn up?"

Robbie shook her head. "Nothing of value. The room's been cleaned out. I don't know what to tell you, Tim."

"What are we gonna do, John?" Tim propped himself against the wall and dropped his head in his hands. "We've got to do something, anything."

"We still have agents searching the grounds and interviewing the students." John leaned down, hoping to get a clear look into Tim's eyes. It didn't happen. "She's gonna turn up. You have to keep telling yourself that, and praying."

"Oh, I've been doing that." Tim finally pushed off the wall and regained his composure.

"Me, too." Robbie rested a gloved hand on his shoulder. "And we're not done yet. Keep it together, big guy."

The team slowly assembled in the administration building lobby. Dr. Simmons, Cliff, Todd, Chief Bennington, and Moses stood at one end of the room. John huddled with Alan, Tim, Robbie, and Byron at the other end.

"Several dozen students have been interviewed." Alan read from his notes. "They all related the same story about her being onstage and then taken off. No one has seen her since. The grounds have been searched and re-searched. Every closet and every room has been gone through. There's no sign of her."

Tim forced his hands into his pockets. "She's here, and these scumbags have done something with her."

"We've done everything the scope of the search warrant has stated." Alan lowered his clipboard. "We've looked everywhere, and she's not here. Tim, I'm sorry, but there's nothing else we can do. We have to leave now and figure something else out. Maybe Ruby has left, as they said."

Byron's fists shook at his side. "She wouldn't leave without contacting me. No way. She wanted out; she told me so herself. They're all a pack of lying dogs."

"That may be." Alan rubbed his beard, as if trying to scrape it from his face. "But we can't prove a thing...yet."

"We can't leave. We need to tear this place apart brick by brick until we find her." Tim stomped his foot on the highly buffed floor.

"It's over." Alan sighed. "I'm calling it now. We took a shot and were wrong. And now I'll have to explain why we served a search warrant on this place and came up empty. That's not going to be fun. You can trust me on that."

"But she's my daughter." Tim held his hands out, as if he were cradling the lifeless memory of his child. "My little girl."

Alan's eyes were weary. "I'm sorry, but we have no more legal standing here. We'll back up and figure another way to deal with this, but for right now, we're done."

Tim dropped his hands and looked like his soul had been snatched from him, leaving only his shell.

"Stay here and behave." Alan turned to John. "You and I need to close this thing out."

They ambled across the long lobby; Dr. Simmons's smirk tormented their every step.

"We will be leaving now." Pangs of failure racked John's body like a swift punch in the gut. He should have had things in place to work the warrant faster—a prewritten warrant or better surveillance. Handing a copy of the search warrant to Dr. Simmons,

John battled a noxious mix of rage, nausea, and fear. What had they done with Ruby?

"So you didn't find what you were looking for?" Dr. Simmons beamed. "What a surprise. I'm sure when my attorneys are finished suing your sad little agency, you will probably be seeking employment elsewhere."

His gloating fueled John's rage, but what could he say? He couldn't care less about his job now. Ruby's safety and Tim's sanity were all that mattered.

"Chief Bennington," Simmons said with his chin raised. "I would like trespass orders issued against Mr. Porter and Byron. They aren't welcome here."

"And you and any of your buddies at FDLE aren't welcome here either." Chief Bennington pointed his finger at John. "I told you to leave this man and his people alone, but you wouldn't listen. You big state boys had to come down here and open up a can of trouble. Now you're gonna eat it."

"Fine, Chief." Alan's hand went up. "Give it a rest. We're leaving."

"Moses, escort these *gentlemen* off Dr. Simmons's property."

"Glad to, Chief." Moses motioned to them to head to the door. "C'mon. Time to go."

John had one trump card left, a little tidbit of information he wanted to see Dr. Simmons's reaction to. Debating whether to play it, John thought through his options. He didn't want to let Simmons know what he knew, but he had nothing to lose at this point. And he needed to see Simmons squirm a bit.

John turned and walked backward. "Oh, Dr. Simmons. I met a friend of yours. Bill wanted me to tell you hello."

With the cocky smirk still pasted on his face, Simmons nodded at him. "Oh, really now. Bill who?"

"Bill Patterson. We had an in-depth discussion about you,

Lesley Ann, and Lake Tarpon. Very interesting stuff. And what a tragedy. Have a nice day." John winked at him and sauntered toward the front door.

Simmons staggered two steps back. "You…you…get out now! Get off my property!" Spit flew from his frothing mouth.

Bull's-eye. The Lesley Ann comment struck its mark as Dr. Simmons's shrill voice echoed throughout the hall. John, Tim, and the others gathered as they headed out the door.

Tim met John halfway. "What did you say to him?"

"Just shaking the tree, partner." John kept his pace to the doors. "Now we have to see what nuts fall out."

Moses hung back just behind them. "We'll meet tonight back at your place. Now look like I'm being all tough on you." He waved his hand like he was ushering them along. "Keep moving."

43

The parking lot of the Gator Lodge & Inn was packed. John, Alan, Robbie, Tim, Cynthia, and Moses all crammed into the musty motel room. A smile couldn't be found on any face; the somber mood surrounded them, uniting the team in defeat.

Tim didn't know what to say. The adrenaline dump of serving the search warrant earlier had long since faded, and he battled the fatigue.

"We're done here." Alan spoke the words everyone feared but refused to give voice. "I just got off the phone with Director Lyman. It seems our friends at the FBI have already been in contact with him, as well as Dr. Feelgood's attorneys. Tomorrow we're packing up and heading back to Melbourne. After that, I've got to drive to Tallahassee for a meeting with the director. He wants some blood."

"I can't leave." Tim sat on the edge of a dresser with his head lowered and feet dangling like his hope. How could this have happened? Here he was a cop, and he couldn't even save his own daughter from a maniac. Didn't matter what Alan and everyone else was doing now. This was far from over.

"I can't just let this go. These crooked scum aren't going to get away with this. And Ruby's still there and still alive...I can feel it. I'm gonna do what I've gotta do to find her. I'm not going anywhere."

"Tim, we've pushed the envelope on this case already." Alan crossed his arms and propped himself against the wall next to the door. "I've allowed things that under normal circumstances I never would have. We took a shot and tried to solve this case. But it's over, from our end anyway. The Feds are still here, and hopefully they can turn up something."

"This ain't a case to me." Tim stood as a flicker of energy sparked in his spirit for the first time since they'd left the learning center. "It never was. It's about my daughter. She's lost, and I must find her—I will find her!"

"I have a ton of vacation time saved up." John shifted on the bed and faced Alan. "I need to use some now. A couple of weeks maybe."

"Me, too." Robbie smiled and nodded with John. "I'm thinking about doing a little fishing this week. Maybe take in the touristy areas of Glades County, if there are any."

"I'm takin' some time, too." Tim caught Robbie's and John's gazes. The message was loud and clear: They were staying to find Ruby, whatever the outcome. He couldn't ask for better friends.

Alan hesitated and scanned the room, a low grumble emanating from his inner parts. "Fine. I'll approve your *vacations*, but any and all official FDLE duties from this point forward are quashed. Whatever you do here, you will not be doing as police officers. Do you-all really know what you're opening yourselves up to? Lawsuits. Criminal prosecution. Are you ready to face that?"

Robbie moved over to one side of Tim while John walked to the other. "We know the risks. Just like we know the risks of doing nothing."

"I won't bail you out, and I certainly can't be a party to this. I've got two boys in college and can't throw my career away now. You-all are on your own. I'm sorry."

"So am I." Tim gritted his teeth. "You gotta do what you gotta do, Alan, and so do I. I'm not leaving without Ruby."

"C'mon, Alan." Robbie eased toward him. "We're going to need everyone here. You know in your heart they've done something with Ruby. We can't leave Tim hanging like this. Help us."

"I'm sorry, Tim." Alan's eyes cast down toward the carpet, and he shook his head. "I just can't."

"Well, I've never walked out on a friend before, and I'm not about to start now," Robbie said. "Friends don't walk out on friends, no matter the cost."

"Alan, I'm staying for as long as it takes." John laid a hand on Tim's shoulder. "We need your help."

"I'm packing my things and will be gone tonight." Alan swung the door open and hurried into the parking lot. "You-all should do the same."

The slamming door announced the first splinter in the team. John massaged his face, hoping he could rub some wisdom and insight into himself. How long before they would completely unravel? What if it took weeks to find any leads? What if none were found at all? Marie always told him he clung too tightly to his cases. What else could he do?

Tim was right, though; this was more than just another case. Tim's only child teetered in the balance. Should they just wait for the FBI to possibly hear some useful "chatter" or see something on their loose surveillance? The hopelessness overwhelmed John. *Lord, please help us. The gloves are off now.*

"I'll still keep my eyes and ears open." Moses broke the painful silence. "I'm here for you-all, but I'm at a loss. I don't know what else we can do."

John's phone chirped; he looked at the number. Sweeney.

Great. Just what he needed. John flipped his phone open. "You did keep your word."

"I told you I would." A little less sarcasm than usual carried in her voice. "And for what it's worth, I'm sorry you didn't find her."

"So am I." John turned his back to Tim. "What do you want now?"

"Nothing. I just wanted to let you know that we're still here. And the chatter has been long and loud since you left."

"Anything of value?"

"Not yet," she said. "But we're on it. It seems that you have certainly stirred the hornet's nest."

"Look, we're off the case." A lemon-sized lump formed in John's throat as he spoke the words. "But will you at least call me if something shakes out? This is personal for us."

"I'll see what I can do. Now go home. We've got it from here, and we're not giving up on this yet." She disconnected before he could answer.

"FBI?" Tim asked. "Was she gloating?"

"Not exactly." John closed the phone slowly. "It seems we've gotten 'em a little shaken up at the Higher Learning Center tonight."

"Please, Walter." Cliff held his hands out, palms up. "Let's get rid of Ruby and move on. She can only be a hindrance now. They came here with a warrant, for goodness sake. What if they return? What if they had found the safe room? We can't risk all the good you're doing, not again."

"Don't be so spineless." Walter led Cliff down the steps to the basement—the second basement. The three-room design mirrored the other underground set of rooms. "I told you they would never find this." He searched his pockets for the key. "They'd never even consider the possibility that we had built more than one basement into our plan."

"I hope you're right." Cliff's voice quavered.

"Of course I'm right." Walter inserted the key into the metal door and unlocked it. As they entered the room, Ruby clambered to her feet. "Ah, my dearest Ruby. Your father sends his regards."

She remained silent, her hands clasped in front of her. "I want to leave."

"Clifford." Walter slipped the key back into his pocket. "Give us a private moment please."

Cliff hesitated and then backed out of the room, closing the door.

"Ruby, dear." He approached his cherished but obstinate flower, reaching for her lovely hair. She pulled away. "Have you come to your senses yet? Have you realized that I'm your destiny? I had such great plans for us."

"There is no *us*. I'm leaving and will never, ever have anything to do with you again. You lie and manipulate, your *system* is evil...and you're insane."

He seized her throat and slammed her into the wall. "No one leaves me, Ruby Porter. No one ever leaves me. I made you. You *owe* me your loyalty. I own you."

No matter how captivating, no matter how gifted she was, if Ruby continued to deny her destiny, he would pluck her from his garden like a malignant weed threatening to choke the life from the blossoms he'd so carefully planted. She would not defy him.

"I gave my heart and soul to God. My body is only temporary. You own nothing of me."

"You better pray to your so-called God," Walter hissed. "Because if you don't turn back to me, you'll be seeing Him soon."

"So be it." Ruby's eyes bulged as he constricted even more. "Anything He has to offer is better than being here with you."

44

"I don't think I can stand to look at his face." Tim walked back and forth across the motel room floor.

"Think of it as case preparation." John flipped through the television channels with the remote until he stopped on the weekly news program *American Journal*. "Trust me, this could prove to be…instructive. Here we go."

"I'm Megan Conrad and welcome to *American Journal*." The attractive woman introduced the show. In her midthirties with dark brown hair, a full figure, and thick glasses, she sat in a swivel chair on the set. "We have as our guest tonight Dr. Walter Simmons, founder of the Higher Learning Method, bestselling author, and motivational teacher."

"Oh, great." Tim wiggled his fingers in the air. "He's just gonna cast his little spell on her. In two minutes, she'll be swooning over him. None of these reporters are ever gonna ask him the tough questions. Let's turn this off, Russell. It's makin' me sick already." He was tired of this man manipulating and working the crowds. It seemed pointless.

"Be patient, partner." John rested his hand on his chin, covering his mouth. "You never know what you're gonna see."

Russell was acting weird. He was up to something. The

man should play poker; he kept his cards close.

"What's up?" Tim plopped into the retro-seventies green chair in the corner of the room.

"Just wait." John lifted a hand but kept his gaze fixed on the television.

"So tell me about the Higher Learning Method." Megan rested her elbows on her crossed legs.

Dr. Simmons, dressed in his usual sweater and jeans, beamed and launched his prosaic description of the wonders of his system. Megan nodded and smiled at appropriate times.

"You're killing me, Russell." Tim massaged his forehead. The man's voice always gave him a headache. It was all he could do not to kick the TV in. *Lord, I'm tryin', but I need help. All I want to do is hurt that man.*

"Wow." Megan adjusted her glasses as she cued into the camera. "That all sounds so amazing."

"It really is." Dr. Simmons bent forward and touched her hand. "You should really come down and visit us sometime."

"That's very kind of you, Dr. Simmons." She turned back to him. "But my film crew has already been to your *campus*."

"Is that so?" He bent back, raising an eyebrow at her.

A film clip flashed on the screen of the front gate of the Higher Learning Center with a guard driving slowing by with a rifle strapped over his back.

"I think this is where it starts getting good." John's shoulders quivered as he giggled.

"All of what you said about your system sounds nice." Megan uncrossed her legs and pulled a notebook from the side of her chair. "But a number of serious allegations have surfaced about your system and your methods."

"Why, whatever do you mean?" He forced a grin while facing the camera.

"For instance, at least two of your students have been missing from your facility for some time—their whereabouts unknown. And isn't it true that just a few days ago, agents from the Florida Department of Law Enforcement raided your campus, looking for these students?"

"Well, I…I…" He alternated his gaze between Megan and the camera. "It wasn't a 'raid.' What a poor choice of words. We've been assisting law enforcement in their—"

"Isn't it also true that you were the only *witness* in the tragic and suspicious death of your childhood girlfriend, Ms. Lesley Ann Patterson?" Her high school picture rolled onto the screen. Her radiant blue eyes and gregarious smile still effective after all these years. .

"Who…who told you that?" He squeezed the arms of the sofa, his knuckles ivory. "Who have you been talking with?" The whites of his eyes radiated his rage.

"Isn't it also true that many people are now referring to your *system* as more of a cult of celebrity than a serious course of study?" She ignored his inquiry and folded over her first page of notes. "That you and you alone are the sole influence upon your students? There seems to be a plethora of accusations and odd occurrences that surround you and your system, Dr. Simmons. Do you have an explanation for that?"

"Lies! All lies and distortions from those who fear me. My enemies are everywhere and want nothing more than to destroy me and stop my work. They fear progress. They fear what my system is capable of." His head whipped back and forth, flipping his hair in wild directions.

"And just what is your system capable of, Doctor?" Megan didn't budge one bit.

"Every man's dream—Utopia." His hands raised as if he'd

scored the winning touchdown and was reaping his adoration. "Man's perfection of himself."

"With you in charge, I assume?" She canted her head, ready for the answer.

"Of course." He shifted in his chair, attempting to regain his composure. "There must always be one who leads. I am the only one who can lead the way for man's escalation to the next level of human evolution, and I will not let anyone, and I mean anyone, stand in the way of that."

"Can you understand why most people might find that a little disturbing?" She scrunched her nose at the camera.

Dr. Simmons drew in a deep breath as he glared at her. "You're one of them, aren't you?"

A confident smile adorned her face. She was tough, determined, and not fooled by this deceiver. She had drawn him in perfectly, and it was great TV. Tim really liked this woman.

"So, Dr. Simmons, that leads me back to the question of the missing students." Pictures of Mitch and Ruby covered the TV. "Do you know what has happened to these kids?"

He unclipped the microphone from his shirt and tossed it at her, then stomped out of the studio, kicking the back door open.

The camera returned to Megan, who grinned and shrugged. "After our commercial break, we'll be speaking with Bill Patterson, whose daughter Lesley Ann drowned mysteriously over twenty-seven years ago while on a trip *alone* with her then sweetheart Walter Simmons."

John hit the mute button and smirked. "I love this show. You never know what you're gonna get."

"I can't believe that!" Tim leapt to his feet. "Did you see what she did? Someone finally exposed this guy. Now everyone will know who and what he really is. This is fantastic!"

John laughed. "Yeah. I don't think that was the interview Simmons was hoping for."

"What did you do?" Tim wagged a finger at him. "You've done something. I can see it in your face."

John shrugged. "She takes e-mail at her website. I just sent her a little information and pointed her in the right direction. Megan did the rest."

"You can be a very bad man, Russell." Tim nodded. "Very bad. You've been hanging out with me too long."

"Maybe so. He had to be exposed, Tim. I debated whether I should tell you or not. I finally decided to surprise you. We couldn't let anyone else be sucked into his twisted worldview, and we needed a little extra push here in town."

"So what do we do now?" Tim felt like sprinting to the Hideous Lying Center right now and causing more trouble. Russell had really fired him up, but he had given him some hope as well. It was good timing and well needed.

"Well, we'll see if there's any more 'chatter' for the FBI." John's cell phone chirped. He checked the number and then flipped the phone up. "Your ears must have been burning."

Tim could hear the screaming on the other end. Kate Sweeney must be a fan of *American Journal*, too.

With her back against the cold, hard wall of her cell, Ruby folded her hands on her stomach and stared into the oblivion of her dark room. Cliff called it her "meditation room." She was only here for time to "reflect" on Dr. Simmons's teachings. It was locked and she couldn't leave. Regardless of the euphemisms used, it was still a cell.

But no matter how locked down she was, for the first time in her life she felt free; she knew who she was and what she wanted.

Peace dwelled in her soul now that she'd never known before. An odd woman with an open Bible had turned everything Ruby knew or thought she knew upside down—Jesus had died for her sins so she could make peace with God. Little else mattered now. Dozens of her grandfather's stories flashed before her, suddenly making sense. The Scriptures China had given her took on new life.

Her father and mother, how they must be yearning for her return, like the Prodigal Son she'd read about. Their faces burned indelibly into her mind. "Lord, whatever else happens, let Mom and Dad know what You've done in my life and that I love them and have returned home in my heart."

She thought of Byron. Did he make it out? Had he tried to help her? Or did he fall in line with Dr. Simmons and throw her off as well? She hadn't seen him in several days and was tempted to believe that he'd abandoned her.

She closed her eyes and remembered the walks and conversations they'd had, the times they'd shared. Warmth wrapped around her: The same feeling she had whenever Byron was near her. Byron didn't walk out on her. God was letting her know. She could not wait to share the Truth with the man she loved.

Raising her hands, she lifted praises and prayers toward the heavens. No matter what happened from this point forward, her life could never be the same.

45

Everyone move back, please." Moses herded the throng of reporters to the sidewalk. As stressful as it was keeping up with the craziness in town, he rejoiced that the truth about Simmons and this place was finally coming out.

The front of the Higher Learning Center resembled a war zone. Satellite trucks representing news and tabloid agencies from around the country had poured into Highpoint, camping out across the street. Reporters circled the front gate like sharks stalking their prey and would intermittently dash to the fence to snap photos, only to be chased back by the Highpoint PD.

Moses and two other officers labored to keep the reporters in the area designated for the press. He prayed that John and Tim were tracking down some leads to end this soon.

Anchors were going live with varying versions of Dr. Simmons's meltdown and the goings-on at the learning center, with stories running nonstop on the twenty-four-hour news channels. Dr. Simmons had gone from media darling to the news chum of the moment in just a few short days.

The Higher Learning Center's security was out in full force with ATVs patrolling the fence line. Monster trucks tooled around the complex, while two guards armed with rifles manned the front post.

Chief Bennington swaggered through the sea of reporters, cutting in front of an *ABC News* reporter filming a segment. The correspondent shook his head in disgust. "Let's try it again."

"I can't believe this circus." Chief Bennington removed his Stetson and regarded Moses. "All these vultures here, looking for fresh meat. It turns my stomach."

"You gotta admit, the guy's getting stranger by the minute." Moses probed the chief, hoping he could really see what was going on. Moses' heart was broken that the chief had gone so blind...or worse. There was a time when he really respected the man.

"I don't have to admit anything." The chief worked his hat back onto his head and continued his walk. "This is all a load of nonsense."

"Chief Bennington," a short African-American reporter called. She hurried toward him, microphone out. "Do you have any comment on Dr. Simmons or his students?"

"Only that these people should be left alone." He planted his hands firmly on his hips. "They're not bothering a soul."

"Are you currently investigating the disappearances here, and is the FBI involved?"

"There are no 'disappearances.'" The chief spit on the ground at her feet. "Some kids left school, and that's all there is to it. Now, you people need to pack your things and leave our community."

"Some are comparing Dr. Simmons's group to cults like those of the Branch Davidians in Waco or Jim Jones's group. What do you think of that?"

"It's absurd." He tossed his hand in the air. "And we're certainly not gonna have something like Waco here. So you-all should just leave our fair town and let these people go about their business. You're only making things worse."

"So you don't mind having the Higher Learning Center in your town?" She held the microphone almost on his chin.

"Not at all." Chief Bennington stared defiantly into the camera. "Dr. Simmons and his students are fine citizens, deserving of their privacy just like anyone else."

A cameraman sprinted across the street and stuck his camera through the fence, taping the front of the complex. A guard sped toward him on an ATV from inside the fence line.

"I told you to stay away." The guard raised his pistol over his head. *Crack.* A round fractured the air. The reporters ducked in unison, and Chief Bennington fell prostrate on the sidewalk.

The stunned cameraman shrieked and sprinted back across the street, nearly getting waffled by a passing news truck.

The reporter still held her microphone out toward Chief Bennington, who lifted his head from the pavement and gazed at the learning center.

"So you were saying, Chief?"

Dr. Simmons prowled around his desk. Those degenerate detectives were behind this; they were the only two who knew. And that seditious Megan Conrad would be made to pay, someday, somehow. She would be held accountable, and he would enjoy every second of it.

Cliff poked his head around the door. "Is this a good time, Walter?"

"Of course not, you imbecile. But come in anyway."

"It's been a couple of days, and I hoped you'd had time to calm down."

"Did you think about that before you said it? Now, have you gotten what I asked for?"

Cliff paused. A "yes" finally escaped him.

Walter waved his hand. "Tell me. Don't take all day."

"Well, I contacted your publisher. You have to understand

that a couple of days doesn't make a trend, but it appears that the sales of your books and materials have…well, in their terms, cooled off."

"What does that mean?" Walter trained his eyes on him. "Cooled off?"

"Since the airing of that *program*, the sales have all but stopped. There has been a large quantity of returns to the publisher as well. It seems to be happening worldwide."

His enemies had plotted, planned, conspired until they could finally find a way to stop him. They would never be satisfied; all they wanted was his blood. They would get blood all right, but their own.

"And that's not all." Cliff pursed his lips and then continued. "Requests have flooded my office for more interviews."

"They all want to get their claws into me now." Walter grabbed the top of his chair and spun it around. "That's how these people survive, by chewing and gnawing and ripping apart anyone they can. They are as ignorant and wanting as the rest of the world. I won't be speaking to any of them."

"That's what I've been telling people." Cliff walked to the front of his desk. "Walter, why don't we just graduate this class and lay low for a while until this passes over? Then we can pick right up where we left off. In a couple of months, this will all just be a bad memory. We can start the college tours again and work our way back."

"Graduate them? They're…not ready. I have more training for them, more classes, more growth. They haven't even touched the surface of what I have to offer. There's no way they can go out yet. It's just not possible." He shuffled papers on his desk.

"Over a dozen students have left the campus already." Cliff braced his hands on the desk.

"Left?" Walter canted his head. "Left! Why didn't you tell me this right away? Why have you been hiding this from me? Get that idiot Todd in here, and tighten security. No one is to leave, Clifford, and you know that."

"Walter, let's just let the Porter girl go and start over fresh."

"Let the Porter girl go?" Walter strolled over to him and walked his fingers across Cliff's scalp. "You need to think, my friend. Who do you believe is responsible for all of this? Ruby and her wretched father. It's all their fault. I can't just 'let her go.' If I did, what kind of wild tales do you think she'd tell everyone? What fantastic stories would she share with the Megan Conrads of the world? No, Clifford, we'll have to take care of her in another way."

"I can't go through this again." Cliff's head dropped. "I can't do it."

"You have no choice." Walter stood so close to Cliff that he could smell his mint mouthwash. "We're in this together, my friend. We can ascend to historic heights together, or we crash to the ground in a furious inferno together. Either way, our destinies are inextricably linked now. Never forget that."

Clifford stared at the floor and didn't move. He was weak and pathetic, lacking the spine and the capacity to do what was necessary to move forward. He could be replaced when the time was right.

Walter turned from him and wandered to the window, laying his hand on the warm glass. He gazed out at the choppy, angry waters of Lake Okeechobee. Riotous and belligerent, the voices in his head pounded and screamed, demanding to be let out. They hungered for their vengeance—and they would be fed.

46

Tim could hardly see through the thick, murky haze. He had no idea where he was, but he could still hear her. He swam through the thick fog, and that's when he heard it for the first time. A growl so sinister, so evil, it rocked him to his spirit.

Ruby called to him again. "Daddy, help me. Help!"

Tim fought through the soup of clouds and sludge. With each new step, he sank deeper and deeper into the soggy ground until he was mired waist deep in muck, inching his way forward.

"Daddy!"

"I'm coming!" Tim yelled, fighting with all he had. "I'm coming, Ruby."

The hazy veil lifted at his approach. Ruby was trapped against the side of the mountain. The huge beast prowled and paced in front of her. Its four legs were a combination of muscles and scales, and its long, sharp talons dug into the ground with each step, throwing dirt behind it as it stalked about, taunting its cornered prey.

Tim plowed toward the dragon, which swung its massive head toward him. The beast sported thin whiskers that hung down its face like a mustache, and green venom oozed from its jagged teeth. Its wings spread reflexively as it howled, and a small red ridge ran the length of its body down to the tip of its whiplike tail. The noxious stench of the dragon and fuming sulfur scorched Tim's nostrils as he slogged toward the Beast.

"Nooooo!" Tim screamed.

The dragon screeched a soul-twisting cry, freezing Tim where he stood. He was unable to move, could barely breathe.

The beast swung back toward Ruby and growled a low rumble. Its gigantic paws crept ever closer to her, the ground cracking under its feet.

Tim tried to yell, but nothing came out.

The dragon loomed over Ruby as she cowered into a ball on the ground. The beast smiled and coiled its hideous head. With a flash, it seized Ruby in its mouth, shaking her viciously. The Dragon devoured Ruby as Tim watched helplessly.

Ruby pleaded once more. "Daddy!"

Her voice trailed off as Tim sat bolt upright, the bed shaking as he trembled in horror. His muscle T-shirt was drenched and his heart throbbed, drowning out the air-conditioning window unit. He threw off the covers and stood, wiping the sweat from his face and brow. The torturous nightmare had ended in one sense, still raged on in another.

John was asleep in the bed next to his; Tim didn't want to wake him. There was nothing he could do anyway. Tim had failed Ruby in so many ways. Where was she? Was she safe? If he knew she was actually on a spiritual sojourn, he could at least rest knowing she was alive. He couldn't bring himself to even think of other options.

What had that beast done with his little girl? Cop or no cop, laws or no laws, Tim would find out what happened to her. He crumpled to his knees in a heap of emotion, fear, and anger.

The room was dark, foreboding. John lay just feet away, but Tim felt more alone in that moment than he'd ever felt in his life. Was the dream a sign? Was God trying to warn him? He had to know.

"Lord, show me what to do. I am Yours now. I'll follow whatever You would have me do. But please let me know that You're here."

A presence descended into the room, which suddenly felt bright and alive. Peace fell on him. Someone else was here with him.

"My Lord?" Tim whispered.

The time for waiting was over. They were going in to rescue Ruby, even if they had to pluck her from the belly of the dragon.

John woke as the first evidence of the sun slithered through the grimy curtains of the motel room and chased the stupor from his head. Tim rested on the lone chair in the room with a blanket wrapped around him, looking at the map of the Higher Learning Center still pinned on the wall.

"How'd you sleep?" John rubbed his eyes.

"You don't want to know." Tim was still dressed in his boxers and muscle T-shirt, his thick arms folded.

"I can make a coffee run." John hurled the blanket off him. "As a matter of fact, I *need* to make a coffee run. I'll get us both a cup."

"Fine." Tim's gaze never left the map.

John rolled out of bed, stretched, and slipped on his jeans. He walked toward the map as well. "What's up?"

"We're missing something." Tim rose with the blanket still around him. "I don't know what it is. We've been over everything. I can't explain it, but I keep feeling in my spirit that we have all the information we need. I don't want to sound hokey or crazy, but I think God is trying to tell me something. I just don't know how to listen."

"Who do you think you're talking with here?" John held his hands on his chest. "Remember, your fundamentalist wacko partner? It doesn't sound crazy at all. You got any ideas of what we need to be doing, because I'm fresh out?"

"I had a nightmare last night." Tim pulled the blanket tighter around him. "It was awful, just awful. I think it was a vision, John. Ruby's alive and in terrible danger. When I woke up, I started praying and the love of the Lord came to me. I'm telling you. Ever since then, I've been sitting here drawn to this map. I've been staring at the thing for over two hours now, but I'm not sure what I'm looking for. It's just a topical infrared map of the center."

John smoothed out the photo with a brush of his hand. The red, orange, and yellow hues identified the hot and warm areas by degrees. The concrete walkways could be clearly seen; they were orange, hot from the sun's warmth. None of the foliage showed up, but rather appeared as varying shades of blue or cooler areas.

John propped one hand against the wall. "I don't know what it all means, partner."

Tim regarded the map more closely. "Turn on the light. I didn't want to wake you before, but I see something."

John hurried over and flipped on the light. They surveyed the map; Tim skimmed the right side of the complex with his hand.

"When we were in the basement area." Tim ran his finger along the side of the building. "We were about here, correct?"

John leaned forward. "Yeah, that looks about right."

Tim took the grease pencil from the table and drew a rectangle coming off of the building at the approximate angle and size of the basement they were in. "What do you see here?"

"I see what you just drew."

"But look inside the box." Tim pointed to the addition. "Right where the hallway is that we were in." Two red disks about as round as pencil lead sat inside the box. "Do you see them?" Tim smiled.

"Yeah, but what are they and what do they mean?"

"Look at how perfectly they angle out from the building right in line with the basement. Perfect red-hot circles in line with the basement."

"I still don't get it." John shook his head.

"Air vents." Tim let the blanket fall to the ground. "Hot enough to show up on the infrared photo. Hot enough to leave a trace, but hidden in the foliage and out of sight while we were on the grounds."

"Okay, I understand." John shrugged. "But that doesn't tell us any more than we already know. There's a basement there."

"Exactly, but look over here." Tim went to the other side of the picture and drew the rectangular corridor on it, jetting out in the opposite direction, in perfect alignment with the north building of the Higher Learning Center.

"Oh, man." John grabbed his chin. Two small circular heat objects were on the other side of the complex.

"That's right." Tim tapped the map with his finger. "There's another basement. And we missed it."

"Are you sure about this, Porter? We might be moving too early." John sat on the bed with his elbows resting on his knees.

Tim sat on the other bed and Robbie on the chair. The team's meeting had come early, but there was no more time to waste.

"I know this is a sign. And we're not doing anything too early…maybe too late. I'm telling you, we've got to move as soon as we can set everything in motion, tonight if need be. She's in trouble. Something wicked is coming, and we have to stop it."

"I don't know, partner." John dropped his head. "You're under a lot of stress and emotion. Are you sure you're not misreading this thing? Maybe your dream was born out of that?"

"It was no dream." Tim stood and opened and closed his large fists. He knew what he had seen and how the peace of the

Lord had come to him. But how did he explain it to them? Russell would probably understand, but this could drive Robbie away. They couldn't afford to lose her, too. "It was a vision. And I believe with everything in my being that God has sent me a message that time is short. If we're going to save her, we must move now."

"I'm trying to be there with you." John locked eyes with Tim. "But this is huge.We can't go back for another search warrant. We have no credibility, so we're doing this on our own. And if you're wrong, we stand to lose everything—our jobs, our freedom, and maybe our lives. It's not a decision to make lightly. We're basing our decision on a couple of dots on a map and a nightmare."

"I told you that I trusted you in this, Russell, and I have. I don't regret a moment of that decision. But now I'm asking—no, begging—you to trust me, too. I know I'm right."

"Do you have a plan?" Robbie's hair was pulled back in a ponytail, and she wore a pair of gray sweats, her usual morning attire. "We can't just run up there armed with only good intentions and harsh language. They have two dozen mercenaries with fully automatic weapons and who knows what else."

"I have a plan." Tim nodded. "At least part of one. It's a work in progress, but it's the best chance we have to get Ruby back."

John stood and passed his hand across his thick black hair. "You both need to know that if we do this, there's no going back. We'll be on our own. We could get in some serious trouble, especially if the less-than-gracious Ms. Sweeney has her way."

"I have no choice." Tim faced John. "Byron said she was in there against her will, and I believe him. I'm goin' in with a butter knife if I have to." Tim paused and caught his breath. "But this is my fight, not yours. I understand if you want to back out now. There's no shame in that."

Quiet filled the room as the team searched each other's eyes for strength. Tim prayed quietly. He couldn't ask more of his friends than they'd already given, but if they didn't help him, he was dead in the water, most likely somewhere in Lake Okeechobee.

Robbie smiled first. "I'm in. I could use a little Fed-time anyway. It'll give me a chance to work out a lot and get in great shape."

Tim regarded John, who grinned as well. "I better call Marie and have her get some bail money ready. We're going to the Higher Learning Center."

"Russell, Robbie, you're both good eggs." Tim's voice quivered and his eyes moistened. "I can never repay you for this." What kind of friends would risk everything for him? How did he deserve that? Russell was right: God was showing up big on this case.

"No need, my friend." John placed his hands on his hips. "Now what's your plan?"

"Robbie, I'm gonna need you to pick up and arrange for the supplies we're gonna need." Tim handed her a list.

"John, I'll need you to have the support elements in place." Tim gave him his hastily scratched-out instructions. "Timing is crucial if this is gonna work."

Robbie scanned the list. "We could use more people."

"I know that." Tim sighed. "But we're all we've got, so we'll have to make the best of it."

"We need to pray." John stepped up and bowed his head.

"I thought you'd never ask." Tim grinned. "I'm ready when you are."

Tim and Robbie followed with their heads bowed as John prayed. "O heavenly Father, guide our hands, hearts, and minds. Protect Ruby, bless her, and let us pull this off without anyone getting hurt. Give us Your cover as we seek to save her, Lord. We cannot do this without You."

"And, Lord." Tim's voice cracked. "If we must defend ourselves, make our aim true." He was getting used to this group praying thing.

"Amen."

"We all know what we need to do." Tim drew a purposed breath. "So we'd better get moving."

Tim opened the door and Alan stood outside, just preparing to knock.

"I thought you had a meeting with Director Lyman." Tim held the door open for him. Alan must have come to talk them into leaving. He was too late for that.

Dressed in his blue jeans and a workout shirt, Alan shoved both hands in his pockets and shuffled his feet. "I did. But I told him I needed to take a few days off to work on my boat." He grabbed his suitcase and breezed past Tim, tossing it on the bed. He glared at Robbie. "I don't own a boat. And I've never, ever turned my back on a friend either. Where do we go from here?"

47

Cliff wavered under the stiff breeze off the lake. Perched on the rooftop of the Higher Learning Center, he kept watch on the storm brewing just off the horizon. He surveyed all that he and Walter had built together. He remembered coming to this place and seeing little more than a glorified swamp. Walter had seen the potential, though, and convinced him that this was where their future lay.

The seeds of a worldwide human revolution were germinating on the shores of Lake Okeechobee, the roots of which would spread to every nook and cranny around the world. An exquisite vision—but one he could barely remember now.

"Todd, you need to have all your men on tonight." The warm, steady wind blew Cliff's hair into a chaotic mound as he shifted his attention to the mob of reporters camped out across the street. How far away that vision seemed now. "We are in complete lockdown. No more students leave here, and no one comes in."

With his hands on his hips, Todd grinned, his shirt flapping around his solid frame. "What if the cops come back?"

Cliff worked his lower lip back and forth. If the police returned, everything they'd created would be lost, and the keys to saving the world from itself would be lost as well, probably forever. They were fortunate last time. How he wished it went differently. He understood Walter, but the media made him out to look like some kind of monster. He must be protected, no matter the cost.

"If they come back, you do whatever—and I mean whatever—you need to do to stop them. Do you understand?"

Todd beamed. "Absolutely. I've been waiting for this chance."

As nightfall chased all remnants of daylight out of Highpoint, Demetrius ambled up the rickety steps of the Mount Carmel Worship Center. Dressed in his usual dark suit, tie, and polished leather shoes, he entered the sanctuary. He'd considered wearing jeans and a comfortable shirt, but tonight was time for business, so he dressed accordingly. Brave men and women marched ahead of him, and he must keep up his end of the bargain.

China knelt at the altar, a place Demetrius had seen her often. When did she have time to sleep? She was committed to freeing Ruby and the others in that place of deception. The young woman had no other life than to serve, and she didn't mind it at all. Most women her age were starting their careers or getting married and having babies. She interceded for prisoners of the soul, and Demetrius admired and respected her greatly. What a mighty testament to her Savior she was.

He approached her quietly, not wanting to disturb her.

Lifting her head, she smiled and extended her hand. "It's gonna be a long night."

"Yes, Miss China, it is." Demetrius clasped her hand in his and knelt beside her. "But there are a lot of people counting on us. We must be faithful."

The sanctuary door flung open, and the four prayer warriors of Highpoint hustled toward the altar, with Ms. Isabel pulling up the rear. The floor of the church creaked and groaned as the motivated prayer team pressed forward.

"Sorry we're late, Reverend." Ms. Florence was out of breath, and her purse jiggled from side to side as she hurried toward them. "Satan's tried to slow us down all evening, but we're here now, ready for war."

Just before the door closed, Marie Russell caught it and pushed it open again, jogging just behind the prayer team.

"Marie." Demetrius clapped his hands together. "So glad to have you here with us."

"I wouldn't miss this." Marie joined everyone at the pulpit. "I want to do anything I can to help."

The seven gathered at the front of the church, clenched hands, and formed a circle that would not be broken until they got word from John that all were safe. The weight of their task struck Demetrius as he considered the irony. Here, in their broken, dilapidated house of God, they were going to battle against the power, the money, and the influence of the Higher Learning Center and its chief prophet of deception: Dr. Walter Simmons. By the world's standards, they were outmatched and outgunned. But they possessed a weapon the world rarely considered.

Demetrius bowed and opened their prayer.

48

He can't be that stupid." Cliff zoomed the camera in on the black BMW that pulled off the side of the road just past the front gate of the Higher Learning Center.

A black man and woman jumped from the car. Mrs. Porter was in a short dress and throwing her hand wildly in the air while yelling at Agent Porter, who wore a baseball cap, baggy shirt, and jeans. He looked to be screaming back at her. A few seconds later, he rushed toward the fence and started climbing. Seizing the back of his shirt, she yanked him off and held on to it as she tried to drag him back toward the car.

"Security, it appears that Mr. and Mrs. Porter are back. They're just north of the front gate, and he just tried to climb the fence." Cliff kept his radio in one hand as he adjusted the picture on the security camera on his desk with the other.

"Do you want me to intercept them?" The guard at the front gate called.

"No!" Todd interrupted on the channel. "Stay put. He might try to crash the gate. Patrols, move up front and get ready to grab him if he hops the fence. He's probably armed, so do what you gotta do."

"What are you up to, *Agent* Porter?" Cliff reclined in his chair, rested the radio on his stomach, and watched the spectacle.

Porter would run toward the fence; then his wife would grab him, keeping him from making it over.

"Control, I want you to call Chief Bennington and let him know what's happening. I want that maniac arrested this time." Cliff considered telling Walter but then thought better of it; he didn't need to know anything yet.

The fracas continued at the fence, and several of the guards on ATVs drove into view, parking on the other side of the fence, blocking the way if Porter made it over. At least Todd had his security people in place, or this could get quite messy.

The crazy Porter yelled at them, his arms flailing about. Mrs. Porter pushed him by the chest toward the driver's side of the car. She turned and looked down the street. She ran around the back of the car, and Agent Porter jumped into the driver's seat and peeled out.

Ten seconds later, a patrol car whizzed by the camera, red and blue strobes blazing.

"Chief Bennington's on the scene. This should be over soon." Cliff rested back. There was certainly no need to tell Walter now.

"We're traveling north on 26 out of Highpoint." Chief Bennington gritted his teeth and growled. "It doesn't look like they're gonna stop for me, Dispatch. I'm in pursuit."

"10-4, in pursuit. I'll contact the sheriff's department for backup."

"Porter, you moron. What in the world are you doin'? Cop or no cop, you're going to jail tonight, and when I get my hands on you, you're gonna go in a real painful kinda way."

The black BMW veered off the highway onto a dirt road, a trail of dust blinding the chief for a moment. "Where do you think you're gonna hide? This is my home. I know every rabbit trail here. You're not gonna outrun me."

The BMW slowed down, flashed a turn signal, and eased to the side of the road. Bennington's pulse spiked, and he yearned to wring Porter's neck. He lit up the Beamer with the spotlight.

He marched to the front of the driver's window. "Porter, get out with your hands up." Bennington trained his .357 on the driver's head. "You're under arrest. Get out now!"

There was no answer from the car. He shuffled a little closer and shone his flashlight into the driver's face. "I said get out and on the ground, Porter!"

"Porter?" Moses removed the baseball cap. "Who in the world are you talking to, Chief? I was just giving Cynthia here a tour of our wonderful little town."

"Moses? What in the world are you doing?" He lowered his pistol and holstered it, glancing at Moses, then to Cynthia. "Oh no! They couldn't be!" He sprinted back to his car and squealed the tires as he turned back toward town.

"Wonder where he's going in such a hurry." Moses snickered as he pulled a pillow from underneath his shirt. He turned to Cynthia. "Please don't tell Tim I had a pillow under here. He'll never forgive me."

"I'm putting you in for an Academy Award." She applauded. "You did Tim well. You had that whole 'angry man' thing down."

"The chief didn't say so, but do you think I'm fired?" Moses scrunched his face.

"Oh, you're most definitely fired."

"Could be worse things. I was gettin' tired of that job anyway. Maybe I'll see if FDLE is hiring. Come on." He jammed the car in gear. "We have to get moving."

"That's the last one." Tim watched the sentry scoot around the back side of the building on his ATV toward the front gate. He had bet that when the clash started, the guards in the rear wouldn't be able to resist running to the action. He owed himself ten bucks.

Alan, Robbie, John, and he manned the twelve-foot black rubber boat and rocked with the light breeze on the lake, the tiny waves licking at the sides. About two hundred feet offshore, they were just far enough away that the Higher Learning Center's floodlights didn't illuminate them but close enough to be on the grounds in seconds.

The back of the complex was stunning, with the beautiful courtyard and the horseshoe design of the buildings reflecting off the water. In any other circumstance, it would have been a magnificent place to be.

Tim and Robbie were wedged in front, paddles in hand, dressed in black with camo paint across their faces. They each had a minibackpack strapped on tight with all the supplies they'd need. John and Alan had the rear, oars at the ready.

Scanning the darkened faces of his friends, Tim fought to keep his emotions in check. In three minutes, they could be in the biggest firefight of their lives—all for his daughter. Cops and friends, through and through.

Lord, I know You don't owe me anything. But I'm asking You to bless this mission—in spite of me—and give us success and protect my friends. If anyone has to get it tonight, Lord, let it be me, not Ruby or any of these brave people. I'm ready for whatever You have. Amen.

"All clear. Time to move." Tim dipped his paddle in the water, and the others followed suit.

"Hey, Robbie," Alan whispered as he stirred the murky waters with his paddle. "You said you wanted to do entry on our next operation. Well, welcome to entry."

"Beats dressing like a hooker." Robbie lifted the paddle out and eased it back into the water, her face focused.

The raft skimmed alongside the alligator security fence in the swimming area, and they followed it around, beaching in the shadows. They dragged the boat onto shore and huddled just in front of it.

"All right." Tim raised his MP5 submachine gun and checked the chamber. He adjusted his raid vest, which was loaded down with stun grenades and extra ammo.

John sported an MP5 as well, along with his pistol and a vest packed with toys. If they got pinned down, the submachine guns could lay down some serious fire. Robbie and Alan carried M16s and their sidearms in case there was a heavy firefight.

"Quick in and out. We extract Ruby and Mitch, then we leave. Does everyone understand?" Tim made eye contact with each person. They had gone over the plan again and again, but he had to be sure they understood.

They all nodded. "Good luck and Godspeed," Tim said.

Tim and John crept up through the shadows to the side of the north building. He was confident they could make it in without being detected. Making it out was another story. Alan and Robbie crouched low and darted across the courtyard to the other set of buildings, using as much cover as they could.

If they didn't hit their objective, the whole plan would fall apart, and the likelihood of them getting out, much less finding Ruby or Mitch, was slim to none. There was no turning back now.

49

Ruby attempted to sleep…again. She wasn't sure what time it was since she didn't have a watch and there wasn't a clock in her room. The hours morphed into each other in a jumbled series of thoughts, feelings, and emotions. Keeping focused was becoming more and more difficult. Only prayer kept her calm.

Ruby prayed for her freedom and prayed for her parents, for the hurt and pain she'd caused them. What she wouldn't give to sprint down that long road to them like the Prodigal. She could dream.

A thunderous explosion rocked the building, and Ruby rolled out of her bed and onto the floor. The lights dimmed and went out. Darkness chased any traces of light from the room.

Groping around on the floor, her heart leapt with expectancy. *Daddy?* She smiled. He was coming for her.

"What was that?" Dr. Simmons called on his radio, which he normally kept off when meditating.

Cliff had no idea what to tell him. He was in big trouble. "I think Agent Porter is here." Cliff was unable to hide the stress in his voice. There could be no more pretending.

"What!? Why didn't you tell me this?"

"We have it under control." Cliff stood and walked to the window and peeked out. "The backup generators should be kicking on any second." The lights flashed and flickered back on as the hum of the huge backup generators rumbled throughout the campus. "See, now we can find them and remove them, Walter. Everything will be fine."

Another explosion rattled the building; everything faded to black again. The generators were gone now, too. The students' screams reverberated down the hallways and throughout the campus.

Cliff fumbled his way to the intercom. "Everyone, stay in your rooms. Intruders are on the premises. Let security deal with them."

Staring into the darkness, dread sucking the breath from him, Cliff held his chest. His worst nightmare was coming true—they were coming.

Tim trained his subgun on the door to the north complex as the second explosion leveled the generators. Robbie and Alan were right on time. Now it was John and Tim's turn.

He had studied the map so many times. Once they were in, they could find the stairwell that led down to where his Ruby was being held. It was laid out in exactly the same place as the south building. Ruby was close; he could feel it. He forced his mind back to the task at hand. He couldn't let emotion overtake him. Not yet.

"Let's go, Russell." Tim pulled his night-vision goggles down. "It's party time."

The power outages had shut off the cameras as well, he

hoped. That would be one less worry. By the time the guards found them, it would be too late. He and John breached the door, inspecting the long corridor. Nothing moving, although intermittent screams greeted them like an eerie chorus from a horror movie.

They tiptoed down the hallway, which showed up as a series of green hues as they hugged the walls. The middle of the hall could be bullet central at any moment. Still no movement. Not yet anyway.

Tim guided the way with his MP5 in a three-point sling around his shoulders. The gun was pushed out tight, so he could look down the barrel even with the night vision on. He scanned back and forth, the night-vision goggles drastically limiting his peripheral vision. He didn't want to lead them into an ambush or trip over something like a fool and announce their arrival. They stopped at the auditorium, next to the backstage door. Both men slipped into the doorjambs for cover.

"It's here somewhere." Tim lifted the goggles and unfolded a small map, spreading it out on the floor. He illuminated the map with his red-lensed miniflashlight. "Within this small hallway here. We're right on top of it. Now we gotta find the door."

John and Tim opened several rooms and closets in that location. The entrance was nowhere to be found.

"Where is it?" Tim whispered. "Lord, help us."

50

Kate Sweeney pawed around in the darkness to find the mind-numbing ring that violated her slumber. She slapped the receiver and pulled it to her ear as she lay facedown.

"Sweeney," she mumbled into her pillow. "This better be good."

"What?" She rolled to a sitting position. "Tell me you're kidding. You heard this with your own ears?" She brushed her red hair to the top of her head and held it there.

They can't be that crazy…or maybe they can. She held the phone to her chest for a moment and collected her thoughts. Those insane cops were going after Ruby.

"Group page everyone. Yes, I know what I'm doing. Call everyone now! We've got a situation."

Walter gazed out the window of his office into absolute darkness. He couldn't even see the lake; the gloomy blanket covered everything like a burial shroud. Porter was here. The rotten, filthy, foolish man was in *his* domain.

He'd come for the precious Ruby—Walter's Ruby. If Walter

was going down, everyone was going down. Ruby Porter would never leave him.

He picked up his radio. "Herb!"

"Yes, sir."

"We have intruders." He squeezed the radio firm. "I want you to get rid of the Porter girl, now!"

"Sir? I don't quite understand."

"Kill her, you imbecile. Kill her now, and kill every one of those cops you see. Do you understand that? They're here to get us all."

After a short pause, Herb answered. "Sir, the door's locked, and you have the only set of keys."

"Shoot through the door. Kick it off its hinges. Do whatever you have to, but kill that girl!"

"Yes, sir. Over and out."

Walter fumbled toward his desk and opened the top drawer, removing a Colt .45. He would take care of Agent Porter himself.

"It's got to be right here." Tim pushed the button on his watch, illuminating it for a moment. "We're running out of time. Lord, help us please." Tim opened a closet door, which was nearly as large as a bedroom, and rolled a floor buffing machine into the hallway, then two buckets that had crashed onto the floor, echoing down the corridor as loud as cannon fire.

"Keep it together, partner." John used a doorjamb for cover as he kept a watch on the hallway. "We don't need to broadcast where we are."

"All security personnel." Cliff's sketchy voice resounded over the intercom. "Start sweeping the buildings for any possible intruders. Our perimeter has been breached. Consider all intruders armed and dangerous, so shoot on sight."

"Tim, you've got to hurry." John glanced back at him while keeping his MP5 pointed down the hallway. "We're running out of time."

"It's right here." Tim knelt on the floor. "It matches the exact place we went in on the south building. It's in this stupid closet." Tim yanked the shelving off the closet and kicked it twice.

Voices and approaching boots reverberated down the hallway toward them. "We've got company." John crept back as far as he could against the doorway, raising his weapon.

This was going to get ugly, quick.

Muffled noises and clamor drew Ruby's attention outside her door. Tucked in the corner of the room, she couldn't see anything but the mantle of darkness. Icy fingers raced down her spine. She was in deep trouble. Dr. Simmons wouldn't let anyone find her, no way.

"Please, Lord." She rolled to her knees. "Forgive me. I've been such an idiot. Protect me and my dad. But whatever happens, I'm Yours."

Herb trained his flashlight on the door at the top of the stairs then over to his partner, Jim, a twentysomething giant of a man with a blond flattop haircut and poorly fitting camos.

"The cops are raiding the place again. Dr. Simmons wants us to kill her." Herb chambered a round into his Berretta 9mm.

They could hear the commotion upstairs and someone kicking at the door.

Jim held up his hands. "Hey, I'm just an employee, not a believer. Do whatever you want to do, but I'm not going to Club Fed for killing some girl. Or worse, a cop? This ain't my bag, man."

"What do you want to do?" Herb lowered his weapon.

"Get outta here as fast as we can." Jim looked to the stairway. "I'm not going down for some nut."

"Me either." Herb holstered his weapon. "The good doctor can do his own dirty work. I quit."

The two hustled up the stairs toward the door.

Flashlights bounced off the walls at the end of the hallway. Security was sweeping the building. They would surely find them—and soon. Tim and John eased all the way into the closet and slowly closed the door.

Tim aimed his machine gun at the door. If they opened it, he and John would have to shoot their way out. This wasn't going to end well.

"Please, Lord," Tim whispered. "Help us. We need You now."

He was sure John had been praying the whole time. He'd dragged his partner into a no-win situation. They were trapped in a closet with no back way out. What would happen to Marie and the boys if he got John killed? What about Ruby? His stomach churned and his arms trembled. If the door opened, he would charge forward and place his body in front of John's, taking whatever came. Maybe John would have a chance to make it out then.

A thump came from the shelf behind Tim. He swung his weapon around and lit it up with his flashlight. The shelf jiggled, rolled forward, and canted open. Tim's heart danced at answered prayer. A figure stepped through the passage. Tim wrapped his arm around the man's neck, covering his mouth and placing the MP5 against the side of his head.

"Shhh. Don't move, big fella." Tim pulled the man behind the shelf. A second figure appeared, and John illuminated him.

"Get your hands up." John's MP5 rested just off the man's chin.

"No problem, officers." The man's hands were nearly tickling the ceiling. "We're not gonna resist. We don't want any part of this."

Tim released his grip on the man and removed the pistol from his holster. "Where's the girl? Where is she?"

"She's right down there." The big man motioned down the stairwell. "Honest, we don't want no part of this mess."

"Lead the way now and quietly." John disarmed the second man.

John shone his light on the two as they descended the stairs, Tim and John on their heels. The footsteps stopped at the door of the closet. Tim eased the secret door shut, hoping they didn't know about it either. He'd soon find out.

The hallway was an exact replica of the other basement, with three doors on the right side of the corridor.

"Ruby," Tim called but not too loud.

"Daddy!" he heard from the center door.

"Oh, praise God." Tim laid his face against the door. "Praise God. I'm here, baby. We're going home. I'm takin' you home."

"I love you, Daddy. I'm so sorry for everything."

Tim spun around and rested the barrel of his weapon on the guard's cheek. "Open this door, now!"

"We can't." He shrugged and glanced at his partner. "Only Dr. Simmons has the key."

John turned the big man around and cuffed him with plastic flexcuffs and did the same with the second. "Where's the young man?"

"What young man?" The guard cooperated as he turned around and placed his hands in the small of his back.

"There's another young man here." John zipped the cuffs closed. "Mitch Garrow. Where is he?"

"She's the only one here." He looked over his shoulder at John. "You can check the other rooms. I'm telling you the truth."

John forced both men to the floor and shone the light at the end of his MP5 into two other rooms. John's look told Tim everything he needed to know—Mitch Garrow was still nowhere to be found.

"It's okay, sweetheart." Tim slid his backpack off and rummaged through it. He removed the det-cord. "We brought our own key. John, I need your help."

John hurried over to Tim.

"Ruby, honey, I need you to get out of the path of the door. It's gonna blow straight back." Tim pressed his face against the door as he spoke. "Lie down flat on the other side of the room. This door is history."

"I'm out of the way, Daddy."

"Once we blow this door—" John pushed the last edge of det-cord into place—"everyone's gonna know right where we are. We'll have to fight our way out."

"I know." Tim pulled his machine gun tight against the sling. He was glad Russell was by his side. He couldn't think of anyone else he'd rather be with in this situation. "But we don't have much of a choice. We're gonna hit it and move."

John nodded.

Tim inserted the probes into the det-cord, and he and John backed up to the stairs. Tim nodded to John.

"Here we go." Inside such a small, enclosed place, this blast was gonna be deafening. Tim and John plugged their ears.

The explosion rocked the room, the concussion smacking them both.

The door disappeared into the darkness, smoke and debris rolling into the corridor.

Tim sprinted through the gaping hole. Ruby lifted herself from the floor, and Tim scooped her up in his arms and squeezed her.

"Oh, baby, praise God." Emotion quaked in his voice. The river of tears he'd held back burst forth as he quivered with his only child in his arms. "I'll never let you go again."

"Daddy, I'm so sorry I got you into this." She wept also. "I love you with all my heart. Please forgive me."

"Tim, time to go." John stood at the door, lighting up the hazy room. "You can make up later. We gotta get her outta here. Now!"

"Stay with me and do everything I tell you. We're going home." Tim snatched Ruby's hand, and John lit up the stairwell. They stepped over the two guards on their way out and sprinted up the stairs. "When we get to the top, we're gonna go with the night vision again. We don't want to give them a target. Just keep your hand in mine, baby, and we'll be all right."

John found the lever at the top of the stairs, flipped it, and rolled the door forward, then open. No one was in the closet, and the door had been shut all the way. Security must have missed the hidden door in their sweep.

Tim turned down his goggles. "We're going dark. Just keep a hold of my hand." He squeezed Ruby's hand as tight as he could.

"I'm never letting go again." Ruby returned her father's squeeze.

John opened the door to the hallway. He peeked out, looking left then right. "Let's move."

They scooted into the hallway and hurried toward the back exit.

"They're down here," a voice screamed in the hallway. As least a half dozen men sprinted toward them, flashlights jiggling and weapons drawn.

"Go!" Tim screamed as they rushed toward the exit. Two gunshots rang out behind them.

Tim spun around and let loose a three-round burst, the muzzle flash illuminating the trio like a strobe light. The security officers dived to the ground. Tim could have hit them all if he wanted. But he only needed to slow them down. They would be free soon.

Pop. Pop. Pop. More rounds sailed their way, this time from directly in front of them. Tim, Ruby, and John ducked into a doorway. A valley of rounds knocked chunks out of the doorjamb, sending splinters flying. They were cornered.

"Watch out." John stepped past Ruby and Tim and rolled a stun grenade down the hallway toward the back door, where they needed to go.

Boom! Followed by a brilliant flash. "Aaaah!" The attacker backed down the hallway and out the very door they needed to exit. He must have thought the grenades were real. Tim would use that to his advantage. He stepped out and lobbed one down the hallway in the other direction. Another thunderous explosion shook the building.

"Go now!" Tim and Ruby raced down the hallway toward the door to the outside. Several more gunshots trailed them.

Russell twisted around and cut loose with a blast from his subgun. A yelp of pain and a collapsed guard told them he'd hit his mark.

"Now!" Tim screamed into the radio as he kicked open the back door. "Come in now!" It was a hundred yards to the water; the raft was in sight. He and Ruby were hand in hand running toward freedom. *Step it out...*

The rifle report caught him by surprise as a round ripped into his shoulder, like a spear searing through his back, knocking him over, nearly dragging Ruby down with him. The scalding hole gushed blood immediately. Not again. Fire rolled across his back and shoulders.

The second round came from the roof and scooped up a rut next to Tim's head.

Robbie stepped from the shadows by the raft and emptied her M16 magazine at the sniper on the roof of the complex.

"That'll keep his head down." Robbie and Alan dashed to Tim, who wobbled while trying to stand.

Two ATVs rounded the corner at full throttle. Alan hoisted his rifle up and chewed the ground in front of them with a burst, stopping them cold. The guards spun around and fled back to the front of the buildings.

John slid his arm under Tim's shoulder and lifted him up. Alan took the other side and wrapped his arms around Tim's waist. "Let's get him to the boat." Robbie backpedaled and scanned the back of the Higher Learning Center with her rifle, covering their retreat.

A high-pitched hum closed in on them as a Jet Ski rocketed out of the night toward the shore. Just before hitting land, the driver turned hard and idled just offshore in the shallows.

"Ruby!" Byron called from his Jet Ski. "Get on. Now!"

"I can't leave dad." She stopped at the shore's edge. "He's hurt."

"Go, Ruby." Tim held his wound, which was warm and slick with his own blood. "I'll be all right. You gotta go."

She shook her head. "I'm not leaving without you. Not again. Ever."

"We'll be right behind you." Tim reached up and grabbed her arm. "We did all this for you. Now you must go."

She hesitated and glanced at the faces of the people who'd risked everything to rescue her. She kissed Tim on the head and ran into the lake, wading to Byron's waiting Jet Ski. He reached his arm down and scooped her onto the back. She wrapped her arms around his waist. Byron throttled it, and a rooster tail sprayed toward the shore.

"Thank You, Lord." Tim collapsed by the boat. She was free. No matter what else happened, Ruby was free. Darkness swallowed Ruby and Byron as they escaped into the night. Tim's head swam as the pain throbbed from his wound.

"Get Tim in the boat." John and Alan lifted him and walked into the water. Just a few more feet.

More gunshots violated the night, but these came from the front of the learning center, nowhere near them.

"What in the world is going on?" Robbie tossed her M16 into the raft as she pushed it in the water. "That's not us."

"Let's not worry about it." John treaded into the water with Alan and Tim. "That's their problem. We need to get out while we can."

"Don't move." Dr. Simmons crept from the shadows, his .45 caliber aimed at Tim. "If anyone moves, Agent Porter dies."

Todd emerged next to him, night-vision goggles strapped to his head, aiming his rifle at Tim's chest, his finger on the trigger. They'd been flanked.

"Put Agent Porter on the ground, and step away from him, please." Dr. Simmons waved with his pistol. "And keep your hands away from your weapons, or this could get quite messy."

John and Alan walked Tim back onto the shore and eased him to the ground. John's pistol was holstered, and Alan's M16 was slung over his back. Robbie's rifle was in the boat, and her pistol was holstered as well. No way could Tim get to his weapon in time. Simmons had the drop on them.

"It's over, Simmons." Tim panted, struggling for breath. "Everything is finished, including you. Ruby's free. And if you kill a cop, you'll get the death penalty for sure. Put down your weapons and give yourselves up."

"I don't think so." Simmons hissed as he lunged forward. "I decide when this is over. You...*you* have ruined everything I've worked my whole life for. All of my visions have been destroyed, and now you're going to pay for it. You *all* are going to pay."

Todd inched closer, his rifle locked on Tim, who stared into the barrel. He should be scared, but he wasn't. They had no power over him now. *Lord, I'm ready*.

"Kill him." Dr. Simmons waved his hand. "Then kill the rest of them."

Todd smiled and leaned in. "Say good-bye, cop."

Crack!

As the shot fired, John tackled Tim, covering his body; Alan and Robbie dived and rolled forward—all guns pointing at Todd and Dr. Simmons.

Todd dropped his rifle and staggered back, blood surging from the hole in his chest. He touched the wound, looked up, wobbled, collapsed to his knees, then fell facedown in the mud, the night-vision goggles rolling into Lake Okeechobee.

Kate Sweeney sprinted around the corner with a dozen FBI agents behind her, weapons drawn. "FBI! Drop your gun, Dr. Simmons." She marched toward him, pistol trained on him. "Drop it now!"

Dr. Simmons shook violently but didn't release the pistol. He glared at the agents, who all had him in their sights.

"Please, give me the excuse." Kate's 9mm tickled the side of his head. "Nothing would give me more pleasure than to turn your lights out…forever."

The pistol thumped onto the soggy ground as Dr. Simmons raised his hands. Two FBI agents grabbed his arms and cuffed him.

"Nice shot, Sweeney." Alan holstered his pistol. "I can't believe you hit him from that far away."

"I didn't shoot him." Kate still covered Dr. Simmons as he was being cuffed. "We handled the guys in the front. It got a little hostile, but we just got back here."

"Who fired the shot then?" Tim scooted to a sitting position. John and the team searched the FBI agents' faces and the grounds. No one could be seen.

"I did," a voice called from the shadows where Dr. Simmons and Todd had emerged just minutes before. Chief Bennington came into view, his .357 down at his side, smoke still tumbling from the barrel.

He walked toward Todd and stood over his lifeless body. Bennington shook his head, snapped his pistol back into its holster, and turned to John. "I might be dumb, I might have been deceived, but I have never, ever been dirty."

"It's good to have you back, Chief." John knelt next to Tim.

"How's Porter?" Kate lowered her pistol and hurried to Tim. "He gonna make it?"

"Other than a bullet wound in my shoulder, I'm doin' great." Tim grunted as John applied pressure to the wound.

Kate squatted next to Tim. "More important, Porter. Did you find Ruby? Did you get her out?"

Through winces of pain, Tim grinned. He'd never been so happy to answer a question from a Fed. "She's safe now. We got her out."

"I guess we've got a little bit of cleanup to do then." Kate stood and scanned the small group of tired, grimy cops. She snapped her pistol in the holster and wiped her hands together. "This is the sorriest looking task force I've ever seen."

"I thought you said we weren't a task force." John raised his eyebrows.

"Think about it, Russell." She snapped her fingers twice. "If we're gonna make this thing work, you'll have to keep up with me here. Just work with me on this."

51

Three airboats skipped across the water, winding through the clusters of cattails and reeds, the roar of the propellers violating the serene morning on the lake. A flock of egrets took flight as they closed in on the small island, more like a glorified sandbar, tucked away in the swamps of Glades County.

Cliff held his cuffed hands in front of his face to keep the reeds from slapping him as they passed. John sat behind him with Chief Bennington perched in the driver's seat, which was anchored a good five feet off the deck of the boat.

Two other sheriff's department airboats followed the chief's path. FDLE evidence technicians Barry Watkins and Dawn Worthington sat with Tim in one boat. Alan, Robbie, and Kate Sweeney were in the other.

"Are you sure we're in the right place, Chaffin?" John yelled over the blaring engines. "Remember, no body, no deal."

"I know what I'm doing." Cliff held his glasses to his face. "It's right here."

Chief Bennington lurched the boat forward, beaching it on the shore, rocking everyone. The other boats followed on either side. John jumped out and grabbed Cliff's arm, helping him from the boat. A chain ran from Cliff's cuffs down to the shackles on his feet, and he wore a bright red prison jumpsuit.

He took several measured steps onto the shore. "You really don't need the leg shackles." Cliff did the felon shuffle onto shore. "We're in the middle of a swamp. Where am I going to go? "

"It's policy, Chaffin." John continued to hold Cliff's elbow. "Just watch your step."

"It's just over there." Cliff pointed through the underbrush, his complexion pallid. He faced the water, his back to his crime. "And for what it's worth, I never thought any of this would go this way, and I'm truly sorry for what's happened."

"It's not worth much." Tim sat on the edge of the boat and planted a leg on the earth, then swung the other over. "But it's a start. At least you did the smart thing by cutting a deal. Life without parole is a whole lot better than the death penalty. You're gonna have plenty of time to get your soul right with your Maker. I suggest you use that time wisely."

If Cliff's directions were accurate, just over the small mound on the island they would find what they came looking for. Dr. Simmons had given the order; Todd carried it out with ruthless precision. Cliff was just along for the ride, or so he said, believing a lie like everyone else. But he was still culpable and did a whole lot more than just believe. He helped perpetrate that lie. He would have the rest of his natural life to consider the damage he'd done. Cliff had agreed to testify against his former boss in the first-degree murder trial. Todd was already facing judgment.

"Are you sure about retirement, Chief?" John kept his hand on Cliff's elbow. "Seems like you'll be missed in Highpoint."

"I've stayed past my welcome." Chief Bennington remained seated on his airboat. He wouldn't be getting out at this stop. "I'll help clean this up, and then it's time for me to move on."

The man slumped in his seat as if he were melting in the

morning sun, the past events wearing on him. He'd believed a lie and was tainted by it. In spite of their problems, John felt sorry for him. Years of public service washed away in a tide of controversy and mayhem. The news accounts about the chief had not been kind.

"Well, Chief, had you not shown up when you did, Tim would probably be dead, and who knows how many of us would have been wounded or killed in that shoot-out. No matter what happened between us, you came through when it counted. You honored your badge. I was wrong about you, and I'm sorry about that."

"I've got no beef with you, Russell." The chief nodded. "But I still feel like a fool. Shoulda known better. Shoulda seen it coming. Highpoint needs me to move on. Besides, Chief Harris will do a fine job."

"I'm sure he will." John couldn't wait to congratulate Moses; he would make an outstanding police chief. John turned to Agent Sweeney. "You coming?"

She grimaced and glanced off the bow into the black, mucky waters. "I'm wearing hundred-dollar shoes and a two-hundred-dollar suit. I'm not getting out of this boat."

"Don't worry, Fed-lady." Tim adjusted his sling. "The state boys will do all the dirty work *again* so you can sit back and get all the glory."

"Glory?" Agent Sweeney scowled at Tim. "Evidently you've never had to explain something like this to a U.S. Attorney. There's no glory in that, Porter. Gettin' shot was the easy stuff compared to cleaning up this mess."

"What did you tell your bosses?" John guided Cliff to a dry spot on the island.

"The same thing I wrote in my report." Agent Sweeney crossed her arms. "Acting on fresh information that a potential victim was being held against her will at the Higher Learning Center, state agents, in conjunction with the FBI and the Highpoint Police

Department, moved quickly to protect her life. They entered the compound and rescued the victim, while at the same time shooting several suspects." Dry and matter-of-fact, Agent Sweeney sounded like a news blurb, even smiling like an anchorwoman at the end of her soliloquy. She was polished and going places, that was for sure.

"So that's how your report's going to read?" John asked.

"Not only that, I'm going to say the same thing at the press conference today. You-all are welcome to come, but you'll have to stand in the back, behind the FBI, of course." She smirked while adjusting her dark sunglasses.

"Thanks for the invite, but we're gonna have to decline. That can be your show." John shook some mud off of his boot. "We've got other things going on."

"We're ready," Barry said.

Barry and his assistant Dawn were the most experienced crime scene techs in the agency. John had specifically requested their help. It was going to be a long, tedious day, and he only wanted the best out here with him.

Barry and Dawn jumped out of the boat, both loaded down with marking equipment, cameras, and shovels. John and Tim joined them as they ambled over the mound to the location of a recently dug grave.

They'd come to take Mitchell Garrow home.

Tim slid past several reporters on the front bench of the Glades County courtroom. He wouldn't miss this for the world. The side door of the courtroom opened, and Walter Simmons shuffled in with two bailiffs escorting him. Walter's hair lacked even basic familiarity with a brush as confused clumps rebelled in different directions.

The room erupted as reporters stood to capture the best

picture of the disheveled leader of the Higher Learning Method making his first appearance in court. Walter panned the crowd with a scowl until his eyes met Tim's. They locked in a battle stare. Then Tim winked and grinned. It was a good day.

"What's the next case on the docket?" Judge Tonya Grey called. Her hair was as black as her robe and hung down to her shoulders, with only a few wisdom streaks running through it. Her stoic expression and solid reputation told everyone present that there would be no shenanigans in her courtroom.

"The State of Florida versus Walter Simmons," the bailiff said.

"That's *Doctor* Walter Simmons." He faced the judge and baby-stepped to the microphone in his red jumpsuit, cuffs, and leg shackles. Two bulky bailiffs in green sheriff's department uniforms hovered just behind him. His attorney stood to his left.

The judge thumbed through the charging documents "Today and in this courtroom, you are Walter Simmons, defendant. And you're being arraigned on the charges of kidnapping, false imprisonment, sexual battery…and first-degree murder. You are also being held on a warrant from Pinellas County for first-degree murder there. How do you plead?"

Walter's attorney approached the podium. "Your honor—"

"I can speak for myself." Walter's rage vibrated in his voice as he spoke to his own lawyer. "I'm not a child." He focused back on Judge Grey with belligerent intent. "Who do you think you are that *you* can judge *me*? I'm above your petty judgments. You have no authority to hold me. You have no—"

"I'm going to take that as a 'not guilty' plea for now." Judge Grey closed the case file. "But I think we're going to need a court-ordered psychological evaluation before we can move forward on this case. Does the state agree?"

The young male assistant state's attorney rose from his desk for the first time since the proceeding started. "The state agrees."

"*You* evaluate me?" Walter hobbled around to face the assistant state's attorney. "I'm not insane. You're the ones who are insane. You need the evaluations—"

"Bailiffs, please escort *Mr.* Simmons back to his cell." She handed the file to the clerk. "This hearing is finished."

"Take your hands off me." Walter jerked away from one bailiff. The second bailiff seized his other arm, and Walter twisted his body around. "You have no right. I order you to release me this instant."

With a deputy on each arm, Walter writhed and his feet scuffed the floor as they dragged him to the cell area, screaming the entire way. Reporters scampered toward the courtroom door with all the grace and order of a hockey mêlée. Today's news day was going to be big.

Tim paused to let the frenzy pass and then walked to the back of the courtroom, where Ruby and Byron flanked Kara Carson against the wall. The young woman kept her arms folded over her stomach and bent over slightly, her red hair falling in her face.

"You doing all right?" Tim stepped out of the aisle and over to Kara's side.

She nodded and brushed her hair back. "It was good to see Dr. Simmons like this. It helps to know he's gonna be punished for what he has done."

"We'll be there for you, Kara." Ruby wrapped her arm around her friend's shoulder. "No matter what it takes."

The young woman had shown a lot of courage. She'd come back to Highpoint to help Ruby and to tell the truth about Dr. Simmons. Tim would do everything in his power to see that justice was done.

"It's time to finish this up." John parked the car in Bill Patterson's driveway. Before all the mess with Dr. Simmons, Lesley Ann's file had consisted of a two-page medical examiner's report and another page with the detective's narrative. It had been buried away in storage and long forgotten, by some anyway.

Now it was a full volume of work containing pictures of the murals in Dr. Simmons's psychotic chamber of horrors and the carefully photographed copies of his journal, in which he had written in grotesque detail how he murdered Lesley Ann.

The well-worn pages of his journal told John that Walter had revisited his writings often, recounting the incident time and time again. The prose was graphic and often bizarre, the uncloaked evil nature of Dr. Simmons showing clearly in the writings he thought no one else would ever read. It had been enough to convince a grand jury of his guilt. Who knew how the trial might turn out? But for the moment, they had closure. Now it was time to pass it on.

John gathered the file together. "This part is never easy."

Tim adjusted his tie. "No. It's not. But it's necessary."

"Well, as hard as this is going to be, I hope Bill can finally find some peace." John shifted toward Tim. The case, while solved, had taken its toll on John, and he was exhausted, mentally and physically. "How come when we get to deliver the 'good news,' it's never really good news?"

"I don't know, partner. This is our calling I guess." Tim grabbed John's arm before he opened the car door. "You've done right by this man and his family. Don't lose sight of that. It might be painful, but you're giving him the gift of the truth. He's suffered for twenty-seven years in limbo, not knowing what really happened to his daughter. Believe me, I have an idea of what that's like. It's about time he finds out for sure what took place that day so he can make his peace with it. That's a gift you can't put a price on. Maybe he can pack up her room after this. You never know."

John nodded. "Thanks, partner."

Bill Patterson opened his front door and waited at the doorstep for them to come to him.

52

How come I'm the only one in the room who's ever been shot—not just once, but twice?" Tim stood in the center of the office cubicles and fiddled with his sling. At least this wound didn't cause near the damage the first shooting had. A little more rehab and he'd be back to his old self.

It still smarted quite a bit, though, but he'd keep that to himself. This time he wasn't slipping into that dark place again. Been there, done that. He was different; everything was different now.

"It ain't right for the new guy to have to take all the punishment. If I didn't know better, I'd think God was trying to tell me something. Maybe it's time to get out of law enforcement."

"Well, Tim." Robbie punched his good shoulder. "You are the biggest target here."

John covered his mouth with a file folder to hide his laughter. Alan rolled his eyes and shook his head. The team was back.

Tim wagged an angry finger at her. "That's just wrong, girl. I'm in fine shape. Will be in even better shape when I can start slingin' weights again."

"Five months." Alan raised the steaming coffee cup to his mouth. An aromatic veil of his soothing vanilla mocha mix wrapped around the team and the rest of the office. "That's all I have. Then you get a new supervisor to come in here, clean up this mess of an office, and corral this pack of feral detectives."

They were definitely back, and it felt good to be in the office again. The luxurious Gator Lodge & Inn hadn't quite filled the bill. Now the grand jury investigations were over, and their actions at the Higher Learning Center had been declared justifiable. The Fed-lady had cleaned up her end well.

"I want to say something for the record." Tim focused on his feet and took a deep breath. "I…I just don't know what I woulda done without you-all these last couple months. A man couldn't ask for better coworkers, for better friends. You risked everything, even your lives, to help my Ruby and me. I will never, ever forget that."

"I think the medication is making him a gushball." Robbie wrapped her arm around him.

"Maybe." Tim laid his good flipper on her shoulder. "But I've got the best friends and family in the world."

"Well, I think we've emoted enough for one day." Alan winked at Tim and flashed a wry smile. "We are way backed up on cases. I divided them up fairly, so I don't want to hear any whining. Let's get to work, people. Crime doesn't take a vacation, even if we do."

Everyone scurried to their workstations, and Tim eased down in his chair and spun in a circle. Life was good. Ruby's picture held its place of prominence above his computer. Just beholding her beautiful, loving face stirred joy in his soul that he could hardly put into words. She was back, too. Back to him and Cynthia and forward to God, which was new for all of them. The world seemed bright and alive.

A cleverly crafted paper clown sat next to Ruby's picture, compliments of the devious but talented origami bandit. He snatched the clown and looked around. Then he thought better of interrogating any would-be suspect. He crumpled it up and tossed it into the wastebasket. What was the use? Children will play.

"Tim." John smacked the top of his cubical twice. "He's here."

"Let's go get 'im." Tim stood. John looked worn out, and he was heavier than Tim had thought. When John had jumped on him at the learning center, it nearly crushed the life out of him. But he wouldn't tell Russell and hurt his feelings and all, especially since he did it to take the bullet meant for him. Russell was a good egg.

"Hey, John." Tim caught up to him in the hallway.

"Yeah."

"I want to walk God's way now. I've messed up enough on my own. But I'm gonna need some help. So if you're hankering for a fundamentalist moment every now and then, just let me know. I'll take anything I can get."

"Be careful for what you ask for, because you just might get it." John flashed his goofy Christian I'm-gonna-tell-ya-about-God smile. "Now let's go let him in."

They moseyed down the short hallway to meet with the state's attorney to review evidence in the case, and a mountain of evidence it was. As they approached Gloria Davis's desk, she glanced at them, then shoved something underneath her desk. She feigned typing on her computer.

"What are you hiding?" Tim canted his head.

"Nothing." She didn't look his way. "Nothing at all. Why do you ask?"

Tim spotted his book *Origami: The Beginner's Guide* resting on her knees under the desk and a fresh creation next to her computer—a blooming rose.

"Gloria Davis!" Tim stalked toward her. "You're the origami bandit? How could you do this to me?"

She smirked and retrieved the book. "It started out as a joke, but this is so fun. I didn't think I would like it so much. I've made a whole collection for my grandchildren. I'll show it to you sometime if you'd like."

"You're breakin' my heart, Miss Gloria." Tim's jaw dropped as he turned to John. "You never really know people, do you, John?"

Demetrius guided Nora Garrow down the aisle of the Mount Carmel Worship Center on his minitour of the sanctuary. Not that he could ever give a major tour, but he so loved the haven God had called him to. He'd arranged for her to stay at the church for as long as she needed. She wanted to be close to the investigation.

China walked from the back room and hurried toward them. "You must be Mitch's mother."

Mrs. Garrow extended her hand. China pulled her close, embracing her. "I'm very sorry for your loss."

"Thank you."

"China has been working with many of the Higher Learning Center's former students." Demetrius folded his hands in front of him. "She's started a support group and is helping them with the transition away from that place. She's a blessing to a lot of people."

"Sound's like you're doing a lot of wonderful work." Mrs. Garrow forced a smile.

"I had the privilege of knowing your son. We spent some time together. The last talk we had, Mitch told me that he had given his life to Jesus Christ. Mrs. Garrow, I know you're grieving, but I believe with all my heart that Mitch is walking with God today."

Nora nodded then wiped her eyes with a tissue. "I'm not a real religious person, but I want to believe what you say is true. I want to believe he's in a better place."

"He is." China nodded. "I would like to share with you sometime why I believe that."

"I'd like that very much." Nora sat down on a pew. "I want to know about Mitch's last days. Anything you can do to help would be greatly appreciated."

Mrs. Garrow took China's hand and then glanced around the sanctuary. "Look's like you-all are going to have a party."

"Well, we are, of sorts." Demetrius had just cut some fresh flowers and hung them on the end of the pews. The pulpit was lined with candles, and a white cloth ran the length of the railing. "Two lovebirds are getting married here tonight. It will be a glorious event."

The Mount Carmel Worship Center hummed to life as Miss Sylvia played the organ like a master with her gnarled but nimble fingers. Ruby was so beautiful in her flowing dress, her hair pinned back with small pearls interwoven through it. She'd come into her own as a woman. Tim could hardly keep the tears back.

Byron stood next to him at the front of the sanctuary. A fine young man. He'd shown a gargantuan amount of guts and would've given his own life for Ruby. He'd earned Tim's respect, although it would still behoove Byron to treat his little girl with the utmost love and admiration—or the man would be answering to him. But Tim was ready now to cut him some slack.

Ruby stepped slowly down the aisle, taking a stride, pausing, then taking another step as Miss Sylvia belted out the wedding march. Cynthia emerged next in the aisle. Everyone stood to honor the bride. Her white dress shimmered, and a smile engulfed her face.

When was the last time she'd smiled like that? Tim loved this woman and would never, ever do her wrong again. But things were different this time. They were starting fresh, on solid ground, together.

Thank You, Lord…for everything. Bless us to do it right this time. Your way, not ours. Our lives are Yours now.

Cynthia joined Tim at the altar and wrapped her hands in his. Demetrius held their gazes, his Bible at his side. Marie, Ruby, and Robbie were at her side as bridesmaids, while Byron, Alan, and John were the groomsmen.

"Please be seated." Demetrius motioned with his hands. "We are here to unite this couple in holy matrimony…again. We are so blessed to serve a Lord who is the Lord of second chances, of undying love, and of a fierce loyalty to His own that we can scarcely understand. We praise Him for that today."

Demetrius opened his Bible and read a passage from Genesis about a man leaving his family to join his wife and create another. He then stretched out his arms and brought Tim and Cynth together.

"Do you, Timothy Porter, promise to take this woman to be your lawfully wedded wife, to honor and cherish, in sickness and health, until death parts you?"

"I do. I do. I really do."

"Do you, Cynthia Porter, take this man to be your lawfully wedded husband, to honor and cherish, in sickness and in health, until death parts you?"

"I do."

"What God has joined together let no man put asunder." Demetrius bowed. "You may kiss the bride."

Tim and Cynth kissed, and his spirit fluttered under his new covenant with the love of his life. His father had married them the first time. Tim imagined his pop rejoicing in heaven for so many reasons now. He and Cynth were restored and following the Lord. Ruby, his precious Ruby, was walking with God. They were a family again. He'd be pleased, Tim was sure of that.

Tim cast his eyes upward. *You were so stubborn and determined about the things of the Lord, Pop, that you haunted me with it from the grave. And I can't thank you enough. Now I'll get a chance to do it in person someday.*

Tim turned to Cynth, and everyone rose as they marched down the aisle again, as one, toward the greeting room.

China had decorated the room off the sanctuary for after the ceremony, white streamers hanging from one end of the room to the other. A three-tiered cake was decorated and sitting on a folding table covered with a white cloth. Several presents shared the table as well.

Byron's arm was locked with Ruby's as the festivities continued. Tim's heart swelled that she was so happy.

The four prayer warriors caned, hobbled, and walked their way into the room. Chief Moses Harris joined the small but joyous cadre.

"Come here, child." Miss Isabel waved to Tim. "I have a message for you from the Lord."

Tim grinned and approached her, standing just out of reach. "I'm not falling for that again. Last time you had a 'message' from the Lord, you about slapped the taste outta my mouth."

"Oh, this is a sweet message, child. Come closer."

Tim paused, still unsure. Her hand of chastisement could be vicious and might render him unconscious for his own honeymoon. He took a deep breath and decided to risk it. Bending down, he scrunched his face in anticipation of another wallop.

"The Lord loves you and will keep you all of your days." She kissed the very cheek she'd battered before and massaged it with her fingers.

Tim held her hand. "Thank you, Miss Isabel, for knocking some sense into me."

He joined Cynthia as they prepared to cut the cake and open presents. Sitting on top of the presents was an origami statuette of a man and a woman with a small child with pigtails in between them. They were all holding hands, and a small cross was lofted above them.

"Wow!" Tim lifted it carefully and placed it on the table next to the cake. It was a masterpiece and should be treated as such. "This is beautiful. Thank you, Gloria, even if it is a little bit sassy. I love it. This must have taken forever to finish."

"I don't know what you're talking about." Gloria shrugged. "I got you a new set of towels. I didn't do that."

"Really, I'm not upset." Tim tapped the cross, which jiggled. "It's okay. I love it."

"Truly, Tim, it wasn't me." Her eyes were wide and innocent. "I would tell you, and it is quite exquisite. It must have taken hours, maybe days, for that much detail."

"Well then who?" Tim scanned the guests' faces. Everyone seemed as perplexed as he was. He regarded the statuette again. His family was restored, even better than he'd dreamed. The folds of the new creation were sharp, crisp—strong. Not ever to be broken again. It was truly a work of art.

"Looks like now I've got to be on the lookout for the origami angel."

Reader's Guide

1. Tim and Cynthia's relationship fell apart when they tried to handle life on their own, outside of the will of God. How should their marriage be different this time around?

2. What made Ruby vulnerable to the teachings and influence of Dr. Simmons?

3. Does spiritual warfare play a part in our daily lives? If so, in what ways?

4. Is it possible for a Christian to become involved in a cult or fall prey to false teachings? Why or why not?

5. Why are Dr. Simmons's teachings of human perfection and Utopia so attractive? Is that teaching counter to biblical doctrine?

6. What do you think of China's approach to witnessing?

7. John, Alan, and Robbie put aside their professional responsibilities to help Tim and Ruby. Is this unscriptural? Can you think of an example in the Bible of someone doing the same thing? What would you do in the same circumstance?

8. What excuse did Tim use to reject the Christian upbringing his father spent so many years trying to impart to him? Have you ever known someone who used the same excuse? Could there be another underlying reason?

9. Is it possible for someone to be raised in a Christian home yet still not follow God? Why or why not?

10. John, Tim, and the rest of the law enforcement officers had to fire their weapons to defend themselves during the rescue mission at the Higher Learning Center. Should a Christian ever use physical force to defend himself or others? What about Christian police officers and military personnel?